ANNEX

Book Three of ARTORIAN'S ARCHIVES
A DIVINE DUNGEON Series

Written by DENNIS VANDERKERKEN and
DAKOTA KROUT

TABLE OF CONTENTS

Acknowledgments..5

Prologue 6

Chapter One 8

Chapter Two 16

Chapter Three...23

Chapter Four..31

Chapter Five...38

Chapter Six 43

Chapter Seven...50

Chapter Eight..58

Chapter Nine..66

Chapter Ten..73

Chapter Eleven 84

Chapter Twelve..92

Chapter Thirteen 104

Chapter Fourteen...113

Chapter Fifteen 123

Chapter Sixteen 129

Chapter Seventeen..137

Chapter Eighteen 144

Chapter Nineteen...150

Chapter Twenty 157

Chapter Twenty-One..166

Chapter Twenty-Two...172

Chapter Twenty-Three 180

Chapter Twenty-Four 187

Chapter Twenty-Five 194

Chapter Twenty-Six..204

Chapter Twenty-Seven 212

Chapter Twenty-Eight...221

Chapter Twenty-Nine 229

Chapter Thirty 238

Chapter Thirty-One 246

Chapter Thirty-Two 253

Chapter Thirty-Three 261

Chapter Thirty-Four 269

Chapter Thirty-Five 281

Chapter Thirty-Six 290

Chapter Thirty-Seven 298

Chapter Thirty-Eight.. 306

Chapter Thirty-Nine 314

Chapter Forty... 322

Chapter Forty-One 329

Chapter Forty-Two 338

Chapter Forty-Three.. 345

Chapter Forty-Four.. 353

Chapter Forty-Five... 360

Chapter Forty-Six 367

Epilogue 370

Afterword... 375

About Dennis Vanderkerken 376

About Dakota Krout 377

About Mountaindale Press 378

Mountaindale Press Titles.. 379

    GameLit and LitRPG.. 379

Appendix 381

ACKNOWLEDGMENTS

From Dennis:

There are many people who have made this book possible. First is Dakota himself, for without whom this entire series would never have come about. In addition to letting me write in his universe, he has taken it upon himself to edit and keep straight all the madness for which I am responsible, with resulting hilarity therein.

A thank you to my late grandfather, after whom a significant chunk of Artorian's personality is indebted. He was a man of mighty strides, and is missed dearly.

A special thank you to my parents, for being ever supportive in my odd endeavors, Mountaindale Press for being a fantastic publisher, Jess for keeping us all on task, and all the fans of Artorian's Archives, Divine Dungeon, and Completionist Chronicles who are responsible for the popularity allowing this to come to pass.
May your affinity channels be strong, and plentiful!

Last of all, thank you. Thank you for picking this up and giving it a read.
Annex is the continuation of a multi-book series, and I dearly hope you will enjoy them as the story keeps progressing.
Artorian's Archives may start before Divine Dungeon, but don't worry! It's going all the way past the end of Completionist Chronicles! So if you liked this, keep an eye out for more things from Mountaindale Press!

Prologue

Grandfather,

It was practically silent in the Fringe cloister without you around, until Ra became old enough to get around on her own. Now I am chasing the rambunctious little nugget around with my rolling pin daily. Somehow she figured out how to get at the cookies, but luckily she has not yet figured out how I find her no matter where she hides. Those lessons with you are paying off even years later, ha!

Keeper Jin indulges her, even going so far as to sweep her up and run when I am attempting to enact discipline! He always runs toward your massively oversized pillow, so oftentimes I am able to cut them off before they arrive.

As much as I want to continue my pretend complaints, things are well in the Fringe. Wuxius has gained some more... *fatherly* features, making me think that it is not only Ra who is making off with my cookies! On a stranger note, *things* have started washing up in the salt tides, not dangerous things, but odd things all the same. Ra has been gaining little dolls nearly every tide, and is making quite the collection. Frankly I find them somewhat creepy, but she adores them and I do not have the heart to take them away.

Ra asks after you frequently, which I suppose is our fault for telling her stories about you since she was born. I can only hope that Yvessa is correct when she says that you will be back. We are still getting letters from you, and we do treasure them.

I am sure that you will appear when we are least expecting it, likely with the rest of the family in tow. Or, who knows, perhaps you'll fall from the sky like a certain lovely song that has become popular in recent times.

Whichever it ends up being, I'm sure no one will be disappointed.

Your Granddaughter in love,
Elder Lunella.

CHAPTER ONE

"I'm... *disappointed,*" the smoggy voice full of hungry shadows mused to itself, failing to savor the culmination of what should have been a tantalizing and *delicious* plot. Instead, its palate was fouled.

Years of scheming, dark plots, utmost guile, well-executed strategies, quips and snappy retorts prepared and practiced en masse... all of this shouldn't have resulted in anything *other* than a decadent downpour of exaltation and battling wits.

"Such *time* I spent snacking on scrumptious Sequoia. I savored every *nibble* torn from that mind, even as its final spices were *denied.* How he *withered* while *I* progressed, and *your* ilk scoured and ruined the landscape for my connoisseur canines and swallowing throats," the voice drawled, monologuing to itself even as its target remained *unapproachable.*

"The fact that you and your deep-rooted entourage blasted, busted, and broke the landscape *itself,* merely to close my tunnels, was a *treat.* How I *longed* for challenge and cadaverous cacophony to expend my efforts against. Such *inspiration* you gave me! Now, at the closing of the curtains... here you lie at my feet. Yet I feel no satisfaction; in fact, I *despise* you for it!"

It was difficult to see in a cavern without natural lighting. When Artorian ever so barely opened his eyes, it wasn't any different from the existing fugue states he was shifting between. Reality wasn't yet on the schedule, and the academic remained caught up in his thoughts. Currently, he was thinking of a kitten. Soft, fluffy, will accept *exactly* three-point-one-four pets before mauling the living daylights out of your entire hand.

The cat sat sphinx-style on a square sheet of warm light while luminance streamed through an imaginary window. Within those exact confines, the kitten sat as if trapped within a box of its own making. The box could be inferred, but was it truly there? Could there be both a box around the kitten, yet *not* at the same time? It was a paradox box.

Such considerations had swamped his senses as they ebbed and flowed like great ocean waves. Both impossible conundrums and flippant conjecture screeched at him from opposite sides of a room that didn't exist, with voices that weren't there. All of this from one single event: his glimpse of *the beyond.*

The sight of the heavenly had been so jarring that even his mind was grasping at straws to find a way to reframe it into a way that made sense. It may have been one thing had he merely *seen* it with his normal eyes. Perhaps his mind would have simply turned away or ignored the *being.* But no, his *foolish* mind had experienced the event directly, thanks to his empowered eyes, which made the after-effects slap him harder than a Dwarven granny with an explosion-empowered slipper.

The voice awaiting him in the dark was malicious and full of smiling hunger. When the shapeless mass noticed its stirring companionship, its elation instantly grew. "Ar*torian...!* You wordy, *delicious* thing. How *are* you?"

"S! Equals one-one-seven."

The darkness blinked in bewilderment. All subtle movement in the area had ceased entirely as the mass of thought attempted to process the utterly ridiculous answer it had just been provided. *Oozing* charisma, it voiced its thought just in case. "Come again?"

"It's the calculation for luck. I figured it out!"

One blink was an accomplishment. The flutter of eyelid flapping that followed, required this dark aspect to take on physical form purely so it could press hands together and reassess its priorities in existence. Something had clearly gone awry here. "Certainly, you meant 'why can I not see', followed by screaming, gasps of disbelief, a drama with a crestfallen collapse at the inevitability of defeat, culminating in begging to have your suffering swiftly ended."

Artorian was used to being blind. He remembered it well enough that this temporary setback didn't faze him one bit. Had the unhappily familiar voice not monologued its evil plan like a third-rate villain seeking desperate attention, he would have likely mentioned the fact. But no need to give an enemy more information than they had! He found that cycling Essence wasn't improving his ability to see, and echolocation only outlined a vacant cave network.

The answers came easily enough. In comparison to the mysterious nature of the universe, this puzzle was only as difficult as figuring out who ate his evening pie in the Fringe longhouse; as if honey wasn't sticky and children were clean eaters.

Creepy self-entitled voice. Check.

Dark underground conditions. Check.

Villainous idiot that was going to get beaten into the ground?

Check.

The old man touched his beard, only to find that he may have been the one who had eaten the pie. His otherwise groomed fluff was sticky and wet. It also smelled unpleasantly of... iron. Ah. Not pie. Doesn't take more than one battlefield to gain an innate knowledge of when you're covered in blood, and he'd seen more than his share of battlefields.

This did not bode well for the people that had gone down here to hide. *Down*? ...yes. Cavern aesthetic, musky wet air, cold, dark. Down. Why were people hiding? He was having a rough time recalling... it was all such a jarring blur. "How did I even get down here? I was on the mountain *top*."

An attempt to brighten the area filled him with incredible dread. While the hum of the energy building in his Aura could be heard reverberating through the cavern, no light graced or filled his Aura. "*Tsk*. Oh, come now... you couldn't have known about that. Surely a little clarity on your situation would be *illuminating*."

The unpleasantly familiar voice bounced off the thick sheet of his presence, preventing a mental assault by sheer virtue of an Aura being present. The attack felt like nails screeching along a chalkboard, except that his Aura was the board.

Something about the tone gave Artorian pause. That sentence had not been in response to his question; rather, a response to what he'd almost done, and *didn't* do thanks to his sudden discomfort. Unsettling as the situation was, it provided questions. Questions that pulled resources from his panicked mind still enraptured and terrified by the glimpses of the divine. His thoughts were diverted to the here and now, and the old man could feel himself relax as those extraneous considerations dimmed enough to be shelved for later.

His sigh of relief greatly displeased his unseen host, but not half as much as the following commentary did. "Even a blind man can see the truth when it is so *obvious*. What more illumination do I need when you've told me everything?"

The darkness hitched and fractured with crackling energy. Artorian would describe it as the sound of lightning, if it happened in reverse. The voice came again: "You know *nothing*."

Artorian nodded at such a sagely statement. "Truer words were rarely spoken."

Irritation clashed all around him. Not in flashes of light, visible clues, auditory snippets, or sensory stimulation on his skin. He didn't have to hear the psychic wailing to know it was there. Silence was not the strong suit of the personality he was undoubtedly surrounded by. In fact, silence was a sign that all was well! If he could hear the voices... his defenses were breached.

Since he could not, Artorian safely inhaled the stale cavern air as his thoughts leaned to the conditions required to bring him from the top of the mountain. That's where he had last been, as far as he was concerned. The shift to somewhere *much* further down was jarring.

The emergency escape plan, the one that would bring him here without him doing so himself was only for the direst of circumstances. If he'd woken up down here, it should have been with a significant portion of Jian, or at least the students. The stench of blood was an indication that Jian had certainly accompanied him... so why had he been excluded from the event that put them in this state?

"I will rend your flesh, tear your bones, break your muscle, and chew you until you're goop. All that's going to be left of your mind is chunks of wispy screams that neither remember fresh air, nor the tenderness of a kind hand."

The voice was too physical. It carried a similarity to a different familiar voice. One devoid of charisma, steeped entirely in jealousy and self-entrapment. Artorian couldn't see, and so couldn't be certain, but the idea had manifested and would likely hold true. Artorian's reply came as a whisper. "...Cataphron?"

After a moment of silence, a heavy footstep fell onto the bloodied floor. A second footfall joined it, the weight behind it nearly nonexistent. Enough to *be*, but not enough to mimic true corporeality. The charismatic tones responded in a mixture of voices, each morphing halfway into the next. "I despise you *so*. The name you call both is, yet is *not...* present. Alive, but dead. *Assimilated*."

The arrangement of voices made Artorian clutch his robe. Not *merely* Cataphron mixed in the whirlpool of voices, but the three prior masters of the academy each lent their own voice to the amalgamation of sound. It seemed that Cataphron had found his old masters after all. Or what there was left to find, at least.

Still, the amalgam did not pursue him. How strange... had the positions been reversed, he would not have allowed his opponent to wake from slumber merely to trade words or deliver a fancy speech. An idea struck Artorian: what if it was not a matter of choice? Were there any circumstances that would make this action so unfavorable that it gave merit to avoiding it outright?

The fresh puzzle set his mind alight. New information could be pulled from recent happenings and important events. Think, old boy, *think*. What had the amalgam said? What does an old man not know about, and why is illumination encouraged? This was the Caligene of blight, phantoms, and shadows. Light would be its *bane*, and the creature's words seemed to instigate him to activate abilities that would cause it harm. Artorian straightened as a piece clicked. He was upright, his fists balled up even though he could not discern his surroundings, still the anger flowed. "*Cataphron!*"

The surreptitious smile schmoozed out a very un-Cataphron-esque response. The kind of delighted smirky tone that signaled a plan was about to see fruition. How the Blight craved the satisfaction of seeing its plan come to a rewarding conclusion. "*Ye~e~ess?*"

Artorian stomped the ground with his foot, splashing a wet wave of 'red water' all around. "You blithering *fool!* You absolute *squirrel!* How could you let the Blight take you? Why didn't you *fight!*"

What had been a slimy smile dropped to flat unamusement. The old man just wasn't playing along. Come on... light up the place. It knew the old man wanted to do so. It's what he was *good* at; he made that awful lance which caused shudders of unpleasantry and destroyed his reaching thoughts! Had this *clown* been any better at the skill, there might not have been enough information returning to formulate the plot. Some *persuasion* was required, and the amalgam slipped right back into the drawl of a charismatic salesman. "Oh, he *tried*, old student. He tried."

The voice swirled around Artorian, not bound by bodily positioning or physical factors. Clouds of blight shifted and moved within the cavern they fully occupied. They just had to make sure that they didn't cross the rules, and they'd be fine. "See, I ate him *easily*. There was no external Aura to prevent me from gulping him right up. You already know nothing else defends from mental assaults! That's why you've layered it on so *thick*. You didn't wake to any of my *normal* words, but when I began using the mimicry of a voice box, here you are...!"

Artorian had not expected to learn anything from this conversation. Especially not that a thick enough external Aura blocked out mental prodding and assaults. He'd file that away for a time where that knowledge could come in handy. "I... I see. Did you also eat whoever got me down here? Let's not pretend it's not blood I'm standing in. Hmm. Hopefully nobody I know.

I've grown tired of mourning again and again. It's more of a dull ache at this point."

He cut himself off as he started to ramble. It was a *terrible* time for reflecting.

CHAPTER TWO

The cave laughed; at least what was *in* the cavern did. There was no distinction. The general area rocked and reverberated the age-old pathways. "They were all snacks to savor, and savor I *did.* Though I admit I had *quite* the gluttonous streak while waiting for the main course to wake. There is nothing that compares to a truly unburdened mind."

Artorian folded his hands behind his back. "Unburdened *indeed.* Can't help but notice I can breathe decently. How odd that an entity controlling and occupying the entirety of the space I inhabit is allowing me such a relaxing awakening. *Uninterrupted,* even. Why, for all that talk of eating me, it doesn't feel like I have as much as a scratch on me. *Curious...*"

The Blight bit its lip, monologuing in attempt to throw the academic off balance while regaining its own. "The greatest curiosity has yet to come across your notice! If *only* you could see the complexity of what I'd prepared for you. Were you not on the menu, you might have even found it beautiful. Art only an *advanced* mind is able to appreciate..."

It was too late; Artorian had the amalgam by the hanging satchel. "I suppose that hinges on a single question."

Phantoms wailed in disgust, but none of it reached the intended target. No screams of mental anguish could breach an Aura that was changing to increase in effectiveness against their specific influence. What a *terrible* matchup this old man was. In disdain it spat out a retort, using a body to utter the guttural vocalization. "That *being?*"

While the Skyspear headmaster wasn't at all pleased about the current situation, it did bring a smile to his face to test the conditions under which this war was operating. "Who *are* you?"

The cavern trembled and shook. The Blight hated, despised, and *loathed* this terrible, annoying, unyielding living *creature*. Could it not just *die* already? The Blight knew all too well that the answer to this question meant two things. One, this despicable wrinkled cockatoo *knew*. Two, the reply would determine vulnerability. Being an amalgamation of every mind it had consumed, who it *was* remained a matter of... sensitive nature. A fact so crucial to its own preservation that it knew *better* than to reveal the unembellished truth.

Deflection was in order. "Who am I, *indeed!* Who but the stuff of nightmares? The walker of the pale? The whispers one hears in the dark? The reason one does not remember why they entered a room? I am the missing sock in the wash, the full stomach after someone becomes lost in the woods. I am that which one bumps into when there should have only been empty space, and I am what watches you from the creeping corners of the dark. I am the reason one cannot fall asleep at night, for danger is nearby and it is unsafe to rest."

Pausing a moment to relish, it regarded the aged old bat. "I am hunger. I. Am. *Death.*"

Artorian cackled; that was good enough for him! "*Not* Cataphron. Confirmed...!"

Relish turned to ruin as the sound of a heartbeat coupled with an outward pulse of plasmic light rippled in spherical form from the starlight cultivator. Refined Essence was compressed into the effect as Artorian combined several ideas. Costly, but if he was only going to get this single effect off... it might as well be one for the ages!

Echolocation, luminescence, moss, and stickiness exploded from his presence. The Blight shrieked as thick, crawling, growing patches of light developed over the smoky layers just like lichen and moss did. Simply much, *much* faster.

The effect clung to the walls, spreading, glowing, shining. Providing a natural illumination to the cavern as his pulse extended in reach, until eventually it struck the ceiling. What a *colossal* hole in the ground this was. Artorian almost wished he'd remained ignorant upon being greeted by the sight that awaited: thousands of bodies littered the ground that must have once been a pit. While he indeed stood upon a layer of blood, he somehow hadn't guessed that the soft ground he was traversing... was bodies. Bones littered the cavern halls as far as he could see, and he knew in his heart... that if there was *one* thing he should not do... it was to *look up.*

For all the love contained in the heavens and the earth... do *not* look up.

The effect of his Essence hadn't ended when it left him. There were instructions contained in the pulse that still tore through underground pathways, sticking its effect to the walls where it could self-replicate in limited form. Costly, sure. However, if his guess was correct and he *shouldn't* attack his foe in the near future, the near-natural lighting hopefully would not count as such. Artorian wasn't going to get away with this twice, and he needed all the information he could get his hands on. That meant...

Artorian's chin tilted before his eyes did.

He should *not* have looked up.

What does an amalgamation of several tens of thousands of minds, corrupted, blackened, and blighted look like? Turns out, like they still had hands and faces contorted in screams as they tried to escape a slimy, moist, glossy leather bag that stretched but never broke. It wasn't even a physical, solid body. Yet the shadows were so dense, and the infernal energy harvested from the torment and continual anguish so packed, that it may as well have been.

"Ew."

The 'burning' effect of his pulse of Essence was superficial, and had been extinguished by the Blight. A body in the endless, sickening floor-pile of meat... no... *Cataphron* rose. His eyes were the same ghastly hollow that had been so prevalent in Artorian's nightmares that very first night in Birch's company. With the candles... how sweet the candles made by the Wood Elves had been. But much like oils, they did nothing to alleviate the true problem.

Cataphron's steady, familiar voice spoke up in the charismatic cadence of the Blight. "How. In the name of the Abyss. Did you figure it out?"

The academic snapped to the question. The words had been so... human. So steady. So believably from a real body that, had he not known better, he'd have thought the body walking towards him without a shred of effort was actually alive. "Oh, Blighty... *you* told me, by *not* telling me. Unsurprisingly, waking up at all was the first big giveaway. Being able to breathe the second. Threats without action the third."

"The only true course of action would have been for me to be part of this meat-floor you've decorated your hole with. It sickens me, and I wish I knew how to tear you from existence with great vengeance for what you've done to all these poor people... all the Elves you've hunted and harmed... all the lives you've consumed and cut short!"

Cataphron gleefully smiled a sickly grin, snickering. "But you *ca~a~an't..*"

Artorian didn't move from his spot as a Blight-infested and puppeted Cataphron came face to face with him. He held back a wince; what a few years of rot and decay can do to a person. Hiding his rage, Artorian mimicked the mocking tone right back at the 'creature'.

"Neither can you~u~u..."

The Blight laughed through fleshy vocal chords. "Oh, the land law you have with this man may prevent me from ravishing your mind like a snack bar at the royal palace, but unlike before... you're in *my* house now. You can't leave unless I want you to leave." The Blight sucked in a breath, and it felt like all the air in the room moved into it. "Perhaps I can't harm you directly... but I don't have to feed you, or let you sleep peacefully, give you time to think or explore the caverns. I can rearrange them, loop them, *maze* them. I can befuddle you while I deny you the light from your star, and walk a few paces behind as every day I slowly watch. You. Die.

"Maybe you'll even make mistakes and drop your Aura too low, and then... I'm in." Cataphron practically giggled, "What *fun* we will have."

Artorian *tsk'd*. The land law was exactly what was preventing the Blight from tearing him open, and what was preventing him from full bore erasing the heart of this thing with the butt of his starlight pencil. "Someone else will come and get rid of you."

Cataphron smiled from ear to ear and laughed like a mad hyena, cackling in delight at the absurdity of the claim. He bent over, slapped his knee, and enjoyed the visceral feeling a body provided through infernally-altered senses. This body was *perfect* as a physical host; no external Aura to prevent any takeover or interference!

Cataphron had been the cleanest snatch up ever. No damage to the host, perfect for replacement and inhabiting. The Blight *adored* having a body this suitable to play with, and play with it he *would*. "Oh, you can't *begin* to understand how wrong you are there... You *might* have had a chance, but the memories from your 'old friend' told me everything. A flawless counter against my most *specific* problem? How could I resist? Sure, *you* achieved the position of Headmaster, but what threat is that when I have you so conveniently in my box?"

Artorian raised an eyebrow. Achieving Headmaster was a threat? Now *that* didn't fit any narrative so far; why would that be of note? Earning the position itself is likely due to being quite powerful, but *type* mattered more than amount for this problem. Catty here had also mentioned quite snootily that 'he' might have had a chance.

The power of erasing starlight was *good*, but while it accounted for some of the facts, it didn't account for *all* of the facts. Time to dig! "*Ha!* I could have defeated you as an academy *student!* I don't need some fancy title. Had Cat and I gone another round before he went under, I'd have won!"

The laughter burst out once more; bubbly and thick as the raucous hilarity struck the multiple minds contained in the Blight, all using Cataphron as a mouthpiece. "First of all, Shinebug... no, you couldn't have. Secondly, this body would have wiped the ground with you so hard, you'd have been the courtyard's new paint scheme."

Artorian grit his teeth. "Where there's *one*, it's usually not done."

The Blight ignored the strange phrase. "I can't wait to see if you cave in to your baser needs. There is food for you here in plenty... I've left the bodies for you. They were never for *me*. I eat *minds*. No, my 'old friend' these..."

The infernal body moved its arms about, gesturing at the thousands of bodies. "...are for you! Will you go hungry, or will you force yourself to suffer, and survive? I don't have to feed you, but can you stop *yourself?* I've learned that you're as big of a glutton as I am! Think of *that*, we have something in common after all...

The academic felt poorly for all these people, but he couldn't help them now. Not even to clean up their bodies. His most common Aura effects would incur the land law violation. Any use of cleansing effects or something similar were going to harm the Blight, and since the Blight was currently *Cataphron*... that was the first snag. The second snag was that there wasn't just *one* land law at play.

He surmised there must be a second one that specifically had to do with the Headmaster position, or rather, the landowner. If he was the landowner of the Skyspear above, this Blight must be the owner of the below. That created quite the tension, and while the details were unknown... needing to be a landowner to face a landowner had a reasonable sense to it.

Artorian recalled an old passage from the Skyspear creation myth. He'd thought it was silly for someone to carve a menhir from the moon and launch it planetside to... entrap? An enemy. Not *defeat* it? How... annoyingly fitting. Sounds like someone else may have lacked a means to kill ol' Blighty before. He recited the memory in a whisper while the phantom Blight cackled at him. "Only the highest spear may pierce the deepest depths."

That was good and all, but he was stuck in the kitten's box. Blighty still had him trapped, and his light-moss didn't have a long duration. Still, it had given him the information he needed. That was generally worth the cost. Next came the hard part:

Waiting.

CHAPTER THREE

Several hours in a deep dank cave did much to dim the spirit. There was a fringe benefit to this, as the initial panic had faded from the Skyspear student body. Those that survived, anyway. From a rough headcount, a third of the students had survived. The whereabouts of the remaining two thirds remained unknown until some rudimentary exploration, then telltale blood streaks leading down sporadic and numerous paths took away the hope that they would find the students alive.

From the drag patterns, their bodies looked like they had been dragged away at high speed. Based on the impact splatters, what had killed them hadn't been the *attack* so much as the journey into the dark depths themselves. Sharp turns through rough caverns left many walls stained sanguine, and the sharp tips of stalagmites and stalactites were considered responsible for anyone that may have aggressively bounced their way down the tunnel network.

What exactly had done the dragging was unknown. No footprints marred the flawless streak patterns and impact stains. *People* hadn't done this. A *thing* had grabbed everyone down here, likely one at a time, then dragged them with force and velocity to their graves like a kraken pulling a ship into the depths of the ocean.

Jiivra sat defeated on a stair step, the great majority of a frightened student body huddled nearby. Her Aura emitted a faint light, having just taken over from a few of the fire students too exhausted to keep their illumination active. They'd run out of torches an hour ago, and their planned supplies were soaked beyond the point of usability.

The way out was barred by a landslide, not that they could have used it. Even now they could hear pick and bone nick and peck at the makeshift blockage. It was only a matter of time before the tireless undead made their way through. They didn't know *exactly* how long they had, they just knew they were tired, didn't have the planned supplies, and had failed everyone they'd pushed down here.

Only a few of the students managed to speak. Even then, it was in short supply since the drab mood cut short their willingness to speak. They were responsible for leading an entire town down here. They'd been so *sure* it was safe; so *certain*. Nothing bad had *ever* happened during explorations! This was an *abandoned* cave system.

They'd never guessed that there was a lurker with an appetite sizable enough to consume the entire populace. *Why* hadn't they known? They should have *known*! The realizations were eating away at them, and their instructors didn't have any way to make them feel better. They were all equally responsible as far as they saw it, and they too blamed themselves.

Astrea frowned and lifted her head. There was a *tingle* in her ear. Speaking wasn't a popular option, but the buzzing only got louder. *Closer.* "Does anyone hear that?"

A groan erupted en masse from the huddled air Essence students, and the head boy spoke in a monotone. "We hear the undead slowly clawing their way in, yes. Hard *not* to hear with how quiet it is in here."

Astrea dismissed the snarky retort. "Not the *ticking*, the *buzzing*. The crinkling of paper that is just getting louder and louder?"

Alexandria perked up at the mention of paper. That was her playhouse, and she pressed her hands around her ears to make them bigger. She squinted, thinking that would make her hearing better. It didn't, but it lifted the corners of many a mouth that spotted her antics, making them forget for just a *moment* how awfully cold it was down here.

The tiny librarian shook her head, she couldn't hear anything. It made the students grit their teeth until Jiivra shot up sporting a similar frown. She reached out to Astrea, trying to match information. "Crinkling paper that pops and then gets wet?"

Alexandria pouted at being left out. Glaring between the two older girls, she again tried to squint-listen. Agitation struck her as *again* she heard nothing. She was being played with by the tall-sisters! Not fair! A few of the Skyspear students stood, copying the librarian's ear-cupping attempt. Still, they also heard nothing and instead sent a questioning look at the highest-ranked master and... the *plus one*. How was the *newbie* doing something they couldn't? This was either a pitiful attempt at a distraction, or a joke in poor taste.

The cave lit up in a flash as crackling plasma light hurled its way through the open space like a bulldozing rhino with its tail on fire. It left a bioluminescent moss carpet that rapidly grew in its wake. It sucked up the moisture clinging to the cavern walls to sustain itself after the sudden accelerated growth, and the albino foliage crinkled as miniscule roots dug ever-so-barely into the rock to hold itself in place.

Students gawked in bewilderment, whispering mumbles between them that shared the same uncertain tones of confusion. That confusion intermingled with a spark of hope as Jiivra punched the air hard enough for her fist to create a *thud* by compressing the air. "*Yes!* Chalk one up for Skyspear, not all is lost!"

Jiivra's smile was wide, and the only one returning it was an equally excited Astrea. They both deduced that there were limited sources which could pull off that oddball effect. The remaining student body got to their feet with a hastened heartbeat as they picked up the details from the conversing pair.

Astrea proudly pressed her fists into her hips. "Grandfather lives! That's good news for everyone. I'd say that pulse was a good indication he's snapped out of whatever mental quagmire he was stuck in on the way. Though I'll admit I have no idea what the effect was supposed to accomplish. A means of telling us there's a fighting chance? I'll take that as a 'crack on'!"

Jiivra dropped her illumination effect. The cavern was visible enough with the new low-light. Unfortunately, it also let everyone see more paths where bodies had been dragged. The difference was that more popular paths were no longer obscured, and it was easy to tell by the sheer amount of viscera and 'paint' which cavern tunnel became the most likely candidate to find the culprit.

The celestial combat instructor wasn't convinced. "Did our old man do this? *Probably.* Do I know what it means? No. This never came up in the discussions, and I don't even know what the intent is."

Her Essence-cycled eyes scanned the surroundings, but she didn't grasp any hidden meanings. "A pulse of heavy celestial to be sure. It revitalized plant life that previously thrived here, which I can safely guess is the moss. The conditions are good for it. There seems to be a change in what it's supposed to *do* though. Because... well... it's glowing."

Astrea had a sudden memory of something her Elder had said well over a decade ago. She parroted his words and took a deft few steps closer to the wall for her own inspection. "*Don't* eat the glowing moss."

She received some looks that wordlessly said 'duh', including one from Alexandria. Even *she'd* read that it was a dumb idea to eat things that seemed unnatural or weren't properly prepared. That's how you got the screams. It's what people did shortly after they ate something they shouldn't have and rushed to the latrine. Don't eat weird things. Don't get the screams. Easy.

"I know I heard it, the wave passed, and I felt incredibly uncomfortable as it bounced off me and shot back." Astrea shrugged at the nonverbal reply from her surroundings. "*Erghh*. It took a chunk out of my cultivation too. Oh, that just feels awful."

She wrapped her arms around her stomach at the realization. Groaning internally as she kept her complaints to herself, though the momentary discomfort was a good uptick in the general mood of the students. Their head instructor hadn't been too fond of the newbie when they'd first brought her up, and the gossip that she was an infernal cultivator reflected poorly on the daughter of the Fringe.

Astrea didn't care about any of that. She had just pulled herself together when Jiivra softly held her shoulder. "How are you feeling, and can you tell me more about what you mean with 'bounced back'? I didn't feel that at all."

The infernal cultivator nodded, having an idea or two. "You said the majority of that pulse was celestial? Well, I don't need to know two sticks can make a fire to figure out that was not great for me."

Soft pats followed on Astrea's back, and the students were a little confused. Didn't they dislike each other? Those who remembered their flirtatious fighting outside of the cave said nothing, distracted by their need for answers and direction. Abyss if *they* knew what to do or what that pulse meant. "You're alright..."

The infernal cultivator nodded. She was, and Jiivra's support went a long way. "Bounced back. I mean *directly*. That pulse thing hit me, shaved off a chunk of my cultivation, and repelled off and away from me like it was one of those rubber tree-sap orbs the kids started dropping down the Skyspear steps. You didn't feel that?"

Jiivra shook her head 'no'. "Nothing of the sort, if anything it went right through me."

A few of the boys snickered but went ignored. The celestial instructor decided it was time to crowdsource for information. She turned and spoke with her usual militant poise. The school snapped to attention and without being prompted arranged themselves into a square formation. Fun and games were over when certain voice tones came out to play. No amount of feeling diminished was going to allow them to get one over on their combat instructor; she was still a C-ranker.

In fact, her rank was popular gossip material. According to the most reliable sources they had, it was supposed to take *significantly* longer to hit the C-ranks. On the mountaintop, their instructor simply had all the conditions working in her favor. Not only was she the prime source for connecting celestial Essence during her chants, but she was the prime benefactor. As a Master, she could cultivate unrestricted. Just about all of the Essence type the area gathered was hers to claim.

With a wide and consistent support network of students, her daily needs were seen to with advanced frequency. Most of all, it was a popular topic that she didn't have their dual-ring cultivation technique. The students all had a 'containment ring' and a 'cultivation ring'. One trapped their corruption until they could find a suitable means to get rid of it, while the other allowed them proper cultivation progress.

Their celestial instructor didn't just have rings, but a cultivation technique *personally* constructed by the Headmaster. A lower grade copy of his own, significantly advanced method. While it had taken their Headmaster five years to recover from Echoing... Jiivra had spent those years gathering her power.

Not spending it on improvements, or Essence techniques, or infusion, or Aura building. Nothing except gather, and gather, and *gather* as the sun-Core refined her celestial Essence as fast as she could take it in. That technique was designed to take a multitude of Essences and refine them all at the same time.

Having it focused on a single affinity spiked the efficiency. Jiivra innately grasped the difference between her prior fractal and this new, three-dimensional method. On a surface level it looked deceptively simple. Yet, the method moved in ways that you just didn't expect, and the complexity and nuances involved an entire category of difficulty higher than what she was used to.

A twenty-split fractal was easier than this, and she'd gotten to thirty-plus before the Vicars had stripped her of power. Jiivra was pulling in celestial Essence as hard and fast as she'd been able, and the cultivation technique might as well have been relaxing on a beach with a coconut drink in hand. The only reason she managed to handle the technique was due to its nature. Unlike her prior fractal technique, the gyroscope balanced itself.

Starting and stopping was the hard part, since it would pull in passive gain when you didn't want it to unless you *really* put effort into clamping it shut. Though, even with all of that, nobody knew the *real* secret of how she was breaking through the ranks so fast.

Jiivra clapped her hands now that she had everyone's attention. "This is what we're going to do."

CHAPTER FOUR

Artorian saw a ring of light return to his position through the illuminating moss, bouncing back from one of the tunnels right above him that he couldn't conveniently get to. The bioluminescent moss didn't faze the Blight. It was too weak and too minor, and based on the absolute lack of response from the unpleasant shapeless mass... it hadn't noticed the *extra* bit. Artorian spoke with bemused wit. "We're going to play a game!"

"The game is how long it takes you to figure out what mistakes you made. Without me telling you, at least until it's too late. I will, however, give you a clue when you ask for it."

Cataphron started beating a dead horse. Specifically, using one of the bodies of a Jian resident. Mostly out of sheer frustration, as at every turn this delusional, irritating fogey worked around his decade-long plan. The old man was supposed to *run*, to attempt to flee and *hide*. He was supposed to discover that no path he could take led to his freedom. No path led to salvation. All paths would lead the codger right back to *him*.

Upholding this first-person viewpoint was difficult. He slipped into sentences with 'we' instead of 'I', and the twinkle in the old man's eye was dangerous. That idiot-pulse had been harmless, but it had confirmed something both of them had been uncertain of: the land-law only worked while the Blight was *Cataphron*. When enough mind, similarity, and identity was invoked to trick the vow into believing the soul of Cataphron still belonged to the original body, rather than a mimicry.

Crunch

The Blight snapped its considerable omnidirectional vision to the old man. Once again, confection crumbs flaked from the sides of his cheeks, marring the edge of his lips as another 'cookie' had come from nowhere to be consumed. The man was supposed to eat the flesh of the fallen! To fall into *despair!* The Blight was *seething* for satisfaction.

How did this field mouse have so much *food* on him? Artorian crunched the delicious cookie, swallowing with a wide smile before thumbing the corners of his mouth to lick them clean. A very thin and veiled starlight Aura surrounded him, excessively cleaning without harm to the Blight. The identity slider had been completely moved to 'cleaning' with a little leeway for 'light'. Not enough to harm his adversary, but certainly enough to annoy the deathly *abyss* out of it.

Artorian had spent *years* honing his ability to get under Cataphron's skin in letter format, and easy *decades* of consistent sass practice. The cherry on top? He was living and doing this purely out of spite; purely to aggrieve and annoy an entity that likely wasn't even from this world. Just to stick it to 'em. Artorian knew that his survival was... unlikely.

The **ping** he got back let him know some of his students had survived, unfortunately he didn't know who, or how many. Just that they *had.* Since the ping had returned, the effect must have reached them. Though that wasn't the intent of his little... charade.

The truth was in the moss. Artorian didn't know it, but his Fringe-daughter had been absolutely right on the gold coin: Blighty here was a glutton. It liked to *eat!* Eventually, it was going to eat some of the moss in counter-spite. Artorian *knew* it would. It would think of it eventually as a way to get back at a creature it couldn't touch, since it wanted so *badly* to see him suffer. Specifically, suffer *slowly.*

If the Blight dropped the entire sadism routine, and went after him in earnest... then it could not do so while maintaining the method by which it was somehow holding the land-law vow together. Much like the armor that was currently still of no use to him. Artorian just didn't have a good grasp on how the *blazing heavens* that worked. Why did land-laws even work at all? How does a patch of ground have the ability to punish someone for breaking a promise or oath?

That just didn't make any sense, because that's not how it worked in the Fringe. He knew *well* how rites of land ownership functioned, but not abyss-blasted *why*.

Cataphron spat back at him. "*Burn* you and your games."

Artorian raised a brow. "You're hurt by fire... I'm surprised to hear you make such a comment."

The Blight infesting Cataphron's body reeled unnaturally. Cracking the spine to bend the body in twisted ways before aligning it to face Artorian with sickening pops. "No, I'm *not.* I'm *immune* to that annoyance called fire. It's just a distraction. A dumb. Paltry. Minute. Irritating distraction. I care not for any temperature. I don't feel it. I care not for the damage their extremes *supposedly* accomplish. They don't function against me. Of all the compound Essences, there are but *two* that have ever given me any thoughts of doubt. Once you are dead, none will remain in this world."

Sagely nodding was the old man's reply, a mystery cookie pressed between his fingers. He spoke with flat snark, but played it off like he meant his words. "Oh. *Well,* then. My sincere *apologies.* I never realized I was in the presence of such greatness."

Cataphron threw his arms into the air as the untenable mass above him shifted with bubbling agreement. "Finally, some *sense!*"

An idea struck the philosopher, and he stowed the cookie for now. He had planned to take a loud, interruptive bite at whatever the response was going to be... but something better came to mind. "Ah, well. Yes, I suppose I should have noticed earlier. I didn't really make the connection before now. I did see a high ranked Mage throw power at you, and it did... well, it did nothing. Given such invulnerability, I shouldn't be surprised by an entity that's two hundred years old."

The Blight recoiled as if it had been grievously insulted. The entire room shifted as smooth shadows became jagged and edged. Some even creased and dug dimpled lines into the moss-coated wall. So, shadows could become solid? Good to know!

The room, rather than Cataphron, replied. "Two *hundred?* You wound me with your poor estimations. I am no wet-eared whelp. I am two *thousand* years into my glorious eternity. I am from the peak, the pinnacle, the *apex* of the Golden Age."

Cataphron's body stilled, and Artorian was hard pressed not to test an attack. It was too likely that was a ruse, a purposeful moment of weakness to eke out an aggressive response that would spur his own demise. Cataphron's neck cracked and his face did a full-moon turn to regard him, sad to see there was no flicker in the old man's Aura.

Artorian let out a calming exhale. Close call. He'd nearly done it. Best to pry a little more. "Two *thousand!* My word, were you ever human? Or always... actually I'm not sure what you are. We've just been calling you whatever comes to mind at the time."

"Whatever comes...!" Cataphron pressed his undead hand to his chest, appalled once more. "What do you *mean* you do not know of me? I exist in every history book, every folk tale, and every dreadful story mortals use to still their children at night. I, the eternal transcended of the dark. Wondrous, vast, and all-reaching. There is nowhere my tendrils do not spread, no underdark my bleakness does not tread."

Artorian pressed thumbs into his temples, then rubbed them in slow circles. "I'm... no... no, that doesn't sound familiar. I thought it had to do with a story about the mountain being tossed from the moon, but of course *that* was preposterous."

"It. *Is.* Not!" The cavern shuddered and violently shook as the intensity of the phantom's words cracked stalactites, and the old man went diving for cover. Sharp sky rocks would certainly do some harm, and even though he was staving off infection and disease from all the dead via his Aura, it was too big a risk to take a hit.

The Blight *fumed*, roiling like an angry swarm; buzzing with the silenced screams of trapped minds trying to push free from its entrapping blubber. "My last fray with the first Aran was a battle of *legend*. We scoured the planet and fought on the three moons, back when there *were* three. How the balance *twisted* when the third was sent to the great unknown, merely to force me into underground entrapment and slumber. The brightest of the Golden Age destroyed their prosperity merely to buffet me like a wailing *child*."

Cataphron scoffed, contained enough to talk locally again. "*Human?* Nay, I was never of such insignificant filth. I was Elven before my Apotheosis, as *all* the greats were. A *true* Elven, before the fracture. Before the fall. Before our race was shattered."

The old man sat down on a large rock, watching Cataphron move wildly and talk more with his hands than even *he* did during an enthusiastic lecture. The Blight really loved talking about itself. Maybe he could do something with that... another nudge? Another nudge. "Here I thought you were from the great beyond all along, since nobody can figure out what you are."

Cataphron faltered, a near weeping expression on his drooped face. "Oh, how the histories have muddled. The deepest knowledge is *lost.*"

The droop quickly flicked to a maddened ear-to-ear smile. "How I look forward to *correcting* such maladies. For I *feel* it. Claws hack at the outside of the mountain; they seek passage within. I need but *one*. But *one*... then my connection shall be powerful enough to resurge once more."

Artorian once again had a cookie in his hand, though he looked at it disinterestedly. "So, just an Elf then. Odd body for an Elf. Very wispy, like a smoked pipe."

The Blight snarled, swirling again as its irritation returned. "Do your ears serve only as repositories for *wax*? Was! I said I *was* an Elf! I have become *more* than Elven prowess. Even back *then* I was special. I survived the Ripping where others did *not.*"

The old man nibbled at the edge of the confection, repeating the words of note to make it sound like he was invested in the conversation. "The ripping, you say... but of course."

Cataphron scoffed, as if such a young mortal could possibly understand the significance. He smiled, knowing that he could lord his knowledge over the old fool all he wanted. Like always, he would outlast any mortal. This tale calmed him and reminded him of that fact. He would win in the end. Victory would be all the sweeter when he watched this moth wink out against its dark flame.

"Oh yes... knowledge of Essence channels was so commonplace during the Golden Age that even *peasants* had their centers cleared of corruption. Yet I... *I* was special. My infernal channel, during an event of Ibis Ta—a gathering of power—went wild. The overabundant influx of the infernal ripped my channel open, forcibly closing all the others. They thought me dead, but I lived. I lived, and underwent apotheosis over the course of a scant few years. Why, it went by so swiftly that I barely remember the *agony.*"

Artorian no longer half-nibbled at his cookie. His eyes sternly locked on the hollow dark flames alight in Cataphron's sockets. "You *jest.* You merely say this to deny me truth. If you had truly survived an affinity channel rip, which *all* sources say is fatal... you jest. There *is* no apotheosis, that means to become a *divine.*"

The dark, charismatic voice cut him off, "Or to *become* something else, beyond that which you were. Three *years* I suffered as the infernal took me. *Replaced* me. Yet as I changed, I learned things unimaginable. I tapped into power my peers could not reach and my tutors could neither grasp nor comprehend. I moved infernal in ways so natural that *monks* sought *me* out for guidance. My connection was so strong, *Ascended* sought me for answers. Do you truly not grasp what becomes of those who survive ripped Essence channels? We become something else.

"We become elementals."

CHAPTER FIVE

"Tychus, did you have to kill another one of our retainers?" Grimaldus flipped a page in his book as he walked closely behind his brother. They had been evicted out of the ziggurat until they'd 'regained enough honor' to be seen by the Vizier once more.

In any other situation, this would have been a gift from the heavens themselves. They were out unsupervised, surrounded by thousands of refugees, and were far more powerful than the standard person they would encounter.

Grim looked down at the bone bracelet he was wearing, grimacing as he recalled the Vizier's words: 'While you wear these, you have my protection, and I will always be able to find you. There is nothing that will unintentionally break them, which means the moment it happens you will have proven that I can no longer trust you. Then, I will have no use for you. The Mistress, on the other hand, can always use more bodies.'

His brother *tsk'd* at the reminder. "I already told you, it is not my fault that their bodies are so frail!"

Tychus currently stood at six and a half feet tall, muscled so heavily that he nearly looked obese. "I gave him a supportive pat on his back when he was yelling at you, it is not my fault he died from a suggestive nudge!"

Grimaldus flatly accused his brother. "We both know that you have trouble controlling your body cultivation. We both also know that your control is not that bad. Just because someone is yelling at me does not mean they need to die. I know it is frustrating, and hard to understand, but it is better to serve the evil you know than an unknown."

Tychus rolled his massive shoulders and shoved yet another refugee-turned-raider out of his path. "Well, at least we get to enjoy some fresh air. I am certain that you are as sick of the pits as I am. Any thoughts on what we can do to get back in the good graces of the sublime Vizier?"

Grimaldus narrowed his eyes. Sometimes his brother truly did not know how to hold his tongue. "You must realize that your voice booms, and we are surrounded by literally thousands of people who would do anything to get in his favor?"

"I would love for someone to report me for calling him 'sublime'." Tychus chuckled at the very thought. "What is going on over there? That seems promising."

Grimaldus followed his brother's gesture, his eyes locking upon a massive sprawling arena that was currently under construction. On one of the completed arena rings, two people traded blows. "That must be the Vizier's recent bid for the Mistress's favor. He had recently mentioned a foolproof, unbeatable ranking system that he had designed."

"Unbeatable? *Arena?*" Tychus allowed a wide smile to break out across his rectangular-shaped face. "Perfect! We will become the champions of the arena, and by then not only will we have proven ourselves, brought honor, and given everyone plenty of time to cool off... but also gained a hefty sack of silver if I am reading that prize board correctly."

Grimaldus shook his head. "That may work for you, but all my cultivation allows me to do is kill. There is not very much I can do to someone beyond simply dissolving a chunk of their body, and I feel like that would not be taken very well."

Just then, the fight in the arena concluded in a spectacular fashion. The spear of the winner entered the front of the loser's neck, exiting the back. The loser dropped to the ground, and the onlookers erupted into cheers. Tychus smirked over his shoulder at his smaller brother, "It appears that the matches can be to the death."

With a dark gleam in his eye, Grimaldus nodded along, now on board with the idea. "It appears I have found a way to progress my cultivation even while exiled from the pits, brother. Shall we register?"

Tychus just giggled.

Over the next few weeks, the brothers took on all challengers. The only time they refused to fight was when the arena matchmakers attempted to force them to fight each other. After the first two matchmakers were killed in lieu of one of the brothers, the others finally seemed to catch on.

After a month, the two were officially on the top one hundred list where they finally began to encounter dangerous foes. For the first time since they had begun, the duo were up against more than just simple F- or very low D-rank combatants. Still, they prevailed.

The reputation the two of them created for themselves was one of no mercy, no quarter, and that anything and everything would be used to win. After opening a position on the list for themselves by drenching the ground in blood, their next opponents and the ones after that simply bowed and forfeited.

During a match where Grimaldus' opponent didn't flake out, Tychus roared in appreciation as his brother's opponent screamed when swarmed by skeletons. All opponents were given the opportunity to surrender, but after the initial refusal not a single one had ever been granted mercy. Grim was all smiles when a day later, he left the dais with another victory. "All of that reading is finally paying off! I saw no Essence loss today! Even better is that I do not need to burn yet another set of robes."

Grimaldus laughed along with Tychus as they stepped to the side and prepared for the next and final matches of the day. "Perhaps we will finally be taken seriously when we tell them we will only give them one chance to walk away without joining my growing horde."

A matchmaker walked up to the two of them, a cheeky smile brimming on his face. "It seems that the top fifty is as far as you go for now! I have just received orders from the Vizier: you are to present yourselves to him immediately."

The two brothers stood and turned as one, but the matchmaker had not finished, "Of course, since you are leaving right now, you will have to forfeit this match and the earnings from today's winning streak. Oh, abyss!"

The man dove to the ground as a boulder-sized fist lazily swept through the air where his head had been but a moment ago. "All I am doing is explaining! I get nothing out of this!"

The emerald-eyed brothers were already walking away, not sparing the man a second glance. When the Vizier gave you an order, you followed it on the spot if you wanted to remain alive. Grim chuckled at the memory of the pudgy matchmaker flinging himself away. "It appears we have gathered enough honor to regain our positions."

"Sooner than expected, in my humble opinion," Tychus rumbled.

"You just wanted to continue spending your silver on the lovely camp followers," Grim teased his bulky companion. "And here I thought you would..."

He trailed off as he saw the expression on the quasi-giant's face.

Tychus had narrowed his emerald eyes at the sea of humanity around them. His voice lowered and quivered as it only ever did when they knew they had privacy. "What are we doing here, Grimaldus? Have we become irredeemable beasts? Look at me! Day by day I continue to grow, within a few years I will be a monster... what would Elder have-"

"*Enough*, Tychus!" Grimaldus demanded, his equally pained emerald eyes dangerously flashing. "You know we will do *whatever* we need to do in order to survive. It has been years since we came here, and it may be years before we can escape. We can only hope that when we do, we can forgive ourselves for doing what must be done."

"The fact of the matter, Tychus, is that we are the only ones that will *need* to find forgiveness. Well, perhaps Astrea is still out there, but the simple fact of that matter is that the Elder, just like everyone else we knew in the Fringe..."

"...died *years* ago."

CHAPTER SIX

"Elementals." Feeling very alive, Artorian cautiously repeated the word like he was tasting it in his mouth. He found it... encouraging. It served only to whet his appetite, though he held firm so as to not fall into another ruse. "The very basis of the Essence, given form, mind retained?"

Cataphron shouted in elation, pleased with the development. "*Yes!* See, even *you* can think if your betters spoon feed you the components like the little mortal baby you are..."

He paused as he saw the old man hold his chin, deep in thought. "Lost *already?* That's not unex-"

"I'm counting."

Cataphron gleefully allowed a partial smile as the left side of his lips curled upward. "Don't hurt yourself too much for my sake. Actually..."

The Blight didn't get a response from the hushed counting that was furiously happening on the old man's fingers. He could make out a muddled mention of 'two thousand', see a head scratch, and then another attempt to start from the top. "Now you're being worthlessly annoying again."

Artorian looked up from his mathematics. "It just doesn't add up. There's no history dating back more than... maybe a few hundred years? Everything before that is just *gone*, or didn't *happen.* This 'golden age' of yours. It never *happened.*"

The Blight's mood soured, and it was visible on the possessed face of the undead infernal cultivator's corpse. Artorian thought that was awfully *expressive* for a dead man. "Merely because you don't *know*, doesn't mean history didn't *happen*, fool! Perhaps a lesson will make you see some stars."

A malicious grin followed, and without waiting for a retort the Blight launched into a full 'I know better than you' tirade. Perhaps he could *bore* the codger to death with history. "Don't worry: unlike *mortals*, I have done well to keep up with what you have so *wastefully* cast aside. If we say that the point we are at now is zero BC, Before Cataphron, then the years work as follows:

"Two thousand BC, the height of the golden age. The apex, the midpoint, the glorious spread of the Ever Empire. Knowledge of the Tower was at its zenith, and the Heavenly ascended near once a year, leaving this mortal coil for a greater purpose. My favorite of which was an old *friend*. He became the Heavenly of **Order**, keeper of vows and promises.

"It is through his magnanimous will that concepts such as land-laws, ownership contracts, and Mana-promises hold power. By your own might you make the vow, and by *his* oath, keeps you to yours. It is in this time that I transcend, and face unfair and unjust *punishment* for what I've become. It is here the third moon is sacrificed, and it is *here* we ring the bell of decline. For the age of plenty has ended."

"Twelve hundred BC, the golden age comes to a screeching end. Gnomes go into seclusion due to persecution from the rise of the major Elven super nation. *My* nation. Currently they're just called 'Ancient Elves', but we used to be so, *so* much more. Grand political struggles tore apart the accords of unison, and with their destruction... Essence knowledge is no longer shared; it is now *hoarded*, rather than kept as a cohesive whole. Species fracture amongst themselves, entire lineages and houses are lost in pursuit of safeguarding what little they can save.

"This was the last age where a Node was added to the Tower, and knowledge of the Heavenly made the rounds. No more have ascended to the heavens since this day, as no more iridescent borealis have graced the entirety of the sky.

"One thousand BC. One of my favorites... the Endless War. Due to horrendous strife, what becomes known as 'the Endless War' breaks out as attempts to secure the world's best resource deposits come to a head. *Gone* are the days of politically agreeing to share basic needs. The strong survive, and the majority of higher end cultivators begin lineage feuds that will last for centuries.

"To the survivor... it's nasty. It's awful. Border slaughter runs rampant as the supernation starts to collapse. The call goes out, the last try for unity and peace. All remaining high-powered leadership gathers in the Socorro capital.

"Nine-fifty BC. The *Meteor*. After some serious infighting, a common cause is discovered when a space rock comes to say hello. It turns out that when you kick a moon out of orbit, it just comes back for revenge. It impacts the capital smack-center. The majority of the effects are mitigated at the cost of the lives of thousands of Mages and a grand majority of S-rankers and up.

"They saved the world as a whole, and I have my first taste of sweet vengeance. They lost *their* world, no matter that the world itself survived. The Elves shattered into splinter species. Ancient Elves become 'Wild Elves' since their entire civilization is gone. Only rubble and ruin remain, their ways of life split along with their self-aggrandized species.

"Knowledge of cultivation retreats into the recesses of the world, and those who have it become the new nobility as the Endless War comes to an end. There are none left to fight, and those who do remain are broken. It is time to consolidate, and plan anew!

"The old world is dead... long live the new world. A mere *century* afterwards, the new generation of mortals that have come and gone have no clue what came before. *History* is different. The old ways are taught no longer. It is *taboo* to do so, for those teachings brought only ruin. The powerful are reclusive, despising intervention into their personal affairs. Interlopers are silenced. Scholars are culled. Knowledge is scoured and stolen between ancient houses for *scraps* of a monument that no longer stands.

"New ways of life spring up, and the old world ignores them. New wars break out, and the old world lets them happen. Undead march the lands, and the old world *lets it happen*. Conflicts are waged between forces not their own, and those who survive remain of the opinion that the new world is not *their* concern. Hundreds and hundreds of years, and the old world remains passive; culled by their own hubris. Locked in their own torment. All who live from that age are mad, lost, broken... or *me*." The Blight savored that last syllable with a succulent slurp.

How it had eaten, and eaten, and *eaten* the minds of *eons* of people. How each mind added to its intellect, even as it added to its propensity for distraction. The Blight remained distanced from madness, for there was always another passion in which to indulge. A passion of hunger, for existence was to feast, and all the world had been laid before it on a table.

"So yes... *elementals*. We are endless and unbound. Our minds kiss the fabric of the universe, unshackled by flesh. I do not bend the infernal to my will. I *am* the infernal."

Artorian tapped his chin. Pleasant history lesson, but nothing about what was preventing this supposedly 'mighty elemental' from leaving in the first place. If he was truly all-reaching, remaining stuck under the rock you'd been cast down with seemed a nearly *ironic* choice. So the only conclusion was that the Blight had omitted important information: specifically on why it was stuck here.

No, it had let slip a few things. A few... *crucial* details. "That's quite a children's tale. So your attempts to lure me into violating the land-law came about due to your friendship with a person that *became* the reason such laws are enforced in the first place? Devious."

If the Blight didn't know his plan had been seen through before with certainty, it did now. Its entire speech had saddled it on a high horse, and it felt *great*. Superior. Atop the world and preparing to crush a mortal speck between its elemental foot. Then *that* got mentioned, and it was right back to feeling lemon-sour as the scrumptious crunch of a cookie being loudly chewed echoed in the darkness.

Cataphron's voice was flat. "I *hate* you."

The reply was a joyful *mmm* of a thoroughly enjoyed confection. The Blight considered just flattening him. Just ending it. The long game was going to be satisfying... but he *could* just quickly end it.

It squinted as it noticed an anomaly. A suspicious flicker hung on the academic's Aura. That *brat* was *baiting* him! His Aura held a counter attack, fueled and ready to burst. That weasel! "When I reach the tender groves of your precious friends again, I'm going to consume so many of their trees that the Wood Elf S-ranked elders will have to wake up just to contain the damage."

Artorian waited a moment before sassily regarding his next cookie. "*More* jesting. Wood Elves don't have S-rankers."

Cataphron slid unpleasantly close to the edge of Artorian's external Aura. "Of *course* the Old World has S-rankers, and not even their Soul-ranked dimensional shifts are effective against *me*. They are merely a deterrence at *best*.

They're *all* bound to the Nature Law, all three of them. That's the limit with any given Node. *One* S, one double-S, and one triple-S. Their terrible naming convention that describes how many steps one has taken towards the heavenly ascension."

Remaining steady in the face of what was intended to be disheartening discomfort, the old man leered into the ghostly sockets of a man that used to be a peer. "Very well then. I take it you're on the last step? Given you've had such *vast* lengths of time to develop your power, and all. The souls you must have eaten along the way likely mean you're going to be meeting your friend soon, no?"

The flickering phantom eyes looked away. Oh? Curious... the infernal cultivator's form followed soon after, and the body walked with the waltzing rhythm of a self-important noble. "I... oh, what's the harm? You won't live to tell a soul. Speaking of, I consume and entrap *minds*. Not *souls*. That requires being tied to the gluttony node in the Tower of Ascension. Also called the *devouring* node, or the hunger node. No. I *was* Ascended, but such connections are lost when one transcends into an elemental.

"Had I successfully made the first step into the S-ranks... maybe. Unlikely, but maybe. Had I turned during the portion of the S-rank where initial actualization occurs, then *certainly!* Unfortunately, becoming the full incarnation of an Essence doesn't sit too well with stable concepts. I am able to do anything the infernal **Law** can. It doesn't like not being *needed* and all its effects being freely available. So, it threw me out of my Ascension, and the ripped channel consumed me."

The Blight reflected on the moment like it had been yesterday, though time had long since ceased to hold meaning. The expression plastering his captive's face enticed a smile. The

Blight tasted the seasoning it had just poured over an impending meal.

The old man was *shook!* Artorian pressed his hand to his heart. His body angled back and away, and his face was carefully contorted in an expression that conveyed shock, awe, disbelief, and appalled rejection. "A person can *cease* being a Mage? Surely that's a one-way road with all the effort one goes through to get there!"

CHAPTER SEVEN

The Blight merrily laughed. This was causing destabilizations. It *liked* that. "Ha! Just what do you think nodes *are*? How they come to exist, refine, and function? In the day when the Tower was still building, this knowledge was so common that even *children* knew. Of *course* you can be rejected! Do you think the **Law** of Ice would let you retain your connection if you lost your water Essence channel? It does *not!* It strips you of your Ascension body and kicks you back out to the low mortal realm. Do you believe an Actualized, your S-rankers, to be any different? *No!*"

The phantoms sneered in delight. The wounded whimpers from the old man were *candy* to its senses. More. It needed *more*. "It takes much *longer* for an Actualized to be punted to the curb, but it certainly happens. Waste away too long without benefit to the **Law**, and it may judge you unworthy. It will find more suitable candidates to replace the waste of space, and if you fail the challenge it sets forth... The **Law** siphons your power, breaks it into itty-bitty little pieces, and channels it to the worthy that *did* pass. It will fuel and fatten them up with Ascension energy until they reach the breaching point.

"When they do, and the Actualized is nearly bottomed out, the judging concludes. Death or graduation. The Actualized return to being Ascended, and if they attempt to use power as they did before... they will *destroy* themselves from the exertion. So used are the powerful to their measure of ability, that they ofttimes forget how to *function* if they lose it."

Artorian held his face with both hands, mentally recording this information with rapt attention even if it was false.

He had to know. He *needed* to know. The perfect opportunity for a sassy quip came and silently went, spent instead on the acquisition of knowledge while upholding the clever ruse of being in agony from the proffered lessons. Pretending made Cataphron keep talking. So pretend he did, with dramatic flair.

"Affinity channels are *everything*. They determine everything from growth rate to potential. They are used by the Tower as first measure to check who you can even speak with. Not that the Nodes retain much personality once they become such, and I've found the prospect dull and wasteful. Just *think*... triple S-ranks. *Centuries* of work and toil, only to remove yourself entirely from all that progress and become a fresh node in the Tower as the first step of becoming 'Heavenly'. An absolute *waste*.

"For any concept that already has an existing node, or Essence combination you'd wish to occupy, an Actualized has to replace the entity in said node. Which can't even be done *forcefully*! The node has to *desire* transference to the heavens, completing its journey into a full and proper Heavenly cultivator. Then *poof*. They're gone! Never to be heard from again as they become incapable of interacting further with this realm. They become so intertwined with the functions of the universe that they no longer have eyes for the realm they came from. *Never* has a Heavenly been contacted that didn't address the one who did so with *disdainful* dereliction and disinterest."

Artorian didn't interrupt what had become a full-on rage-vent. The Blight didn't appear to have noticed it was serenading the fumes of its agitations now that it had someone to listen. Like a toddler that spoke at length merely because someone was present in the room to hear it craft a calamitous cacophony. "The Heavenly have lost all care. All the wants of this realm are foreign to them. As an entity without body, and freed will, I... _understand_ how they view such things now.

"Time erodes connections and lack of communication burns all bridges, much as I care _only_ to absorb ever more scrumptious minds. Those conceited _things_ only care to uphold their function. Even their slight _nudge_ towards this realm is appalling, releasing celestial Essence onto the land like a dumped sack of glitterdust!"

Cataphron quirked a curious brow at his captive. The academic was sweating. Beautiful. _Suffer_ you little twerp! "Something _wrong?_"

Rubbing his chin, the lecture attendant *_Hmmmm'd_* to himself. "So, if there was an 'error' in the universe. A rip, a problem, an inconsistency. They would... fix it?"

Undead groans sounded awfully guttural, and Cataphron lurched away excessively. "If those interest-devoid grown-up-nodes _don't_, what's _above_ them will. If there was ever something truly egregious—such as a time loop or tear—they attend to it quickly. Resolving the issue as soon as the Essence reaction runs dry and stops being able to sustain itself.

"It happened _painfully_ often anytime celestial and infernal were used together in great quantities. Chaos is a **Law** that several Heavenlies angrily hold by the scruff of the neck. Chaos, Entropy, and Discord... there have been _eons_ of discussion about why any time there's a significant problem, it _always_ comes down to those three."

Artorian wished he could write this down, but he'd have to settle for burning the knowledge into his memory. His sweaty outwards appearance wasn't a ruse; the bodily reaction happened in response to a great weight falling from his shoulders. "So... when in the scriptures it mentions the progression path, and 'Godly' is mentioned after 'Heavenly' there is *really* a...?"

"A divine-tier cultivator?" The Blight was right back to superiority boasting. It was thoroughly enjoying grinding the scholar's face into the ground. That type did *poorly* when their beliefs came into fundamental question.

"Back when the Heavenlies could still be enticed to turn back enough to spare us a few graced words... that's when the Golden Age truth delvers were told of the rank above theirs. Grasping the meaning was just utterly *impossible*. We *already* can't grasp the full power of a Heavenly. There was something *higher*? Something *more*? Entire *schools* went mad trying to puzzle it out, and even made a Node for Madness simply to be able to cope. The *fools*.

"They made the base layer of necessary potential thought intricately complex and equally impossible to *understand*. With so much group-mind unity and Essence behind it, that the Madness **Law** burst through the Tower and made a home for itself all the way up on the Seven hundred and twentieth floor! The top! What were they *thinking*?"

Cataphron composed himself as he reached the answer to their own question. "Well... Madness. I suppose they weren't thinking at all, if they were even able to at that point. At least it barred anyone who didn't have *all* the Essence channels from tapping into that awful *mistake* of a node. Locations are *precious*! Don't make nodes in the Tower unless it follows the pattern! Six per floor. It was six per *floor*!"

The old man sassed, "Odd, I was told *seven* was the correct number to aim for."

Phantoms screeched at Artorian for that inane comment, not knowing he'd said it on the fly, lying through his teeth. How *dare* he assume he knew better with outdated and incorrect knowledge? The old man's off-the-cuff statement made the ceiling-body *roil.*

"How would *you* know? You weren't *there.* You didn't take the lessons, or attended the equation lectures, or scribe the reasoning for why having more than six nodes on any given floor would destabilize the inter-constra-pattern of the Tower-matrix itself! Oh, *sure*, you can put seven nodes on a floor, but at what cost? You can't add a floor after that! When one of the nodes in the Tower loses their concept because it's outdated entirely, it can lose its place if the Heavenly in it goes on to finish his cycle! Without anyone to replace it! That kills the Node and connections, and opens up a slot where it used to be, but it's not like the Essence combination will be *different!*

"This is the entire mess that led to nodes carrying multiple concepts for a single Essence mixture. Suddenly *everything* earth and air is in the same place! *Lightning?* Earth and air node. Easy. Simple. No problem. Mud, slime, clay, quicksand. *All* of that suddenly the same blasted node! If they were going to just let that slide, they could have at least made the growth additive and *sequential.* No! They threw Nodes at the Tower like monkeys throw feces!

"As soon as the Prime Six were down, they went on a Heaven-cursed race to fill the slots! No thought was given early on to adding Nodes in a *reasonable* method so that climbing resulted in a pattern that could be *expected.* First floor: water. Second floor: water and air, for mist. Then do *all* the combinations of two's, and once you're done with them *all*, proceed adding the combination of *threes* in higher levels.

"Reasonable, yes? Did they *do* that?" Cataphron punched a corpse so hard that the channeled might of the blow created a twenty-foot deep hole in a perfect cylinder. His voice was breaking, and the personality of Cataphron faltered as a mélange and mixture of several other voices all spoke and aired their grievances at the same time. It was like with the Wood Elves, but without the soothing quality, and a reverb that was more... doom-y. "*No!*

"Second floor! What do those idiots slot? Infernal and earth, water and earth; air and water; water and celestial; fire and celestial; then water, earth *and celestial*. What? That's a tri-combination! Then I turn the page for the next tier, and the first thing I read is an infernal, fire, *and earth*. What is another triple combination doing on the second and third tiers? *Who* thought that was a good idea?"

A second cylindrical crater joined the first. Everything in the area disintegrated within the affected region. Artorian was watching this time. It was the goose effect! Goo wasn't what was eating away at anything in the zone this time, so it must have been... infernal touching it directly? Not through a medium, but directly? This must be the prime benefit an elemental had over its cultivator counterparts. A cultivator gathered and then expended. A Mage *channeled*, based on Ember's lectures. It seemed that an elemental *generated*. They were a *source* of their relevant energy.

Wouldn't that mean elementals were cultivation sources for a whole *host* of people? That was a very good reason to keep knowledge of them tightly shut in a box; an advantage people would not want to share. Did Artorian know anyone that could benefit from this?

Why, yes. Yes, he *did* know of one.

That knowledge was mentally shelved for later. He paused his musings and calmly unpacked his hookah, preparing it while the seething Blight worked to reclaim the hold over itself. Artorian *could* attack now, but it appeared there was... surprise company. He looked up to blow out the first smoke ring, and noticed a patch of cavern moss was brighter than its resident counterparts. His Essence sight was what picked it up, and the written message was a deviously intelligent ploy. Someone needed inside knowledge of the infernal to get *that* past a being made entirely from it.

Astrea, you clever girl. Yet It wasn't the right moment. Keeping a note of the message, he turned his attention back to the screaming phantoms now present in the large, empty cavern. Not counting the dead. Multiple see through wispy forms were arguing with one another. The multitudes of minds were having a row since they couldn't reach a consensus. So, it *did* work similarly to Wood Elven unity? *Interesting.* He wondered if... "So what happened to your cultivation technique? Did you lose it when you transcended into a superior being? An Elemental?"

The soothing brush of ego from a hated foe snapped away the shades. They all huffed into a nonexistent breeze as the collapsed and crumbled dead body of Cataphron refilled and wrested itself from the body pile. "That is not your concern... or did you mean to gauge the quality of techniques we had in the Golden Age? I bet you wish to ask if we used 'Royal' techniques."

Phah!

The infernal body spat dissolving goo at the ground. "What a *sullen* naming convention. Everything of this era is just so... *crude*. Limited. The entire point of separating the core-cultivation techniques into their own tiers was so we could track how quickly that variable would affect someone's time until Ascension. 'Royal' is at *best* a third tier understanding of the glorious compass counterparts we had at our fingertips.

"A better core technique was something you received because you could handle it, *when* you could handle it. At least until that awful pearlescent *curse*. That was a terrible thing during the decline of the golden age, it locked people into their technique and broke it entirely if they attempted to swap it. It ruined an entire cultural lineage."

A heavy cloud in the shape of a circle puffed out from Artorian's carefully parted mouth. He wanted to know more about the pearlescent material. It had done... *something* to him. Asking directly was going to be suspicious. He needed a way around to broach that subject.

CHAPTER EIGHT

Artorian clapped his hands together. "I'm going to need you to slow down, you're going to cause me to bleed from my ears if you keep telling me things that fast. So, if I'm following on that last topic, then the amount of Essence channels contributes to how quickly one becomes Ascended, and the core technique is just a part of that math."

Slow *down*? Had the Blight heard that correctly? How it *loved* the idea of watching his captive bleed just from being overburdened by mere *words*. Oh, there *would* be no stopping now. "Mortal bodies come with roughly the same limitations when it comes to cultivation. You're trying to make yourself into 'something else'. A person with one Essence channel will usually take around two hundred years before they can enter the Tower from sheer Essence requirement alone."

"The requirements drop by roughly three to five decades for every additional channel. Some variation is accounted for based on channel quality, but none in my Era had anything *other* than perfect channels, which cut the time down by an additional ten years per channel. Opening new channels you didn't start with was... tightly regulated."

"On average, a three Essence-channel individual can knock on the Tower's doors in a century if they do things 'decently well'. Assuming that you have nothing special boosting you during that time frame. Average *everything*. So 'a mostly-okay fractal spiral cultivation technique' at the minimum, with a spiral quantity of ninety-four. Or your basic third-axis internal helix."

The Blight tasted sweet succulence as Artorian groaned loudly, and rubbed his pained forehead from all the word choices and difficult concepts wracking his mind. It didn't pause to let the aged academic catch a mental reprieve. "This coupled with a 'mostly okay Essence source' classed as non-curator. I suppose you'd call that a non-dungeon. With a 'mostly alright cultivation time allotment' but nothing special. As in a day job between cultivating time, while you're trying to have a social life."

Artorian groaned again, long and with stuttered pauses. Cataphron betrayed an enjoyable shiver. It didn't notice that each expelled groan matched gently glowing patches of moss directly above them each time it altered its illumination pattern.

"If all you have is the basic Essence string or single spiral chi technique. Well... you *can* reach Ascension from there, but the time requirement is going to double, if not *triple* at the minimum. A 'Noble' or 'Royal' technique is a misconception. It's not special because it's 'Noble'. It's higher grade because it capitalizes on cultivation functions the average technique *doesn't*. Single strands? Bottom tier. Shaped strands? Mid-bottom tier. A *spiral?* Paltry, but you're at the top of bottom-tier along with center webways."

Its sorrowful tone increased in distaste. "I'm aware the *fractal* is popular this era. It's a bottom to middle *parlor* trick. Mid-tier *only* if you reach ninety-four spirals. That's *literally* in the book as the *average*. Perhaps Zibonacci spiraling all of them would make it reach the top of the middle tier?"

Another muffled yelp from its captive was soothing, so it slid in extra detail like the prick of a needle as it explained that complicated Z-word. "It means 'perfect spirals'. Keep up, human!

"How about core-techniques worth our time, yes? Bottom of the high-tier is where variation and creativity starts to *really* show itself. The basic requirement of all these core-techniques capitalize on using all three dimensions, rather than limit itself to two axis' worth of direction. They use available center-space far more efficiently, and that directly translates to Essence influx and refining speed. This is the level of complexity your 'Noble' techniques have managed to replicate. The *bottom* of a high-tier, or *slightly* above average. Nothing *impressive*.

"Adding proper interconnectivity and layering in the design bring them up to the middle of high-tier, and having that combination in a Zibonacci sequence brings it to the top of high-tier. Cramming more of a core-technique into a small space isn't *necessarily* better. That's still limited to the core-types that *can* undergo Z-sequencing. Abyss help you if you attempt the absurdity that is joint-cultivation with a Beast-Core. Helix patterns and function-specific core-tricks don't need the Z."

Artorian drank some water from a flask. "Bernoulli?"

"Bernoulli *indeed!* He..." All sound ceased, and Cataphron leered at the... was the Skyspear headmaster snacking on fruit and puffing from a *hookah*? How had it not *noticed* this? That was *absurd!* It caught some of the smoke and... dissolved where it touched. *What.* The Blight blinked and inspected the smoke. It felt awful, but was overall harmless. It... *ah.* Celestial Essence with an ingrained dispersal identity. Clever. It couldn't eat that. This required retribution.

The Headmaster continued to communicate in smoke signals, counting small victories against the oblivious Blight as his camouflaged and Essence-hidden students lurked in the passage above. They were planning out their next moves using methods that eluded this *beast.* They were also listening in, and Cataphron was nothing if not chatty.

Now they were waiting for a signal, and what would happen next was still being planned. Artorian needed to buy time, needed to keep the attention on him. Under no circumstances could he allow the Blight to look up or intercept their messages. So, some Essence was purposefully wasted. If this failed, it didn't matter if he lost it *all.*

"I'm not going to ask how you know that word. Yes, Bernoulli's containment principle is a direct example of a core-technique that is crafted to perform a *function* rather than concentrate on Essence refining. Since you clearly have no issues with the High-Tier... this is what the '*Worthy* tier' looks like. Only those who are *worthy* and mentally capable can reach these. This one is called the 'Penrose triangle' and it is classified as an impossible object. With Essence, in a place that both exists and does not, it *is* possible; but the mind must be *twisted* for a concept this reality-shattering to be maintained at all times."

The Blight crafted what it meant using infernal shaping. The twisted triangle glowed a corrosive, corruptive violet. It wasn't an intense glow, but touching the object would cause deepest horror. A torus twisted into agonizing existence next to it, the shape an affront against nature. A Möbius strip bubbled violet as it bent into being as a third exemplified shape.

Artorian held his head. What in the *Heavens* was he looking at? That worked, but *how?* How does that make a core cultivation technique? Does it *spin?* Are there multiple shapes? Do they interlock?

"Auw. My *head...*" He closed his eyes out of actual pain, and a drop of blood ran down his nose, staining his salt-colored moustache. That pleased the Blight to no end. *Words* had made his enemy bleed.

"Oh, my dear academic..." oozed the charismatic, nearly *sultry* voice. "This is but the *Worthy-tier.* For the upper-echelons of the Ascended... imagine *this* next one. Inverted-"

Artorian blinked and came back to himself a long moment after the Blight stopped speaking. It was laughing at the blood that now freely flowed from his nose. "Ah yes... S-ranked core-techniques... they will break a mind."

Granted, the Blight couldn't use these either. Messing with dimensional layers was S-ranked territory. It had only gotten to the height of the B-ranks before crashing down into elemental-land. But the mention *alone* had caused his guest severe pain; that made it all worth it as the impossible shapes were dismissed. The Blight had to stop there and backtrack. It had but a scant few minds that could uphold an impossible object, and it was expending them quickly; which forced those minds into a state of rest.

The Caligene could afford this cost. The wellbeing of his companion was far more limited. This exposure to abundant information was beating Artorian to death without causing direct harm, successfully subverting the land-law! The old man was hurting *himself* with the inherent difficulties of grasping these topics. Cataphron was *blameless*!

Artorian wiped his nose with a part of his sleeve, and a light twinkled in his eye. The Blight was incredibly prideful about its superior knowledge base, and he verbally stabbed it right in the metaphorical kidney. "I think you missed a step; you mentioned the pearly stuff?"

A hiss cut back at him, "Pearlescence is theft! That curse is nothing but a demerit! It provides a mimicry of the layer between cultivator and ascended, but steals part of your progress without your knowledge. Worse, your entire journey can now break to brittle ruin. Most of the energy isn't even returned, it is *taken*. It didn't *used* to be taken. What is now a necessary step and lauded as the mighty 'C-rank' is nothing more than trickery by a particularly insidious dungeon Core. The effect will never go away now that it is in place, even if the originator is slain. At best, the siphoning effect could be *redirected*. That snively little *cheat.* Can you guess, just *guess*, what the affinity connections on that cryptic miscreant are?"

Crunch.

The grandfather chewed on a grilled sandwich while thinking it over, downing a chunk with some water. With a full mouth, Artorian tried to reply, not expecting to have been put on the spot with an actual question. The Blight had seemed content to just monologue eternity away. "Celestial and Infernal?"

"Plus *water!*" Cataphron corrected him, but the initial assumption had been on the nose. That mixture was nothing but problems, on top of that: it just shouldn't exist. Except it did, and it could.

Artorian ran a hand down his spotless beard. His Aura cleaning up any lingering crumbs or bloodstains. "So it just siphons some progress, and improves the power of the core? That still sounds like an improvement. It's not much of a curse unless one specifically considers the no-return issue. Not much of one if you never knew the freedom of swapping cultivation techniques in and out beforehand. It does nothing to your progress otherwise? Doesn't it make the C-rank... special?"

Blight spat at him. "*All* cultivation progress is preparation for Ascension. *Nothing* matters until then. The Tower is the personification of 'purpose'. It is sought above all else, until you realize purpose is self-chosen and not found within a poorly built Tower of another's making."

The mass turned ashen in coloration, but Artorian had heard what he needed to and more. So that *hadn't* been what made it feel like his C-rank had stifled and essentially done nothing. It was still something else. Abyss! He'd gotten the listed improvements while he lay in the raider camp. His Core 'improvement'. Faster Draw. Better refining. All marked and crossed off on the checklist. So why hadn't his improvement *felt* like an improvement? He was loathe to ask directly, that was giving information to the enemy.

He'd dallied long enough. Packing his treats, hookah, and other sundries that had been pulled free to annoy the abyss out of this self-absorbed creature. Artorian got to his feet on the rock, and began rudimentary stretches. "By the way... do you sleep?"

Cataphron crossed his arms and squinted vacant eye-sockets at the man. "None of your concern."

Artorian smiled from ear to ear. It was time to drop the ruse. "Oh? Good. I had a question. Have I told you about my children? I'm *awfully* proud of them."

Cataphron already didn't like where this was going. What was this ridiculous segue? "...No. You haven't, and *shouldn't.*"

The grandfather was beaming. "As example, one of my youngest! She has this nickname. I didn't know what to make of it at first, but I love her, so I wasn't going to raise a fuss. However, it has struck me that names have power. Shall I tell you what it was?"

He spoke the words with flair and pointed a single digit to the sky, spinning in place on one leg like a top. The old man's stunt caused Cataphron to take a cautious step back. Falling silent, the Phantom Blight searched around the cave system. It tasted touchable air, and prodded the general local region. Just in case something was... odd.

Cataphron's sockets burst with violet infernal flame, his chin tilting up to regard a piece of space it could not access. There was an oval dome of some sort. Abyss! It consumed the infernal Essence he was creating! His infernal presence was absorbed so slowly and gently that it hadn't noticed the drain while distracted.

With all the boisterous fever of a performer, Artorian channeled Essence into his voice and legs. His explosive, boosted words rang loud through the cavern. Reverberating off the walls as he announced the next performer; the star of the show.

"Introducing: *Astrea, The Nightm~a~a~are!*"

CHAPTER NINE

"Three. Two. One. *Bounce.*"

The Blight's viewpoint centered upon its aggressor as the thrumming waves of Astrea's Essence-laden voice reached the elemental. Expecting some vocal shenaniganry, infernal defenses slammed into place in preparation of something meant to induce a cave-in. It's what *it* would have done: an indirect attack that didn't violate a spoken oath. A list of such events had been meticulously prepared, and strut-supports to prevent exactly such an event came into being.

The truth of the attack was *far* more nefarious. Had the creature perchance had more than the span of a moment to grasp what his enemy had said, it might have grasped its crucial mistake. The words hadn't been an attack at all: they were a *distraction.*

Astrea's technique slammed into place. With a plethora of targets that had practically no defenses against unexpected mental assaults, she felt *invited* to attack. Her nightmare technique had never possessed such power, and had never been *this* effective. Where there was usually one mind, or perhaps a few napping in a dormitory or barracks that she could spread this effect, here minds were packed like sardines.

Her practiced nightmare ability spread like a wildfire in drought conditions. The technique drank *volumes* of infernal Essence to fuel itself, but for once it didn't even need to take it from her. Free energy bloated within the Blight, so the supplied nightmare rampaged unabated.

To the Blight, the initial assault was akin to having its face grabbed without warning, only to have it sharply snapped upward. Even though it saw with sight beyond sight, the landscape orientation and associated gravity turned a full ninety degrees. It saw the old man flying sideways as it heard the *sound*. An awful, dirty wavelength. "You can *fly?*"

A gnashing claw made of lacerating mouths lashed at his captive, but the complete alteration in its frame of reference made the strike miss by a large margin. The old man caught the hand of a woman in white, who hoisted him the rest of the way. That insufferable academic spared him a smirk. "Nope, I just jump good!"

The new 'down' trembled as the fleeing group of academics booked it down the cavern hallway. The Caligene's outcry turned into a tarry, howling roar. Its ability to respond with reason had been temporarily stripped as internal problems wrought havoc on the otherwise carefully controlled mental prison.

Looking inwards, the Blight found a riot. One did not need walls or doors to trap minds that had no will to escape. It was but a few who sought sanctuary that were kept at bay, denied their futile attempts to escape. Those shapes against its near physical outer layer? That was his method of letting minds wail against the inevitable before they broke and stilled like the rest.

Where typically there was a stretched void occupied by the downtrodden that would obey when called, now there was *screaming* it hadn't induced! That was unacceptable! Only *it* was allowed to make the screams! How *dare* that infernal-dabbling whelp!

It was that very difference in its prison that caused the elemental such grief. When it controlled the stimuli, it also controlled how occupants could react. Nothing had ever penetrated it mentally; that was what he did to *others*! The soon-to-be-dead girl was thieving his tricks! The Blight had been thoroughly unprepared for such an event, because the act itself was unthinkable.

Ah, but wait. Had his nuisance guest referred to the whelp as 'his daughter'? The elemental felt his frustration growing. His detainees were rioting, fighting back, refusing commands, and worst of all: *dancing*. The Blight couldn't apply complicated efforts in the world around it when it couldn't even properly control the prison of its own mind.

He'd regain control in time, but for now his near physical body uncontrollably thrashed around the caverns. The elemental raged as it fought the technique, cutting off the nightmare's Essence supply once the effect was isolated. Just so it could actually make some *progress* against the percussive festival. That one-trick whelp was at least true to her name: dealing with this was a *nightmare*.

***

Dodging incorporeal infernal tentacles was a surprisingly taxing bit of parkour. The energetic arms ranged in type and size, from spindly string to kraken-sized slappers. While some bashed aimlessly into the cave walls as they thrashed, others came into being only to whip out from an unexpected angle.

They'd have been sliced thin enough to slip through a fishnet if Astrea hadn't been calling out incoming attack vectors as if she were a seasoned sergeant. Artorian pondered that last thought. It was entirely possible she *was* used to commanding people, given where she'd been on the totem pole when he finally managed to whisk her away. As per usual, Artorian had chosen a *terrible* time to ponder.

"Duck! Throat level horizontal slash from the left!" All heads dipped moments before a violet blade, looking like a guillotine, whiplashed from the left wall and slammed into the right, only to get stuck and dissolve the space around its impact point while the group ran on. They didn't spare even a moment to look back.

Artorian felt tired. He hadn't had time to restore his Essence reserves, and that last little jumping stunt had taken what little he had remaining. That high of a jump from a standstill was costly. Even the mapping pulse he'd sent through the caverns had been cheaper, and *heavens* had charging that jump been slow.

He'd forgotten how excruciatingly awful it was to move Essence through his body rather than through his Presence. The downside of hookah-assisted cultivation was mostly mitigated thanks to his functional Presence, but he'd needed to use his body both so that he could keep his plans secret... as well as actually *perform* the jump.

He wouldn't have tried it at all had he not known Jiivra was ready to catch him, as well as pull him along if he stumbled. He flinched as Astrea spoke again. "Split and hug the walls, fat one coming through the middle!"

Artorian's thoughts got pushed to the side as the floor they used opened into a ravine. Several dozen thinner 'hairs' bristled up from the opening like a fish breaching the water's surface with its dorsal fin. They went right back to running the second Astrea pushed away from the wall, the brightness rising when Astrea called out that she needed more.

Of the group, Jiivra and another student, Ronan, provided lighting. Jiivra used her normal body-illumination method while Ronan held a concentrated cube of fire in each hand.

Artorian locked his vision onto the object. Cube? Yes, six sides. No, don't question it, there's running to do! The fiery cubes shone with light one would expect from a healthy fireplace, and the boy himself appeared a dexterous fellow. If anything, the old man was pleased as punch that the odd reactions to his daughter had stopped. Then again, that tended to happen when someone was saving your bacon. There was a life lesson in there somewhere.

In fact, it went on Artorian's list of the three kinds of people never to disrespect. Those who handled your food, those who handled your gold, and those who handled *you*. His lips twitched into a smile as he recalled Tibbins and Yvessa.

"Abyss! Entire front is all black. I don't know. Stop. *Stop*!" The five skidded to an unwanted halt. They could hear a wet surge rushing behind them. They knew it wasn't water filling the cavern, but it didn't need to be. They could all imagine seas of grey goo flooding the empty space behind them. Their heads turned when the pathway before them squeezed shut like a violent muscle spasm, crushing solid rock into gravel.

Ronan brightened his cubes and squinted at the 'muscle' blocking their way. "Did we get *swallowed*? That looks like the inside of a throat in the diagrams from the *Second Volume of Medicinal Practice*."

The others looked at the fire practitioner with quirked brows, and the discomfort made Ronan blast the barrier with a stream of fire. Something shrieked in response. They didn't like *that*, a shriek meant a physical thing. The throat released its hold, and at Astrea's push they all continued their mad dash for freedom.

Tired, frustrated, and on edge from avoiding dungeon-level death traps. Jiivra snapped at nobody in particular, "Someone tell me that wasn't a real thing that just happened."

The Headmaster hopped over a pothole and fell into step next to her. "Still the same creature! Smoke signals aren't exactly good for long explanations. It's an infernal elemental, it can go physical under the right circumstances. No, I don't know what those conditions *are*! Just run! Stick to the plan!"

One of the other students in the group of five, Ishtar, swiveled her head around, and her long braid nearly smacked Ronan in the face. Her voice was soft in comparison to the guarded and borderline panicked tones of the others. She'd been brought along to keep their movements quiet, but the air essence student was out of gas. "What *is* the plan? You forget we do not all speak glow-moss or read smoke-signal. How do you even *do* that? No, forget I asked—plan! What is?!"

Astrea agreed. "I know all the bits of how we get to granddad, but the rescue was improvised and I didn't hear anything about a plan!"

Jiivra's face turned sour. "I said we'd think of something when we *got* to it!"

Ishtar sassed back, because that was in no way an answer, "Well, we got to it. Now what!"

The silence from the glowing combat instructor didn't do their morale any favors. She bit her lip. Just getting to the correct cavern so they could recover their Headmaster had been the extent of her plan. They were up an unpleasant creek, and didn't pack spare paddles. "It's not like we can leave the mountain! It's crawling with undead out there!"

Astrea skidded to a scared, sudden halt. "Everyone on the ground! *Now!*"

They all almost made it as they hit the ground. Tearing through the ceiling, an infernal mouth bit a chunk out of Ronan. Everything from his torso on up was gone in a crunching flash, including the illumination his cubes provided. Only the legs remained. The remaining four didn't have the liberty to remain as still as those legs as their infernal guide screamed at them to get up and run.

Astrea glanced at something behind them right before her scream, and nobody dared to look. There was only running. They soon came upon the large domed cave where the rest of the students awaited them. Welcoming cheers turned to shrieks, and expressions of joy quickly turned ghastly at seeing whatever was behind them. The four didn't halt, yelling in unison: "*Run!*"

CHAPTER TEN

An aspect of Favor checked a very fine gnomish pocket watch for the sixth time. What was taking so long? You'd think that a vast workforce of countless undead toiling without pause—and with strength their previously living counterparts could not have mustered—would be able to make some kind of tangible progress.

Click.

The lime green sigh fogging from the skeleton's mouth was proof that even he was tired of waiting. The aspect clicked the contraption shut and held its perfectly bleached skull with a bony hand. Seated cross-legged on an appropriated palanquin, it watched the minimal progress. It's not as if the 'princess' had any use for comfortable seating when her bones were scraping at dirt and rock the same as all the others.

It was *just* a forced cave in. Even if the blocks were sizable, excavation should not take this long. Just how deeply had the entryway collapsed? He dearly hoped it was not particularly far. They had a schedule to keep... oh. Wait. No, they didn't. This assault on the mountain was significantly ahead of schedule. They weren't supposed to be *able* to take the region for... what? Another decade at *least* before they'd even been slated to try?

Favor counted his blessings that no demons were present. That would have altered this entire engagement. It also would have meant he'd not have gotten the credit for what was about to happen. Him, a mere Favor, succeeding in an assault that the bigshots hadn't seen as possible. What an upset! He'd felt strung along at first, and hadn't really wanted to come. It was a known suicide mission.

Alas, favors are favors, and they were merely a currency for the powerful. Whatever insidious plot the Vizier had finagled was certainly working out, and the credit would be all his! Sure, the sudden... *disappearance*, of the Favor before him was... worrisome. Yet a bargain once struck is final. The aspect sharply looked up.

After that freak rainstorm, it had turned out to be a very nice day. The sun was shining, and barely a cloud stained the sky. Had the Favor still been able to feel the heat on its skeletal frame, he might have even called it pleasant, had the threat of eternal torment not laid so heavily on its soul. Alas, such was the fate of a skeleton, and the reminder was always there; where you'd go if you'd fail. How *easily* failure came to pass. All it took was a little pull from a displeased caster and *pop*! An unimpressive pile of bones clattered to the ground and off you went, screaming back down into the abyss.

As an undead, one really needed to work and show results to stay connected to your summoner. Especially as an intelligent undead; those were expensive and problematic to raise. Having been a necromancer several hundred years before this raising, this particular bag of bones was *exceptionally* keen to show immediate fealty.

It was what had landed it in the ranks of 'Favor' instead of being stripped down to a ghoul, or ghast, or other near-mindless undead that would have *guaranteed* a downfall. Even undead, Favor shuddered from that thought. His bones rattled unpleasantly. *Anything* but going back to the abyss, and he did mean *anything*.

The abyss was entropy personified. Infinite, yet contained in the worst of ways. The place was timeless, yet you could *feel* the seconds grind past. You didn't have a body there, therefore you couldn't *do* anything. Yet one could experience the violent, unknown, chaotic changes that occurred there. *Things* existed, but they were named such because they were otherwise indescribable.

The aspect had no clue how he'd held onto even a scratch of sanity. It might have been the type of energy involved when he was fished back out? It had certainly been nothing like his own vague recollections of being a Mage. He never, not *once,* brought an undead into being which was something other than an angry, mindless murderpile. Your mind is one of the first things you lose in the abyss. Then when you come back, the return to a lack of pain is...

Favor didn't know how to describe it. Maddening, perhaps? He heard a chunk of rock cave in, and a glance let him see a fresh dust cloud obscuring the crushed bodies of easily a dozen undead. Maybe *that* was the problem? His poorly controlled army was digging a hole that just kept collapsing in on itself from above. A 'two steps back' scenario. His bony hand pressed to his forehead. Some intellect was certainly lost; how had it not noticed that sooner?

Craving a distraction from failure, Favor glanced the other way. Some infernal geese honked at one another, having a tiff with undead c'towls. The c'towls! Now *those* were things of beauty. Sure, they're the puffiest little monsters alive, but dead they're all murder and no fluff. He *loved* them, which was an odd concept for a creature not actually capable of love. Was an undead skeleton even a creature? Probably not. A worry for another time. He scratched the losses and rough time of day onto the vellum.

That's odd, hadn't it been barely morning? Why was it so *bright?* Forget that question, why was there a second sun, and why was it getting closer? Favor pressed the sleeve of its robe over empty eye sockets out of habit. Not that it did anything.

The blindness only grew, and something suddenly enraged Favor. It didn't even know what, or why; it was just so, so *angry*. That a skeleton could feel anger wasn't considered. All higher thought was tossed out. Similarly, the other undead in the region also reacted in the same way.

Favor reached out a clawed hand towards the incoming meteor, and saw his hand... melt? What the *abyss*? A creeping, awful feeling crawled over its being. It felt... soothing? What an agonizing, terrible experience! No soul that spent time in the abyss that acclimated to the normality of pain and discomfort could accept this *atrocity*. This feeling wasn't just harmful, it was *insulting*. Being basked in this glow was akin to being afflicted by an Essence healing effect. Those tore undead up like a salt block in water, and the light from the fireball was no different.

Something about the descending ball of doom made all the afflicted undead in the region howl bloody rage at the object's impending planetfall. The burning meteor turned sharply in the sky, veering down at a forty-five degree angle to steadily whistle towards them. They wanted to attack it, rip it to pieces, charge it en masse and tear asunder whatever *dared* to take pity on them and take away their pain. They had earned their resilience!

They should have known to hide. To seek cover. To do anything *other* than charge towards the depths of peril. Such considerations didn't happen. There was only wrath, and only vengeance was accepted. The light had to die; they would *make* it die. It didn't *matter* that their legs melted away to soup. They would crawl. It didn't matter that their arms broke to brittle pieces like sugar cubes in hot tea. They would hinge forward on their jaws and *bite*!

The enraged hordes didn't get to do any of these things. They, along with all the vegetation, nearby land, and most other objects not bolted down with the weight of a mountain were wiped from the map. The mountain, unsurprisingly, was the only thing that didn't budge. Everything else wasn't so lucky as the full force of a meteor impact wiped the slate clean. The previously hilly and wall burdened city of Jian was reduced to flattened wasteland in a bright flash.

Nothing remained as shockwaves uprooted and tossed matter out of the way. Stone wall sections flung far into the distance, sure to give whoever was below them an exceptionally bad day when it was time for the projectiles to come back down. The burning wreckage would be one thing, but the thousands upon thousands of Jian made swords and spears that zipped off into the distance like glimmering dots of glitter were sure to cause all *sorts* of strife.

What would a lone adventurer think when a shining blade flicked through the sky, only to split the clouds and stab deep into the ground before them? So it was for a great many people. They thought that the heavens had suddenly destined them for a new calling; for the weapons didn't just retain their Jian quality luster, unique shape, and honed craftsmanship. With the meteor's impact, something *more* imbued itself into the crafts.

The resulting dust plume mushroomed the sky. Mana crackled and flared into being as the impact point drenched the region in aberrant fire Essence that set aflame any wreckage and uprooted any greenery it could get ahold of. The landscape of waste and ruin was soon a raging caldera; a pyre that fueled itself. The inferno even caught lingering clouds of dust aflame.

What had, a few minutes prior, been a war won ahead of its time was now reduced to a total loss. An explosive wave of Mana repelled rogue particles, and an orb of incinerating swirls helixed around a rising figure at the center bottom of the newly born caldera. The impact had crunched and packed earth much more than anticipated. Unknown underground tunnels that wildly sprawled were all empty space, and didn't hold up as well as solidly-packed ground did when a several-ton object comes knocking from the skies above.

Ember brushed off her shoulder and took a single step before looking at the devastation she'd wrought. Her power absorbing body emanated visible waves of burning energy. She was actively trying to pour as much of it into her environment as possible, and she'd taken the opportunity to sink several A-level Mage ranks into energy expulsion on impact.

Securing her own well-being had been worth the cost of the resulting nuke she set off. Gathered walms of power released fully, and she now stood unharmed in the ruin of what had once, *probably*, been a place.

When she'd noted an unpleasant lack of life during her descent, Ember had upped her output. There was no reason to hold back and attempt to save lives when there were none to hold back for. She didn't care for the abundance of undead either. One stone. Two problems. Or in her case, one Ember-shaped meteor. Her rank ticked up again as she looked around. She'd bought herself precious minutes with that outburst, but it wasn't good enough.

Ember had spent far too much time looking for her friend, and she had more than a limit; she had a *dead*line. She was sure the current S-rankers were enjoying the few extra moments of game time, but she didn't have time for that. Calling out seemed pointless, and since she'd only gotten a single response from her Mana fueled echolocation tracking, she was happy to have even gotten this close.

Who gave up when so near to victory? Certainly not her! Yes. Good. That was a stable personality trait. Hold onto it.

Keep it. Hold it tight and don't let it go. That was one more thing that could provide a basis of her S-ranked actualization. The new body that would come into being couldn't survive or thrive under the shaky self-image she currently had. Where in the Abyss was...?

A *ping* reached her Mana, and Ember's vision snapped straight down. A wave equivalent to a solar flare burst from her body as that tiny motion was performed at Mage speed while at full emanation. Ordinarily this was so wasteful one would die from it, but she was in a *Judging*.

"Below!" Realizing what she'd said, and what she'd done to the ground made a chill grip her heart. Oh. Oh no...

Panicked, Ember grabbed empty space above her head and spat blood. *Blood?* Yes, blood! Sure, it was mostly Mana, but Mages *did* still bleed! It was that darn ripped fire Essence channel, and the new celestial one wasn't exactly helping. The channel had previously mended to a perfect connection, but the sheer mass of energy moving through had torn it right back up. The injury to her affinity channel was throwing her off. If she wasn't currently being gorged in energy influx, she'd have no idea how to cultivate now that such affinity channels were present. How was she even going to cultivate as an S-ranker? Did that even work the same?

She tried to push through the panic, which only caused increased blood loss. Her Aura laughed at the cost, shifting into the horribly expensive starlight variant even if it did little. Expensive was *good* right now! So was thinking she'd make it to the S-ranks! She *would* make it. She could do this, and Ember screamed to build herself up. "Come on, You're a *Yaran*! Yarans can do anything."

Rogue firestorm Mana wreaking havoc in the region, and starting to do its own thing, stopped when it felt the pull.

Turning, it hurried to fill the space between the A-ranked Mage's hands. Ember squeezed her eyes shut, trying to think of something, *anything*, that could help her find the mind that she needed right now. Think. *Think!* What was connective enough? What would be a message that could be recognized when she couldn't directly talk to who she needed? What would be the *one* easily recognized thing that would make someone realize she needed help, and either rush to her or let her find them easily?

She glanced up and winced. Manastorms were no joke.

Manastorms actively being *fed* without a solid intent were even worse. It crept into surviving material, and upon being called, sought to find form and meaning before answering to a hierarch. Mana was no different than Essence in that regard. It needed direction, or it would go wild. Ember's pull was enough for it to adhere; for *all* of it to adhere. Some, however, had already self-generated things it was going to accomplish.

While the Mana gathered, so did all the objects and items it had crept into; similar to the distance flung weapons, but on a far more deep and intense scale. While the weapons that flew far and wide had been ingrained with a Mana that changed their internal composition and structure to allow for a randomized fire-based effect, the effect in Ember's immediate vicinity was far more profound.

Entire suits of armor dug their way from the ground. Rising to heed the sounding bellow of the warhorn. Weapons burst from scorched earth to freely float to her beck and call. Circling around Ember's being in a wide ring before being grasped by the empowered gauntlet of living armor, adding to their collective intent. Because Ember's intent was to find anything that could help, her Mana did its best to improvise.

Like a toddler trying to be helpful by bringing you a handful of mud when you casually mention needing plant food.

Storming the region, Mana lashed out in its wild search. What was the region plentiful in? Weapons. Crafts. Creatures. Such *scant* options. Crystal cobras remade with Mana now sported three, rather than two, affinity beast Essences. They herded in a manner Ember was used to, adhering to a tactical rank and file. Each of them rose up once in ordered place, hoods flaring. They felt threatened because Ember felt threatened. Her power, freely emanating from her panic, bled over into everything she was wantonly calling.

C'towls with fire instead of fur traipsed into formation with their common catlike grace. Owl intellect shone in their eyes as the geometric symbolism on their foreheads absorbed rogue Mana, forming into B-ranked Beast Cores as they sat on their butts. Geese rose... but exploded, burning to cinders as the infernal basis of the creatures couldn't hold up to the trickle of celestial that was present in the raging, jagged lightshow pervading the area.

Ember closed her palms around something, and it filled her with the sensation of relief. All the other entities nearby mimicked the Mage's behavior, calming as she did. "Yes. You, *you* are perfect."

Ever so barely parting her hands, she kissed her chosen creature sweetly. "Fly. Find. Give, and let me know."

She released the chosen just as a blackened skeletal arm punched its way out of the ground. Angered by how the undead thought it was wise to delay her further, she altered her vision. Ember saw a great multitude of unfriendly shambling shapes come up from the ruined, burning ground. Survivors that had been buried instead of having the decency to be crushed. There was an unpleasantly great number of them, and most were crawling from the place Jian had once stood.

She didn't have time for this, and she was seeing thousands, and thousands more crawl from the ground. Some of them didn't stand up to the Manastorm, but far too many did. While Ember didn't know it, removing 'Favor' as an intermediary had latched the skeletal control of the fallen horde to someone a tier higher on the rung. Someone with *actual* power was now holding the reins of these puppets, and the increased power tier connecting to the undead boosted their power, blackening their bones in the process. What Ember did know was that she'd seen the effect before. This wasn't her first anti-undead war.

Unlike the last time, she looked around. Where previously she'd faced such a group alone, this time she had an impromptu army of her own; eager and willing to receive identity. Her words were terse and with her little sweetling carrying the fate of all her hopes on its tiny wings, she did something she was good at. No, something she was *excellent* at. It was time for war. "Destroy all undead. Everywhere. *Forever.*"

Sapience burst into being within the army of the Eternal Pyre. They chose to call themselves this as they received Ember's strength through an utterly overabundant stream of Mana. While it was ordinarily folly to give anything enough power to self-sustain past the point where easy control was ineffective, Ember did not care. She was not here to babysit, she was here to *survive*. Her hand slowly reached out, and a blazing suit of armor dropped to a knee, offering fealty and blade.

Ember had wanted a swordspear, but subconsciously she knew that it was swords that were held by the hand of a leader. She didn't know *why* it was that weapon specifically which inspired such a connection, but that is what her subconscious told her. Ember took the jian. Granted by a soldier that knew no fear, knew not what it was like to tire, knew not of disloyalty. It, like every other scorching entity was an inferno of purpose. Together or not, they would fight and persist to the last drop of their Mana before fizzling out.

Their duty was paramount. It was prime. The Eternal Pyre turned to face its enemy, and a spark of righteous might flickered with the touch of celestial influence from within them. Lifting the jian, Ember rose the tip to the sky and twisted on her heel. Her order boomed through what was now a valley, and individualism bloomed in each burning warrior as they set forth to carry out the order.

"*Charge!*

CHAPTER ELEVEN

The world caved in. Blight was crushed, entrapped, and smothered in the avalanche of dirt, rock, and... heat? The Skyspear survivors didn't have the luxury to really think about it as the massive cavity they occupied decided to cease being a cavity.

Huddled together, screams and outpoured Essence were all that kept a hexagon shaped area of space from collapsing in on itself. Earth Essence students and anyone with even a *hint* of an earth affinity was pouring out energy to support those who were trying to keep them all alive.

The shape they occupied cramped and crunched to become smaller and smaller, but now was not the time to be picky. People were shouting as emergency backup ideas sprung into existence. Ideas certain people had never wished to use again; had *hoped* they'd never use again.

Ali had been the saving grace, shouting the intended hexagonal shape out with the idea of repulsing earthen matter in that particular formation. It was just a shape, they could *do* shapes. All the earth Essence students had been through the ringer when the self-important Cataphron had still been a quasi-instructor.

That man wasn't one for treating his students like anything other than expendable workhorses. However, it did make for exceptionally gifted students that had been forced to work their butts off in an attempt to sate their instructor. A feat much harder than the critical predicament they found themselves in now, and this was do or die.

Everyone was tired, but tired wasn't a good enough reason not to challenge fate when it was bearing down on you with unknowable tons of dirt. To Astrea's surprise, it had not been the impending threat of being crushed to death that was the most dangerous thing in their little hexagon. Oh no, that had come when her Fringe elder spat out an idea—or maybe an imperative—that made them believe he may have gone insane. A real *Fringe* order.

"Everyone give me your refined Essence so I can give it to the earth affinities!" While the earth affinity students led by Ali didn't see this as too big of a problem, considering they were all holding the ceiling up, everyone *else* did not like what had just been demanded. Another student snapped at their Headmaster.

"That's not possible!"

Jiivra was far less inquisitive on the how or the why. If there was anyone who could pull off such a strange idea, it was certainly the codger. Worst of all, deep down in her soul, she somehow felt responsible for this mess.

"Explain how, now!" While most others were still coping with personal concerns, Jiivra lived in the moment. If they could get enough refined Essence to the people currently keeping them alive, the only bottleneck given they were *plenty* motivated, they could make it out of this! Seeing the looks sent her way, she snapped back at the students. "Personal growth is worthless if you didn't live to use it!"

Artorian responded, his left hand pressed against the back of the earth student showing the most physical strain; a good indicator they were bottoming out. "Razor! When I tell you, drop into active cultivation! I need you to *pull.*"

Concern washed over the young man's face, as his current efforts were entirely dedicated to preventing imminent death. Active cultivation was going to force him out of helping, and stuff him full of corruption. This was *not* a place to turn the technique on!

Even if it was underground, and otherwise likely perfect for earth Essence, underground was still just too dangerous, you had no idea what sort of rogue elements could be at play. He also was one of the students with *two* affinity channels: earth and fire. Starting his cycle without fire present was just... *abyss!*

"Headmaster, I don't think that's-"

His reply was cut short by a surprisingly calm voice as the Headmaster spoke. "My boy, do you *trust* me?"

Razor felt his teeth click together as his jaw snapped shut. He closed his eyes, reassessed his life, and exhaled a reply. This was a hill, and he might have a chance to save people even if it meant... oddities. He chose to fight and die on this hill. "Just say when, Headmaster."

A nod was all the reply he got before Artorian's right hand reached out for anyone willing to grasp it. Jiivra clasped it and felt the pull. What a... *familiar* sensation. She could do the opposite of this. Healing was giving, and this... this was *taking*. She didn't have the time to ask what she needed to do; instruction flowed from the old man like water down a stream.

"Drop your Aura, all of it. Let my Presence connect to your hand, and just *shove*. Shove refined Essence into your hand like you're trying to charge grip strength. You're going to feel like you're losing it... because you are. I'm going to channel all your refined Essence straight into Razor's spine so it floods his center."

Jiivra got the jist, but Razor froze up. "Do... do *I* need to drop something?"

He felt a supportive tap against his spine. "I'm already through the little you had in place. You didn't get to the stage where Auras are important yet, just don't resist, and pull! In three... two..."

Jiivra dumped refined Essence into her hand exactly as she would if trying to vastly empower her grip strength. Since Artorian had only specified 'refined', that's all she fueled. Her ranks dropped so fast that she felt nauseous and sick, but the glow on the old man's Aura strengthened. Soothing comfort washed over everyone present, and that did wonders for morale.

"One... now!"

Razor took a shuddering breath, and prepared to get wrecked. He dropped his support to the group technique, but his addition had been so minimal that the loss wasn't noticed. Can't help without Essence, even if the structural pattern of the effect was boosted via inclusion. While in his center, Razor began to pull, dipping into active cultivation.

The shuddered breath hiccupped into a sharp inhale. His ranks jumped! Again and again his power flooded until he felt like he was drowning. His entire center was drenched in refined Essence, the influx ending when there was roughly no more room left for it to go. It could have gone into his cells, but while it was in the center it was ready for immediate use. For a cultivator at Razor's level, that's *exactly* where it needed to be for him to be useful.

"Razor! Stop cultivating! Hexagon!" The student snapped out of it, reactively slapping his hands back on the hexagonal shape of their little self-made prison cell. He flooded the technique with enough juice to suddenly be of significant assistance to the rest of the team. He smiled wide; now *this* was helping!

"Ali, you're next! Don't pretend I don't see that sweat! Jii, let go! You're too close to dropping below your death plane Essence level. You dying is not worth the rest of us making it. Someone else grab my hand!"

Jiivra weakly trembled as her hand released. Her hand felt desiccated and cramped. Letting go was so, *so* difficult to do. A great amount of Skyspear students couldn't give Essence without hitting the death plane, but since their combat instructor had set the example, those who could, did. Astrea stepped in to follow suit.

Her ability had been forcibly cut along with the destruction of their surroundings, so she knew their foe was going to quickly recover now that she wasn't actively causing problems for it. She'd likely not manage to fire her nightmare effect off a second time. The chance the Caligene's mental defenses would be 'as down' a second time was unlikely even in the *best* circumstances.

Astrea grabbed hold of her grandfather's hand, and joined Jiivra after a weakened tumble. Seven ranks had vanished from her body in a flash, and the loss had been violently disorienting. She dropped like a rock, caught by now prepared students after seeing it happen the first time. Their little hole wasn't much of a hexagon right now; more a squeezed down bubble that was trying to bounce back into shape.

Ali's improved output became a turning point when she woke back up from active cultivation. Slamming fresh Essence into the technique once more. Alone, this would not have been successful. As a group? It made all the difference.

Sharing their ranks wasn't something they wanted to do, not *really*. Still, refined Essence was transferred to the students whose skills were directly relevant to all of them making it out of this predicament. When the ground tremors ceased, the strain on students holding the hexagon together visibly lessened. Razor and some of his friends groaned, falling to their butts to recover. Ali exhaled out relief, and coughed out the first spot of good news: "The crushing stopped. We're stable."

Astrea pushed herself up against the slanted dirt wall, very much aware they weren't out of this yet. "What's next? We might not be doing so well on air."

Eyes turned to their Headmaster, who was doing something... odd. Then again, judgement was withheld since odd might be exactly what they needed. He was whispering to some of the moss? Alright, maybe not *that* kind of odd.

Touching it with a finger, a luminous plasma wave sparked along the bleached greenery, which glowed in response as a pulse shot through the rock and stone surrounding them. He grit his jaw, borrowed Essence cycling in his eyes. "Abyss. I have the worst of it against earth. Earth affinity students, which one of you can cycle Essence into their eyes well enough to find the closest cavity or passage?"

The huddled mass of students broke into hushed arguments amongst themselves, pointing out strengths and flaws. Boasting was no good here, as they needed to pin down exactly who had the skill set for the next task. They were also aware they were about to lose whatever refined Essence they might have left, so it was a swift game of pass-the-baton.

Jiminus became the final choice. Artorian couldn't say he was surprised, given the lad was the second earth and fire affinity mix. He did not like the Blight, but there was something to that one statement it had gleefully lectured him about: affinity channels were *everything*.

That thought was dismissed. No amount of natural gifts could beat out sustained practice and hard effort. Artorian momentarily considered a well-trained single-affinity user and an untrained all-affinity user, and didn't like that he'd probably just... proven the Blight correct.

He despised how much accurate information that awful mass had given him. Lies would have easily been dealt with.

That annoying blob likely deduced as much, and had told him *mostly* truths, successfully unseating him from a position of comfort. The gall. He *loved* comfort! "Jiminus, you're up. Do you know what you're doing?"

The boy jumped up and shuffled closer. "Find a cavity or open space closest to this position so someone else can tunnel to it before we run out of air."

That shut the Headmaster up. Both because it was grim, and... right on the nose. No other explanation or questions were needed, so Artorian channeled refined Essence into Jim's spine. The boy needed as much Essence as his eyes could hold.

It took a few minutes, but the announcement arrived nice and quick. "I've got something."

The congregation thought that was... too fast? They didn't complain, fast was good! Artorian's curiosity still got the better of him. He had to know. "So swiftly? How did you accomplish this?"

Jiminus pointed at a hexagonal corner going down. *Sharply* down. Down was not a good direction to go, but if it meant a new source of air... new sources of air were a positive.

"While it's not the closest, there's a tunnel network there that has remained mostly intact. It's a metal tunnel rather than an earthen one, so it held up against the crushing. When I cycle my vision, I normally see all the rock. I had the thought to invert it instead, so instead of the rock, I see the empty space as big black blobs while the earth is just see through. I couldn't do this without so much Essence powering me."

Razor frowned as Artorian cut in. "Why aren't we taking the *closest?*"

That sentiment was shared by a few, but Jiminus started moving his hand in a wavy circle. "The closest one is actually right on the other side of that part of the hexagonal wall, but particles of dirt are somehow very wildly swirling inside of it. It reminds me a lot of..."

"Blight," Astrea pitched in, finishing Jim's sentence. She was squinting at the wall, confirming the worry with a thumbs down. She was cycling the bare minimum she could, but it was more than enough for her to pick up the flailing infernal cloud on the other side. "Definitely Blight. Very active, not happy. If that came into contact with something it could consume... that's the end of our road. Jiminus did a good job not choosing that direction."

With that information, Astrea pulled some of her refined Essence back. There was a limited amount to go around, but that was incredibly important information for their survival. She regarded her grandfather, and swallowed, "Call it, old man."

Artorian smiled and nodded at her. His hands went to Razor and Ali's backs, and Essence fluxed into their centers. "Get us to that metal tube."

CHAPTER TWELVE

Fresh air met them as Ali and Razor pried apart the stubborn wall of metal. The headache they all shared began to fade as the influx of breathable space provided exactly what they needed. Air students had pulled the breathable oxygen along with them, but were glad for a break as the tunnel behind their backs filled in. There was no other way to make a tunnel, that dirt needed somewhere to go.

Skyspear students spilled into the sizable metal tube as soon as they were able. It was malformed and difficult to traverse, but they didn't care. This tunnel offered one more step on the path to survival. Jiivra called out, "Jiminus, Astrea, where to?"

"Not *that* way, for certain." Astrea tiredly pointed at the tail end of the dark tunnel while holding the side of her head with her free hand. The lack of air hadn't done her any good, and she was the only one who didn't currently benefit from her grandfather's soothing Aura. Sure it was... *nice*. Her infernal Essence simply didn't agree.

Jiminus spent a little longer looking around as the rest of the students spilled in. He had less Essence to work with, but made due. Some of it needed to go back to the tunnelers for them to actually make it. Well, they'd made it. "I'm seeing nothing from this position, I can't even see what Astrea is talking about. If we can walk to the mouth end that goes up a little, I might see something after some climbing. For now, it's all bad in all directions."

With no better options, they made their way up the tunnel. The passage lacked the expected cave thematic. No stalactites or stalagmites, no damp walls or anything of the sort.

Just a big, fat tunnel that seemed to go on forever in an upwards direction they were happy about; it meant plenty of air.

"Hold up... I see an opening." Jiminus pointed at the ceiling, but Astrea didn't agree.

"No good. *It* is there, just not moving. There's a big patch of nothing past that though."

The earth and fire affinity student grumbled, "Also no other open space that I can see nearby. We..."

He stopped when Astrea squeezed his shoulder, her head snapping to look behind her. Her voice carried the same tone from when she was calling out instructions to avoid infernal tentacles. "We need to run. It got in, and it's catching up *fast*."

Cursing under their breaths, every student and instructor made a run for it. Artorian and Jiivra took up the rear, Astrea and Jiminus led the front, with Razor and Ali directly behind so they could work some stone if needed. Jiivra saw the violet cloud worming its way up the tunnel behind them at a glance. It was aglow with infernal energy, angrily bouncing off the metal tube confines as it thrashed forward. She didn't need to hear the shrieking to somehow be aware of it. "That looks *unfriendly!*"

Ali's voice called out loud from the front with good news. "Cavity dead ahead! Get through, we'll seal the way!"

Earth students were already closing the gap they had to squeeze through long before the back of the line was close to making it. If they didn't, even rough mental math said they would all be dinner. Jiivra shared a glance with Artorian. It didn't look good for them if they didn't hurry up.

Artorian glanced over his shoulder mid-hustle. "Doesn't look very intelligent, or like it's anyone we know."

Jiivra shot him a look of fury and confusion. She was *not* okay with him risking a foolish ploy to buy them time, they needed him to funnel Essence between them. "Don't you *dare* old man!"

She didn't say more as a quick glance revealed some... unpleasant realities. There wasn't a lot of refined Essence to go around anymore. They were all running on fumes, and the old man didn't have much to spare. She was tapped, and far too close to her own death plane to really say anything.

"Grab those last in the line. Get in the cavity and work it from there. I'm going to buy you... those extra few seconds." Jiivra bit her lip at the academic's words. Emotion was breaking her, but she couldn't afford to do so much as stop running.

"We've got fresh airflow in here!" one of the students yelled through the closing metal pipeline. That passage was getting awfully small. "We can get outside!"

Artorian smiled at one of his favorite people and pressed a hand to her back. His Aura winked out of existence as the Essence needed to sustain the soothing effect dropped below the minimum requirement. The light in the tunnel literally went out, and when Jiivra flickered on her own Aura... she was no longer running next to the old Elder from the fringe.

She bit her lip to silence herself, swooped up the two stragglers in an arm each, and hurled herself through the metal split and into the cavity behind it. She hated herself for shouting her next words... even if she knew it was necessary. "Seal it!"

As the metal creaked to a smashing close, a tiny, buzzing, red dot zipped through the final remaining inch of the passageway. Artorian turned. His back facing the closed metal seal. He was panting, sweating, sore, and out of breath. He relied fully on his Presence to carry him through life, and now that it was teetering... there was no point in running. He sucked in a breath, and his external Aura just *barely* sputtered back to life.

"There we are, a little extra light to keep the violet worm at bay—*gah!*"

A violet claw was three inches from his nose. It had moved so *fast*. Based on the speed the Blight had been going, he *should* have had easily another seven seconds. He'd been deceived. While watching the tendril retreat, the charismatic, oozing voice clicked at him. Abyss. *Cataphron.* "Tut... tut... *tut.*"

A familiar shape crept into being as the amorphous worm shaped blob took on an appallingly familiar violet body of infernal energy. Cataphron soundlessly clapped his hands together. Why didn't it make a sound? Ah. Right. No real body present to make sound *with*, probably just the voice box. "All that running! Look at where it brought you. I was so close... you were nearly on your knees. I thought 'I have him'! Alas, it appears that I'll have to wait, oh... maybe a *minute* longer?"

Artorian's Aura sputtered, and in that blink of time the infernal violet body flashed forward, as close to the old man as it could get. The elemental ended up a scant three feet away, compared to the... *thirty* it had been before. Not good.

"I told you I was willing to wait for my sweet, sweet satisfaction. I had prepared follies and fogies as distractions. Pathways and prefectures of dead ends. *Years* of quips and one-liners. Here it was all... for naught. I'll have my vengeance, and so much sooner than anticipated. Can you hear it my friend? The rumbling of my stomach? I wonder what you taste like..."

"Salt and vinegar." The old man took a deep breath and steadied his Aura, regardless of how weak it was. He heard something, a sound the Blight clearly wasn't making. It was distinct, and utterly out of place for their location. His attention broke away from the Blight, and it was *not* happy about that.

"You're a clown, I bet you'll taste *funny.* No matter, it all goes to the same place." Though it couldn't see what had distracted its prey, Cataphron saw Artorian hold his hands up and clasp something invisible. The old fool was playing a trick on him again, but something about the fool's expression made it feel... wary.

Artorian couldn't believe what he was holding. It was living fire, but didn't burn to the touch. If anything, it was soothing. *His* kind of soothing. The familiarity was making his heart pound as he held the tiny, single... bee.

It crawled around on his hand like a real bee, just like all other bees had loved to crawl around on him. He still didn't know why they did it, but the sensation was heartwarming, and it brought a softness to his previously dim and dour face; a smile that was half sadness. "Well... will you look at *that.*"

The bee fluttered its wings at him. Undisturbed by his surroundings, Artorian pet the little beasty with a single, tender finger. Brushy brush...!

Cataphron screamed at him, but it only resulted in the barest minimum of reactions. "Look at *what?* There's *nothing!* You think you can steal my victory by pretending to go senile? I *have* you, old man! You're *mine!*"

A small set of chuckles left the Headmaster. His eyes rose up to regard the personified Blight. If he'd been wearing a set of glasses, he would have looked over the rim and adjusted them to cause a glare to shine off the glass. "No... so long as I have my moss in place, you'll *never* have me. You'll *never* find my last little trick, and it will strip you of *all* victories."

The chuckle became laughter. His Aura weakened, but it was worth selling his last little distraction ploy. His enemy took the bait. The Blight found every instance of that odd, harmless looking moss and devoured it whole wherever it was found. It wouldn't allow a single thing to taint his satisfaction. "I *will* have the last lau... why are you smiling...?"

"Oh, Blighty..."

Cataphron took a cautious step back as Artorian plucked a patch of moss from his pocket. "I hope you packed your bags, because you're going on a *trip*. You *don't eat* the glowing moss."

Lifting the bee to his lips, he exhaled fire Essence onto it. Speaking with a whisper. "*Honey...*"

The bee lit up with Mana, and finally the Blight could see what had been hidden as the celestial shell coating the insect peeled away. The opposing energy had hidden the creature from its gaze! The Blight felt *wrong*. Its ability to see was going through a worse psychedelic phase then even Astrea's nightmare had caused. Cataphron's reality was starting to go through an odd inter-twisting kaleidoscopic set of landscapes.

Exploding in a harmless burst, the bee sent out a pinpointing shockwave of Mana, loudly heralding its exact position. The cavern filled with ambient Mana, providing the general region an outburst of fire Essence as the Mana followed the direction to 'give', and purposefully disassembled itself. Artorian's eyes shot open wide at the realization. Kicking his sun core into gear, the confined fire Essence slammed into the cultivator. This was in part a terrible idea, but Essence was Essence, and he was almost out. The C-ranked cultivator's skin turned red at the rapid absorption, and his pearlescent core became hot, hot, *hot!*

The Blight wasn't doing too well. All that awful moss had been imbued with celestial energy. It didn't take being a scholar to know that a creature made entirely from infernal didn't do so well when ingesting a material that was its pure antithesis. The identity trapped in the moss only made the effects worse. What had this terrible geezer *done* to this stuff? Where in the world did glowing moss exist which wrought havoc directly upon the mind? It didn't have the ability to think any further, and blindly charged the old man.

Visibly unable to uphold the Cataphron identity, Artorian deduced there was no threat of triggering the land-law. But while the Blight could no longer reason, it was still bigger and had more Essence. It *would* win.

Against Artorian, yes. It *would* have won. Against the burning thing that split the earth from ceiling to sky like it was ripping apart a cardboard box? No, *there* it could not win. It also could not stop itself from trying. Infernal masses flooded the crevice and shot upwards in the form of countless gaping mouths.

Ember wasn't interested in the defiant mewling of a fake B-rank incorporeal creature. Her left hand was raised palm up, and a tiny bee made of incarnate fire hovered a few inches above it. She regarded the scene below with sclera as dark as the deepest void in space, her body cracked and covered with searing spatial tears.

She leaked Mana like a shredded waterskin as she descended, yet her density only increased. Ember hit A-rank eight, causing a wave of energy to explode outwards. Her Mana easily burned away the oncoming darkness storm, and reached out to grip the culprit. A Mana shaped hand comprised mostly of flame and a *touch* of celestial squeezed the life from the Blighted cloud.

Phantoms shrieked, and her light shifted from torrential pyrostorms to radiant starlight. Artorian gasped in relief, feeling *invigorated*. His active cultivation drank in the Essence generated by the rapidly deteriorating Mana. Except that this variant was already in the configuration he *desperately* needed. He'd been a *toe* away from his Essence death plane, and he collapsed upon the ground, no longer even attempting to uphold the charade. The ploy had worked in the nick of time.

While he was certain the Blight would recover from consuming celestial Essence sooner than he liked, Artorian had known that in terms of raw power... the Blight was going to win out sooner or later. He was still stuck in a hole in the ground, living on a timer that was ticking toward 'done'. When he squinted his gaze to look upon his savior, his hopeful smile bled away to horror.

"*Ember!*" he called out to her, hoping that the fractured creature in her shape was actually her. It was getting hard to tell, and it had been a taxing few days. From rescuing Astrea until now, life had been a nonstop wild ride of activity. He was *exhausted*. Still, from the look of it, the rest would need to wait. There was no rest for the weary, nor the wicked.

He tried again: "Ember!"

The spaced-out Mage blinked, her head jerking back an inch as she *saw* rather than merely *looked*. Mage speed was incredibly swift, and Artorian hadn't finished his second call to her by the time she hovered before him, her arms embracing the old man as softly as they could. He still felt a rib creak in complaint. He spoke with great effort. "It is good to see you... my dear."

Ember's inhale drew in enough breath that all the air in the cavern moved. She was aflame, but didn't burn to the touch. That, or his core was so hot he wasn't feeling the singe. Hmm... little of both? His cultivation slammed shut as she hugged him; he couldn't let Mana in.

Ember released him slowly, and a burning field in the shape of an orb surrounded them. It countered the Blight when it blindly attempted to swamp over them, but she didn't seem to care. Her voice was as cracked as her skin, and Artorian gently took her by the shoulders. "You t... too. I n... need help."

His nod was sharp, and he mentally caught up faster than her Mage speed could move. "Details. Short."

Ember tried not to break her friend's arms when she gently squeezed for support. She'd found him. She'd actually *found* him! But she was out of time. Ember would hit A-nine shortly, and then she'd have *seconds* on the clock. Her voice was hasty and frightened, her tone streaked with gasping tears as she tried to get the words out at the right speed.

"S-rank. I'm... Actualizing. I'm Incarnating. I don't... I don't have a stable self-image. I don't know *me*. Who am I? Artorian, who *am I*? I'm going to rip apart without a proper personality, and I didn't have the t... time. I don't have the t... time."

He'd never expected the knowledge from the Blight to have been such a boon, especially this soon. His arms shook off her uncertain grip, surrounded her shoulders in a hug as his mind raced. "I've got you. I *have* an answer for you. It's not the answer you want, because it doesn't answer the question you *want* answered. A philosopher does not find the right answer, they find the right *question*."

"The correct question for you, my dear, is not who you *think* you are. Nor who *I* think you are. The right question, is who do you *want* to be. Those values, those viewpoints, those core patterns. Grasp those. Think of that which you would want most in this world, and claim them. Grasp them tight and hold them close. Find that which you would promise yourself forever and ever, and never betray. For *that* is the core of a person."

She swallowed away a panicked breath as tears stained her cheeks; they were vaporizing as they touched her skin. She was here, listening, because she was placing her trust in the hands of a frail little human that wanted the best for his world. She desperately wanted to believe that she was part of that world. "W... where? How do I even begin?"

Artorian clasped her hands and closed his eyes. An idea came to mind, but he didn't want to tell her. He considered it a violation, but... if it might save her... he had already prepared to die just earlier, what was a few extra minutes with a friend? "Ember, tell me again. Please, if you ever told me before. What was her name? The name of your youngest, the one they called the Fire Soul?"

Ember frowned; that was a sharp left turn away from a useful topic, but there was no way in the Celestial Heavens that he wasn't asking for a good reason when the timer was so close to ticking. She hit A-rank nine, and swallowed as she diverted the energy away from the confinement of their safety sphere.

Everything outside of their sphere became molten slag, but that detail would need to wait. She closed her eyes, and sent her mental hand reeling into her heart to open up a box she did not wish to open. Gritting her teeth as steaming tears ran freely down her cheeks, she opened the box and pulled free the memory of her child. Her precious, dearest little one.

Her jaw moved, but no sound came out. He spurred her on, adding volume to his concerned words. "In your language..."

Her breathing became hectic, sporadic, shuddery. She snapped her eyes open, and within them Artorian saw only the void of space. The depths of the unknown, and blazing irises that swirled as a mighty supernova. She was different. Something had happened to Ember, and it was tearing her apart on more than just the S-tiered level.

He had a thought... it was a *terrible* thought. Ember swallowed, and this time her mouth moved, and words were spoken.

"Dawn. I wished to name her... *Dawn*. For she smiled bright and playful. She greeted the world with a noise of elation, and when I held her... she was at peace. At peace until the end. Until her last breath, my little one was the first ray of light on a new day. She was my hope. The first, and last Zaran. Taking the name of Yaran one iteration further."

Artorian held her tight. This was taxing, heart-rending, and a deep burden. Yet he had to say it; he *had* to. "Think, my dear, of how you would have raised her. What values you would have taught, what lessons you would instill over the *centuries* of her growth. What would you have said, if she stumbled? What would you have done, had she been hurt? Where would you have been, had she needed you? For she needs you *now*. She needs her mother to think of her and all the things you would have done. For the soul of fire is named Dawn. The Incarnation of the will of flame awaits her calling." He squeezed her harder, though she would never know it.

"Who, my dear, is about to *become* the Incarnation? Who better to honor the daughter that embodied hope than the one who holds tightest to her memory? You have named the soul of fire, and she awaits you in the spirit of the **Law**. Greet her. Give her the life you wished to give her. None knows those values, those lessons, those desired personality traits better. Than. *You*."

He swallowed hard, trembling. "You are not stuck being what someone *else* wants you to be! That's not *their* choice to make. A sense of identity, who you are, is decided entirely by you. Let me meet you again. Let me meet the soul of fire. Please, let me meet Dawn. For that is the name of hope you have *always* embodied."

The cracks on Ember's body tore wide open.

A-rank Nine.

Zenith.

CHAPTER THIRTEEN

'Death or graduation'. This was the universal motto by which the S-ranks functioned.

Pagacco and Duke hadn't moved an Ur-piece on their board in over an hour. They just sat there and watched, unable to speak. They didn't want to admit the failures they'd gone through to be so thoroughly stripped of their remaining S-ranked power. They could feel the inversion looming; it was just a matter of time before Ember was completely topped up and the judging concluded.

They knew the outcome to their ranking decrease. They were about to suffer incredible, horrific pain as their Incarna bodies turned inside out, reverting to the original A-rank bodies they'd had so long ago. Neither of them liked the idea of those forms after eons of being what they *wanted* to be, but it was inevitable. They had no good ideas on how to keep their current niveau of power.

Even the dungeon Karakum was silent... albeit for different reasons. The fire **Law**-bound dungeon Core knew something was afoot; it just didn't have the intelligence to puzzle out *what.* The silence was... palpable and intoxicatingly depressing. Its two annoyances were about to lose something. It didn't know what, it just knew it had to hide its unbridled joy. It had plans. Several, since it recently had a Mana influx that let a dungeon of its type and color actually *do* something.

If the duo became weaker, such as in the areas of suddenly being a Mage rank... why, then it would no longer be vastly overpowered by either of them. Oh, the games they would play! It didn't have time to consider further. The dimension it occupied—the one considered 'reality'—froze in a world made entirely of greyscale.

It could not hear, but it could see. It saw the agony of the wailing figures. They held themselves and fell to the ground. Roiling. Writhing. Twisting in unnatural, incomprehensible ways as their bodies seemed to turn in on themselves, collapsing onto a single point in space while simultaneously having a form spat out from the other direction of the spin.

The judging had concluded. Their **Law** had found them wanting.

It restructured the proper order of the world within the field in which it had dominion. The gavel had struck: the **Law** had judged. Mana made bodies coated in a shell of Incarnate energy lay twitching on the glassed desert floor. The greyscale effect bled out of reality; neither of the fallen beings would be able to make it happen ever again. They were no longer Incarnates; they were Ascended. They were Mages. Both Ancient Elves sat up with a displeased groan when the pain stopped.

Karakum could tell they were happy to be alive, but just who were these geezers that looked a thousand years old? These methuselahs didn't remotely look like the two playthings it had expected. Karakum was so startled, it didn't know what to do as it shifted viewpoints to look between the two; experiencing the emotion known as 'flabbergasted'.

The two ancient geezers got to their feet. Wobbly and uncertain, but to their feet nonetheless. "Ha! Look at you! Your beard reaches the ground!"

Pagacco was having none of Duke's banter. "Says the hunched over corpse with bent ears!"

Duke felt his ears. Oh abyss, they were actually bent. He waggled his bony finger at his old friend, a hand pressing to his lower back to get used to a body of... Mana. *Ugh*. How awful. He had to deal with *bodily functions* again. He didn't want to~o~o! It didn't matter. He smiled as Pagacco had trouble walking.

They quipped back and forth until Karakum the dungeon Core got the gist of it: these *were* the creatures that had tormented him! For the first time in centuries... Karakum smiled. The mana around its core cracked like glass. Reforming to create the expression as it was trapped as an orb no longer. Finally free to form its own body, Karakum grew. A ruby-armored crystal scorpion once more.

***

Es-illian-Yaran held her head and howled. Not with her voice, but as an emanation of power to the endless void. Ember's lament was filled with memories of her little girl. Of her body crumpling into a single point in space, directed at the very middle of her cultivation's center. She shifted to and through a small, indistinguishable pinprick as her mind and body were moved into her Soul Space, as her Soul Space *inverted*. Her center spilled out into the real world using Mana as an intermediary. The energy of her soul became manifest, and the first thing it demanded in order to exist was shape and personality.

Over the eons, Ember had encountered many theories of the soul. Many were suspect; most were flat-out wrong. Her favorite was that the soul served as a mirror image of the traits one had as a person. If one was a good person, then it was to be said they had a good soul. The theory was named HunPo, after the scholar who came up with it in the Golden Age. She passed before her time could truly shine, but by the age of thirty was said to have grasped the will of the Heavens and Earth.

Hun's peerless mind divided her writing into conjoining segments. Yin: vital force expressed in consciousness and intelligence. Yang: physical nature expressed in bodily strength and movements. When the Yin and Yang move in unity and harmony, they express themselves as the nature of the soul.

A person is how they carry themselves, think, react, and act. These reflections are carved into their soul, and the soul reflects it on the endless lengths of a still ocean; silent and unmoving for all to see.

Ember's soul was no lake. It was a twisting helix of rampant fire. Her pyre. The Soul energy needed immediate information on what she was. She realized... the old man hadn't been wrong, even if his words had been the epitome of recollected pain. It wasn't who she was at this moment that needed to be actualized; it was who she *wanted* to be. The person about to come anew into the world did not need to be broken, and didn't need to be a war torn Yaran. It did not need to be a Zaran, for that was a title afforded to only one... one who had passed.

The shoes of her daughter—however tiny they were— were a pair too big for her to fill. Still, the words of the wise resonated to a soul that needed them most. The person going back out into the world did not need to be her. It did not need to be her grief, her loss, her damage. It could be... *Hope.* A new perspective and horizon.

Yet, how could she do this? She couldn't just-

A memory played before her. It was small, and it was weak. It was haphazard and frail. It wasn't... hers? Her mind latched to it, absorbing the information in less than a moment as she experienced the Wood Elf technique of memory giving in a fashion so direct and profound that she was assured her Incarnation energy was somehow involved.

In the space between worlds that Ember currently occupied, the **Law** of **Time** snapped its fingers and acted in accordance with the rules. An Incarnate would have all the time in the world to Actualize. So it was written, so it was agreed, so it would *be*.

Yaran blinked. The pain was gone? No. It was not diminished, it didn't disappear. The ticking time bomb that was her Mana-made body simply no longer applied as the first droplet of Soul energy blossomed into the real world. Cracks still coated her body, and while she was unable to move, this was her soul space. She looked at herself from outside her own perspective, and found everything frozen in a landscape of grey.

Her eyes closed, and she absorbed the gifted memory. A footfall on a bridge that didn't exist stepped into her vision. A walkway of darkness without borders or walls squeezed into being, and at the end of it... there was a bonfire. There, she saw her friend. Then a younger version, and younger still. All were seated on stumps around the fire, versions of personality that were partially discarded.

She watched and listened as the Elder of the Fringe sat and surrendered. He could go no more; he could live no longer. The task ahead required someone... not *better*. Different. Traits and choices that would lead him to a path his current self could not walk. As that Elder looked to an empty stump, Yaran saw a new man appear from nothing. Perhaps... not from nothing, but from the traits needed. The traits wanted. This person, she recognized: *this* was Artorian. Her Artorian. The version she knew. The nosy, distractible, excitable, gabby, foxy, playful old man.

There had been... something else. Beneath it all, that veneer of personality was hiding core traits. The required curriculum. She looked deeper, and the memory allowed her to see; where she expected resistance, she found only welcoming warmth. Where people would ordinarily wish to hide the truth of their being from all others, Artorian trusted her to see the truth. The awful truth of who he really was beneath it all; what he sacrificed to become 'him'. Ember had to see. She *needed* to see.

Peeling away the coat of paint, there was wrath, rage, fury... and there was *war*. These aspects, she knew ever so well. Dropping a layer deeper, she found something unexpected. She found that the previous layer of action was built upon a layer of reason. She couldn't believe her eyes when three moving pictures played over, and over.

In the first, it was the old man. The Elder of the Fringe, holding his adoptive children from families not his own. He smiled, and they beamed back. How he *loved* them! They had bright minds with bright futures, if only he could give them the opportunity.

The second, a youthful, spry warrior decked in the imperial regalia of a commander. A practice before he ever needed to go to war, the first preparation before the first battle, a young woman smiled at him and held a tiny baby in her arms. His baby. He'd never spoken of his child, nor the woman. How he *loved* them! Even when they were gone forever.

In the third, and last, he was a youngster himself. He was playing around with... some kind of animal? It pounced on him, and he held it tight. It licked his face, and his childish hands rubbed down the bristled mane of what by all rights should have been a dangerous beast. That didn't matter to the little boy. How he *loved* it! How sad he'd been when he'd buried the creature under the cover of rain.

A layer deeper. Ember fell. She understood now, that his wrath, his rage, his war... they were not the driving force of his being. They were the tools to accomplish his means to an end. A willingness to do what had to be done. The Incarnation of a good man, going to war to protect that which he loved; even when it was gone from this world.

Her feet hit the floor. A hard, unforgiving floor. There wasn't a moving image here. Instead she found two replicas of her friend. Yet they were scarred, bleeding, dying. Falling to the ground once again, their broken forms stirred. She tried to step closer to help, but found herself unable. The sheer force of the absolute core of his personality rebuked even her.

Even broken. Even battered. Even pushed to the brink of losing all that was worth living for in the world. A single, shining trait did not quit. It did not stop. It did not surrender. It would get up, get up, and get up again.

Ember was moved beyond words. He'd said it to her before. A hint, perhaps? Never had she taken it to mean anything with such incredible willpower. At the very basis of her friend's psyche, the bottom most fundamental core of his being, the truth he wanted to show her. The truth he needed her to see was that through endless trial and tribulation, there was a trait he wanted her to have. The only gift he could grant her that could possibly have some meaning. There, at the very basis of a little human's mind, Ember discovered what it meant to be unyielding.

She looked up, and saw that the figures had stopped falling. The bloodied, broken, tired, and identical exhausted men looked over their shoulders at her. It made her freeze, or feel the sensation of frost. It passed when they smiled at her, the second core trait with an arm around the first showing itself. It was the truth: that he could not do it alone. The figures mouthed words at her, and while unspoken, she heard them loud and clear.

"I believe in you."

A strength filled her. A knowledge that, while this was the most difficult tribulation of her life, she wasn't alone. The core personality traits watched her go, keeping fists to the air in solidarity of her journey as she moved back up the layers. The three stilled images moved no more, they only regarded her. All three versions of her friend smiled at her, a companion in all walks of life as they raised their hands to wish her well. The tools of strife did not quarrel or shout when she ascended to their layer. They saluted her proudly, as a fellow compatriot of endless trials.

She opened her eyes, seated at an empty stump at the bonfire. The pleasant, foxy, playful personality smiled at her. It took her hand, kissed it, and gave her a playful wink just to be coy. It was nothing serious. A pleasantry designed just to serve as a reminder that she was lovely, and had not a shred of judgement to fear from her friend. He mouthed words at her, and she could hear him clearly.

"I leave this place to you. May you find yourself in the exact place you need to be." With those parting words, she was alone in the bonfire construct. The mental room where an old philosopher came when he'd failed and needed to try again. She took the idea, and left the memory.

Back in her soul space, she squeezed her metaphorical hand into a fist. Ember imagined and built her *own* bonfire. Hers was the helix of her cultivation technique, but it functioned all the same. Opening her eyes, old versions of herself littered the camp by the hundreds. She was, after all, much older than her human friend. Feeling far less alone, relief washed over her at seeing how far she had come. She smiled, and they all smiled back.

Taking a few steps, Ember exhaled deeply and seated herself on an available stump. The others around her said nothing as she turned to the empty stump next to her, and spoke from her heart. "I can't do this anymore. Can *you*?"

A copy of her current self manifested slowly, and smiled as it regarded her. The new self looked younger. More vibrant. Full of life. "I can."

The new version reached over and grasped Ember's shoulder. "It has been an honor, and a privilege, to have *been* you, Es-illian-Yaran."

Yaran swallowed her worry, and shuddered as the next words trembled out. She knew the answer to her question, but she needed to hear it. Just to be certain before she passed her torch. "Thank you. What is your name?"

The new version steadily gained the perspective that the old one lost. It beamed at Ember, and took her hands into theirs. "I am the one that will finish what you have started. I will be who you wanted me to be, with the lessons you wanted me to know. With the memories and sights you wanted me to see. With the actions you would have wanted me to take. I am the life you wished you would have had, and I can't wait to show it to you. I am the hope you always wanted everyone to see. My name, mother, is Dawn."

Ember's viewpoint dimmed as her personality came to an end. She let it go willingly. Made anew, Dawn Aran rose from the stump...

And became certain of herself.

CHAPTER FOURTEEN

Artorian could have sworn he'd heard the snapping of
fingers as his connection to Ember closed. He didn't have the
luxury to ruminate the fact that his last-ditch effort to give Ember
information was cut short before he felt he had gotten it across.
Abyss! He had hoped that if words failed, a memory dump of a
key memory that could help might be of some use.

Alas, he didn't know if it had gotten anywhere. Artorian
watched the flaming orb that was their protective dome fade and
thin. On the other side, Blight hungered; it beat against the
shield now and again like an animal testing for weaknesses. It
lost some darkness in the process, but it had plenty to spare.

Worse still, the moss effect was either in the end stages
of fading, or had fully expired. The academic couldn't tell while
the shield was up. Though, in truth, he didn't really want it to go
down. His core had cooled since he'd stopped the influx of
Essence gathering, but he'd accrued more fire corruption than
he'd liked. He'd need to be careful in the short-term future as he
now had more of it than any other. Artorian knew he could be
quick to anger now. Even if it was contained, corruption wasn't
that easy to just stop.

When her shield flickered and showed an obvious gap,
Artorian closed his eyes and took a deep breath. He could
flicker on his starlight Aura, but that was only good if the
personality present wasn't Cataphron's. From the look of it that
wasn't the case, but he'd still be overwhelmed by the sheer
amount of infernal energy. That would be the end of the story.
He didn't have the Essence to go toe-to-toe with an elemental.
He might as well be challenging a Mage to fisticuffs while in his
skivvies.

To his surprise, no flood of infernal came. Peeking open an eye; he saw all of Ember finish collapsing into a single point in space. She was gone, and only a black dot remained at chest level. Her shield followed suit in the next instant. Artorian's arms fell limp to his side as a figure he didn't know made its way forward; some Ancient Elf with long ears clapped as it approached him. He could hear the claps, so it was a fully physical manifestation.

It was here to gloat, no doubt. *Clap. Clap. Clap.* "So close! Yet no victory..."

Artorian dejectedly dropped his eyes down to admire the black hole. At least he had something he'd never seen before to look at before he got... eaten. His words carried that dejection in his defeated, insulting tone. "What's with that ridiculous body? Who are you supposed to be now, someone exceptionally good at gloating?"

The phantom laughed to itself, and that Artorian could hear even more clearly. It was a cruel, clever laugh. "Oh, *this* body? Well, since you aren't exactly a threat, I had to reconfigure against that which was. You see, just in case I heard right, and that person was a Yaran, I have to uphold the land-vow that protects me from attack by that particular lineage. After all, it never hurts to be too careful when it was Es-Arcturus-Aran that knocked me from the moon using a mountain as a club, then trapped me beneath it."

This was a part of history that Artorian did not know, and it... countered some prior information. A flicker of an idea played behind his eyes. Ember was gone, but he didn't know the details of S-ranking. Just some... hearsay, by a possibly disreputable source. "Too bad... I hope that hurt."

The Blight reached its clawed hand for Artorian's neck at the speed of darkness. Still, before it ever touched his throat...

the world stilled. None could move, and Artorian couldn't even slide his eyes sideways. He could, however, see that the new color of the world... was grey.

The black hole ripped open, and just as a body had been sucked in. A new, advanced form slowly manifested and came out. A bright mocha-skinned beauty freed herself as Soul energy constructed her desired body. Black and burgundy cloth clad itself over her young features, and metal rings that appeared to be gold fastened about her upper arms, sealing the cloth in place while exposing her shoulders. A matching ring on her middle finger kept the material across her fiber taut as it vacuum-sealed into place.

Lush lips matched burning orange eyeshadow as a flock of fluent, wavy locks spilled from her head. The coloration began as bright yellow, and with ombre smoothness turned orange, then red, until the tips showed a soft, deep-dark tyrian purple. The hair ends had no color. They were dark as the void, and sparkled like the depths of space. Shorter than expected ears grew into being, still elven in design... but, dare he say... cute? Two cuffs sealed themselves on the top lip of her ear, and a thin halo of burning white circled into place around her head.

The crux came when the woman before them opened her eyes. Accented by long, thick, dark lashes, her sclera were the black of endless space. Her irises shining as mighty supernovas that spun in the void. The difference was that Artorian believed with certainty that was what he was actually looking at. Only then did he notice her perfectly done dark eyebrows. He'd never pegged Ember as the overly aesthetic sort, yet this body was the textbook definition of sexy style. She flexed her hands, showing off bright orange stiletto nails that shifted to match her most prominent ombre hair color.

Yup. Definitely went hard on style. She didn't just look like she'd manifested from a black hole, but all senses screamed that she *was* one. There was nothing she couldn't fatally attract with a look. Nothing she couldn't crush under oppressive infinite pressure, which was exactly what happened to the Blight as it flattened into a paste against the floor.

Artorian remained unharmed; not feeling any such deadly pressure. Exhaling, the world trembled as 'Ember' took and released her first real breath. The greyscale ceased to be, and a wobbly old man was caught by... nothing? Space was just holding him up. He couldn't tell *what* space, or where. Just... space, which gently brought him to his feet where he could steady himself.

"Oh... well. Thank you, and hello. I am Artorian. It is lovely to meet you."

The girl smiled wide, and extended a hand. Her voice was milk and honey, carried over the space of a dozen galaxies that played with planets as instruments; like the music of the spheres descending to grace the mortal world with their perfect tune. "Dawn Aran. It is good to meet you, my old, and new friend. Please, call me Dawn. I have been very excited to meet you. Thank you. For everything. I know you didn't have to do all of that for me, nor show me the memory of who you are. Please do know that in your venture to reclaim your family. I offer my full support. It is the least I can do."

Artorian beamed and tried to keep a steady face. He had expected to die, not regain so incredibly much. "My dear, I am just happy that I could see you again. It would have been a long road without you, my friend."

Dawn gently hugged him. "I'm sure you would have told me all about it, when I saw you again."

The old man brushed under his eyes with the back of his wrists. "Oh stop, you're making me weepy."

Dawn smirked and winked at him. "As if you didn't do that to me with your little pre-Actualization speech. That hurt, you know..."

She released him just to pout and turn away, holding her own shoulders as the tip of her toe left the ground. She remained there, floating in place. Was... was she playing with him?

A different trait. How very... new. He smiled and poked her in the shoulder, giving her a little push. Sure enough, she just floated along like gravity didn't matter in the slightest! She turned from the push, her eyes shooting sweet daggers at him as her pretend pout gave way to a beaming smile.

"Had *enough* of this disgusting reunion?" The Blight's Ancient Elven body reformed from the ground up. The pressuring effect on it had expired, and the regional darkness was swelling in strength once again.

Dawn pressed a finger to her lips, loudly musing. "Hmm... that's funny. I was sure I'd crushed you like a bug."

Artorian frowned and crossed his arms, turning to face the S-ranker. "Aren't we all bugs to you at this point? How does Soul energy work? Just how much more powerful are you than you were?"

Dawn popped her finger from her lips. "Oh... significantly. Compared to a zenith class A-rank nine, this is *so* much more powerful. A full category higher. Yeah, I'd say a categorical difference, at least. I could *sneeze* and release A-nine power; it would be nothing. Which is why I'm... confused why Blighty here—who I remember getting rid of with the Wood Elves—*isn't* paste."

Artorian filled her in before the phantom could. "He's got a land-law covering his butt. It's why he's in that elven personality. When he was in the previous Headmaster of Skyspear, we couldn't attack one another because the land-law would do us in. Or at least, it would smite the aggressor dead on the spot. Whatever he has with you must be different, he doesn't seem... phased."

The Blight laughed and did a... twirl? This personality was a jester.

"Close again! However, I won't tell you anything. I'm more than aware she's got the power, and you've got the mind. As if I'd tell you anything after that trip you sent me on. Clever boy for hiding that trap... I'm afraid you're all out of tricks now, and your Essence count can't be doing well. *She* can't kill me, and you're unable. Sooner or later she's going to look away, and then it's bye-bye Headmaster, and hello afternoon snack."

The violet Blight rubbed its hands together with a self-assured grin. It stopped smiling when it saw the academic ponderously running a hand down his beard. "C'towl got your tongue?"

Dawn quirked a perfect eyebrow, leaning on empty space as she patiently smiled at her friend. She knew what she was good at, she knew what he was good at. Dawn was just... waiting for it all to fall into place. She had an eternity. First thing she learned: S-rank lifespan? Permanent unless killed. It was intrinsic knowledge.

The Blight leered at Dawn. "Since we're all still figuring out what to do. Why aren't you... on fire? I vividly recall from the forest days that you were a Fire Mage. So there should be... more *fwoosh*. Less 'mystical'."

Turning on an axis in the space she occupied—she defied gravity just by existing—she spoke aloud. "Well, S-rank of the **Law** of **Fire**. Correct. There is just a minor difference between ordinary Actualizations and the one I went through."

She pointed at her chest. Even the Blight thought it rude to stare at the given location. "Ripped fire affinity channel. Though that's to blame for another problem I'm going through. What you likely can't get your widdle head awound... is my new celestial affinity channel. Got it from trying to copy an ability from my thinking friend over there. Oh, looks like he didn't even hear me. That's fine, he's going to do his thing."

The Blight spat at the S-ranker. "An affinity channel? That *late* into your Ascension? That's paramount to suicide!"

To his dismay, the floating woman agreed with him. He didn't know he would hate her agreeing with him! "Oh yes... having multiple affinities doesn't prevent a low-tier law from accepting you. It *does* however open up additional options when Incarnating. See, it offered me two choices freely, out of three. The first is your average S-ranker. Nothing special, just as normal as they come. The second... well, you're within proximity. I know you're an elemental."

She opened her hand, and fire sprung freely into being. "You have also been denying yourself the innate feeling that you know that I am also one. At least partially. Maybe fully? Don't know. I *was* only born today..."

"*Third?*"

Dawn righted herself and did a little side-to-side shimmy. "Third is a little bit of this."

She snapped her fingers. "A little bit of that. And a whole lot of look at me, because I'm a fancy cat!"

The Blight thought she was crazy. "So you're a cat? Could have gone for c'towl, they're superior in every respect."

Dawn beamed a smile at the creature, and something deep within it became unsettled as the woman phased out of reality. This caused some sort of void that started sucking him towards it. Just him. Nothing else. Only her supernova irises were visible in the absolute depths of the void. They were so pervasive that even as a creature of the dark he feared this space. *Never* should he go there. Not even the land-law might protect him wherever that black hole led. Then it clicked, and he understood. "The **Law** conspired with a higher **Law**, because it couldn't account for your peculiarities!"

Dawn manifested back to reality and blew him a mocking kiss. "Got it in one! The **Law** really didn't want to give me the option, but being quasi-elemental made quite a stir in the Tower. It had to contend with a higher tier **Law**, **Holy Fire**. I was bound to **Fire**, but the higher **Law** outright gave me the option to Ascend. Special circumstances... you're right, it is suicide to unlock an affinity channel that high into the Ascended ranks. Given how much I'd done for the **Law** of **Fire**, the other Heavenlies existing in matching nodes were all in an uproar. You should have heard the **Law** of **Celestial**. Oh, it tried hard, but unfortunately it has active S-rankers."

She danced around the air like a ballerina. "The **Laws** came to a compromise. So long as I took on an Aspect of Incarnation that didn't conflict with existing Incarnates, I could do it. The **Law** of Fire was ecstatic to keep me. To conform to the rules, I gave **Holy Fire** a big hug, and whispered sweet thoughts into its ear. I wanted to send a message to a higher **Law** that I knew wouldn't want to talk to me. Yet I was surprised at how the bigshots pay attention when you least expect."

She *giggled*, of all things, while hovering in loose geosynchronous orbit around the violet manifestation of Blight. "See, the big contribution I made to my **Law** was how to replicate my friend's starlight effect using Mana. I was surprised to find there is no **Law** of **Sun**. I was hoping my message was going to go there, since the Incarnation idea I had directly correlated to the concept. Even if I have but the measly two. Yet, two was enough. For the concept involves no air, no earth, no water, and no infernal. There is nothing to further break down.

"Whereas the sun is a star, there are holes in space where no light can escape. I wanted to be what happens when a star reaches the end of its lifespan, and comes into existence anew as something else. My best friend is my sun, so I will be the dawn of the endless void that comes after." Her grin widened; intent clearly evil.

No, there was no *evil* in her smile, it just felt as such from the apparent malice she was directing toward the Blight. She'd answered his question in a way that guaranteed he understood that however long it might take... she would end him. There was indifference. Apathy. Her expression was heartless, emotionless, and callous. She was the void where things went to end, and she had chosen to hunt him.

The Blight wriggled as its bodies shuddered with temporary deformations. They recovered quickly enough as Dawn's expression returned to normal. He might have been a monster, but this wench was on another level. Luckily for him, he was untouchable...!

"I think I figured it out!"

Dawn beamed her smile at the Blight, her body language and posture slowly turning towards Artorian. "Oh? Please do tell me... and welcome back! You were gone for a bit there."

"Oh, well. Yes. Sorry about that." The embarrassment was apparent on the scholar's face. He pretended not to have been aware of the entire interaction while he'd been puzzling. "Though it turns out it was rather simple, there might just be... side effects."

The Blight threatened him with an accusatory finger. "Not. Another. Word."

Artorian challengingly turned his eyes on the virulent mass. "Hmm? Or *what?*"

CHAPTER FIFTEEN

Jiivra and the student body made it safely to the surface only to find an all-out war.

Tired students ducked for cover as a blazing c'towl catapulted over their heads and tackled into a group of skeletons that just wouldn't stay down. A flash of burning light blocked their vision as an earthquake struck, a massive ravine opening nearby in the location where that metal tunnel had been. Something shining and bright jumped down, and the blinding effect ended.

"Instructor! What do we do?" Jiivra's students were panicked, and rightfully so. In need of a swift plan of action, she looked around and saw... indescribable devastation. Everything was flattened, gone, reshaped, or... she didn't know. There used to be a city here, now she couldn't even see traces of ruins. Just... things she didn't believe, like animated armor or floating swords autonomously attacking skeletons with blackened, almost glossy looking bones.

One problem at a time. The mountain was still there, better than nothing. "Back to the mountain, dodge the... *everything!*"

Her half-hearted words—while shouted—were acted on by jumping hastily back down the hole they'd crawled out from as a slashing sea of swords sundered the space she was in only a moment ago. The burning blades whirled in place and flung themselves around like a school of fish. They became discs of hot, spinning death that tore up undead in their path. Mostly.

"Nevermind!" The snapped change to her own command forced her to hold back students that would have blindly charged forward. There were always some, but a jian-storm was reason enough to wait it out.

Astrea offered her two coppers. "I like the safety cave. Safety cave is great."

The news and decisions spread down the group well enough until it got all the way to the end; the message had devolved into 'steel swarmy boys ahead'. It was confusing, but once they'd gotten clarification from the front it didn't seem all that incorrect. When razor sharp clouds of sapient weapons wrought unholy abyss upon endless fields of slash resistant skeletons, hanging back was a *fine* idea.

Skyspear was exhausted regardless. With plenty of fresh air and the passageway sealed with no further pending threats from below, most of the student body collapsed and lay down to rest. They were wiped from running, being Essence drained, and something about the mounting stress from fighting to survive.

The sheer concept of 'living weapons are having a tiff with animated skeletons' made the majority of the student body throw their hands up and check out. They were aware of some crazy concepts, but that one took the honey cake. That was with knowing about their Headmaster's antics. Going down was death, going up was death, and there was no sideways. Seemed like a good time to nap.

Astrea sidled up next to Jiivra, who had her face buried in her arms while seated and hunched over. Her weariness matched that of the students. Her Essence count was equally low, and while she had a C-ranked cultivation technique, she was still heavily deprived. Her effective level was currently closer to the low D-ranks. "You getting by?"

Jiivra half grunted out a response with genuine effort. "I'll live."

Astrea snorted out a half-giggle, her hand muffling her mouth as the tired combat instructor glared at her beneath heavy eyelids. "That's something my Elder would say, after he arrived to the longhouse after a long day of suffering through our pranks."

Jiivra snorted back. She believed it, having been present in the Fringe during the early days after the Salt village was raided. The years of Skyspear life had only further ingrained her thoughts on the old man. "Yeah, that sounds like him. With a dumb little smile on his face, trying to pretend he wasn't horribly bothered over something incredibly minor that wouldn't have annoyed anyone else."

The celestial cultivator turned her head, laying it on her arms as she regarded her opposite. "How about you? Holding up?"

Astrea's smile was a carbon copy of the everything-is-okay-but-it's-not smile that was just described. She tried to hide the pain behind her smiling expression, but the twitching gave the lie away. She got fist-nudged calmly in her shoulder; it worked on the old man. To Jiivra's surprise, it worked equally well here. Astrea took a deep breath and spoke.

"I'm afraid. I'm out of Essence and hiding in a hole. It's likely the grandfather I wanted to go home with just threw himself to the beasts to buy us time. I'm tired. I hurt. My vision keeps flickering and if Blight comes, I won't notice it before it's too late. I'm shaking, I'm cold, and the only reason I'm not falling apart is because there's too much going on and my heart won't stop pounding. I just. I can't... I can't..."

She fell sideways, or was pulled. Astrea couldn't tell. Her rant had quickly deteriorated into tearing up, but a tight squeeze surrounded her. Ordinarily she would have complained all the way from the abyss, all the way up to the heavens from being hugged by someone she'd only known for days. Today it didn't matter. She wasn't the only one that needed comfort; plenty of other students had huddled up, and so she said nothing.

Being held helped tremendously. That hadn't evoked comfort since her Fringe days. Jiivra held the back of Astrea's head, keeping an arm curled around her back. She said nothing about the huddle. This was fine. It helped them both. Within the confines of support, Astrea managed to mumble, "I'll live."

Jiivra nodded. They'd be alright. "We will. Just have to wait out the bar fight on the surface. I bet when we get up there, your old man will be standing there with one arm behind his back and a hand on his beard."

"Oh, *there* you are. What took you so long?" She sassily mimicked Artorian's speech pattern. Astrea snorted again, a little smile playing on her lips. Jiivra continued: "I've got some confections in my pocket! Stuff this in your face so I can stand here and look bemused, nodding to nobody while asking you questions to make you talk with your mouth full. I find your embarrassment... humorous! Fufufufu!"

She received a minor jab to the ribs. Alright, maybe her gag had been a touch embellished past the truth, but Astrea was smiling. That was worth the entire affair. Jiivra would have said more, but a tiny, familiar snore came from the curled-up bundle sleeping on her chest. She smiled, and wished she had a blanket. Wait.

Jiivra's hand reached for her shoulder and found the soft, familiar brush of a snoozing, oversized sugar glider. Had this snooty little mongrel slept through the entirety of their nonsense, remaining so still and silent they'd forgotten he'd been there? She pressed her lips together in the patented Tibbin's squeeze. Because yes, yes it had. "You cheeky little..."

She tickled it under a wing, and the sleepy C-ranked beast stirred. His celestial ignore-me field lifted. Blanket mewled upon waking, chittered, and licked its nose. It had a few seconds of looking around, released Jiivra, and stretched. After a few of the still waking students jerked from the sound of the chitter, Blanket made a loud squee. While everyone else was dead tired, Blanket was happy as a clam to go around and meet absolutely everyone. There was petting to be had!

Group morale improved drastically when there was a creature of pure fluff that wanted nothing more than to give you some kisses and love up on you. Those who were awake adored running their fingers through the incredibly soft fur. It was soft, and comforting. Most importantly, it made them smile.

A harsh crunch repeated as something scorched, and glistening dark color tumbled down the crevice that would get them outside. The ones that were awake felt momentary terror grip their hearts as a skeleton shambled to its feet. The drop hadn't killed it. The attacks above hadn't killed it. They were out of Essence. They were abyssed.

Blanket blinked at the entity of hate and murder that looked at its family like it was about to tear them asunder; mostly because the mindless thing was about to do exactly that. The sugar glider took *exception* to a threat.

Jiivra didn't quite believe her eyes at the sight that came next. The waking students were silently glued to the... fight? That couldn't have been called a fight. It was easy to forget that, between the love and sweetness, Blanket was still a C-ranked beast. The glider zipped over in a celestial flash and clamped jaws on the back of the undead's glossy skull. One *crunch* later, the pile of bones harmlessly collapsed into a pile. They watched as individual bones dissolved into misty black sand.

Blanket bristled. Standing up on his hind legs, he looked up to the crevice the undead had fallen from. Oh, it was not having any of this. Slowly, the Glider sat on its haunches. It chuffed at the ceiling light, daring another to try and come down here. A few glances told Blanket that his family was tired. They needed sleep. Blanket was awake, and strong. When it saw Jiivra smile before weakly nodding off against Astrea, it took on the mantle of responsibility.

Blanket defends.

Blanket protects.

CHAPTER SIXTEEN

The Blight glanced up to the ravine above. All it needed was one undead. Just *one*... to fall close enough for it to grab. Since its vision couldn't be seen by others, it was confident that this plan wasn't something his... company... had seen through. There were things it wanted to do, but it had held off on wantonly attacking in favor of a higher priority. As usual, distractions were getting in the way.

"What was it you said?" Artorian rapped his knuckles against his forehead. He recalled, and mimed the words with as much insult as he could muster. He disliked parroting the Blight's words, but it was all for the sass! "Oh, you can't begin to understand how wrong you are there... you might have had a chance."

A cruel smile crossed his lips, so unobstructed and visible that Dawn quirked an eyebrow. She didn't know the old man to be one for malice. Her senses felt the change on his skin before his lips pursed into an expression of cheeky amusement, like a child that knew something a sibling didn't and couldn't wait to tell mother.

The violet Blight elf hummed as it pressed a hand to a nonexistent hip. "Shame that you really don't... you're more drained than a twisted rag, squeezed dry of water and left to hang in the sun. You're holding on... how, exactly? You should be crumpled."

The academic laughed back with a mocking 'Oh, hoh, hoh!' "A comment on my well-being? I'm in better shape than that pitiful excuse of a body you're trying to form. Your ears aren't even... even. Might want to work on your shaping technique, boy-o..."

The Blight elf snarled and lashed out a dissolving violet whip of desiccating energy at the irritant. There was no reason to let the mongrel keep talking. The desire of watching the bug suffer over a long period of time to savor his slow demise had been fully replaced with a need to just shut. Him. Up.

A pleased smirk graced the Blight's locally formed body, but it faded and dropped to dissatisfied agony as its attack was blocked by... it didn't know what. The invisible orb surrounding the old man had stopped whiplashes from twenty differing directions and bent angles; all the hostile energy stopped dead in its tracks.

He shot a glare to the Actualized hovering nearby, but she silently blew the Blight a kiss. Of course she wasn't going to let her friend be threatened. The protective energy wasn't even visible; like it occupied a part of space not active in the real world, but still prevented his assault all the same. S-rankers were known for their greyscale effects, yet it had perceived none needed to put the shield into place. Wasn't it a requirement that the field activated if they used any Soul energy?

Clap. Clap. Clap. Artorian mockingly copied the clap Cataphron had given him shortly after he'd first woken in that awful pit of despair, filled with countless dead. "Look at you, trying so hard... really though, fix those ears?"

The old man winked and pointed to his own left ear, whispering, "I'm sure you've heard this plenty of times but... it's a little short!"

Dawn covered her face to stifle a brutal giggle. The Blight wasn't remotely as amused at the two-millennia-old stab. "There is nothing wrong with my ears. They're supposed to be like that. It's... stylish. I won't have my favorite technique be spat upon by a creature such as you."

Artorian brushed his ears and nodded sagely. "Correct, and you saved me the need to ask a question... awfully *kind* of you!"

The darkness screamed at him with a hundred raging mouths, but didn't advance. Its attacks repeated, only to be equally rebuked as the hot orb made his Essence whips catch fire. Essence, catching fire? Soul energy was a cheat.

Artorian held his hands behind his back, face aglow with maximum snootiness. "You see, you're right. I am awful at techniques, absolutely terrible at them. I've been relying on a trick I learned from my dearest friend here to get the Essence back by creating a zone of sovereign Presence. A space owned by me. Mostly I just throw Essence out, carefully crafted with identity, purpose, shape, intent, and a myriad of other factors. However, if I throw it out, it mostly isn't coming back. Not much of a technique if it isn't stable and fails to reel in the majority of spent energy."

He trotted towards one of the energy tentacles bearing down on an invisible shield. Yet his walk seemed to move the shield, forcibly altering the attacking whip pattern as well. He wouldn't be able to inspect it closely. A shame, but he described the knife the Blight was about to get shanked with.

"Yet... for all my ineptitude, I could not have even attempted such a feat if I didn't have one, particular thing that let me do it. To manipulate Essence, I need a cultivation core. A refining technique that lets me gather, store, and use relevant energy. Why, I would venture to say even Dawn still has one, and so did the Wood Elves! Strange thing, that last one. You see, theirs weren't in their actual bodies. Yet still, they use and refine techniques with skill I haven't had the time to replicate."

He paused in his stride, and winked at the floating S-ranker, who promptly pretended to react as would a shy noble lady to a troubadour playing beneath her window. "So that leads me to a simple conclusion, Blighty. As you just so kindly confirmed for me, you've been using *techniques*. Honestly, you think you're brooding and clever but your ideas have as much spice as a salt sandwich."

The Blight didn't like where this was going, but couldn't do much about it. That abyssal Actualized was hanging around, stifling his wick so it could not burn. That failed student from the mountain was also still not shutting up, and electric distaste sparked through its mind when Artorian asked a question that no one ever should. "Sure, you generate Essence, yet that isn't enough to satisfy the requirement of control. So, my dear boy... you say you can't be killed. *I* say, where is your spiral?"

The Headmaster pressed fingers to his puffed-out chest like a guest lecturer at a public forum, adding more pomp to an already pompous, purposefully aggrieving choice of words. Meanwhile, the Blight was sending an impressive, diverse array of differently shaped and identity imbued attacks at him. It didn't like being looked down on, in fact it actively despised it. It was just more proof for the academic that the lack of self-control was indicative of having poked a sore spot.

Dawn was having a great time. Fresh from the inversion, she was still 'cooling off' and coming to terms with just what exactly she now was. It was thrilling. She knew borderline nothing about what to do from this point; beyond the fact that she'd need to learn new things all over again. The age of stagnation was over for her, and she delighted in the thoughts of future opportunities while lounging about. So she indulged in a show of verbal backhanding while still 'waking up.'

Watching her friend lambast an ancient... evil? Well, it was elven in the golden age and thought it was doing well for itself now. So... evil idiot? The correct term was ancient idiot.

There was also something annoyingly familiar about the way the violet body was shaped, and Artorian's mention to the ear had made her pay attention. There was a poem in her family concerning the sacrifice of the first Aran; the person whose lineage she had taken the name of, as she intended to start it anew.

She tried not to hum as she recalled the verse.

'In depths of void, and coldest spite.
There lived a creature of darkest night.
It spoke with haste such that it spat.
A tale of an ego that could fit within no hat.
The first of Aran fell to lay it low.
Yet none under the sun could deliver a fatal blow.
If ever the dark would see the light.
All those lives shall be granted respite.'

Dawn mused over the verse a few more times, but found no wisdom in it that she could offer to her friend. The first Aran had been like her, a fresh S-rank, though one tied to a higher **Law** than her. If her greatest forefather hadn't been able to extinguish this stain from the world, she wasn't going to do it either without help. Yet that was just the thing: she had help. A memory flashed of her time within the bonfire. The lesson that one couldn't, nor *needed* to do it all alone.

Dawn's smile flashed at her wordy friend that was quipping back and forth with the Blight; both untouchable as they flung poorly veiled insults at one another. They were each trying to step onto some higher, more noble platform of moral superiority. The dark one was going to have difficulties with that challenge... if you wanted to wax poetic, you could not come ill-prepared. Unfortunately it appeared 'Blighty' over here hadn't just been idling time away. As amused as she was over the verbal destruction being swung about with the subtlety of fish being used as clubs, she cleared her throat.

Space warbled. Grey exploded from her being, and Dawn frowned as she found that she was the only one capable of moving freely. Everything else was stuck, stopped. She hadn't done anything different? Why was there a field now? Could she make it go away?

Space stabilized as she thought about making the effect disperse, but the grey remained. Oh. It was even worse than not tightly controlling your Mana at all times. She hadn't held too much Soul energy before, but now the trickle was building bit by bit, and her thoughtless action had caused some to... leak? No, not leak. She'd lost nothing. It had just... forced its effect upon the world? No. Still wrong.

She nearly snapped her fingers, but stopped herself as she realized she'd cleared her throat at S-ranked speed. Not Mage speed. Mage speed was sluggish in comparison. Where was the sound she made in her throat? Oh, it was still here, traveling as a visible ripple of sound waves. Not very fast, but in motion. Dawn realized the effect of those tiny waves might... utterly reduce anything within in a sneeze's radius to fine particle dust. The grey field was preventing an effect from being unleashed upon the world.

It wasn't an attack, or some special feature. It was a defense, a precaution! Well, a little late now, it was out in the world. Her own fault, really. So it was her task to stop it. What to do... more energy wasn't going to fix this. A voice played in her head as she tried to ponder. "You looked, but you didn't see."

Without trying to physically do anything, she looked around. What was different? What was new? Aside from the world being grey... grey. It was grey. *Why* was it grey?"

She could feel a smile in her thoughts. "Now that... is the correct question."

Dawn was imagining Artorian's voice, but it helped. The region of space she occupied didn't defy the rules of nature currently in progress. It more... took them elsewhere? This was her space, and the earlier mention of sovereign territory came to mind. Not exactly the name using Presence should have. It was just Presence. It also just happened to make it easy to reclaim resources spent in an area. Like taxes. *Oh...* sovereign territory. She got it now. Clever.

So, what was here, and what was 'elsewhere'? Motion in the space wasn't present. The world was still. Her grunt was still 'here'. Could she... move the grunt 'elsewhere'? She focused on it since the world was essentially not moving anyway. She could see the soundwave fade into obscurity, and successfully move... 'elsewhere'. Well, that was going to need significant exploration in the future, but as soon as the threat she hadn't intended was gone, the grey effect on the world dropped. Much like her friend did.

The Blight brushed itself off, then pointed at the fallen academic just to laugh. It had experienced S-rank pressure before, and Artorian hadn't. Gasping for air, the Headmaster heaved in a breath and sat up on his butt. "Great Woah! What in the name of cultivation was that?"

Dawn pursed her lips and said nothing. She was keeping up a shield of Mana around her friend, since that's what she'd had available at the time. Yet her control was starting to crack as her Mana was fed into her soul space, and her Soul-ranked... something... gulped it down to trade it in for Soul energy. It was just like trading Essence for Mana; except she couldn't discern the source.

A world of grey washed over them all again as Dawn turned. Just *turned*. Oh, this was hard! Even just thinking of the Mana shield made the orb suck away from its current position, leaving Artorian vulnerable. No! Not acceptable! With a wave of her hand, a new bubble formed in place. She'd done it hastily, and had forgotten something. Still, protections were in place!

Artorian was on the ground again when the grey field lifted. He heaved a deep breath again. "Dawn, my dear! Please do be careful with those, I can't breathe when you do that!"

Controlling herself, she really pressed herself to drop to Mage speed, then mundane speed. Working on it, she realized that the confines of that bubble didn't have a replenishable air source. She altered it to allow for some imperceptible holes to allow filtering. She kissed out the words, "Sorry, bee-bee..."

She got the conversation back on track. If she was losing control of her abilities the more powerful they got, a quicker resolution was better. He'd been onto something early on. "So, why is the location of Blighty's spiral important?"

CHAPTER SEVENTEEN

Artorian brushed himself off. He could have sworn something odd had occurred in the space around him. It felt cramped, but he was already mentally trucking along. He too, wanted to give this annoying foe a fatal back of the hand.

"Do you recall in the Grove, how Wood Elves retained their Core techniques outside of their personal bodies? I am convinced Blighty here is no different. There's no way this fake body before us, or messy amalgamation-mass down below, holds a cultivation core able to hold enough Essence energy to make our boy here 'all-reaching'. Words from his own mouth."

The academic pointed an accusatory finger at the arms-crossed violet Blight; who was snarling at being picked apart like this. It needed an undead to *fall* already. "The techniques in use don't appear too cheap either, and I'm a wasteful fool when it comes to expenditure. I can tell. So given your flattening earlier didn't do him in. It means the vulnerable part isn't what we're looking at. Like we're facing a phantom of the original. He hasn't been defeated because nothing has been attacking it somewhere it can actually be hurt."

The Blight snapped at him, "So what? Theories aren't going to help you! If there was such a thing, it could be anywhere. Maybe even on the moon!"

The creature bent backwards to laugh, but it petered out quickly when it saw the foxy smile the old man had plastered on his face. "Awfully strange that you mentioned waiting on an undead to come by, so you could escape. Your Core isn't anywhere far, it's *here*. There's no other place it could be, because of the very thing supposedly protecting you from Dawn."

She picked up on that cue, but said nothing. It was better for the attack strategy to be laid out entirely.

"A function of starlight definitely hurts you. Yet if it's not affecting anything except rogue fumes. Not very effective, yet Dawn supposedly can't harm you because of a land-law. Why else take that ridiculous elven body and personality? Not that much of a personality is left. Now, to be immune from whatever she can do to actually hurt you, you need that land-law. Funny thing, that; do you know where land-laws don't work?" He was beaming. The Blight wanted to tear his throat out.

"Outside of that land's area! When you leave the relevant territory, the rules in that place can't express themselves upon you anymore. You should have seen the books available on the topic in Alexandria's library. Interesting stuff... so if the only place you can be protected by the land-oath is here, then *here* is the only place it could be relevant. That means your Core, your real body, is here. There is also a second, incredibly important aspect to consider." He brushed his beard. The Blight was desperately looking for ways to silence the man; and it noticed something. A tiny space in the shield, just enough for particles... and particles is all it would need.

"I was wrong before. There can only be one land-owner of a given area. You were right, and I repeated the sentence just for this reason. 'I' could hurt you. For 'I' am the landowner, and a land-rule that prevents you from harm in general will not function if the land-owner rescinds the ruling. I just have to say that **I revoke y**..."

Chhlggg! Artorian fell to his knees and grasped his throat. Tears of pain ran from his eyes as he turned red. Unable to breathe or speak after inhaling... infernal particles? Abyss! He flickered his Aura to life and switched it over to affect his Presence, filling him with the effect as the heavy celestial Essence in the Aura trashed what was preventing him from breathing. His voice, unfortunately, had taken a severe toll. Blood dribbled from his lips as he coughed. He saw that Dawn was already purging the area with... he didn't know what. Fire? It was probably fire, but it didn't feel hot to him; it was also bright neon blue.

He could just see that Dawn was raging mad, like the Blight had exploited a weakness she thought had been foolproof. On second thought, that's likely exactly how the Blight must have been feeling this entire time: stripped naked as its protections were explained and peeled away like the skin of a fruit.

Without the ability to talk, he couldn't rescind the rule in place that was preventing the Blight from true harm by Dawn. Even an S-rank can't defy a ruling that was being upheld by a Heavenly. He would have said it sooner if he'd put the abyss blasted dots together! He thought of it, and had immediately turned his sentence to declare the change.

His throat wasn't healing internally. Why did it have to be infernal that dealt this damage? It was significantly more difficult to heal since he relied on celestial involvement. It wasn't his fault he'd only focused the best one for the job! Okay, fine, perhaps it was. Artorian had a backup in mind, it just wasn't one he wanted to use. It carried terrible... side effects. He soundlessly bashed on the inside of the shield. Unable to make sound, and still not being good enough on Essence to cause a sound effect, he was down to just trying to get Dawn's attention the old-fashioned way: wild flailing.

The damage an S-ranker could do was the kind of thing stories were written about. Her first punch into the Blight-mass drilled a hole so deep into the ground that only her shield had protected him from the viscera it churned out. One needed an awful lot of room to store a city's worth of dead bodies... and it turns out that blood is still a liquid, and doesn't accept being squished.

He wasn't going to get her attention in time. Artorian pulled free his hidden pouch on the small of his back, nestled neatly under his robe. He opened it fully and desperately dug around in it. Armor. No. Weapons? He hissed at himself, his throat still not allowing words to form, "No! Vellum, paper! Give me something to write on!"

Artorian had nothing. A scribe and scholar, and he didn't keep so much as scratch paper on him? "You fool, you're going to be a laughingstock!"

He glanced at his robe... it was material. He had no ink to write with, but his orb-shield was covered in... red. Red that was oozing into the tiny openings meant to let him keep breathing. Ah, no wonder Dawn was so mad. He fished around in the spatial pouch. Not a single quill? Artorian felt the bundle of Sequoia's bow. He'd never had the heart to unwrap it, but he pulled it free now. For with a bow, comes arrows! They were thorn arrows, fine tipped, and perfect for impromptu delicate applications.

It would do!

Hastily throwing his outer robe down, he scraped up a red line from the inside of the shield, and carefully got to writing. That it was written in blood... surely it wouldn't affect anything. It's just a medium, yes. Don't overthink it, old boy. Just a medium. Just ink. Don't think of where it comes from. Focus. Focus...

Dawn was deep underground by the time she'd even slightly calmed down. She brought her might to bear upon any part of the phantom she could find, and even bedrock was but brittle sand that burst apart if she moved through it. Her greyscale flashed on and off underground; her unchecked rage not as caring what overbearing effects she let free upon 'the real'.

The entire time, the Blight mocked her. "Is that all? Harder, oh yes, *harder!* You pitiful worm! Even your grand-forebear struck me with more force... and still accomplished nothing!"

She beat him to ash and dust, her surroundings a living inferno. It was to no avail. It made no difference. The phantom reformed, reshaped, and returned to mocking her, spurring her on. Her fist stopped an inch in front of the next iteration of the Blight. The sheer force behind it still evaporated buildings worth of space, but the strike itself halted as her mind caught onto the situation. Spurred her on? It *wanted* her to hit him. It was doing nothing but mocking, but was still pulling her far away from—*abyss!*

Artorian belched out blood. The raw amount of infernal Essence pouring into the shield orb was overwhelming his flickering sunlight Aura. Raw amount was all the Blight needed. With the ability to be in several places at once, a little distraction was enough. Left vulnerable, that shield did nothing. The convenient blood to write with dissolved, and a very hunched over Artorian had needed to find... alternative sources of ink. This was the work of folly.

Putting the final touches on the robe, he felt weak and pale as his lifeblood ran down his arm. Unable to use the blood falling from his mouth as it boiled away, he'd stabbed the arrowhead into a place without a great many nerve endings. This didn't mean it did not *hurt.* To his great displeasure, his Aura was also healing him up as much as it was rebuking the smothering infernal cloud. So when he needed more ink... there was more pain. "Finished!"

He pulled the robe close to his chest and curled up into a ball, protecting as much of the written text as possible while making himself as small as could be. Less Essence was needed to protect a smaller object, but the amount he gained was barely enough to keep staving off the death plane. Each slammed strike from within the shield wasn't harming him directly... yet. It was still driving him ever closer to complete Auric failure. Once that went down...

Blue fire washed across both sides of the Soul-shield as Artorian's Aura flickered. He was tired. So, so very tired. Everything was heavy, and dark, and cold. Fire or no, he was cold. His vision was hazy, and as light once again filled the bottom of the ravine he peered up with tightly squeezed eyes. Dawn. That shape reminded him of Dawn. It could be the Blight, tricking him with a fake body?

Blue fire? Enough information to make him risk it. Dipping his finger on the bloodied arrow as it once again drew ink, he wrote 'Sign' on the inside of the shield, in reverse. His arm dropped to his side in the middle of writing the 'n'.

The soul shield dropped, and a barely breathing academic hung limp in Dawn's arms. She'd seen what he was writing. She'd gathered the gist of it and pulled free what he'd been holding close. Part of his robe? There was text on it. She grit her teeth after reading it. Yes, yes that would definitely solve the problem... with significant cost.

She bit her finger without a second thought, and pressed the dot of her energy to the cloth. There was no blood. Apparently, S-rankers lacked that, in favor of a damage resistance that made Mages look squishy. The contract was signed. It was done; he'd done well getting this ready. The fight wasn't over, and Artorian was still breathing.

Wrapping him in a field of grey, a single step took her from the deep ravine in barren, flattened wastes to the top of the Skyspear mountain like it was nothing. She lay him down, wrapped in a foggy grey mass that dispersed as the body within was 'fixed', and acclimated to the change in elevation. She unfurled the contract, and read it again.

"By my power of land ownership, I, Artorian, hereby grant my title and land-claim to Dawn, Soul of Fire. Undersigned thusly." His signature was messy, but there. Next to it there was a spot with 'Dawn' and a line beneath it. She'd placed her dot of energy there, completing the transfer. An extra line caught her eye, a line that didn't have anything to do with the contract.

'Under the mountain.'

She wondered what that could mean for only a moment. It was the location of what must be the Blight's Core. He'd written it with his lifeblood, and wouldn't have done so if the detail wasn't crucially important. Her friend would rest here in safety, so she declared a changing of the rule as land owner.

"I, Dawn, owner of the Skyspear, hereby declare that I revoke all prior protections that this land might have granted."

The mountain shuddered. Lightning cracked in the sky as her revocation was checked, measured... and approved. For it was the purview of the land owner to make such changes. Dawn folded up the cloth and pressed it into Artorian's hand. He was out cold, but when he woke would be able to see she'd signed it. He'd know what that meant for both of them, after this fight was done. She also saw her old spatial pouch, and dipped her fingers in to retrieve a single item.

Now she could do something she'd wanted for a century: Dawn could kill the Blight.

CHAPTER EIGHTEEN

The Blight didn't like feeling stripped of protections. Literally stripped as entire swaths of Runes were ripped from its cultivation Core beneath the mountain, peeled away like layers of cloth as intricate patterns faded, popped out of existence, or crackled with electricity and shattered completely.

"No. *No!*" Oozing its prior charismatic voice once more, the amalgamation roiled against the changes, trying to hold the Runes together. In place. Something. Not only was it vulnerable, but now, without the Runes stolen from Dark Elves. It was...

"Found you." Dawn's burning voice quaked forth as if a furious volcano was speaking. The ground around her melted. She scanned the underground with Soul-energy-fueled vision, and had seen so much more than basic Essence combinations ever could. The tremor that her words and movement caused finally made an undead trip down the ravine. She had traversed from the top of the mountain, down to next to the Core in a single straight shot, melting a literal hole right through the earth to arrive in exactly the location where she wanted to be.

The undead tumbled. Fell. Broke. Shattering before it could zip all the way down at terminal velocity. The Blight saw a ray of hope, and lunged for it. The mind connected to the skeleton was something that, if strong enough, the Blight could piggy-back all the way back to the caster. There would be a personality battle for control, one it couldn't lose. Or prior to this point, wasn't able to lose. Now it was going to have to take the risk; risk that it could absorb the caster's mind, and that it was a Mage rank or higher. Preferably higher.

An infernal claw shot to the sky, planning to snatch the skull conduit from midair. It was so close! Then the world turned grey. The undead conduit stopped falling, and so did any movements the reaching infernal hand was making. It watched in horror, as the skeletal body dissolved into particles of ash. With the connection severed, and the remains useless, the world of grey dropped away, allowing the residue to harmlessly fall to the ground as soot, where it then started to melt and boil.

"Tut, tut, tut..." The void in Dawn's voice carried over vast underground distances. "When I'm done with you... nobody will remember you ever existed."

The Blight shrieked in fear. It had to retreat. It had to flee. How could it have been such an idiot? This was all going to be for naught if...! The sound of space warbling, or tearing, reached the Blight's ears. It was an awful sound, and the worst part is that he'd *actually* heard it. Not with a gimmicked body, but with its real one. Dawn had located his core.

Dropping the perspective from the cloud, real eyes opened after centuries of being closed. They were orbs of pitch-black tar, but they saw the burning god before them all the same. Dawn's voice caused rumbling earthquakes. "That is the single largest piece of honeycomb opal I have ever seen. Believe me when I say that I have seen some big rocks in my life. I'm going to enjoy squeezing the life out of it."

The Blight's real body didn't have a chance to speak as a combination of pressure and solar heat melted away the gathered layers of infernal protection. It was pulling together all its infernal gas, tendrils, and anything else it could get ahold of at a prodigious rate... just to collapse everything around it as a shield to stave off the torrential, cosmic heat for just a few more seconds. It needed to think of something...!

Like lightning, an idea struck its elemental brain. It was going to perish here; it was too late for anything different to happen. Still... dark laughter filled the area. "Even if you destroy me, here and now, I will return! So long as the Skyspear stands, I will come after you, and all you care for again and again! An elemental cannot truly die, I am bound to this land! You will not wrest me from it! I curse your lineage, and the lineage of Artorian, to be fouled by Blight!"

Dawn swung her arms outwards, as if grasping the piece of mammoth-sized opal from far away. Heat rolled out from empty pockets of space where her Soul-energy was condensing. "So long as the Skyspear stands. I *promise* that you will do no. Such. Thing."

The Blight madly cackled at her. That had been so easy! His assailant was so wrapped up in her fury that she hadn't noticed his last, cruel little ploy. It had no power now; it couldn't actually curse her! But words had power, and promises even more so! "I *accept.*"

Dawn felt a cold shiver in her soul as the vow she'd unwittingly made clasped around her heart. She would die on the spot if she broke it, and realized too late what the infernal elemental had done. She was trapped! Even if the elemental was gone, she had promised against the possible *threat* of his return. Even as land-owner, this was not something she could simply overturn. A promise against a possibility was a no-win situation for her. While Skyspear stood, she could not leave the territory it occupied.

Dawn screamed dark vengeance, burning away the last of the defenses with ease as the Blight's main, actual elemental body became visible. It was person-shaped, of all things, with one ear shorter than the other. It was as black as the abyss, and spewing out infernal energy at a relatively stable pace. Had an infernal cultivator gotten ahold of this... they would have had unimaginable power. "*Abyss you!*"

She pulled the item nicked from the spatial pouch off her back. Grasping it firmly, she squeezed the grip on Sequoia's bow. A string of Soul energy sprung into being between the ends, allowing the wood to bend taut as an arrow of similar make particulated into being between her fingers. The arrow sprung to life as it took on the Incarnation of the sun, and became fueled full of identity meant purely to erase.

Dawn took a deep breath, and for a moment regarded the memoriam bow as she opened up a connection. Distance was nothing to an S-ranker, and she was pouring energy into this effect just to uphold it for a few seconds. A few seconds was all she needed for a reply. "Call it."

Across vast distances, a grove of roaming Wood Elves felt a knock on their forum doors. The familiar warmth that radiated through made several of them toss the connection wide open. Rosewood, Snowbell, Oak, and more held open the strained passageway that was trying to slam closed from the demanding new connection that burdened their communal mind space.

The congregation present looked at what was being shown, saw the reality, and heard the call. The answer was swift; all were in agreement. To gain retribution for untold centuries of anguish. To wreak vengeance upon an ancestral foe. To remember their loved, and fallen.

The will of the grove poured through the connection, and the shape of her arrow burst full of meaning into a new shape as it took on the conglomerate will of an entire people. The answer was clear.

"Lance him."

The arrow pierced the defiantly screaming elemental and punched right into his cultivation core. Not the little fake double it had hastily made to try and trick Dawn; such minor obfuscations no longer functioned. Not against an Incarnate. She saw clear as day that the Blight's actual Core-cultivation technique, along with a myriad of others, were all painstakingly carved inside of the monster-sized opal.

She wanted it. It was so pretty... unfortunately, not even a speck of dust would be left since she was now fighting against the possibility of the elemental's return. So it had to go. *All* of it. Every last speck of crystal would break down from a fully physical thing, to matter, to corrupted Essence, and then she would burn even that to cinders.

Sure, she could grey-zone the entire area and 'place' the opal elsewhere, but that wouldn't destroy it. Just displace it. She needed it gone. Permanently. The Blight shrieked its last vile laughter, pleased even in its last moments before it forgot entirely who and what it was. The luminous erasing effect spread through every connected Essence particle of its being. The elemental vanished with a pathetic *pop.*

Sequoia's bow sprouted a single, victorious leaf. The last, and only acknowledgement of vengeance completed before the entire bow crumpled to ash, utterly overtaxed and overburned by a category of energy it had no business handling. Dawn plucked the leaf and gently set it behind her ear as one would a prized feather. With a snap of her fingers, a makeshift simulacrum of a sun exploded into being, surrounding the entire opal and hastily reducing the object to protomolecules from universal-scale oppressive forces. It took but a few moments, the release of her fingers extinguished the sun as quickly as she'd sprouted it into being.

Even as she ceased emitting light, her surroundings were luminous with sizzling heat. She closed her eyes and expanded her senses. Everywhere the Blight had touched. Everywhere it reached. Everywhere it tried to crawl to... it either burned, or forgot what it was and returned to being base Essence. She ensured it.

Dawn exhaled, the first released breath of relief. A gust of air that could knock a tornado from its path whooshed through the tunnels. This S-rank level was... insane. She was so *powerful*... it was going to take her decades of time to comprehend herself, and everything she had to watch out for. The worst part was that she was going to have to do it alone. Or at least without the direct presence of her friend. They needed to talk about that. She remembered that Artorian was going to be forced to leave the mountain as soon as he woke up, so she addressed it without pause.

"I, Dawn, under authority of land ownership of the Skyspear mountain, allow Artorian and his family to remain without repercussion." Even being deep underground, she heard the lightning of confirmation. It might not be enough, but it was a start. She flew upwards, leaving the vast open cavern of molten slag and terrible memories behind her.

CHAPTER NINETEEN

Dawn was at her bestie's side when he awoke a few hours later. "Hey there, old timer."

Her voice was soft, and Artorian blinked as he saw the sky he remembered falling asleep under... sort of. A few things had happened in between. Was there any chance that had just been a bad dream?

He needed help sitting up, though his cultivation was already rolling. The academic felt less hot, though drained in nearly every sense of the word. He needed days of sleep, tables of food, and... he groaned loudly as he checked. Years of cultivation just to recover. Again. At least it would be faster this time. His poor children. No! They had survived this long, and he wouldn't fail them by dying from rushing their captors too early. They would need to survive a little longer, no matter how terrible he felt about that fact.

"My dear?" His words were so weak he didn't believe they came from him, even if he heard them. His voice was in an awful state. Celestials above, it hurt to speak! His memory was foggy and his Essence stores were pathetic. He wasn't alone, and that counted for a lot. Dawn anticipated his needs, because a water cup easily made it into his hands, followed by a piece of... bear meat? Artorian smiled. She was making a joke. Still the same old Fire Soul he knew from the grove.

He drank water, and ate the actual food she'd gotten together. Yet the entire time he was with her, she looked sad. It was pending news, and it would have to wait until his risk of death was eliminated. A good meal went a long way to accomplish that while his passive cultivation gulped starlight Essence faster than his mouth could accept food.

When his Presence flicked into activity, the soothing waves of healing that ran over the insides of his rasped throat did wonders for his speaking and food swallowing ability. It might be a shame; he was tolerable when quiet! "Get it off your chest, my dear."

He smiled at her, knowing she was holding back bad news for his sake. Dawn carefully drew some air, thankful that at least there was no need to repeat what happened underground. Her hands slowly slid over his, and Artorian supportively held her. "You made me landowner."

"I recall." Artorian nodded sagely, face breaking into a burdened smile. His hand motioned all around, even though all there was to see over the ridge was devastation. "You could have it all. My empire of dirt."

He wiggled his sandals. "I'm actually surprised my feet aren't making me rush out, though I do feel the discomfort, the push, and the unwelcome nature. Nothing might be driving me out for some reason, but I most certainly abandoned my duty here. The land wants me to go, even if it can't enforce it. Your doing?"

She returned his quiet nod, though her frown spoke volumes. "I take it... something happened, and you can't come with me."

Her lower jaw trembled, and she nodded again. She didn't, or couldn't speak right now. Her power would rampage, and even if she had that under control, she wouldn't have known what to say. She'd messed up badly down there. He patted her hand with a loving smile.

"Nothing we can't get around. Tell me every detail when you feel better. Later. Why don't we just sit together for now. Just for a bit? It's a lovely view with plenty of sun. I could use some sun, and it would be a terrible thing to waste."

Dawn moved a finger to his shoulder and carefully pushed him. A quick nudge was too much. This would do. Her friend opened his arms wide. "You think I'm going to let you be sad that you can't make excessive movements? If you can't, don't! I'll hold you."

She frowned at the thought of an S-ranker being held, but was already altering her density to be a weight that wouldn't pulverize him if she slipped. Wordlessly, she curled into his arms and nestled her face into the side of his inner robe. The outer one was missing, but it had perished to a good cause. She didn't mind being held, and could actually hear it when Artorian turned on his cultivation technique. It made music. Like a kalimba. She'd never known it to make music.

The starlight Essence that had been flooding in before rushed through his being as if a levy had been opened on a massive dam. It only increased the volume of calming sounds that Dawn heard, and she adored it. Just a few minutes. This was fine, for just a few minutes.

Artorian said nothing when she fell asleep. No amount of physical or Essence power to shape the universe changed how taxing some experiences were on the mind. Physically, he doubted she'd ever know harm again. Mentally, touchier subject. However, she wasn't alone. He'd find a way to assure that even if they couldn't remain in the same place. He thought about it as his own thoughts descended into his Center.

If there was one good thing about a solidified C-ranked cultivation technique, it was the Essence draw and refinement speed. His reserves were back into the mid D-ranks within minutes of active cultivation. He was absolutely going to need to invest in techniques. This kind of Essence loss was exactly the thing he'd told himself on his bed in the Fringe that he shouldn't be doing. He sighed and got cozy, scratching his head at one particularly extra red containment ring. Survival came at a cost. It was going to take him an extra... ten *years* to lance all of that away.

He had the time. It would be fine. A little cultivation, and he'd get his things together for one last descent down the mountain. It felt awful to be on it. Maybe less so to be off it, yet nearby? Worth a try. When able, he planned to go and find his students. For now, it was cultivation time!

***

Blanket was tired by the time night fell. The sugar glider had stood watch until then, when the first of the stirring students woke up. Many piles of black sand lay strewn all over the floor of their surprisingly safe little hole in the wall. The tubular metal cave had held through earthquakes, explosions, vast torrents of air movement, and sounds that would make a grown man not want to look outside. The beast mewled at Jiivra when she woke up, pouncing her into the ground.

"Morn—*huhg*!" Tackled into the dirt, Astrea woke up in mid-air as Jiivra tossed her in the progress of tumbling backwards. She flailed in the air, a breath gasped in panic as her senses started picking sensory data up on the way down. Falling happened in dreams, it wasn't supposed to happen for real!

"Gotcha!" Astrea's fall was broken by something squishy. Glancing down at what she was laying on, both Ali and Razor groaned. They had body blocked her impact with the ground; they calculated what was needed to catch her on the way down, but *heavens* were they bad at math.

"Still... got you..." a pained whine from Razor wheezed out as Astrea accidentally pressed her hand right onto his spleen when getting up. There were bodies in the way! She had tried not to hurt him! While brushing herself off, the students got up as well; though Ali had to drag Razor back to the wall.

A defeated sigh rang out from Jiivra. People turned to look at her and tried not to giggle at the sight of a very large sugar glider having decided he was going to curl around her for a nap. It was nap time, then after a nap was eating time. He was tired and hungry, and social decorum wasn't something a beast understood. "Blankie... get off."

Astrea leaned against the wall, rubbing her eyes with bemusement. The fall from mid-air had woken her up in a hurry but she was still incredibly tired. "I don't think he wants to do that. He has the face of a content beastie."

Jiivra groaned, actually whining, "Is it safe outside yet?"

The infernal cultivator shared some glances with other students. It was considerably quieter up there, and the light show seemed to have ended. No noises came when she stopped to listen, and it's not like she could smell anything other than terrified people and metal down here. She guessed she was going to have to check it herself since nobody was jumping to volunteer.

Carefully she made the climb only to barely poke her head out of the crevice. She scowled and kicked the wall. "You have *got* to be joking."

"Oh, *there* you are! What took you so long?" A heavy pink puff-cloud left her grandfather's lips after a mighty draw from a hookah. He was set up nearby with a maddening array of culinary crafts. Who... where was he getting this food? How had he gotten this food? How was he alive? Wait... he was alive!

"*Dad!*" Artorian dropped his hookah pipe, his eyes locked onto Astrea with bewilderment as she leapt from the gap to charge him. She was crying by the time she was in a full-on tackle, but her Elder caught her like she had the weight of a lightly stuffed plush toy. He wasn't going to judge; 'Dad' was fine. Grandfather would have been preferred, but Dad was just fine. As if he could say no to his family.

"Hello, my dear. I'm so glad you're alright. I take it the others are in that crevice? Won't you fetch them? I've got some confections prepared. Thought you might be hungry by the time the hubbub died down."

Astrea squeezed the life out of him, or at the minimum tried, but she didn't have the Essence to get very far. He didn't mind, and made little pathetic groaning noises anyway to pretend she was doing a number on him. "Oh, I am defeated! Squeezed by a mighty princess. I have been felled!"

He got punched in the shoulder, and all was right with the world. "Help me get them out. I barely made it out myself."

He nodded and waddled over, leaning on a scavenged scabbard as if it were a walking stick. Poking his head into the crevice, he whistled and called, "Hello down there! Is anyone hungry? I brought pie!"

Jiivra's eyes snapped open, and she was upright so fast Blanket was launched to the opposite wall as if a springboard trap had just been triggered. Blanket did not like this in the least. He hissed at her and chittered, bounding up the walls to escape the crevice. Only to see the face of a very adored old man. Blanket activated its tackle maneuver, and down Artorian went. It was super effective. The old man rolled backwards a few times from the sheer loving force of Blanket's impact. "*Oof!*"

Jiivra was seething, and almost fully crawled out of the hole by the time Artorian was up with Blanket relocated as a cape. Fueled by rage and a need for answers, she threw her leg over the crevice's edge and rolled the rest of the way. "Do you have any idea how worried I was? I thought you were dead, stop hurting my heart!"

She had him by the front of the Gi moments later, and if she'd had the strength, she would have manhandled him and given the old fox a heavy back-and-forth shaking. He couldn't stop laughing when Jiivra threatened him, arms swallowing her up in a hug. "I'm so glad you're well. Now come. Eat. I have questions to ask while your mouth is full! *Fufufufufu*."

CHAPTER TWENTY

The rest of the student body was hoisted to freedom in short order. It took a while to get everyone out, and their reactions of what happened to the surface became repetitive copies of those who'd come before. Some thought they'd arrived in a different place entirely. It was all so devastated, save for the Skyspear.

Large blankets had been brought down from the still mostly intact academy. They served as picnic blankets on endless lengths of desolate dirt. A variety of hookah, fresh dishes, and fruits were strewn out in clay pots and bowls. Piled up tapestry rolls were systematically rolled out to make more room as an ever-increasing flow of hungry, tired students joined the survivor's encampment.

Nobody questioned where the food came from. They were just glad to have it. Stuffing their faces and downing whole vases of water. Surprisingly little was said. Most remained shell-shocked at recent events, and many had suffered great losses. Friends were gone, instructors were gone, and... well. The city was gone. It was a lot to take in.

Jiivra popped a grape into her mouth and clambered to her feet. A quick glance let her find her target, and some wobbly steps led her to nudge Artorian in the shoulder. Silence was fine, but there was a pertinent question that had been bothering her. "How'd you survive?"

Artorian smiled up at her and pointed to the mountain while chewing on a sandwich. He didn't talk with his mouth full, and received a less than gentle sigh in return. That didn't help the celestial cultivator, but her Headmaster's fingers suddenly moved up before sharply coming down. A nearby *thud* hit the ground, softer than a falling object should have any right to be.

She glanced over and went pale in a heartbeat. Artorian grew incredibly confused when Jiivra dropped to a knee. Her right hand kept in a fist while pressed to the open palm of her left. She held the position, moving the hand-greeting above her head while keeping her gaze downcast. Artorian whispered in response. "My dear?"

A hasty hiss spat back at him under her breath. "Artorian what are you doing? Bow! That's a Saint!"

Artorian's confusion doubled as he glanced up to see Ember was here with a fresh batch of food for them. She was the only one that could quickly go up and down, and the only one with actual cooking skills, as odd as that was. Oh, whoops. Dawn! Not Ember. Drat! He was doing so well. Now he was slipping. His face scrunched a moment before getting up.

Upon doing so, he noticed that anyone with a clear line of sight to their combat instructor had copied her pose in an absolute hurry. "I... Dawn, dear. What's going on?"

Dawn set down a hollow rock containing a literal ton of goods. She took in the behavior and dropped her forehead into an awaiting hand; blocking her vision with her palm and fingers. "It's... I forgot about this part."

Artorian raised both his hands to the air. Making an 'I don't know what's going on' motion before loosely dropping them down to his sides so they slapped his hips. "This 'part' being...?"

Jiivra was not amused in the slightest. Her stern hush carried an intense, sharp sense of urgency. Worry filled her expression. "Artorian! Get. *Down.* That lady is a Saint! Show deference. Now! You're essentially telling a Vicar to abyss themselves if you don't!"

The Headmaster heard her, but just slowly moved his gaze back to the S-ranked cultivator. Jiivra had whispered louder than she wanted to. Students who had been equally confused overheard her. They were cultivators too. Even low on Essence, their enhanced hearing went a long way. Not wanting to risk a negative event, onlookers joined the rest without a word. Seeing as a person they couldn't defeat if they teamed up on her was on a knee.

"Please... don't. Please get up. I don't actually like this." Jiivra shot up at Dawn's words, changing her kneeled bow to a standing one. One similar to the standard Skyspear greeting of deference to a Master. It didn't make Dawn any more comfortable, as it turned out that their relative position to the ground hadn't been the problem. The Incarnate realized that this wasn't going to play out the way she wanted, and for a moment slipped into the role Jiivra understood. Just to move the conversation along. "Can y... *ahem*. You can relax."

Heavens did she hate stuff like this. Why couldn't everyone just treat her like a person? This was like her late Mage days all over again. Actually... "Artorian, have you met any Mages? Aside from myself in the earlier days?"

Jiivra didn't actually relax. Her posture did, but her hand motion and bow remained unchanged. Jiivra feared for her life, regardless of the fact that the Saint was talking to her Headmaster with a distressingly casual tone. If she and the students would not have been present at all, that would have been preferable. Holding to tradition was far safer, so she would. Insulting a Mage spelled the end of your entire lineage. Failing to placate even the slightest whim of a Saint spelled the end of your dynasty.

Artorian held his beard, answering the question. "No...? No, I don't believe I have. Why are they all bowing even though you said it was fine for them not to do so?"

Dawn pressed a finger to her lips, her elbow leaning on an arm that she kept around her midriff. How to explain this...? "Do you recall that, as a Mage, I was potent?"

Artorian affirmed with a positive nod, his arms crossed as he tried to follow where this was going. His thoughts weren't coming easily at this particular moment. Since he was paying attention, she filled him in just as if they were having a lesson back in the forest.

"In your measurements, that was the scale of an A-ranked cultivator. Also called a High Mageous. A B-ranked cultivator is just called a Mage. What I keep referring to as an Ascended. To me there is no difference between your B-rank and A-rank, however, to all your students, that difference is one of life and death. A Mage has such power that their desires change the course of history. A body of Mana makes one nigh invulnerable to all the ordinary threats a mortal can face."

Artorian swapped his position to press his arm about the small of his back, free hand pensively resting on the beard. He'd grasped the context well enough to follow along, and nodded for more.

"A Mage is respected by realms as a whole on a fundamental level. One upset Mage means the end of your kingdom, queendom, or tribe unless you have a Mage of your own to counteract this. With Mages, no two individuals are ever truly on the same scale of power. Affinity count, Tower tier, technique proficiency, Core cultivation technique, inherent identity of the **Law** in question, and a few other circumstances are directly important when it comes to comparing one Mage to another."

Dawn held up a few fingers. "As example. The amount of Mana they're currently holding, amount Invested in their actions, or how compatible their abilities are with their personality and Mana Type. Once you are a Mage, you exist in an entirely different world of problems. Even if all your old ones cease to exist." The old man rolled his wrist to ask her to go on, but he was stopped. Getting a look from Dawn in return that meant she wanted to know if he was actually following, before she kept speaking.

Artorian cleared his throat and filled in what she was looking for. "Power translates to respect, because the threat of not respecting those individuals leads to fear out of what they could do if you crossed, disrespected, or otherwise inconvenienced them. So... people bow, or otherwise wait to be addressed even if their social rank may be higher. Social rank plays second fiddle if the person you're speaking to can whistle and turn every stone in the vicinity to shrapnel. I get it..."

Dawn was pleased, and motioned at Jiivra. "Even though I have requested it, your student is afraid because she cannot afford to chance the possibility of an offense. Perceived or not. A Mage would do this to a High Mageous, because that is again such a vast gap in power that the roles take on another category. Think on this: a king bows to a Mage, a B-ranker. Then the person the king bows to shows deference to *someone else*. The social impact of this is heavy. Further factors are compounded when High Mageous types are involved, as their relative scale of power is even wilder when they try to compare to one another."

She grimaced and waved away her next words, "I have avoided the topics of items and equipment so far, for at this rank most cease to hold relevance unless the object is something truly potent. Such as a dungeon Core, or crafts of true significant power. The Soul-item one manifests in their soul space has an incredible impact on ability output. The theme one ties themselves to as an A-ranker directly impacts their Actualization process—their S-ranking."

Dawn made a motion for Artorian to really break up his student's poses, as it was visibly making her uncomfortable. Artorian took a few steps and lay a hand on Jiivra's fist. He hadn't realized she was sweating so heavily. Her breathing was steadied only by sheer force of will. Artorian had a thought as to why that might be. Vicars must be A- or S-ranks, and she had her cultivation ripped out of her once already. That kind of mental scarring doesn't just get glossed over.

"My dear. She's serious. Please relax." He met her gaze and gave her a warm grandfatherly smile. "You asked how I survived? I would like to introduce you to my best friend, Dawn. She just so happens to be an S-ranker."

Jiivra's stared at him and whisper-screamed, "What is wrong with you? How do you know people like this? What *even*, old man!"

She was trembling as Artorian pulled her a single step in the direction of the Saint. She stumbled, and Dawn was eager to help; sadly, her sudden appearance in front of Jiivra hurt more than it helped. Jiivra went from pale to chalk white, eyes flicking between the offered handshake from the Saint, and the... utter otherworldliness she exuded. Her hair and eyes were made of empty space, or something! Her eyes had irises made of fire suspended in black emptiness! This was entire *existences* too much for her.

A weak *eek* left the combat instructor as Dawn took her by the wrist and gently shook it with a smile. Frozen in place with her muscles taut, Jiivra tried to say 'hello' but all that came out of her was a squeal-noise with a *huuu* attached.

Dawn let Jiivra go and shoved a thumb across her shoulder to motion at what she brought. "Fresh meals are in the rock, just take the top off with... nevermind."

She snapped her fingers and the lid of the 'pot' popped off, revealing steaming piles of meat-buns. All that bear had to go somewhere, and steamed buns were easy to make in large amounts. Artorian spoke to fill the silence: "What makes Saint so different from a High Mageous? For a mortal like myself, I'm not sure the difference is graspable. Just another tier of who bows to whom."

Artorian received a nod from Dawn in return that said 'essentially', and she pushed up from her toes to hover in mid-air. Blanket awoke, and did itself a startle! There was a thinger next to it, a floating thinger! Its tiny eyes blinked at Dawn, and it didn't know what to think for a moment, until it got a very gentle scritch under the chin from the floating warmth that smelled of fresh buns. "Do you want some treats too, big boy?"

Blanket's loyalty was bought with honeycomb within the minute, and Dawn beamed at him as he lapped the sugar up with munchy pleasure. Artorian harrumphed. "That little traitor!"

Jiivra nudged her Headmaster in the ribs after an hour. She had to get comfortable while the entire student body lined up to give Dawn a handshake. "The Saint title is the faith version of what adventurers call the S-ranks. Those people are so powerful that... I don't even know if I can make a comparison. They end up ruling countries because there is simply nothing to oppose them. Entire wars have been decided by which side's S-ranker fell first, as that single detail determines an outcome immediately."

She swallowed and steadied her voice. "In the Choir, all S-rankers automatically become Saints. Even if you were an A-ranked Vicar before. The title swap is instant, as are the expectations. There's so few left in the world that you just don't see them outside of positions of incredible influence and reach."

Artorian nodded and motioned for another bun; he was handed a few and copied Blanket's eating pattern of 'more food in the stomach is better'. Jiivra said nothing even though she would ordinarily scold him, since it put a fraction of a smile on the Saint's face. She was glancing over far too often. Also, she was an instructor, not a student! Jiivra quenched that thought immediately; the Saint could call her a piece of *grass* and her only response was going to be a resolute 'thank you'.

She sipped her tea with a hint of spite, and a long slurp. The tiny smile vanished from Dawn's face, and the celestial cultivator just about gagged on her drink. Oh, come on! Jiivra stood with a grumble and quickly took steps away to plop herself down next to Astrea. Abyssal Saints and their abyss blasted preferential treatment.

Astrea enjoyed the addition of the company. Her social status had risen significantly, and she was no longer getting the cold shoulder. Fully included in a very familial feeling unit as the Skyspear survivors paid no further mind to her infernal nature. She was getting buns and water refills with the rest of them. Astrea was included in jokes and jabs, and didn't get flak for returning them.

Artorian noted the interaction, pleased as a busy bee after finding lots of honey that his granddaughter was getting some well-deserved social time. His little one was smiling and laughing. Surrounded by devastation or not, that made his world just one bit better.

"She doesn't look like you." Dawn weightlessly leaned on Artorian's shoulders, curling around his back like a ghost that didn't bother to adhere to gravity's rules. Her hands were atop one another, placed down just so she could rest her chin on them. Artorian smiled with a grandfatherly sigh, matched with an expression that signaled both pain and pride.

"She's my daughter all the same, and I love her so. We've two more kiddos to rescue. I'll figure out the rest from there."

Dawn nodded as she bit her lip. "About that... talk. Is now a good time?"

CHAPTER TWENTY-ONE

Artorian held his chin as Dawn told him about her mistake: that she'd accidentally been fooled into making a land-vow which prevented her from leaving the region. She was full of guilt since she wanted to help his other ventures. It's not like she was otherwise tied down with social responsibility, or the usual confines an S-ranker tended to lock themselves into. She was fresh, with the ability to freely do as she pleased.

He pressed a bun into her hand when she was getting too down on herself. "Eat something, you'll feel better."

She just ended up shaking her head. "I no longer need to eat. Or anything of the sort."

"You'll feel better." He pressed the bun into her hand regardless. His tiny supportive little smile made her take a weak, unnecessary bite from the dumpling. He gave her a look of 'go on' and she took a bigger bite. It gave Jiivra a migraine to watch her Headmaster make a Saint eat.

"So, so long as Skyspear stands, you have to protect it from a possible threat. I've got that right?" Dawn pursed her lips, body language making her seem small as she curled in on herself. Her tiny, almost nonexistent *mhm* squeaked out at such a pitch that Blanket thought there was another animal around. The C-ranked beast momentarily poked his head up out of Astrea's lap, but went back to napping while several people rubbed his fur. Such was the difficult, rough life of a soft sugar glider.

Artorian glanced at the mountain, and exhaled, "Well, alright then."

He leaned back and called to his family. "Alexandria, dear. Those Fellhammers. I mean, the Dwarven group we had come by. Did they mention they were going to come back? What happened to them?"

His spry youngest got up from her group huddle, taking her bowl with because there was no *way* she was done snacking. She plopped down next to her Headmaster as best she could, but Dawn was taking up an incredible amount of space even if she was just hovering around her adoptive grandfather's back. She wasn't bothered, but glared at Dawn while deliberately scooting her butt closer. The entire idea of power dynamics and differences didn't quite... register. Dawn smiled from ear to ear at Alexandria's feistiness. She loved people with fire in them.

"They left after you went on your walk. I had someone write it down, but it's up there." Her tiny hand pointed to the top of the mountain.

The Headmaster exaggeratedly made large upper body nodding motions. "Beautiful, beautiful! I figured you might remember more, without the writ? You are the smart one after all. What did they say?"

Alexandria sat up a little straighter, trying to fit the image she was being given. She didn't dislike feeling smarter than the tall ones, and her chest puffed out a bit even though her eyes squinted and her forehead frowned. "They..."

Both her hands held the side of her head as she tried to remember. It was kind of adorable. "They said they would be back in seven moons with reinf... reinfurt? Reinforcing mints!"

Her grandfather leaned over and whispered into her ear, and the youngest jumped to repeat it. "*Reinforcements!*"

Artorian pretended to not have said anything at all, performing another dramatic iteration of positive nodding as he closed his eyes. "I see, I see."

Alexandria didn't follow. "Grandad, your eyes are closed, you can't see."

Dawn snorted and had to look away, covering her mouth with her hand while Artorian beamed, and peeked through his eyelids. "Boo!"

Playfully screaming, Alexandria jumped up and ran away, ducking for cover into Blanket's grasp. The critter had jerked up upon hearing the outcry. It bundled her up and hissed at anyone in the vicinity trying to touch her, not realizing they were all family. Blanket wasn't exactly awake, so it was all instinct. The interaction got a chuckle out of nearly everyone, but Jiivra's expression remained flat and unamused.

"What's wrong?" Astrea whispered in Jiivra's ear, and the quiet words shook her out of her visual, albeit silent grumbles.

"Nothing." She glanced to Dawn a little long, pouting over how she was just fawning over her Headmaster. "Nothing."

Astrea was doing her best not to giggle. "Uh-huh... don't worry, there's someone out there for you."

The surrounding students said nothing as their combat instructor was being figuratively slain. It was feed for the gossip mill, and the sheer discomfort of their instructor fed them better than any feast Artorian could plan.

The red-faced instructor was on her feet and marching away while Astrea smiled broadly with her teeth showing. Interrupting *Dawn* was preferable to this torture! Sure, it was harmless and nothing was meant by it beyond being the butt end of a joke. Still, she was terrible at handling it. "Headmaster. What do we... what do we do from now on? Everything is gone."

The students quieted down. The answer carried some importance to them. "Well..."

Artorian raised his hand up, and Dawn helped him stand. The answer was important, and he understood that in this case, there wasn't any joking allowed. This was their lives. "I have a *teensy* plan. It is going to sound like an odd plan until you hear it all the way through."

"You've had *normal* plans?" Alexandria's face was hooded by Blanket's wing, but her eyes were exposed, and she saw no problem with butting in to blurt out her comment. A stifled laugh went through the student body.

Dawn decided she *really* liked this one. Her friend was stumbling over his words for a moment. Oh yes... definitely liked that one. Recovering, Artorian began to pace without thinking. Dawn let him go and floated up so as to not be in his way, lying sideways on vacant space to watch the show.

"So, I asked about the Dwarves because I am going to pull off an absolutely bonkers idea." Eyebrows went up. We'd gone from 'teensy and odd' to 'absolutely bonkers.' Oh, they needed to know. Their Headmaster motioned at the devastation all around them.

"We can rebuild on the land, but all of the value, all the gold, all the treasure, really *anything* of value, is under it. When the Dwarven reinforcements come, I expect they're not quite going to expect... this. I want to play on that viewpoint. For reference, I am no longer the landowner." He motioned to Dawn. "She is, and since it's only been roughly a week since they left, they don't know that."

His pacing quickened. "We, as the little family we are, will steadily move the academy down from the mountaintop. We're moving! Now, I know this might sound strange, but that's what I meant with odd. When the Dwarves come, we're going to 'convince' them to build a settlement here. 'Here' including..."

Artorian pointed down. "Under the ground. I'm sure you're all very aware of the tunnels. Now I don't know about you, but I hate the idea of leaving those unguarded; shifted around or not. The promise of free wealth should be enticing, but I want to sweeten the pot."

He motioned at the mountain. "Recall how we've been mining it for wealth and trading the metal to Jian? Well, underground construction takes a lot of stone, and starmetal is no joke. That should get them to salivate. I want to rebuild the academy above ground. With some silly feature, like on a lake or something if we can get a whole lot of water together. It's an idea in progress. Don't look at me like that."

His pacing continued. "While beneath the ground, using the entire mountain as a mineable resource likely means an inquisitorial secret base gets constructed. One able to house an entire—if not multiple—Dwarven clans. They're fantastic at keeping tunnels in check, and who would suspect a secret Dwarven base under a cultivation school?"

He spoke under his breath, eyes flicking to Dawn as he turned so nobody saw. "Skyspear specifically refers to the menhir shaped mountain. If the mountain doesn't stand, there's no land-vow to apply. Contract loophole, found!"

Tiny cogs started turning in the Incarnate's mind. Would... would that work? It was dumb, and taking a vow to the letter. However, if that was enough, she'd be free of the location she'd otherwise forever be trapped within. Her glimmering smile let the old man know she was on board with his scheming. A student's hand went up, and he pointed at it.

"What about a really awesome tall tower!"

An *oooh* resounded around her, and another student filled in. "A nine-tiered pagoda!"

"Why stop at nine? Why not more, like a spear!"

Artorian rolled his shoulders at the student suggestions. Yes, excellent. That was exactly the kind of positive forward thinking he was hoping for. He glanced to Jiivra, and she gave a thumbs up. For her, it was several beasts with one stone. Her academy would get saved, she wouldn't be separated from her family, and she'd make a branch of the Church do work for her.

Now that would be tasty, *tasty* vengeance.

The students had glints of scheming joy in their eyes. They got to be included in one of the plans, and what a plan it was! As a bonus, no more mountain meant no more *stairs*. That was huge for them, and the whispers between them would ensure that detail would be kept quiet, lest someone get the bright idea to add some.

Artorian beamed and rubbed his hands together like an evil villain. "Looks like everyone's in. Here's what we're going to do..."

Chapter Twenty-Two

The Inquisition rolled up on a hill far steeper than they remembered. It wasn't that detail they were bothered about, but that rain the size of marbles pelted them from above. The kicker was that the water was black, like it contained the remnants of a massive forest fire. Even midday, it was dark. Pyrocumulus clouds densely packed together overhead, visible cracks of red lightning snapping between them.

The gloom served to make their trip all the more eerie. A league and a half away from their goal, the entire cohort dropped to a standstill. All foliage and vegetation this far out had been flattened, and some still burned regardless of the heavy pitter-patter of rain. They could see the horizon in every direction because there was nothing left to block their line of sight, save for the hill.

A roughly five-hundred strong force had marched to Skyspear, the majority of whom were grumbly. The reason they'd stopped a league and a half away was the road itself. The trodden dirt patch changed into packed, dense clay and charcoal. Further up, shimmering flat patches of glass could be seen reflecting the scant trickles of light that made it through the clouds. All in all, not enough of a concern to stop a military convoy.

Kiwi Fellhammer pressed his hand over his eyes, shielding his Essence fueled vision from the unwelcome shower. "Those are definitely suits of burnt out armor lining the roadside. It doesn't seem like anyone be in 'em."

O'Nalla's expression was sour, she didn't like the rain. Her arms were crossed while she rode atop the front of the primary support cart. Even though the hooding of the Dwarven caravan kept her dry, it didn't improve her mood any. "So can weh go now?"

Kiwi grumbled in Dwarven under his breath. "Ah think so. 'Bout half a league from the hilltop, there be kneeling suits of armor on either side of the road. There's a destroyed sword in front of each of 'em, and their helmet be resting on the hilt. They're as ruined and scorched as the rain that's fallin', and there be a person sitting at the hill's apex. I can see the back of a robe, and the interesting bit is that it ain't wet in the least. There's a bubble around the bloke keepin' all the water away."

That last spot of news was far more interesting to O'Nalla Fellhammer. Anything that kept water away was a friend of hers. She pulled on the warhorn and tooted the combination for the march to continue. When the Dwarves came up behind him, Artorian didn't turn to greet them. He just sat on a dry pillow in the middle of the road, overlooking the desolation. O'Nalla was pleased as a Dwarfling who'd just gotten her first clan mug to be immune to falling water once she stepped within the bubble, but the sight that awaited her made even *her* hardened heart drop.

"Great pyrites below. What... what happened here?"

Kiwi didn't know what to say either. Several more Inquisition officers joined the convenience of the large water repelling Essence bubble, but they too could not find the words. The impact crater was bigger than any hole they'd ever dug. The entire lower half of the Skyspear mountain was scorched and blackened from whatever heat had been present to scour and break the land. All that farmland they remembered seeing was just flat, or part of the crater. The entire city of Jian they'd passed through days ago was nowhere to be seen... like it had never existed.

Artorian swallowed and started speaking: "Well, I went on an enthusiastic walk through the woods-"

O'Nalla's armored grasp clamped his shoulder before he could continue that ridiculous start to an explanation. It made the old man stop, and seemed to have gotten the point across as he started over.

"So, I was minding my own business-"

The sound of a tea kettle boiling over peeped between the angry Dwarven woman's lips, and the grip on Artorian's shoulder *squeezed*. Kiwi wanted to laugh at the landowner's attempts at humor, but the view was grinding that pleasantry down with mortar and pestle. "Did ya get yer wee one?"

The old man released a heavy sigh. "I did... at a cost."

The question of the cost didn't need to be asked. The view was enough. The teakettle noise ceased, and O'Nalla's grip loosened. "The survivors are in the academy, packing up to leave. We're going to try and save what knowledge we can before burning everything else to the ground, and laying down a land-law so that none will ever be allowed to enter these lands again. We will leave a hoard of wealth and eons of knowledge inaccessible to all, locked away until dust is all that remains."

He tiredly looked up to Kiwi. "You were too late, my friend."

A look from the Fellhammer head made O'Nalla take swift and silent steps backward. The hefty Dwarf plopped himself down next to Artorian, patting a hand on his back. "Don't let it eat ya. It's just how things go sometimes. Think o' yer wee lass."

The old man somberly nodded in an exceptionally slow fashion. "Yes. Yes, that's a good idea. It's just such a shame. I planned to build a new life here, you know? We even had a large number of recent breakthroughs, and... this."

He pulled a sheathed jian from under his cloak, and several of the Inquisitorial commanders took a cautious step back. Even sheathed, the raw power emanating from the gap where the hilt touched scabbard was viciously palpable. A borealis of light poured free when his thumb pushed the grip away, releasing waves of incandescent heat that hung in the air. The old man tiredly looked at the lights, his gaze wistful.

Kiwi swallowed, entranced by the sheer might contained in a weapon not more than two feet away from him. Wealth fever crept up along his spine, and his lips moved before his brain could tell him it was a bad idea. "Could I... see that?"

Snapping his mouth shut, the Inquisitor fully realized no man would hand over a weapon that emanated such vast power. One *leaking* Mana, as if it was a wasteful byproduct of the true potency the weapon contained! Dawn had let Artorian have the jian she'd personally used. It was a crucial part of the initial deception.

Without even looking at the star struck Dwarf, Artorian clicked it shut and handed the weapon over with dejected, downcast casualness.

"Sure. It's the only one I could recover. The rest..." He sighed, motioning with rejection at the crater before him. "Lost. Buried."

Kiwi and O'Nalla's gaze met, a silent conversation taking place with mere looks as the Inquisitor firmly squeezed the jian in hand. The implication that there were more weapons like this... just laying around... even this sword *alone* was a tool that could swing tides into the favor of a C-ranker, or be a suitable gift and sword for any Mage that got their hands on it. If the old man was going to lock this region off... all that power would be wastefully lost.

The Dwarf snuck a peek. Nothing within him could resist a glance as his thick thumb popped away the hilt once more. Freed more than by merely a hint, the blade released a steady stream of iridescent grey energy which flickered and ate through the air like a firework burst. The grey, void filled flame shot towards the closest suit of charred armor, and filled it with a waking wholeness.

The empty suit of armor popped and cracked. The insides were fueled with the growing, silver-grey flame as its charred arm reached out without a body inside to control it. The helm was taken and placed upon the space where a head should have been. Held firm by an unseen force, the helmet remained steady and in place. Four sharp lines burst into bright silver behind the burnt-out helmet; eyes of energy that judged all flaring to life as it sought the eternal enemy.

Dwarves close by drew their weapons and jumped back. Wary troops realized the existence of a possible threat and bounded forward, bearded axes in hand. They circled the kneeling armor, which did naught but place both its gauntlets atop the blade's pommel. It remained there, like a loyal knight awaiting orders.

Kiwi released the blade from its prison no further. His concern stained with worried eyes flashed to the landowner. The man was still and downcast, unaffected by the events that just transpired. Which meant he must have seen it happen before and was jaded to this spectacle. Kiwi connected the dots that there were 'many blades' and 'many suits of armor'. That 'wealth and knowledge' was going to be 'abandoned'.

This was a gold mine for the Inquisition, if he could but claim it. He needed to convince a single, depressed old man that lost the majority of his region not to lock it off. He also wanted to keep this sword. Kiwi *badly* wanted to claim and hoard it. Yet if he did, it would be seen as the act of greed it was. The old man would not take him seriously with any talk if he kept it. Seating himself back down, he bit his tongue and said nothing as a very shaky, unwilling hand returned the weapon.

The old man smiled weakly, took the sword, and pushed on the pommel to fully sheathe it once more. He laid it on his lap like it was a piece of plywood, giving it no further thought as the light within the armor began to fade. Taking its helmet back off, the scorched suit placed it back upon the sword hilt. When it took the position of rest, the same as all the others in a very lengthy line, the four silver lines faded. When the potential foe stilled, the nearby Dwarves relaxed as their commanders gave hand motions for them to stand down.

Kiwi paid it no heed as he leaned sideways. "Y'know. You don't have to leave. Could always rebuild."

Artorian rubbed his forehead. "Y... *yes...* I suppose I could. However, with almost every piece of silver, copper, and gold buried beneath the dirt I can afford no work crew. With the materials to the swords stuck in mountain veins, we can mine them no further. The secret knowledge of the breakthrough of a new kind of weapon empowerment is equally buried in the dirt, along with most everything else of value."

His next words seemed to ring out from a hollow space within himself. "I have no workforce, no money, no goods to trade with for reconstruction. There are no more local resources to rebuild with, and there isn't a human in my academy that knows how to work stone well enough for new housing. I have students, but they are children. Tired, drained, and injured children who just lost their families, their lives, their friends."

Artorian sighed once more and buried his face deeper into his hands. "The time it would take to recover Essence alone, for my tiny group of scholars and lads to recover enough to do work, would leave us starving a good few months before we could commence any sort of work. I have nothing. Nothing. Just an empire of dirt. I cannot hire and cannot pay. I cannot grow on desolate land. I cannot retrieve what is lost, for we don't even have a single shovel."

Those with knowledge on how to build settlements agreed that those conditions were dire. The man before them was a landowner in name only, but that didn't mean he couldn't set the land-law to kick them all out. The wealth fever was creeping into many more of them, having heard the kind of riches that would be there for the taking if they only had the time to unearth them.

"Then, if somehow I could rebuild. I need facilities of such complexity that only gnomes knew how to make. If we cannot store the knowledge of our library safely, against the weatherings of time... better to burn it. I know of none with the power to craft a room sizable enough to store centuries worth of vellum and scrolls. I might know how to *move* them, but..."

He shook his head, hiding his face in the crook of both arms. The robes he wore hid his expression, but he had all the bearings of a man defeated. O'Nalla motioned at the hunched over figure, mouthing angry, soundless words at her superior not to let this opportunity go by. An upset motion at their cohort of troops, and sharp point at the crater was enough for the Inquisitorial leader to get the message that his subordinates were on board with the claiming effort.

They'd come here to fight a war, instead they could go home without a single casualty, bringing the Inquisition a golden platter of resources. The honor they could bring to their clan for such a feat was massive, and such a gift didn't come by every dynasty. Kiwi cleared his throat, "Well, I'd say that's not quite right. Ya know at least *one* who could make that sort of building."

CHAPTER TWENTY-THREE

Artorian placed his hand over his heart and shook his head. "Please don't give an old man needless hope. It will only hurt bitterly in the end."

Kiwi Fellhammer gripped Artorian's non-sore shoulder. "Look, lad. Listen, I've got four hundred and eighty soldiers behind me that came here to help. So we came late to the fight, it's true. That's still nearly five hundred heads worth of smarts, and a thousand hands with Dwarven muscle to get something done. Why don't you tell ol' Fellhammer here what's in yer heart, and we see what we can do. Ya look burdened. Get it off yer chest..."

Artorian's heavy exhale failed to be masked as he pressed his mouth against palmed hands. "Lord Inquisitor, really, I cannot afford your services. No matter how kind and heartfelt they may be. What could I possibly offer you for this boon? I have rocks and dirt. Rocks and dirt!"

The Dwarf slapped Artorian's back and didn't let up. "Humor me. One old soldier to another."

Those words made Artorian's eyes sparkle. He knew that saying, and he knew it well. With a stern breath, he righted himself. Motioning to the crater, he spoke with his hands as much as his mouth. "Oh, very well. I apologize for this old man's childish daydreams. If I could do anything, I would strip mine the mountain tip to base. Crack every vein of ore, find every grain of starmetal, and gather every handful of rock. I would wish to rebuild a brand-new city in the crater from this. The edges mark a perfect city border, and as much as it pains me... the burnt woods will allow for farmland that would yield fantastic crop yields."

He swallowed and motioned lower. "It was joked that we could have a lake now. A paltry attempt to get a smile from the weary. I would dig deep into the rock, reclaim the lost riches, the lost swords, and the lost arts. I would have ordered massive construction projects to allow for an underground library with exact conditions. A hidden city under the surface, masked by a sprawling cultivation school above it. A multi-tiered pagoda at its center, the new Skyspear."

He dropped his hands. "Ah, such dreams I have."

O'Nalla sharply head-motioned at her superior, sending hand signals that translated as 'clinch the deal already'. Kiwi's attempt to say something was interrupted as an interested sound came from the Headmaster, followed by a message that wasn't great for them.

"Though, perhaps you are correct! I *do* know one who could help! It has been quite a long time since I have encountered Modsognir. I don't know the name of his clan, but he was a merchant. He might work out some kind of deal if I... perhaps sold off some land in recompense?"

Kiwi's words were short. "*Don* Modsognir? Fox fur trim gambeson, fine wolf pelt boots, buttons of platinum closing his arctic elk jacket?"

Artorian's eyebrows shot up. "Oh, you know one another?"

The Inquisitor did his best not to grumble, but the sourness spilled through regardless. There wasn't any bad blood between Dwarven clans, but there were frequent... opposing viewpoints that resolved in a violent manner.

"Few do *not* know of Clan Modsognir, which, so you know, is the clan name. They are a kind of... *merchant*, yes. However, the one I was referring to was your connection to the Inquisition. I'm aware you've encountered a Fellhammer brother in the Fringe? It was my hope you were on good terms. Since you mentioned them, I see no reason not to inform you that contract would be acceptable. However, if you would be willing to let the Inquisition do the work, we would be willing to do so for only salvage rights."

He motioned at the sword with a thick finger. "It'll pay for itself with coin and goods you would have owned regardless, and it will save you the trouble of needing to dig it up."

He saw the old man frown and hold his chin with a hand. The landowner was clearly considering it. "Can... can you do anything about the immediate survival of my students?"

O'Nalla stepped in behind her leader. "We could certainly add that to a contract if you were willing to draft one with us. We could speak of terms and conditions, and the like. Not only would it give you a chance to specify your worries so we could address them, but a contract would ensure that we would not back out of assisting you. Your wee ones benefit, you benefit."

The surrounding Fellhammers nodded in agreement as well. They were in on the ruse, and they were going to take as much land and resources as they could get away with. Still the old man had to agree to actually sign the Mana contract. Sweetening the words used even if the contents of the pot didn't change was a perfectly acceptable Inquisition tactic. It was even in the rulebook. Chapter three, section seven. Acquisition without assault.

Artorian released his chin. 'If... if salvage rights will do for your immediate assistance, does that mean to imply that you would be willing to indulge the *entirety* of my childish dream for... more?"

Kiwi's wealth fever struck him hard, and his tone was sickeningly sweet. "Why, my dear Headmaster, whatever could you mean to offer? As a skilled force of the Inquisition, not to mention that we're comprised of Dwarves and half-Dwarves, your dream isn't only possible, it's within reach."

Artorian sat up, and shifted on his pillow. "Land? Land sounds like it would do. Though you'd likely want a duration."

He pensively opened his roughened hands and looked at them. "I'm not getting any younger... it... it might be best for another caretaker to take over in my stead. What... what about a full land transfer? With the caveat that it occurs when the last of the Skyspear mountain is mined away and not a single rock of it remains, and that I see the majority of construction to completion. Particularly the school and main pagoda spire? Would that... would that be sufficient? I'd like the chance to see my children happy before I leave for greener pastures."

Kiwi roared orders over his shoulder. "Fetch me vellum and ink!"

O'Nalla was beaming. That was perfect...! "Aye, this sounds like good business. We can begin right away, after we got some signatures sorted and inform our men."

Even with the heavy rainfall, well over three-fourths of the cohort was already aware of the entire goings on. Essence-enhanced hearing, while it made the rain worse, was plenty for keeping information well gathered. They were the Inquisition after all. Inquiring was their specialty. Those who didn't know were filled in swiftly as events occurred, and the wealth fever spread.

They were building a brand-new outpost and were getting away with hiding it. With official documents to cover it up, and what sounded like an immense haul of loot to take home. The honor they were about to bring to their clan... Blessed pyrite was looking out for them this day! All this trudging through rain had revealed a mountain of gold at the end!

Kiwi tugged at his shoulder, whispering lower than needed. "Greener pastures?"

Artorian leaned back in his direction. "I might be a cultivator, but it isn't buying me the time I expected it would. I have a few years left in me, certainly. However, I'm doubtful that I have more than that. No amount of refined Essence can indefinitely keep my wreck of a body together. C-rank wasn't what I hoped it would be, and I've expended many years dilly-dallying. I have two more children to get back home... and for that I need a home for them. Do you recall when you told us where they were?"

The Fellhammer recalled well, and the thought wasn't pleasant. "Deep in enemy territory. You're thinking of leaving the territory in someone else's hands so you can go on a last-ditch effort for yer children. Can't say that ain't noble. Also, can't say it doesn't make me understand why you'd set the transfer on completion of a task, rather than, say, yer life ending. Ye want yer wee ones to have a home, in the likely case ya don't actually succeed."

The old man pressed a hand to his chest again, leaning back in shock that he'd been so easily seen through. "Am I such an open book to you, my Inquisitorial friend? Here I thought I managed to be clever, if not outright sneaky!"

The Inquisitor could easily tell Artorian hadn't lied about his lifespan problem, it was a well-known issue for older cultivators; they never got the same results youngsters did. That's why so many young adults tended to run the show and go on wild adventures; their physique could *handle* explosive growth. "Well it is mah profession, my friend. An' what father wouldn't want a better life for their wee ones? We'll build you a *fantastic* hold."

Artorian mused it out, a small smile on the corners of his lips. "Imagine that... a Dwarven hold named Skyspear. You'd never even guess it."

Kiwi nodded generously. He was counting on it, in fact. The vellum was delivered, and a small flat surface was prepared before them. As if a small table was a challenge for an entire squad of gifted earth cultivators. "Anythin' else?"

The Headmaster folded his hands and pursed his lips. "Maybe... a small little place. For me. Here on the border, overlooking the crater. It'd let me see the progress, and when the time comes... I can slip away without too much notice. The place could be a little shrine for... when I'm gone. Maybe we can gather up all the statues from the mountain path and plunk 'em here. What an honor it would be to spend my days within the sculpted presence of Woah the Wise, Corey the Mountain, Scout the Succulent, and Danielle the Detailed."

Artorian chuckled. "Who knows, maybe one day we could have a whole host of sculptures with personal scriptures from their lives? Why, I remember a vivacious Choir lad who wanted to be a scholar. How nice it would be for him to succeed. I can see it now, the Obelisk of D. Kota, greatest scholar of his age."

The Inquisition gave the sermoning old man a nudge and a quill. Artorian blinked and looked down at it like he'd forgotten what in blazes it was. Then he took the implement, dipped it in ink, and began scribing. The Inquisitor had no issue making Artorian do the majority of the writing work; his scribing talent and clarity was impeccable.

The cohort was directed to proceed and get comfortable by setting up camp. They each smiled as they passed. Their

Head Inquisitor was securing their clan a hold! As if to herald the success of their glory, the rain slowly ceased and the skies cleared. Rainbows and additional light peeked through, shining honor upon the birthplace of a new legacy.

CHAPTER TWENTY-FOUR

"Do you think they bought it?" Astrea sat hunched over, hands pressed above her knees as she squinted to the crater's edge down below. Every now and again she could make out the pinprick that was her grandfather, but that was the best she could do.

Dawn lounged on a floating carpet nearby. Why bother with rocks as flooring when an anti-gravity hammock was just so much better? Her voice wasn't salty or sassy in the slightest, confident in her assessment. She'd heard the entire goings on through all the husks of armor nearby. "Oh, they bought it."

Students jumped victoriously into the air. They had gotten things set up just in time before needing to flee to the spire to make it look like things had been properly staged without their involvement. "Can we make it stop raining now?"

Jiivra walked by and gave the exhausted group of water and air students a proud thumbs up. They collapsed to the ground and were glad to be done. She sat in the makings of a hedonistic hotspot, glanced over the ridge, and pulled out her pocketbook when satisfied. Astrea quirked a brow when the quill and ink came to bear, watching the woman start scritching words into it. "Does that pocketbook have a title with your name on it?"

She nodded slowly, not wanting to interrupt her writing progress. "It does. Your old man put it together for me in the Fringe. I was a different person then, and would have tumbled off a cliff had this tiny thing not made it into my life."

Astrea leaned forward to try and sneak a closer peek. "You make it sound like that booklet is your child."

The scritching paused, and Astrea's words were considered. Guilt for leaving it behind in order to live panged into her, and her fingers squeezed the pages. "If it wasn't before then it certainly is now. This booklet is the closest I'll likely ever have to a little one of my own."

"Hey! You have us!" a student chimed in, and the group around the speaker smiled widely as instead of being rebuked as expected... they heard a chortle followed by the pleasant *bumf* of Alexandria running to tackle into Jiivra's chest at full speed.

"No making mommy sad!"

Jiivra melted from within. She stood corrected, and curled a loving arm around the youngest student of Skyspear; her little librarian. Alexandria giggled as her head was peppered in kisses, trying to weakly push away at the invading face with tiny hands. It tickled!

Laughter broke all around them. It was good to feel like a family again. Yes, they'd lost much. Yet this was worth the world. They lived, they were fine. They were going to make it and get back up on their feet.

One of the students, Dame, cracked her back during a stretch. It made a few eyes look in her direction, and a pink flush coated her cheeks from the attention. Given that she had it, she shyly raised her hand into the air. "Can... I ask a question?"

At a positive response from the people she recognized as instructors, she formed her question. "What do we do now? That part wasn't in the plan, and there's a lot of small dots moving down there that are getting closer to the base of the mountain."

Frowns replaced the nods, and people scrambled to the edge for another look. Sure enough, there was a great amount of motion in the crater down below. Jiivra snapped her booklet shut and got back to her feet, cradling Alexandria while leaning the child on her extended hip.

"Everyone up and at 'em. Start gathering seeds, roots, and re-plantable stalks from all of our plants and food sources.

We are moving the entire operation off the top of the mountain and down to the crater. We're going to shack up on ground level. Expect a large amount of back and forth trips, especially when we get to taking apart the library and other contents in the special rooms. I'm sad to see them go, but that's the plan and we're sticking to it."

The students each got up, and when their instructor had finished giving orders they got to work. Except for the snoozing air and water students; they were sleeping off their exhaustion. Those young adults would be filled in later. For now, this was fine. She let Alexandria go once the child began to wriggle. "Nobody is doing anything to my library without a proper order of what gets moved when!"

She smiled as she watched the youngling zip off. The child reminded Jiivra of her own younger days, where she too had carried the flag of valiant zealotry. What a young and gullible fool she'd been. She sighed and turned, taking a few steps so she could clasp her fist and bow to Dawn. "My Saintess, may I ask a question?"

Dawn came to a jerky stop. She'd been glancing down at the crater, keeping tabs on her friend and the details of the contract being worked out. It essentially abandoned the region of Skyspear to a faction of Dwarves which comprised a good majority of the Inquisitorial branch of the Church. It also solved several problems they couldn't have otherwise done anything about. "Just Dawn is fine, Jiivra. Please, no more with the formalities."

It was a jarring request. A lifetime of having status differences hammered into you tended to do that. "As you wish. I don't understand why our old man wanted you to remain hidden. That seems entirely counterproductive. Where would you go? You'd be found anywhere in the region if someone did as much as think to look."

Dawn twisted on her lounging axis, gently descending so the tip of her foot connected with the mountaintop ground. Since she was blocking the path of the sun, a long shadow extended. "A feat accomplished more easily than one might believe. Why? Well, if I knew I was going into a land where a Saint resided, I would need to go fetch another Saint to handle that encounter. Considering we are dealing with a faction our darling long beard is holding at the pointy edged distance of a blade, that's not a pleasant endeavor."

Jiivra was incredibly surprised. She, in fact, didn't believe it. "Our Headmaster *adores* Dwarves. He went off on a whole half-asleep lecture once on how he can't get enough of their vivacious energy and rambunctious never-say-never spirit."

She stopped what might have ended up being a long defense had she not caught the edge of Dawn's lips move upwards. The Saintess provided a clue. "What has slighted a vengeful human that does not brook harm against who he considers his family?"

Jiivra squeezed her pocketbook as her hand clenched. "The... the Church. Oh no. Tell me he's not actually setting up something incredibly foolish down there to go to war with the entirety of the Church?"

Dawn chuckled a pleasant giggle before her dainty fingers slid to seal her lips. Her expression amused regardless. "'Going' to war implies the *beginning* of a process. Have you not seen our dearest is already smack dab in the middle of it?"

Astrea decided this was a fantastic moment for keeping her mouth shut, and pretended to nap with Blanket. She tried not to stir while listening in with a sharp ear. Jiivra in the meanwhile was kneading her brows with her thumbs. "Abyss, Artorian. Why?"

Dawn's finger harmlessly pressed against the celestial cultivator's skin. Aimed and held at the exact center of her... Center. "You *know* why."

The veiled protections even a Mage possessed to shield their cultivation techniques and internal workings were a pittance to an S-ranker, so Dawn could see the cultivation technique as clear as day. She watched the swirl of the miniature, simplified version of a cultivation technique she had helped put together. Jiivra's standing had risen significantly in Dawn's eyes from that detail alone. Astrea had it from the daughter title, Alexandria had it for carrying the flame of knowledge, and Jiivra had it from her Core. For never would *anyone* risk all they were to save the life of another... if that person wasn't important to them.

Jiivra's response came as a stifled stutter, but both her hands were taken by the Saintess. "It's alright. Believe in him. As for how I'll remain hidden..."

The S-ranker winked, a minor head motion tilting the point of interest to the ground. When Jiivra turned her vision to see, a sprawl of flaming, burning, blinking c'towl eyes filled the entire space of Dawn's lengthy shadow; spilling out from her foot where she remained connected with the ground. The living flames were being stored in her shadow.

"I once spent a decade in a forest as a *candle*; I just couldn't bear to deal with the world. Reforming your shape is something any basic Mage can do with ease, especially with plenty of practice. The body is no longer entrapping the mind, those positions are reversed for a Mage. For a Mage, their mind becomes the limiting factor. If you can conceive of a concept, and how it would function, you can do it."

Jiivra relaxed when all the burning c'towl eyes closed in unison, reverting the eldritch display back to a common shadow. Dawn's smile held a hint of laughter. "Much like my personal little army of fang and claw, I'll be residing in an entirely separate layer of existence. Per the limitations my specific concept allows. Watch..."

The Incarnate of Fire hovered herself over Jiivra's shadow, and eased herself into it as if it were a portal to another space entirely. When entirely submerged, only Dawn's eyes remained. She winked, and Jiivra shivered as she felt the interaction, rather than saw it. Another moment, and to the best of anyone's senses, Dawn was gone.

Astrea had both her hands sealing her mouth as her wide eyes met with Jiivra's, who was equally as unsettled. The instructor didn't look too good. "I f-f-feel sick."

"I have no idea where she went." Astrea pointed at the shadow. It was just a normal shadow. Nothing odd about it. "Is... is she in there?"

A wordlessly mouthed 'I don't know' snapped back at Astrea with barely controlled panic. She took a few more steps, and her shadow crossed with Astrea's. Neither thought anything of it at the time, but Jiivra went pale when she looked behind her and saw movement.

The combat zealot going pale was enough for Astrea to silence herself, head slowly turning to find a pair of swirling irises in the form of supernovae hovering next to her face. "*Boo!*"

The 'Nightmare' didn't know where the voice had come from, and didn't care. Reason left her as she yelped out a scream, running at full tilt away from the scene. The laughter that followed her was something she'd have to deal with later. Dawn's eyes had gone with Astrea's run for a few meters until her shadow crossed Jiivra's again. At which point she managed to stay in place, and reform back out of the shadow she'd originally sunk into.

Jiivra shuddered. "How are you doing that!"

The Fire Soul ran her fingers through her hair once manifested enough to do so. "S-ranked perk... I just reside on a different layer. I'm not gone, and have perfect awareness of my surroundings. It's like looking through a window, all that changes is which side of that window I'm on. While my bond isn't with teleportation, the specific higher Essence I get along well with mimics many of its functions. I'm still figuring it out as I go." Dawn took a deep, cleansing breath.

"For the most part I'll be staying in Alexandria's shadow. You two can defend yourselves, but the youngest would benefit from an extra pair of eyes. Plus, I would benefit from reading material. It's boring in the other layer; there's a whole lot of nothing."

Jiivra sighed and nodded. It was good for her little librarian to have extra protection. "So what do we do now?"

Looking over the edge of the mountain, Dawn smirked. "Now, we just wait for the years to pass... all will come in due time."

CHAPTER TWENTY-FIVE

"Well aren't ye a sight for sore eyes!" Hadurin Fellhammer beamed a smile so wide it could have illuminated the entire eastward shrine. Situated in the eastern cardinal direction, the 'small' shrine sat on the territory edge of Skyspear's crater border. Three more similar shrines bordered the lands, each in their appropriate cardinal direction. Yet it was in this one where Hadurin had found the long bearded old man from his early days in the Fringe.

"Look at ye! A spry... celestial *pyrite*! Yer in the middle of the C-ranks? I saw you a wee few years ago, and ya could barely crawl!" The half-Dwarf's thick hands shot into the sky, cheerfully swinging around to embrace the old codger.

Artorian laughed and gave the sturdy rock of a man a good squeeze. Not that it did much to him. "Hadurin! My old friend. What took you so long? I've been sitting here and watching the regional development for..."

He counted on his hands a moment. "Three whole years already!"

The Grand Inquisitor set his azure jade hammer in the open palm of a nearby statue's outstretched hand. Artorian raised a brow, and Hadurin had a second look at the statue before hastily removing it and placing it down on the floor instead. "Tha' coulda been bad."

Artorian affirmed the words with a nod. "Indeed, it could have, old friend. Laying any item in the hand of Danielle the Detailed is sure to bring ill fortune upon the item, for it will be lost swiftly as it is broken down into its component parts for study."

The Inquisitor picked it back up and cradled his weapon to his chest like a child. "Not me hamma!"

The old men both saw each other's half smirk, snickered, and then bent over in mutual laughter as the joke concluded. "It is good to see you, old friend. I was concerned on why there had been no vellum from the Fringe lately. Are my youngsters well?"

Hadurin reached into a spatial pouch and pulled out a stack large enough for the Headmaster to be taken aback. The Dwarven man snickered as he heard his fellow warrior's words. "What... what's all this?"

"Ooh. Well. Recall tha' Lu and Wu had a wee one? Well, she's as bad as ye are. Wee one ain't even ten, but she causes trouble for twice that amount. Found your old notes she did, most of these here scribbles are 'notes for granda'. She might not have yer mind, but celestials above does she have yer nose. Specifically when it comes to gettin' inta things!"

Artorian rubbed his forehead. He knew about Ra. Lun was going to tear him one. He weakly motioned for the stack of letters. He received the delivery as the first vellum dropped into his hand. No... not vellum. Was this paper? This didn't feel like paper. It was metallic, and sported a golden trim on the edges. The faint smell of peach and rose hung to the rolled-up scroll, and only then did he see there was a scented wooden log, carefully smoothed on the edges keeping the metal message tightly bound. He stared at it a moment longer in abject confusion. "You got me here. What is this?"

Hadurin reached over and tapped the bottom coronation, popping it inwards like a button. The message went *click* and loosened in his grasp, able to be unfurled. "It's a summons."

Suspicious glances darted across the object before they landed on his 'friend'. "Explain."

The Grand Inquisitor looked around, seemingly to check if anyone was listening in. "A summons. A 'request' for you to show up at a certain place and time. Personally, I'm just glad I got here before the Don did. He's got one of his own and I wanted to make sure you got mine first. You're looking at an eventful year my friend. Hope you didn't get too comfortable cultivatin'! Speaking of, got all yer wee ones?"

Artorian gingerly unfurled the oddly light metal letter and started reading. He half responded while his mind remained elsewhere. Some of the text on this document was less than to his liking. "Two to go, they're just a little difficult to... this is in a year? I can't make it all the way to the Seat of Sorrows in a year! They can come get me if they needed me in such a hurry. That's the opposite side of the abyss-blasted map!"

His friend pursed his lips, silently moving his hands behind his back as his raiment came to bear. Artorian realized that the Dwarf was here on official Church business. This wasn't a housecall, regardless of how pleasant their meeting had started. "Oh, they'll be comin' to get ye alright. Keep readin'."

Artorian grumbled and moved his finger down the writ as his face turned ever redder as he read the ever more irritating information. "*Mages* will come get me if I don't comply? For what?"

Hadurin just looked at the floor and cleared his throat. "Keep readin'."

The Inquisitor could tell when Artorian had reached the best part, because his jaw dropped. "To bestow the Medal of the Divine Order?"

His long beard *whooshed* and slapped a statue from how quickly his head moved. "I'm not even a part of the

Church. Why do they want to give me this? Why the entire list of threats for noncompliance? This isn't an invitation to attend, this is a death missive!"

Artorian was fuming, finishing up the last few paragraphs before an earlier mention finally clicked. "Wait, Don is coming?"

Hadurin made a holy motion across his body to forgive himself. He sighed heavily and pressed his hand to cover his eyes, hunching forward slightly. "Aye. He's got... the other one."

Artorian's concern was instant. "The other *what*?"

Crack!

Wood burst as the shrine door was kicked squarely off its hinges, the voice of a very upset and familiar Dwarf tearing his way through the front easily heard. Inquisitorial guards had not been able to stop the man, and slowing him down had been equally unfruitful. Hadurin had heard the stomping coming through tremor sense, and merely stood there, not really wanting to deal with this right now.

"The other missive! From the family!" Don Modsognir's glimmery platinum coat buttons came into view before the rest of him did. An equally metallic missive was in his hand, and a drinking horn in the other which angrily pointed at his Dwarven brother. "An' the *family* always. Comes. First!"

He stomped to a halt and deeply inhaled through the nose. "Ya know that! So don't be sending mah boy here to yer blasted Vicars. Ah don't trust it, and I knew ya was doing it too! I diverted mah whole caravan and ignored a whole tradin' route to try and cut ya off, and ah still got here too late somehow. An... *Artorian, drop that!* Quickly!"

The academic didn't hesitate, parting his fingers wide and letting the metal message clang and clatter to the ground. Don was nearly in a panic. "Did any o' yer blood get on it?"

Artorian checked his hands, and then looked down at the message. His hands were fine, but now that he was looking for it... at the bottom where his hands would have gone, he saw the golden edge coating was razor sharp. The back of the message also appeared to be a... was that a *contract?* "Those sneaky celestial devils!"

His head jerked up to Hadurin, who was still covering his eyes. He'd known and wasn't able to say. Under his breath he mumbled gruffly at his brother. "Took you long enough. I even sprinkled clues ruttin' everywhere."

Artorian was preparing to lambast his Fringe friend, but the dejected tone and word choice made him hold his tongue. If there was a contract on the missive, then it was very likely Hadurin was under one as well, unable to say or do certain things. "Now I can at least tell 'em that I got here first. That'll have to be enough. Please hand yer's over will ya. I really need tah sit. Been getting dragged around by my oath for weeks."

The Don handed over his message, but the long beard did not unfurl it. It was inspection time first. He carefully handled the prior missive to compare them in structure and hidden message contents. Modsognir went over to his brother and gave him a solid Dwarven hug. Their foreheads knocked against one another in familial greeting; must be a Dwarven thing. Hadurin relaxed shortly after, another heavy sigh of relief escaping him.

"Ah got here in time. That's wha's important. Lemme guess. Yer Vics were gonna 'invite' the old man over and tear 'em to pieces?"

Hadurin shrugged. "Ah can't tell you anything of the sort, but I also can't tell you it's *not* something they'd do. Gimme a bit longer, I feel some oath-chains fadin'."

He got an understanding nod in return, and Modsognir moved to sit down next to a human that was going through every line in each missive like it contained a cypher. "Find anythin'?"

The Headmaster grumbled, glancing up only for a moment before flipping both missives over, pointing at several 'off' geometric lines he didn't understand. "These are identical, but abyss if I know what they are. It looks like a rune, but I know awful little about those things. Best I could tell, and really only because I overheard you both, even a drop of blood would count as a 'signature' which would compel and require me to fulfill the hidden keywords written in fine print. Very clever to hide that text between the sheets of metal. Can't be seen from the outside unless you've got some vision skills or an earth affinity. I bet the Church was counting on my lack of earth channel. Yet, why the summons at all?"

Don pointed at his. "Well, if you sign this one, then you can't sign that one. The dates and times of where you gotta be then conflict, and since you can't uphold both there'd be a wee problem. Which is why ya ought ta do it in that order. So ya can go to the Church but not be stuck under whatever scheme this is trying to entrap ya in."

Artorian lifted the second Missive. "This one says I'm to attend a party? Did I get that right?"

The Dwarves shared a look, and the Don patted his friend's back. "Never been to a Dwarven hold and family gathering, have ye? The Matron wants to see ya. Some of yer exploits got leaked last year. We're aware ya probably don't know. Hadur, can ye fill in yet?"

Hadurin nodded, looking much better. At least his movements no longer appeared stern and rigid like he was a rusty golem. A freedom moved through his limbs, and he stretched them for sheer relief. "Aye. So about a year ago, I get a visit in the Fringe from a person I can't tell ya about. Save that their rank be higher than mine. They be askin' how we got the land, why it's goin against ancient regulations not to build in the Fringe, and why we're still putting a whole cathedral up regardless. An' yes. Ya heard that right. *Cathedral.* In the salt flats, by the way. On the water."

Some incredulous head shaking followed, and Artorian noted Fellhammer was having some trouble sticking to his normal accent. Some of his speech was slipping in and out of Dwarven drawl. Was his fading vow trying to force him into gabbing with proper eloquence? "So some names get dropped, because there's a few folks in the Church that make ya unable to omit the truth. Shortly after it gets discovered a Paladin-aspirant that was personally thrown to the curb by a Vicar is not only still alive; she's doing just fine. The lass lives without help or influence from the Church, and there ain't nobody that knows how a cultivator survived for years without a Core. There's talk of miracles.

"Then we've got reports of a rumor that a Heavenly was holdin' her near-dead body and walked up and out of the city at the foot of the Skyspear. So some folks go to investigate, and come to find out there be a raider incursion coming to flatten the place. Not only do the visitin' Inquisitors get a whole lot of good information, but they personally confirm the Paladin-aspirant's well bein'... as a C-ranker! So not only did she survive, she made it from death back to the C-ranks without dungeon access to boot. All of this in an amount of time that shouldn't be feasible or viable even by Mage standards.

"So for years the Vicar's been scheming. On one anvil, they know that if it's a sign from above, they did wrong by this one. On the other anvil, knowledge of a certain someone's cultivation creation notes were recovered from the Fringe. They look awfully similar to verbal accounts of what visitin' Inquisitors saw. So to cover their bases, someone figured... 'Let's squeeze all possible sources before we announce divine revelation that didn't come from us'. Savvy?"

Hadurin hard nudged his head towards their human friend. "They're in a tizzy from recent events, and the methods be getting more heavy handed. Things be movin in the world. Like somethin' big is goin' ta happen soon."

Modsognir supportively clapped him on the back a few times. "Had the feeling it mighta been something like that. Good call on the not telling the family anything. Especially on the not leavin' clues. Gran'mama will be pleased ya did well by yer own. Be sounding like the Church ain't what it used to be, and there's some... questionable events afoot. Especially in the higher echelons."

Hadurin squeezed his hands together. "It sure ain't pleasant, and *the* Kere Nolsen ran off recently. Something about how he got information on his Da, and now the Saint ain't approachable. The lad may be part o' the organization still, but the Vicars ain't got no leash. They don't like it, but they can't do nuthin. So that leads us here. What's Gran'mama want?"

They both glanced at Artorian, who was going through that particular missive for a third, if not fourth time. A small smile graced his lips, and it concerned both the Dwarves present. From the details the old man was reading... they *should* be nervous. "Modsognir, my friend, can I take it that you did *not* read this message before delivering it to me?"

The Dwarf pressed his fists to his fine belt. "Ah don't go through other people's mail! I ain't mah mother!"

Artorian nodded, and marked the contract on the back of the missive without further thought. That's exactly what he was hoping to hear. "Then I will accept this task, for two reasons."

Lightning cracked the sky outside, and the old man was smiling at both of them. The Dwarves felt unsettled. What had just happened? Modsognir was the first to react. "Long beard... what was in that missive?" What do ya mean... task?"

Artorian exhaled from his nose, thinking of all the time that he had spent cultivating and watching the new city of stone being built in record time. Well, rather than 'built', rock was being 'shaped' with a function that the academic categorized as 'convincing'. He likened it to an argument: one side was attempting to convince the other side something was correct. In this case, a hard headed Dwarven earth cultivator against a literal rock. How the Dwarf *won* those arguments was beyond him.

Rocks and entire patches of ground reshaped into new forms before his eyes, and had for the last few years. Who needs wood when condensed stone worked just as well—apparently *better* after some Runes got slapped onto it. Sometimes literally slapped! He knew construction workers snapped and scowled at inanimate objects, but this kind of shaping was unreal.

The region had been divided into hexagonal quadrants. A little nod to his honeycomb network, even though it was what was preventing him from gaining extra years of life. Each hexagon was dedicated to something specific above ground. Below the ground was a different story, and he thought it fine to let the Dwarven clan moving in do their thing.

The main pagoda smack in the middle of a lake was already twenty-seven layers tall. More, secret layers, existed under the ground. The building slowly rose as new layers were added below. A few of the architects had taken 'Skyspear' as a challenge, so twenty-seven was just the start. That still only took up the middle hexagon. Surrounding hexagons were all dedicated to lake space, for fish. The hexagons next to that were courtyard, and the spaces next to that were housing and essential facilities.

Great swaths of space had been allotted for it all. Not even a single zone had been filled to house all current students, and considerably more were planned for future expansions. Another lake layer bordered housing, followed by another district that was meant to include shops and crafting zones. Bordering that was undesignated, currently set aside for anything growth and production related.

Artorian shook himself and closed the letter with a *snap*. After folding the metal message up, he figured out how to lock it and handed it back to the Don. Modsognir did not like the feeling of Artorian's hand on his shoulder, and he did not know why until the man spoke, and his stomach crashed through the ground along with Hadurin's.

"Here are the two reasons. The main one is that this trip will put me within spitting distance of the two children I have yet to save... and the second is that 'Grandmama' says to bring her grandsons home. *Both* of them."

CHAPTER TWENTY-SIX

The Modsognir and Fellhammer clans got along exactly
as well as could be expected. Nearly the entire trip had been
filled with bickering, the most passive aggressive of quips, and a
nightly brawl shortly after the alcohol provisions were passed
out. The next morning they were all marching with bruised lips
and black eyes as if nothing had happened. Offering to patch
that up for them was taken... poorly.

"Ye'll not be touchin' me battle trophies!" Don
threatened him.

Artorian gesticulated with his hands, upset they weren't
letting him help. "Why not? You look like a fruit that hit every
branch on the way down! It'll feel better and you'll be fresher for
the next brawl, since it appears none of you can live without
one."

The Modsognir Clan Dwarf grasped him by the robe
and tugged him down to eye level. "Don't. Touch. Me.
Trophies. It be against tradition, and tradition be more important
than rules. Ya break the rules, ya just get castigated. Ya break
tradition? Matron be sending diamond-class death squads to
hunt ya down and present ye before tribunal. You'd be lucky to
retain yer skivvies as yer tried in front of 'eryone, addin' massive
shame to yer clan and family. There be worse reasons to flee to
the depths, but I don't know of any. Got me?"

Artorian's hands went up in the air, admitting defeat.
The Dwarf let him go, and the academic dropped the entire
topic of helping them out. This was not how he was hoping the
caravan trip would go. This whole 'tradition' business was news
to him, but the weight it carried was significant. It likely meant
far more than the Dwarf had let on, but he wasn't going to get

anything more out of them. These men and women were immune to his usual wily tactics; he would have more luck getting information by sweet-talking a cliff face.

He plopped himself back into the caravan, hiding away from the ruckus outside. Rubbing at his brows, he sighed as he crossed off yet another idea from his mental list. A whole *year* of travel, and he'd been none the wiser about their destination and customs than when he'd left. It was frustrating!

A massive hand opened up the caravan flap, and Dimi leaned in. "There y'are! Hey, now... ya look ill. Need a poultice?"

Artorian held both sides of his head and groaned. "If you've got anything to fix frustration about tight-lipped Dwarves and not having the *slightest* clue what I'm walking into... then yes, I want that poultice."

Dimi-Tree bellowed out a laugh. He didn't see this as a problem. He had a reputation for being able to fix everything after all. "What's eating yer gullet?"

Artorian was getting desperate for something to work with, so he decided to open up. "What are these traditions? It sounds like even though I'm the one with the mission, I'm in the dark on the social customs that will actually let me complete it. Don and Hadurin aren't giving me a speck of their time, and haven't the whole trip! Did I offend them? How? If I had hair on my head, I'd be pulling it out. My poor beard has been suffering!"

Dimi smiled wide, showing teeth. "I've got a poultice that supposedly helps with hair growth, if ya wanna give that a try. Tastes like a boar's behind, but I won't stop ya."

"Taste...? Don't you rub poultices on?" Given that massive D-ranked boars that were pulling all the caravan sections along, Artorian had gotten his fill of that smell. He just waved it off, because... ew. No. Why would one even make...? Never mind. He didn't want to know. "Traditions? Anything?"

The soft head shake from the massive man just made the elder drop his head into waiting hands. This was hopeless. Dimi shrugged, "You don't need to fret about it too much. We're at the mouth of the Ancestor, so a few more hours and we're home. Expect to get a lot of scowls; they know there's a human coming."

The massive head tugged free of the flap, and Artorian was left alone with his thoughts once again. Abyss! They were specifically telling him nothing... now hold on. Expect to get scowls, because a human is coming? He was the only human on the trip. Would that mean the treatment would be different if his hosts could not discern his race?

His hungry mind grabbed at the concept and shot out ideas like a child made messes. He'd never had much use for this before, but now was different! His Essence reserves were holding strong at the C-rank... reaching into his spatial pouch, he tugged free Dawn's iridium helmet. It completely obscured his face, and he had a full set of this armor! A couple hours before arrival? He could get full plate on with a couple hours.

The Ancestor's Mouth was a gap in a waterfall held open by two humongous statues of Dwarven nobility in regal full armor. Each held a shield that was used to part the falling water, while in their main hands they held a hammer and axe, respectively. Even from behind the iridium helmet, Artorian could deduce that it was likely those statues had moved themselves to their current position, which begged the question: *how?*

A grand hallway awaited the caravan as it crossed over a stone bridge that rose from the river in front of the waterfall. Exquisite, masterful craftsmanship was visible as far as his eyes could see on every square inch of the structures that came into view. Precious metals were inlaid in the walls, and gems twisted in glass containers were giving off an incandescent orange light.

"Aye, I've missed the Nixie Tubes." Artorian tilted his helmet, listening in on the conversation between the caravan drivers. Nixie Tubes? What were those? The captured lights?

A softer, gentler Dwarven voice calmly responded, curious and intrigued rather than excited. "Did ya hear Nix made another thing? Reverse engineered it from some gnomish toy."

The original, hyped voice gruffly waved that off. "Aye, that too. Why is it always gnomish *toys*? Didn' we get a whole *stargazer* from the place we just got back from?"

The caravan shook from how heavily the second Dwarf nodded. "Take two guesses who'll have yer head if ye try and take that apart without the prospectors getting a few years with it first. Even though we got all the doors open, I didn't understand half of the stuff we found. Even those notes didn't make no sense. What in pyrite is a 'solar sailer'? Ain't touching it with a ten-foot axe. So yeah, *toys*, because that's as far as we got with understanding. Even then... even *then*! A gnomish toy be more sophisticated than our best technology. If Nixie says he needs more time, I'm giving the lad more time."

The academic remained quiet, pulling his frame back to be out of sight of the conversation. He was too in-view, and wanted to keep his appearance a surprise as they went through what he understood to be a checkpoint. He sat with his back against the caravan wall, and sat nice and still to mimic an empty suit of armor.

The inspector that glanced into the back of the cart didn't see him at all, and gruffly grumbled a 'go on' before the caravan shook into movement. That was... surprisingly easy. He shifted on his armored butt to the back flap, and looked through it. Dozens of organized, armed to the teeth Dwarven defenders were prepped and ready at the gate they just passed. From what he could tell... they were looking for something?

A little worried voice told him that they were looking for him. They all looked ready to intimidate. Must be one of those traditional things? Strange. Why? Why was it so important to keep him in the dark and prepare troops to give him a particular social image? Was he wrong about this? ...maybe. He shook it off; he would trust the words of Roberts the Ruminating, for his wisdom was vast. "If there is doubt, then there is no doubt."

When the caravan came to a halt, Artorian peeked from the rear flap. Natural light came down from above, so he wasn't underground. Good! From the look of it, they were surrounded by a molded mountain range. One that had been altered to make this perfect oval of a greeting area? Many other grand hall shaped openings dotted the oval wall, likely leading to other important sections inside of the mountain.

Again he saw Dwarves impatiently waiting on something. Except... what's this? Sliding from the back of the caravan, he tested actually moving around in the iridium suit that covered every inch of him. His ability to see was awful, and he grumbled it out loud. "Hmph. Wish I could see better."

He stopped moving at the drop of a copper as panic gripped his heart. The slits providing visibility on his helmet sealed shut, and Essence was pulled out of his Aura. Artorian couldn't prevent the expense, but then again Dawn *had* warned him that the sizing function of the armor couldn't be stopped. It just did its own thing. Had... had he forgotten to ask what *else* the armor did? Abyss, he had!

Darkness and silence sealed away his senses. How was he going to breathe if... colors and shapes flickered into place in front of his vision. What? The landscape he'd previously only just barely seen came into focus before him, and without the slit limitation he'd previously been dealing with. On the outside of the armor, four silver lines seared into activity on the now seamless faceplate, and they moved along with his vision as Runes activated according to his need.

Air Essence cycled bad air out of the suit, and replenished it with a fresh supply without ever needing to create a cavity in the airtight nature of the suit. What he was seeing wasn't an exact copy of what his actual eyes saw, but it was good enough to properly take stock of everything that was around him. "Dawn... what in the Abyss did you give me?"

It took him a moment to recall that her ancestors had fought on the *moon*; a place where there was no breathable air. Armor like this must have been commonplace back then. He bet he could even go beneath the water with this suit and not drown. It wasn't a big leap for equipment that freely reshaped itself to fit the user. Okay, so it cost him half of a cultivation rank. Worth!

He flexed his hands and smiled widely. No issues! Oh, why had he never tried putting the entire set on before? This was amazing! He cursed himself from having close to no knowledge on Runes. His time was precious, and techniques had taken priority while he worked to gather as much Essence as possible to hit the zenith of the C-ranks. Which he'd not remotely managed to accomplish. Most of his plans, going forward, seemed like they needed a body that could handle the strain he was going to put it under.

"Ohohoho I could get used to this!" He paused; his voice was different! It was similar to the gruff, growly tone that Dawn had those first few days in the grove. So the depth of the voice had something to do with speaking from inside of the suit, and it... helping? He didn't know what any of this Ancient Elven craft did, but there was no time like the present to find out!

Walking. No problem? General flexibility? Fantastic. Strength... not the right time for this. Couldn't let enthusiasm take away from the main reason he put this jester suit on in the first place. Looking around again, it didn't seem like Dwarves were giving him a second glance aside from 'is warrior'. Artorian strolled to the front of the caravan, the hooded cart he previously occupied was roughly fourth of fifth from the back.

Arrival was... interesting. Diverting to where a few merchant stands had been erected to sell food to incoming groups, he spun up a conversation. The nearby Dwarf daintily held a fine teacup in hand, his three-headed hound resting nearby as he read something from a tablet. Fine reading glasses perched upon the end of his nose, and he seemed comfortable in his padded stone-shaped chair. "Wonderful creature! Does he... they? Bite?"

The Dwarf looked up, smiled, and reached down to gruffly love on his mutt. "Oh, Fufu here be a downright harmless ball-chasin' fluffball. Don't be put off by the three heads, it was a compromise for the missus. I wanted three dogs; the missus only agreed to one. In a way, we both got what we wanted! Fufu is the creature's name, but each head has their own name, this one here is-"

"Hold up... is that the one with the human on it?" The pleasant Dwarf stopped sipping tea from his glass and squinted at the caravan. Artorian chose not to reply verbally and just nodded, the hasty response he saw from the Dwarf filled in a lot of details. "They're early! Blessed pyrite!"

The tea was quickly slotted into the cabinet next to his work stand, and the glasses were stored. The merchant Dwarf pulled free a bearded axe and a sharpening stone. Slowly, his face melted into a scowl that the man looked like he could hold for days. He gave his axe a practice sharpen, and tried to appear threatening. "Fufu, puff up and snarl."

The three-headed hound bristled. Its eyes reddened and muscles bulked unnaturally. One of the three heads didn't get the message, remaining a tongue-lolling derpy little bundle of happiness whilst the other two turned downright hostile. When snapped at, the third head followed suit. "Good boy, Moon Moon. Faster next time. You! How's me scowl?"

Artorian wiggled his hand back and forth. "I'd half close one eye to really sell it."

The merchant did so, and thought it satisfactory. "Aye, this'll do. Come back and play with Fufu when the hubbub dies down."

The suit of armor nodded and returned the way it came. 'Tradition' was interesting indeed, and Artorian fought against his usual bodily behaviors. He copied how Dwarves held themselves. Where they kept their hands, what gait they strolled with. How did they not notice he was taller than an average Dwarf? On second thought... never mention that. Ever.

It was a great way to get kneecapped.

CHAPTER TWENTY-SEVEN

"Where'd long beard go?" Don Modsognir was looking around after an aide informed him the man was no longer in the back of the fourth caravan. Hearing 'I don't know' had *not been* the answer he wanted. They couldn't let a non-Dwarf roam around the hold. There were rules! At least he'd be easy to spot.

"Lanky man, look for fluttery robes and a beard as long as I am tall. Bald, so ya might be able to pinpoint the lad from reflection alone." Some laughter went around at Artorian's expense, but it didn't help them locate the old fox. He couldn't have just slipped away. He was an obvious standout amongst Dwarves, and the Inquisition had no knowledge of the old man having any tricks that let him hide or disappear... so where was he?

Artorian stood in the middle of the caravan with his arms crossed, more confused than ever. In a full iridium suit, he was a *shiny* man. A tall shiny man. Why wasn't a single Dwarf giving him a second glance? Sure, they saw him, but it was like they saw him and he was someone else's problem. Even the merchant he'd spoken to hadn't noticed.

He took steps to be out of people's marching path, but they didn't do as much as acknowledge him. He wasn't in their way; he wasn't their problem. Was this the suit's doing? This was... the best! He'd never been good at sneaking about, but if he could just walk wherever and not be given a second thought, he could-

"There y'are!" Crackers and toast. The plan sunk like a boat full of holes as Hadurin Fellhammer marched right up on the iridium suit. "What's this chicken fence you've covered yerself with? Whole caravan be looking for ya. I had to cycle me

Essence just to find ya, and I really had to *want* to find ya. We'll talk about that later. Can ya end that effect? I'd prefer to sort this before a centurion shows up."

Artorian sighed. "Well I'd love to *not* be ignored by everyone, but..."

He didn't have time to end the sentence as the 'someone else's problem' effect lifted, and only then did the cultivator realize a Rune had been siphoning away his Essence. It was so minor that he hadn't noticed, and right away did he grasp the value of a well-crafted Rune. While a good technique might recoup Essence used, this Rune stuff streamlined their use and discounted the cost. The Rune must be a technique in its own right, but finished and heavily optimized to really cut down on the Essence draw while accomplishing the same effect.

Had he tried that without the Rune's help, Artorian would have been back in the D-ranks already. A marvel! What wasn't a marvel was the sudden silence that fell over the oval region. Every Dwarf that hadn't given him a second glance became very aware that the human was in their midst, and tradition must not be crossed.

Tea brewing stands closed up instantly and almost *threw* mugs of ale onto a rough wooden slab for people to take instead. Those who had been imbibing the hot leaf juice spurted it out in a misty cloud and snatched up a flagon to down in a single go. A few Inquisitors that had been spending time gossiping and working on crocheted baby booties threw their work into a box and pulled free weapons. They scowled at one another as pleasant banter turned to threatening tones and snarled half-insults.

Gardeners stomped their feet, causing entire flower gardens to descend a foot downwards into a pit as they called for their pickaxes and blamed everyone who was around for taking them. There was mining to do! Those who were knitting did much the same as the crocheters, dropping their tasks just to jump on another Dwarf, scream, and begin a brawl that half of everyone in the oval decided to join without a second thought.

Hadurin held his face with an embarrassed hand, hiding his eyes. He didn't want to accept what had just happened. The Grand Inquisitor suddenly became incredibly polite, dropping his Dwarven drawl. "Please don't tell the Matron."

Taking his helmet off just to make sure he was seeing what he was actually seeing, Artorian's long beard spilled free. When Hadurin peeked between his fingers, the old man was flashing him the widest smile. "Oh, pyrite... no..."

Artorian decided to give his friend some leeway. "Hadurin. You know I can't see so well. What's this ruckus I hear all of a sudden? What's going on? Is Tibbins around? I've come to sneak a meal without Yvessa knowing so I can try and get a double portion. Where are we? It's all so blurry!"

The Grand Inquisitor cleared his throat and quickly waved everyone away before a centurion showed up. The order helped significantly, and all the Dwarves who heard it made themselves scarce. Maybe a minute later, Artorian stood in a far less populated oval entry area. "So... Gonna tell me what I just definitely didn't see?"

Hadurin squeezed the haft of his hammer. "No."

Even with the armor on, Artorian felt Dimi's hand on his shoulder. The pressure was firm and strong. While he didn't feel the squeeze the large half-Dwarf was trying to add, a smiling Artorian turned to pleasantly greet the poultice-carrier. "Hello again, lad. I sorted my headache situation..."

The stern scowl on the mountain of a Dwarf dropped to an expression that bordered on panic, and his eyes flashed over to Hadurin, who pointed at Don Modsognir hastily running over;

he'd been all the way at the end of the caravan looking for their charge. Even though they were both technically *his* charge according to the contract.

Don grumbled at the old man when in complaint range. "Don't you start bein' Oak now."

Artorian feigned innocence. "Whatever do you mean, my friend? I'm harmless. Why, in fact, I wasn't even told there might be a problem on arrival. People I thought were going to inform me kept their distance. Here I am doing my best to blend in, and now you're all sour about something. Who knows what? Anywho, I still feel the pressure from the contract spurring me on. Shall we?"

Dimi said nothing as the Fellhammer and Modsognir leaders had a quick huddle. They occasionally stopped whispering, poking their heads out from the pile to sharply look at Artorian before ducking back down to continue. The words seemed... garbled? Or it was in a language he didn't speak? Either way, Artorian didn't get the chance to understand what they were quibbling about.

With the majority of his superiors distracted. Dimi leaned down, speaking in barely a whisper. Still, the C-ranked cultivator heard him loud and clear. "How'd you do it?"

The iridium armor-clad man tightened the grip on his helmet, whispering back at similar strength and cadence. "Do *what?*"

He could tell the large Dwarf was trying to squeeze him, but it was doing all sorts of nothing to the shoulder of the armor. "Vanish. We were looking for you and suddenly, **pop**. There you are in the middle of the caravan; in a spot we couldn't have possibly missed you."

The old man shrugged, voice just a hint shy of snide. "Try that poultice for hair growth. It might give you the answers you're looking for."

The massive Dwarf rumbled in the back of his throat. It was like a great beast snoring, just more upset and not as asleep. "Don't you be clever with me. I saved your hind in the grove. Give me this."

Artorian's eyebrow raised. "*This* is where you want to cash in? Very well. I owe you that much. Can you even tell I'm wearing armor? Nobody seems to notice."

He got a stark nod from his 'holder'. "Aye, nothing special though. Any Dwarf can have his own customized set, and most all of 'em do. Yer getup is about as standout as a filled flagon of ale in an all-Dwarves-drink-free buffet bar lineup."

A wordless 'ah' left the detainee Dimi had his hand on. "Truth is simple, my boy, I don't know. I planned to use the armor just to try and get informed, since you've all been beating around the bush. I thought the change in appearance might be sufficient for a few minutes. These extra features are lost on me. It seems to be able to do a few things, but none that I understand or would know how to put together. Much less take apart. I could try vanishing again?"

The grunt that came from the mountain answered a definite 'no'. Artorian was pleased with what he'd learned, and didn't press the situation as the huddle nearby dispersed. It wasn't enough, but a start was still a start.

"Artorian." He perked up as Modsognir stepped back into talking range. The rest of the huddle was hurrying off elsewhere. He could smell the words 'damage control' but said nothing. "We're going to set you up in yer room. Then we're having the big moot. Try not to tick anyone off, we're in enough hot lava as is. I know we've been givin' ya the silent treatment, and I'm sorry. I just can't tell ya anythin' at this point. Knowledge of, and about, Dwarven holds ain't shared freely. You ain't got the permission. I know where you're from information is shared freely, but that ain't the case here. Please, for the love of pyrite..."

The Dwarf poked his stubby finger hard into Artorian's armor. It wasn't even important anymore why the man was wearing it; there were far more serious and pressing concerns. "Don't mention or say *anything* about cultivation. Yer school may be yer region, and yer free to share. Here though, knowledge is precious and hoarded, and ye'd be startin' a war if ya shared anything that didn't go through proper channels. I don't even know if it'd be with the Church or the clans. I don't think you'd live long enough to find out. We've put a lot of effort into keeping all our heads attached. Gran'mama is furious, so don't. Do. *Anything*. Stupid."

The spent Dwarven man exhaled through his nose like they were heated smithy fumes. "Now come along, and don't you disappear on us. Still talking to you about that later, but we can't let the elders wait any more than they have."

Artorian followed along with Modsognir and a few members of his clan. "I thought you were your clan head, and in charge?"

Don nodded; such information was true. "Oh, aye, but I've got folk I don't dare cross. A good number of them we're going ta see shortly. You're probably thinking Mages, but no. Worse, far worse. Ain't got nothing to do with cultivation. I know some Saints that will shut their trap in front of the folk you're about to encounter. Don't fret, it ain't royalty. Far worse."

The intrigue mounted. Trying to puzzle out the information, he followed the party through the sculpted hallway numbered 'VII'. Must be some kind of counting system. Nixie

Tube lights increased in number as they passed into the actual mountain, and still the architecture was so noteworthy that more than a few times he wanted to stop and just stare; if only to take in the artworks forged with intricacy into the overall design.

The hall was massive, and he barely noticed the direction the floor dipped. When the path curved, Artorian couldn't quite believe his eyes. They were in a sprawling, city-sized underground cathedral. Yet it was so bright he was under the impression that it was a sunny day, just tinged with a hint of orange. As they passed from Fellhammer section into the Modsognir Clan section, the architecture altered into the form of an exquisite grand mansion.

"The Don is back!" Cheering erupted, and whole families poured from their intricate homes to welcome the returned merchant party. It was always good for them to see family return home alive. Don was cordial where he could be, but hushed whispers replaced the mirth as he reminded his clan that they had company.

The instant difference was night and day. The people of Modsognir left, only to reappear in snazzy... what was that wearable contraption? He was going to call it a suit, as it went over a crimson vest that connected in the middle with metal buttons that the black cloth suit covered. A matching crimson handkerchief stuffed their front left pocket, the Modsognir insignia clearly displayed upon it.

The behavior shifted with drastic effect. A happy, fun-loving people with a penchant for partying and a great love of community were now a well-organized, stoic and silent mob. Gender didn't appear to matter; the Modsognirs wore suits, and kept one hand over the other in front of them, speaking volumes of respect with their eyes and gazes.

"Mah clan is one of staunch virtues. We stand as one, so we dress as one. Check hands if you need to determine status. Number of rings, the type and quality of precious gems upon them, is how we differentiate rank. Try not to speak with anyone wearing more than three diamonds. It's that problem I mentioned before, ask someone with less power to speak to them, and it'll go up the chain."

Artorian assented with a nod, and Nixie Tubes flared to life on a wall before the twelve-foot-high door creeped open with well-oiled precision. Dwarven engineering didn't allow for something even bordering the realm of 'rusty squeaks'. Don motioned. "Yer housing be this way. *Please* stay put till someone comes to get ya?"

Artorian again sighed and assented. He'd had it up to his nose with these mystery rules, but he'd signed the contract and had to make sure it was fulfilled. Otherwise the Church would likely come hunting for his head. Here, the rule of the Dwarven clan was held in higher regard than the status of the Church. That was likely one of the few things keeping his head attached. He might as well figure out the rules and play by them for now.

The housing district was far less glamorous than the magnum opus cathedrals connecting to even more cathedrals. They were... pleasant. Cozy. Warm. That last one was of specific value, as he'd worried it would be cold underground, and memories of being stuck under the dirt with Blighty weren't doing him any favors. He sat his armored rump down onto a springy bed while the Modsognirs waited at the door.

"We'll be bringing ya something proper ta wear. We need to get changed before we're caught in work attire. Don't run off now. Not unless someone says ya can." Don closed the door with a clang, and Artorian was left to his own devices in the resting room. That was clearly a very safe thing to do. Nothing could go wrong following instructions.

Chapter Twenty-Eight

Artorian compiled mental notes. The Modsognir area was laid out like a sprawling network, while the Inquisitorial clan likely owned the more religious designs they'd passed though. It must have been a shortcut to get here... wait. From the sound of it, they were avoiding someone; a person likely residing in the Don's clan area. So coming in from the side was important. They didn't want to get caught.

Caught by whom? Artorian took the time to take the iridium armor off. He'd need to test hidden functions when in more... favorable circumstances. It did so, *so* much more than he thought it did, and that had completely thrown off what should have been a simple test run. Granted, it had gotten him some of the information he was after. There was some kind of rule in place under the guise of 'tradition' that either encouraged, or forced, everyone here to conform to a certain ideal so that outsiders saw only a certain aspect of their society and nothing else.

He made sure to tightly seal his passive cultivation; there was nothing but corruption down here for him. Stowing the helmet into the spatial bag with the rest of the set, he flopped down and held his own hands. Now, what to do? Sneak out? Likely guards at the door. Cultivation was a flat no. Check for hidden passageways? That would look suspicious.

Artorian was still pondering as the front door parted. An older Dwarven woman with grey hair carried linens at a speed that said 'I am busy and don't want to be bothered'. Dressed in slippers and a fluffy bathrobe, her topaz eyes snapped to the half-slumped human on the bed, and she cleared her throat at him. Glancing at the bed, he realized the linens he sat on were dirty.

"Oh, my apologies." He got up in a hurry as the scowling, curlers-in-her-hair Dwarf zipped by him. Artorian didn't want to get in the way of the help. He guessed since everyone was so familial and community oriented here, the elderly saw to the household chores. Based on how swiftly the woman went at her task, he thought it best to keep out of the way. Still, an idea struck: this could be the right person to sneak a question.

Keeping to himself until she was at the pillows, he gently raised his hand up from the table he'd taken a seat at. "Erm... excuse me, young lady. Could I ask a question? I have a terrible concern."

The elderly Dwarf stopped her movement in a heartbeat, blinking to process what she'd just been called. She hadn't been called 'young lady' with such innocence in well over a hundred years. Why, it was downright adorable. She finished pillow casing and raised an eyebrow to regard the human, having a good second look at him. She'd been in a hurry upon first glance, but being addressed by a person who honestly didn't know any better was... charming.

Her voice cracked, but sweet care rolled from her tongue with practiced ease. "What's bothering you, dear?"

Artorian released a heavy-hearted sigh, and the woman was swiftly seated with him at the table. Heavy sighs were universal in meaning, and she flipped open the lid of a small ornate box on the table to reveal some hard-tack cookies. One was between her fingers in a heartbeat, then pressed into the old man's hand. She firmly closed his grip around it; there was no rejecting a grandmother's confection. "Eat, you're bony. Well? Speak, lad."

The corners of his mouth crept up into a smile. Her word choice was harsh, but she was just tugging him along.

'Lad'. Ha! "I'm just burdened with worry that I'm going to upset someone, because I don't know how the rules work. None are willing to tell me what proper social convention is. How do I greet someone? Is there a proper method to say hello without offense? *Should* I even greet people, or will I break this 'tradition' thing by even attempting? I'm told I'm going into a big meeting with lots of majestic, important individuals. I'm just an old man worrying his head off, and it's eating at me. I've been dragged into someone's home, and don't even know if it's polite to wipe my shoes."

The aged Dwarf patiently nodded while keeping her bony hand on the back of his hand, lifting it up and moving it to his mouth so he would take a bite. He did as he was directed, and she beamed a bright smile at him. Oh, good, a smile!

"Where did you hear that tradition was important, dearie?" Her smile didn't fade in the slightest. It comforted Artorian, so he gladly continued. He wasn't going to namedrop, but some generalized details wouldn't hurt.

"Overheard it while I was on the caravan that brought me here. I signed that metal-contract missive to get the boys here, but I've just been in the dark and trying to keep my ears open. I dislike offending people that don't deserve it, and I still have grandchildren to free from unpleasant claws. Making it home in one piece is important, I worry for them."

Her mouth formed an 'O' as her eyebrows went up, having been told something very interesting indeed. There was only one caravan that arrived recently, and it was no secret who came along with it. She believed the old human next to her knew a lot less than needed. "Oh, well, you don't need to worry about that, sugar. You just stick with me and I'll walk you to where you need to be. Don't you worry about offending anyone, alright? You have another cookie, and I'll go fetch something for you to wear that will help set you at ease."

He graciously nodded with relief, having another hard tack. This one was more of a biscuit rather than a cookie, but he wasn't going to not eat it while her gaze was on him. Success! Artorian was eight biscuits deep by the time the door opened again, the same elderly Dwarf strolling in with a spare Modsognir suit. The deep crimson vest lay atop a black suit, and the shining buttons instantly caught his eye.

"Try this on, dearie. Don't worry about the handkerchief, those are for family. You're fine without. Now up! Show me the fit. I have places to be!" Cloth was hastily accepted as a few deft steps placed him behind the table for... decency reasons. He weakly flashed another smile at the woman, and half-caught she was no longer in a cozy bathrobe. Her hair was up and braided, and she wore an outfit that seemed simple in design, yet it was made of something he didn't recognize. Thoughts for another time!

Most of the outfit slid on without issue. It was still too big for him, but they didn't have time to tailor. Still, he looked snazzy! Since he had the extra room, he posed while throwing out a giant smile. "How do I look?"

Mmm. Turning her nose up, her hands were on his outfit and adjusting things against his will to fix some minor details. A button was out of place, and that wasn't acceptable. She sorted it and looked him up and down. "It will do. Now come, we are late."

Artorian hurried along, not knowing if they were actually late at all. Once at the door, he opened it for her since that seemed to be the polite thing to do, and she waltzed through it. Following her into the vast hallway of exquisite craftsmanship, he did his best not to be distracted as he saw the woman hold her hand up, palm open. Without a second thought, he slid his hand beneath the waiting palm to provide support.

Clueless to where they were going, he couldn't lead the walk. The lady seemed more than content to tug him along without a second thought. They strolled through the under mountain Modsognir mansion, encountering few people even though they took—as far as he could tell—major routes for traffic.

When they arrived at the bottom of an immense staircase that led to what the sign indicated as 'The Tribunal', he paused. He knew the stairway must lead straight into the middle of it, while split, fancier stairs veered off towards the side. He gulped and tried to quickly think of something to take his mind off the matter, this was likely where his guide was parting from him. Turning to the lady that had gotten him this far, he slightly bowed.

"Could I please have the honor to escort the wisest beauty in the hold?" It was a bit of a gamble, but entering alone left him vulnerable to mistakes. His worry was misplaced, as she smiled at him and tapped him on the hand.

"Of course, dear. You stay *right* by me. Alright?" Her smile once again put him at ease, and she ascended a few steps so he could properly offer his arm. She didn't need his help, but the offer was just so charming. It was rare anyone let her feel young again, or attempted anything in the realm of romance. The human was adorable, even if he could mean nothing by it.

The stairs were made of lustrous geodes. A thousand rocks were cracked and turned inside out, followed by a thousand more to form each step as they ascended the glowing pathway. The stairs lit up as pressure pressed down upon them, illuminating a piece of Dwarven history carved into the walls with the addition of their shine.

Stone plate guards waited at the top. These men were retired, stationed at a cushy low-risk task after a lifetime of service. These grizzled veterans could stare down a great worm and not blink an eye. When they saw the human come into view, they contained their amusement and calmly stood to attention. Uphold the rule of- *oh, pyrite!*

When the person Artorian was *with* came into view, they felt their rears clench hard enough to form diamonds. Sharing a quick glance, the halfhearted 'attention' stance sprung to full as they rushed to open the doors. They'd planned to let the human stand in front of it awhile. For fun... but fun was tossed into the pit as the solid gold, engraved tribunal doors parted outwards.

Artorian slowed, needing to adjust his support to adapt for the height change when they ran out of stairs. A strong light poured from the opened pathway, and he had to squint to see rows upon rows of Dwarves seated deep within. Passing the threshold, they passed guard after guard that stood against the wall in a long, well-lit tunnel. This path was nearly a hundred feet all by itself, how deep was this tribunal room?

He squinted when they exited the tunnel, and his jaw dropped as he saw they were in a massive... coliseum? Arena? The words felt inadequate on his mental tongue as the area was just so much *more*. Multiple thousands of Dwarves, separated cleanly by outfit and clan, sat in designated quadrants. From the recognizable suits immediately in their vicinity, they'd entered at the Modsognir entrance. Not a soul turned their heads to look at them.

Silence resounded as the human entered. Oh, he felt so bad; this was so embarrassing. Artorian glanced to his right, there were some empty seats in the back row of the Modsognir section. He wasn't particularly important, and should stay out of the way. The back is where he bel...

The lady grasped his wrist and tugged him along. There was no argument even as his discomfort rose with every step. Maybe the middle? Maybe she wanted him to sit in the middle. Sure, that was still out of the way. He nearly paused when they reached a row that had some empty seats, but her Dwarven stride neither stopped nor slowed down. They were going at her speed and her speed alone. Silence had fallen so completely upon the Tribunal that her shoes were the only noise in the space, with every *click* of them echoing through the area.

Reaching the front, Artorian solidly needed to control his breathing. He saw Hadurin Fellhammer between the middle and the front row to his left trying to blend in. He said nothing as they approached the geode thrones. Inlaid with precious metals, the imposing seats of power were arranged in a ring around the middle of the arena. A dais in the middle caught his eye, but he just barely broke his eyes from the sight to look at the single empty seat available in the front row.

Ah! *That's* where he...! The next steps dropped his heart into his stomach. Why were they still walking? Why was he in the throne ring? This was not the place he should be, but the woman dragging him along was undaunted. Not a single person stopped her. He didn't dare say a thing as she motioned for an aide to bring something over. The young Dwarf, full of worry, frowned towards his direct superior that was already motioning for him to get a move on. The young Dwarf scampered from his position and fetched an old wooden chair. With some direction, it was placed next to one of the geode thrones.

Artorian gazed at the seat like a death sentence. With eyebrows raised, he silently looked at the lady with topaz eyes, and her flat expression squeezed into a smile as she motioned towards it. "Sit. Stay. We're having a conversation."

The academic's eyebrows felt like they were about to touch the roof. For most of the walk they hadn't spoken a word. Her saying that they were in the middle of something, and that he was certainly included, made him defeatedly fall into the seat. The tactical section of his mind was blowing the whistle and waving white flags.

The Dwarf who could only be the Grand Matron slowly inhaled a breath, her back turned to the passage they had come from. "Don. Dimi. *Front seats.*"

Artorian had to look over his shoulder to see two Dwarves doing their utmost to sneak into the back of the Modsognir row. Dimi was taking big long steps on his tip-toes to try and squeeze into a seat out of view. The largest Dwarf in the hold wasn't great at being stealthy, and Don had already squeezed his eyes shut; face scrunched as he was following right behind his less than stealthy friend.

Guards winced at the mention of both of them being called out. Dimi mumbled under his breath, completely frozen in place. "How bad is it?"

Don grit his teeth, stuck equally motionless in place. "Matron is smiling. She never smiles. Gran'mama is beyond furious."

A squeaky, chipmunk-like *ah* left Dimi, his voice holding to that peeping whisper. "Great."

The Grand Matron didn't take a seat, and Artorian felt like a slow runner at the track. The lack of being deterred at leaving his chamber. The outfit. The lack of commentary. The silence. He closed his eyes, deciding to keep out of this as the Grand Matron drew another deep, angry breath.

CHAPTER TWENTY-NINE

Gran'mama *exploded.* She was furious, and her voice thundered through the area. "Don Dremurus Mordran Modsognir! You are *late!*"

Don was in the middle, walking up the main aisle as the Mana pouring off his Gran'mama slammed his feet to the ground. His voice hitched; words trapped in his throat as his hands went up defensively. He was going to explain, but already knew the Matron wasn't going to have any of it. Don glanced at a very pale Dimi for help, but he was equally trapped in the sinking boat.

"Dimi-Tree Giant-Blood Wolfram Modsognir. You are also late, but I know that wasn't your fault. You may sit." Don pleaded with his eyes for Dimi not to abandon him in the middle of the aisle, but the giant Dwarf ever so slightly shook his head. He was always there for his blood brother who had adopted him into the Modsognir family. Brotherly bonds, unfortunately, did not beat out direct commands from the Grand Matron. Don stared daggers as the massive Dwarf who shuffled forward, whispering 'sorry, sorry' before sitting in a quickly vacated seat.

"Why are you late, grandson?" Gran'mama still hadn't turned to regard him, and Don mumbled out excuses.

"Erm. We uhh. Came. We hurried, and even, ueh. Followed along with the mandate our friend signed and, so, we brought him over, and..."

"Did it have anything to do... with breaking the rules?" Don turned blue at the Grand Matron's words. 'Pale' was too gentle of a reaction for the blood that drained from his face. He stuttered out his response as he saw Gran'mama fiddle with a slipper between her hands. Pyrite! Not the slipper! "Ah broke no rules, Gran'mama!"

"Are. You. *Sure?*" Everyone in the audience winced, and Don peeped out his reply in the same chipmunk squeak his brother had before.

"...Yes?" The piercing moment of silence stretched.

"Then you may sit." Don Modsognir felt his spirit leave him for a moment as the pressure keeping him pinned lifted. He could properly breathe once again. He didn't think twice, and hurried to sit next to Dimi, their rigid composures a matching shade of tepid pale. Neither of them said anything further.

"Hadurin Azure Eruna Fellhammer." All Dwarves around Hadurin slid from the pew, and before he could blink the Grand Inquisitor was seated in a gaping empty space roughly seven feet in every direction. Dwarves crawled over both pews and their brethren to evacuate the danger zone.

He stood slowly, having been addressed. "Matron."

Gran'mama turned, and impatiently slapped her slipper into her waiting, open hand. Tiny explosions occurred with each impact. "Hadurin, my boy. You wouldn't know of any tradition *transgressions* having happened in the last... day? Would you?"

Pyrite. Did the old man blab? He was hosed. His only way out was to tell the truth as best he could. He may be the head of the Inquisition, but Gran'mama had the kind of mind that ran circles around Artorian's. No way in the abyss that she didn't already know. "We may have... accidentally lost track of the human for a short duration when we were in the oval."

"Oh... accidentally lost... track." The Grand Matron parroted his words. Her tone was calm. Sweet even. It frightened Hadurin to no end. Gran'mama did not smile. "Is that... all?"

The Grand Inquisitor swallowed. "I think so, Gran'mama."

The Grand Matron's slipper hurled away from her. Artorian winced and blocked with his arms to shield himself from the sound and shockwave, but there was no need as it never reached him. The slipper *whizzed* through the air and detonated upon impact. *Boom*!

Artorian blinked. She had *explosion* Mana!

"You *think* so?" The slipper *whizzed* back into her hand from the point of impact. Hadurin had jumped out of the way, and was preparing to do so again. Trying to shield himself, he dove into the crowd to his immediate left. With Gran'mama raising her arm to prepare another throw, Dwarves spilled like water in a stream away from him.

"Do you have any idea what I found? An entire Fringe region that you're keeping to yourself for hidden projects, making your brother Don sneak about for shady business so you can get supplies out to the middle of nowhere! I've got friars from the Church knocking on my hall doors because their self-entitled Vicars are demanding *land* from my clans. They're thinking *their* organization should be above family and tradition, and they demand recompense for the clans not conforming to their beliefs!"

Her thundering voice was accompanied by successive explosions as her slipper flew again and again. Pews turned to shrapnel. Floor chunks becoming rubble. "Why do I have the Church muscling in on family territory, Hadurin? Why is there a massive unsanctioned building project in a crater that your brother Kiwi secured? I received a piece of vellum with a Mana signature that didn't *work*. Then when I tracked down what has been going on, I find that the *same human* is involved with *both* recently acquired regions. Neither of which are by the books, or by the *rules*!"

Artorian squeezed his lips together, trying to become one with his chair as he sank into it; saying nothing. He watched many a Dwarf copy his exact behavior. Or he was copying theirs, hard to tell. Nobody was getting in between Gran'mama and her doom-slipper. "So I asked you to come home, and you ignore me. Then I *ordered* you to come home, and you *both* ignore me. Then I sent messengers to *make* you come home, and neither of you show up!"

She accusingly pointed her slipper at Don, but didn't launch. "I find out one of my grandsons is spending time with a girl he fancies in a Wood Elf grove, and I'm happy for that. About *time* the Modsognirs did something other than endlessly trade, and I'm thankful for the endless influx of high-quality wood."

Her slipper nudged half an inch. "Dimi, sweetie, I'm not mad at you. You've done nothing wrong. I know you got strung along."

The point of her Mana-imbued explosive slipper switched to Hadurin's current position as the Grand Matron spun on her heel. Dwarves protected themselves with Essence techniques even as they dove from the place they'd just been, with Fellhammer still running.

"Then I get a letter from O'Nalla that one of my boys is under a Church contract preventing him from doing what he should be! They treat the *Grand Inquisitor* of the clans like a messenger, making him deliver a document that will wrest the new land acquisition right out of our grasp, along with the human I want to talk to. So I send Don with a contract of my own after I've got all the details. Then, finally, you come home when I've given the lynchpin of your little plan a reason to bring you both here."

Her hand gently came to rest on Artorian's shoulder, and her booming voice was again tender and soft. "I'm not upset at you sweetie; you've *also* done nothing wrong."

Artorian nodded wordlessly, providing a soft smile that appeased her. The Grand Matron turned her head, slipper stabbing in the direction of her troublemaking grandson. "So, my boys arrive home, and I find out within minutes that the human they brought with them is loose, nowhere to be found even with well over a *hundred* of my clan looking. The lad finds out about the traditions that safeguard the sanctity and security of every Dwarf that ever lived! Your ancestors *scowl* upon you, Hadurin!"

The Grand Matron caught her returning slipper and exhaled steam so hot it could boil eggs. "If I hadn't quickly declared and put down in writing that this lad was allowed to know, we'd be having a full tribunal right now. I don't want to hear a word about the lad sneaking away, you had two clans worth of eyes on him, and I blame you entirely for losing track of a single non-Mage human. Now *sit down* in the front pew."

She stowed her slipper. A significantly singed and discombobulated Hadurin groaned out a pained response. His stubby fingers extinguished the fire burning on the end of his mustache. "Yes, Matron."

Gran'mama slid into the geode throne seat, calmly placing her hands into her lap as she watched the Tribunal right itself. New pews were brought in, and the destroyed floor was swiftly mended as clans organized themselves back into proper place. "Now, what is your name, dear?"

The nervous philosopher cleared his throat. "Artorian, Matron. A pleasure to meet you."

She smiled back at him. "I am Ephira Mayev Stonequeen, Grand Matron of all the centralized Dwarven clans.

I go by Matron, or Gran'mama. I don't hold the title of royalty, though they'll listen to me all the same. You can call me Ephira."

Not knowing how to respond, he leaned forward in his chair to make a minor bow.

"A delight, Ephira. My apologies if I've offended in my ignorance." The deference this human offered the Grand Matron pleased the great majority of the crowd. Order was important, and his willingness to fall in line sat well with many a Dwarf.

"It's fine, sweetie. Did you like my biscuits?"

"Oh, I adored them, I think I absconded with eight before realizing it." Artorian perked up and winked, a little drama in his voice as it dipped to a whisper. "I may have nicked a few."

His hand patted his left chest pocket, which did seem a little bulkier than it should have been without a handkerchief in it. A chuckle passed around the crowd, but the Matron got right to the point. "I'm glad. Since I don't want this to come up again, you're allowed to hear privileged information without anyone getting in trouble for it. I really do need to ask a few things. To clarify, a Matron is the female head of a Dwarven clan. While the Grand Matron is the head of all the Matrons. Being Grand Matron means I hold all the land-ownership contracts, and the power that comes with that. Why do neither of the contracts you've been involved with work?"

All eyes bore down on the snazzily-dressed human, and he crossed a leg over the other while lacing his hands together. Ephira was a verbal warrior that knew her way around words, so Artorian chose his carefully. "Well, someone needs to *be* a landowner for signatures to work. It's a little extra wonky in the Fringe. That place has its own rules. Since I am the landowner of neither..."

He raised his hands to the air. Making the 'I don't know' motion, while his face conveyed the same message. Kiwi and O'Nalla Fellhammer didn't feel so good. Both stared at one another from their respective seats. They hadn't known about that particular detail until just now. Luckily for them, the Matron was aware. No explosion slippers for them today. Blessed pyrite.

Ephira easily deduced why her land contracts didn't work with that bit of information. "Why are the Vicars after you?"

Artorian squeezed his beard, pulling down to let the braid brush along the inside of his palm. "Well... I may have upset the Church once or twice. There's also the distinct possibility that your next question of 'why did I sign land ownership contracts when I am not one' might have to do with that."

The Matron leaned down and crossed her arms on the armrest of her throne. "Why, pray tell, did you brand yourself as an enemy to an organization as vast and powerful as the Church?"

Artorian looked up at her with gentle fondness. "I firmly believe it is better to be a friend to Dwarves, rather than be a tolerated non-believer. Which is why—even though the contracts are a little skewed—it is the clans that will receive the Skyspear region. Not the Church, which might make them mightily miffed."

He motioned at the front row. "During my times of need, Hadurin was there for me like a brother when I thought he might barely call me friend. Dimi saved my life in the forest, and while that debt is paid, I would trust him to do so again if needed. Don has a soul so glittering with gold that no amount of coin in the world could amount to his true value. He saw me as a nobody, and yet treated me with love and care. It's only through their kindness that I had the tools to sit in this Tribunal today."

Ephira was taken aback. She didn't realize that the old man could wield words like her smiths wrought works with their hammers. Her hand gently pressed to her chest, eyebrows high. "High praise for my grandchildren."

The old man sat up in his seat, back straightened. "Respect where respect is properly due, Matron. Your sons are responsible for giving me the chance to rescue mine. May their honor light the depths."

A moment of silence hung over the Tribunal; none would speak while Gran'mama was in conversation. "Can you guarantee the clans' acquisition of the Skyspear region?"

Artorian sharply nodded. "I can."

Ephira nodded, pleased with the truth in his voice. Had the old man lied before her, she would have known. "Then I'm going to look the other way on certain problems, and construction can continue as a properly *sanctioned* project. Though I will need a proper contract for it. Can you Introduce one of my sons to the true landowner?"

The human was hesitant, and that didn't go unnoticed. "I... can. I have a suggestion, but have neither the courage nor the position to voice it."

The Matron narrowed her eyes at him. "Tell me why."

Artorian fidgeted, "Could... could I please whisper it to you? It's a... sensitive topic. The landowner is peculiar and she doesn't like... certain things."

Ephira made the hand motion for him to approach, and lent her ear. The aged human shuffled up, cupped his hand next to his mouth, and whispered, "The true landowner of the Skyspear is named Dawn, and she is the S-ranked Incarnation of **Fire**."

"Ah." She dismissed him with a hand motion, and he sat back down as Ephira leaned into her throne. Ponderously, she squeezed her bony hands together while deep in thought. She noted some foul looks angled Artorian's way, and dismissed them. "I'll not accept scowling; the human was right to treat what he just told me with caution."

The admonishment faded. If the human was under the Matron's wing of favor, making a foe out of the man was a poor life decision. Not that many wanted to. Instead of punishment and lambasted castigation, he'd lauded praise and brought honor to their clans. Don, Dimi, and Hadurin all breathed easier.

The Matron made her decision. "I will go myself."

CHAPTER THIRTY

The room erupted with gossip. Complaints were loudly voiced at the prospect of the Grand Matron leaving the ancestral halls. Clans bickered at one another about topics of defense, structure, and safe voyage while others shot down the idea that the Matron was serious—*surely* she would send a son.

"Enough!" Silence fell over the tribunal. "There are many thrones, and many Dwarves who can steward my position while I embark upon this task. I have made my decision. Matron's will be done."

The entire Dwarven gathering stood and slammed a fist onto their chest. "Matron's will be done!"

There was no further argument, and Ephira sat down after her quick rise to snap away the chatter. She was going to continue the chat, but her attention was drawn to a heaving messenger that the guards let through. "My... my Tribunal! Em... emergency message!"

The messenger was provided water and pats on the back, encouraging words were whispered for the message to be given when able. When Artorian glanced at the throne, Ephira wasn't on it. He blinked and scanned the room, but found her in front of the messenger girl, holding her up and adding soothing words of support. Matron or no, she was still Gran'mama.

Artorian got off his chair and tried to get close, but a horde of Dwarves blocked him. He didn't hear what the messenger was telling them. While he could see the messenger's mouth move, his vision obscured too much to read any sort of intent. Drat!

"Artorian." He froze as his name was spoken, and a path of empty space parted in a direct line from the Matron to his current position. He didn't know Dwarves could move like frictionless sand. He was addressed again. "There are Choir Mages in one of our ovals demanding we hand you over, saying you're in violation of a contract. They're here to take you. Is this true?"

Artorian staunchly stood and crossed his arms. "It is *not!* I signed only the missive of the clans, and returned the other to Hadurin."

The Grand Inquisitor chimed in, having dug the object from his spatial pouch. "I have it here! He speaks true! Your plan was a success Grand'mama, the Church has no rightful claim."

She nodded at her boy, extending her hand for the object. Through a sea of Dwarves, the missive made it to her, and she clicked the object open and read it aloud. The contents quickly brought to anger everyone that heard it. This writ was an insult. A demand. A 'you will do this or die'. The clans didn't like people strong-arming their way into their traditions and lifestyle, and this blatant offense sealed it. Tiny explosions popped between the Matron's fingers.

"Hadurin."

The Grand Inquisitor stepped forward. "Yes Gran'mama?"

Ephira crushed the metal document in her hand, and the delicate contraptions *poigned* upon breaking. Sputters of larger explosions between her fingers sent screws and sprockets to the floor. "I am done placating the Church. I have had it. While the Inquisitor profession is one your clan is indeed good at, I no longer assent to Church ties. The central clans are done. I will not accept an organization believing themselves so superior to our family coexisting with us in our lands and homes.

Especially if these are the kind of actions they take against us. Clan heads! Speak your verdict."

They were all so angry that rounds of 'aye' went around like wildfire. Until finally the eyes and ears settled on a very silent Hadurin. "Ma... ye be askin' for half me life... Ye making me choose between me beliefs and me family..."

Ephira understood that this was difficult for her grandson. Still, she needed an answer. Hadurin closed his eyes, and squeezed the insignia on his chest. He thought over his life, and made his irrevocable choice. Ripping the Church insignia from his chest, he crushed it in his hand. "*Abyss* me beliefs. I stand with me family."

A roar of unity rumbled around the tribunal. Hadurin didn't participate, and regretfully looked over to his clan. He'd just ripped half of their purpose away from them. He watched Kiwi stand, rip the insignia from his chest, and throw it to the ground. He was with him. O'Nalla stood, ripped the symbol from her chest, and threw it down. She was with him, and so was the rest of his clan.

A ghost of a smile proudly twitched on his mouth as he bit back tears. What had he done to his family...? He could not express the pride he felt that even in this sudden upheaval, they stood as one. His fist punched the air and his war howl joined the others. His family punched the air with him, following him as the mountain shook.

The clans and the Church no longer walked as one.

***

Friars Fiona, Azral, and Pjotter impatiently waited alone in the middle of one of the large entryway ovals. Being Mages of the Choir, flight was something they'd accomplished ages ago, so accessing the Dwarven lands from above turned the majority of their defenses laughable.

Fiona threw her hands up when an armored party of Inquisitors spilled from the gate to greet them. "Finally! Heavens blessed, you kept us waiting!"

Hadurin squeezed his grip on the warhammer, shield firmly in the other hand as he rolled shoulders in fitted ancestral runic armor. He marched with a good portion of his clan towards the trio. This was their problem to tackle. "Greetin's, Friars! What brings ya?"

Pjotter lazily flopped his hand towards the group. "What is with that gaudy outfit? It's so droll. We are here to pick up the prisoner. Artorian, Headmaster of the Skyspear. He has broken a contract and claimed to own lands rightly belonging to the Church."

Hadurin's helmet bobbed. "So ya say... prove it."

Pjotter blinked as his face squeezed to pure incredulity. "*Prove...?* Prove what? I am a Friar! I am not questioned! I am obeyed! Bring out the prisoner, or we shall go acquire him, and we do not care what we break in the process, Short-quisitor."

Fellhamer's men looked at their leader for guidance, who tapped the business end of his hammer against the armored tip of his chin. "Nah."

Hadurin's shield buckled under the impact as Azral was spurred into action. The quiet Mage wasn't having any of this insubordination against the Church. The Runes on the shield triggered, but Hadurin was still launched all the way back to the door they'd walked out of a few minutes before. His shield was a bent ruin, and his arms were strained to breaking. One punch from a Mage was deadly for a C-ranker, and they all knew it.

Still. Be careful what you hit.

"Celestial *feces!*" The previously silent Friar held his arm and cried out. His fist and fingers were mangled, misshapen. Sure, C-rankers aren't a threat, but equipment powered with Mana fueled runic effects sure were.

The Friars wasted no time launching their assault. If they could be harmed, this was a different story entirely! The Fellhammer Clan roared rebellion into the sky and charged their new foes. Hammers descended as rocks jettisoned them from the ground into a flying leap. Their armor could only take maybe a single hit, but the runic feedback mechanism was going to 'counter' the energy with an equally unpleasant blast. Sure it expended the Rune, but once was enough when they were many and the Mages were few.

Runes blazed with azure light on Dwarven weapons, and the Friars were forced on the defensive. A strike from a C-ranker, even with a potent technique, was laughable. A C-ranker striking with a Mana-infused weapon stopped all humor. It was a measure of countering category with category, and what the Dwarves lacked in cultivation they made up for with fiery spirit, raging temperament, and unbreakable loyal bonds.

***

"Get on!" Don called out orders in a rush. Dimi hoisted the running old man from the ground and heaved him into the cart as the massive Dwarf jumped into the back himself.

Hiyaa!

The boars tugging the caravan cart snarled and pulled the vehicle into a steady trot. With additional encouragement, they got up to a more decent speed. Artorian's head popped up from the hay Dimi had hurled him into, and he glared at the Dwarves. The entire trip from Tribunal to cart he'd been tossed about like a piece of luggage. He couldn't keep it up, too excited by recent events. "Whoo! That was thrilling. Where are we headed?"

Dimi pushed his head under the hay, and picked some up to throw over him. Snazzy suit be burned, there were survival priorities. "Shush! Talk later. Flee now."

He didn't want to mention that he hadn't the foggiest clue. Don was the man with the plan, and the plan was currently... tenuous. 'Don't let the Church have the human' was a fairly broad firing range with lots of room for interpretation. Don, Big Mo now that they were back on the road, filled in as his caravan left from a direction well away from the brawl the Fellhammers were engaged in.

"Can't take ya home. Hadurin breakin' that insignia broke his oath to the Church. Ain't no way they don't know Dwarven clans as a whole didn't just throw them under the cart. There be a storm comin'. So there's likely a Mage headin' to yer Skyspear, and we don't want to be there given the numbers they're going to send. We can't risk gettin' intercepted."

"Hiyaa! C'mon now!" Hadurin wiped his forehead with the sleeve of his black vest. Their combat gear was in the caravan following close behind them, as the Modsognir Clan of merchants moved into action. Other clans each had their own means and methods to deal with the problem they'd just created. Regardless of how it was going to go, this spelled messiness.

"Gran'mama is headed to yer home, so don't worry bout yer wee ones. Mages that show up are gonna get a face full o' exploding slipper. They'll be fine. We can't go anywhere we can't lay low, so the grove is a no-no. Meaning there's only two civilized places we can go, and I like neither of em!"

"Where's that?" the old man questioned, muffled under the hay.

Big Mo scowled and grumbled under his breath. "The Ziggurat where the big raider city is currently building up. Endless refugees, easy to hide in the crowd. Downside, it's the raider society. They're not going to look kindly on our trying to leave with our goods."

He spat before mentioning the alternative. "Or, and I really don't like this option, Chasuble. The seat of the Church and the Paladin's order. It's capital sized, and we're merchants. It's massive and has plenty of people, so we can stay in any old inn and not be found so long as we keep our heads down, while right beneath Vicar noses."

Dimi agreed that both were terrible. "Aren't both of those in the same direction?"

Don Modsognir grumbled louder, doubly displeased. "Aye! They be. Current thought is both the cities are keeping one another in check, and the Church ain't happy about it since the Ziggurat be getting the grand majority of refugees. If the Church attacks proper, they lose all the goodwill of the millions of folk there. Can't afford it. Meanwhile the Ziggurarians don't attack the Church. Vicars are holed up there and they don't want to give those pain-in-the-butts the justification for a defensive war. Politically terrible for 'em!"

Artorian puzzled though it, and a Nixie Tube popped alight above his head. "Why not *both*?"

"What?" Don and Dimi snapped at him in unison.

The academic popped his head back out from the hay, sending stray stems of it flying through the interior of the hooded cart. "Hear me out. The assumption, if I was looking for me and didn't know my personality, is that I'd hole up in the safest place I could find. That's the mountain I'm already in. Entire clans of Dwarves that don't want to give me up? Safe bet. Medium assumption, I'd go home. The safety and security of home terrain means a lot, so retreating to the Skyspear is something I'd send people to try and secure."

Artorian stole a breath before rambling on. "Weak assumption, go to a place with a great amount of traffic, and hide in the crowd like you said. That's the raiders. Unlikely assumption, going on a straight-shot trip to the capital of the people looking for you. *Nobody* expects that, but they might... if they find us nowhere else. So if we shack up in the capital first, we're essentially hidden."

"Then, when they've stopped looking at other sources, we head out to go hide in the crowd unless a better option shows up. There's no better place to get information than literally from inside of their own house. I could easily blend in and walk around and not be noticed in a big city. Especially since only a very specific set of people have clues as to who they're looking for."

Big Mo scowled. "I don't like the plan, but I ain't got a better one. It's going to take us a month to get there. Get comfortable, we're going to change up our caravan's look at the first rest spot that's safe enough. We're not going to get into Chasuble—the Paladin Capital—with our current colors. Lucky for you, the Modsognirs know how to do things under the table."

He flashed Artorian a toothy grin. "Thank ye, for your words of honor in the Tribunal. Hadurin and I would have gotten one deadly punishment if you hadn't stuck up for us. Though I don't know what be the tools I gave ye that ye mentioned."

Laughter erupted from beneath the restacked hay bales. "The sunglasses!"

CHAPTER THIRTY-ONE

The lack of road security caused some issues on the journey. Issues in the form of amethyst direwolves, poison sloths, a rock bear, a silk pheasant, and an invisible blast leopard. None of those were ready for a caravan of grumpy Dwarves. Especially inconvenienced Modsognir Dwarves that were already bitter about the entire deviation from the ordinary.

Scowling constantly, the clan snapped at one another for the slightest transgression, and tempers ran hot. They hadn't wanted to break from their trade route. They hadn't wanted to rush home, and they *certainly* hadn't wanted to run away from it. Yet here they were, being delayed by regional annoyances. At least they had something to take their frustrations out on.

Turns out, almost every Dwarf had both an earth and fire affinity channel. Those who went into the Fellhammer clan, or came from it, also had a great tendency to have a celestial channel, with all the corruption that came with it. Fire corruption? Anger. That didn't sit well with earth corruption's lethargy. Both combined translated to significant grumpiness.

Artorian kept his head down on the long trip. Hiding under the hay accomplished a whole lot of nothing, and the attempt was abandoned. At this point, anything that found them would either be individuals that would serve as Dwarven anger management dummies or would be a Mage they couldn't handle. Neither was a circumstance where hay helped, but keeping to oneself certainly prevented your hosts from diverting their dissatisfaction to you.

"Do we have any electrum coin?" The conversation on the other side of the cloth of the hooded cart made the human perk an ear up. Electrum, why would they need that? It seemed he wasn't the only one with the question.

"Why in the ruttin' pyrite would we need electrum, ya daft geode?" The sound of someone being hit upside the head followed.

The slapper soon became the slappee, with far greater enthusiasm and intensity. "I be older than ye, ya pebble! Ya ain't never been to Chasuble before, have ye? They use their own currency, and don't accept the simple copper, silver, gold standard. Each o' their coins be electrum, with some Essence markin's or another that validates 'em. I'd have *smelted* a sack of coin if all I needed was some ruttin' electrum!"

Slapping contests came to a halt as a third Dwarf stopped the chicken wing fight. "Break it up, break it up! Don's got a chest o' divines, and we'll be sortin that in a bit. Caravan is about to stop before we head up an' over the hill. Now shoo! I need the human; we can't be seen entering Chasuble together. Too suspicious."

Grumbling, the duo walked away from the hooded cart, a few slaps resounding as they did, the fight continuing regardless. The caravan flap flung open as a thin man squeezed himself up and into the opening. Artorian frowned at the sight, the snazzy black suit had been replaced by... initiate's robes? He recognized these from the Fringe. "Hello there, what's with the threads?"

Getting to his feet, the Dwarf brushed himself off. He beat his thick mustache to get hay that stuck to his face away. The man didn't have much interest in small talk, handing over drab brown robes and a leather pouch. "Yer gonna find yourself in a similar set. 'Ere, put these on, and take this satchel."

Taking the delivery, he prodded a digit into the satchel, hearing coinage. "That be a few divines, currency for Chasuble.

All in all, you've got about four to five gold's worth, so don't go wastin' it. That's a year of wage for yer average Chasuble citizen. We're going in as northern Dwarven clan traders. Still practicing accents from the mine of 'sota."

"Try not to laugh too hard." He cleared his throat, providing an example so the human could get it out of his system early. "It's a lot of money, don'tcha know?"

The old man did a double take upon hearing the total twist around in accent. He'd been distracted by going through the clothes he'd been handed, but his eyes were wide at what he'd just heard. *Laugh*? He was speechless.

"What? Was on the spot wasn' it? Bah! Ye got no sense of' appreciation for the culture. Strap yerself into yer new robe when we get to the hill. Yer gonna have to walk over yerself since you can get through the trade as a pilgrim. Divines are for greasin' palms. We're a bit early for pilgrimage, but it's well known they all go to the big temple in the center of the capital. So if you get stuck, just start blabbing about that."

Dissatisfied, the Dwarf slipped from the cart as quickly as he'd come, and a still silent Artorian just blinked. That was... alright then. Before getting changed, he flicked his sunglasses out and smoothly lay them on his nose. Picking up one of the spit-shined shields, he checked his reflection after mounting it. Stylish indeed! Just for funsies, he performed a few poses, just to see which could be more entertaining or intimidating.

Shoulders squared, leaning back, hands held in front of him was a popular choice when including a minor head tilt. Ah, to indulge in feeling young. He ceased his silly antics and changed into the considerably less snazzy robes. Pilgrim indeed, this was some shoddy rag work in comparison. Still. Covered was covered, and he got it on before checking himself. Yup,

Fringe Initiate using auxiliary supplies; likely where this robe was nicked from.

When the caravan fully squeaked to a halt, he popped out and picked up a stick from the ground. Impromptu walking implement to help sell the blind old man look. Don was waiting for him at the front of the line.

"Ah! Artorian, good timing. Got yer divines?" The trekking human held up the satchel, and a grunt of approval shot back at him.

"Good. Ye be goin' first. Soon as we go over that hill, we're gonna be under scrutiny if news travels as fast as I wish it didn't. Ya look solid. Drab, brown, downtrodden. Pilgrim! Excellent. When yer inside, find anywhere to stay that'll take ya. Don't worry about findin' us. We'll easily find you. We know what we're lookin' for. Now, off with ya."

That wasn't a great amount of instruction, but it was better than nothing. He'd been the reason for this absurd plan after all. Artorian sighed and scratched at his chin. "Very well then, I wish you the best, my friend."

Don slapped the old man on the rear, causing him to jump half a foot into the air and get a move on, before needing to rub the injury as he leered over his shoulder. "Don't be sappy, we'll see ya soon enough. On with ya!"

Artorian was going to comment, but could see the burly man squeezing his mouth shut. He was just about biting his lip. Oh. He didn't want to show emotion, nor give away the fact that sending the human out was something he felt bad about. Odd, Artorian didn't recall what would make the Don care for him so. He gave a wave and trekked over the hill. No reason to let his friend get a stomachache from worry.

The sound of a stream struck his ears first, and his path swiftly led him next to it. Humans coated in dirt passed him as he traveled up the road. He had to get out of the way of a large oxen cart holding a grain of some kind; he'd never seen yellow grain before! It was raindrop shaped? How strange!

The other travelers ignored him after a mere glance at how he was dressed. The rough farmers didn't deem him worthy of so much as a greeting, so he didn't press them. A quick and easy to notice similarity was that all the farmers wore the same chasuble, a kind of scarf over their clothing. Interesting, so it was more than just a city name? They were all made of poor material, and had no particularly interesting markings.

A good hour of walking brought him in clear view of what must have been a very strange outer wall, separating city from farmland. The Oddwalls? A good enough temporary name. There was a distinct lack of bannermen walking the wall once he got close enough to check. Flags proudly hung and flew in the wind, but no guards? Another point for Oddwalls. Why was this discrepancy messing with him? He shook it off and got in line for the front gate.

Some merchants and a group of Acolytes lined up before him. Interesting, all of them had chasubles as well. He did not possess one, and that was starting to look like a problem. The merchants wore some with cloth of finer material, and a circle appeared to be embroidered upon the ends. He checked the Acolytes. Two horizontal stripes forming an 'equals' symbol.

"Hmmm." One stripe per rank? Likely. Artorian watched the interactions with the bannermen carefully. No Acolytes seemed to give the gatehouse guards coin, but there was a peculiar hand movement they all copied before passing through. Without hand motions, the merchants handed over electrum without complaint. There was laughter, and there it was again! The hand movement! He watched each occurrence, and thought he had it down by the time it was his turn.

"Hello there. Just me, I'm afraid." Two humans in their early forties tried not to snicker. The guard addressing him nudged his robes with the bottom of his spear, dismissively rebuking him with a half-laugh, as if he was surprised.

"No beggars in the city, old man." Artorian was forced to take a step back. That spear butt wasn't going to do anything to him, but he had to keep up appearances. He caught the smell of hyacinth flowers and his nose flared. Artorian straightened up, leaning on the scavenged stick.

"Young man I am no beggar! I am a pilgrim from the far reaches of the west, and I have come a long way on my very first pilgrimage for the temple. If there is an entrance fee, merely tell me. There's no need to speak such foul words."

The guard broke out into a wide smile, and the expected greed twinkled in his yellowing teeth. One of them was fake, replaced by a sizable golden nugget. "We don't accept silver here, you'd need to fork over a divine, and I don't see a-"

The man was silenced as a coin danced between Artorian's knuckles, finding its way between his fingers and onto his thumb. Flicking it sharply, the coin *tinked* into the air, and the old man trudged forward as the guard dropped his spear, scrambling from his position to try and catch the coin on the way down. Seemed like corruption would have an easy hold over this locale if the guards were that hungry for a coin. "We're not off to a great start here."

The second guard still held his hand up. "While you've paid the toll, I can't let you pass-"

Artorian wasted no time, performing the requisite hand movement that he'd seen all the other Church members do. His copy wasn't perfect, but it shut the bannerman up right quick. Something changed in the guard's behavior, and he moved out of the way swiftly. "Have a nice day, sir Acolyte."

Acolyte? Oh, well, he had copied their symbol. Looking over his shoulder, he stopped moving altogether. Where was the wall? He could see the stone gatehouse, yet the wall was nowhere to be seen from the inside. He quickly snapped a glance back at the guards, but they were handling the people that had come up behind him. An illusion? Should he risk going to touch it? His hand wavered, but his fist squeezed itself. No! Curiosity would not kill the c'towl this day.

Wresting himself away, he meandered stick first through a poverty-stricken district. Ah. So this is what the Dwarves had meant by just finding a place. That might be difficult if the locals were unfriendly, and explained the pouch of electrum. Money greased the rough wills of the needy into being cooperative. Even the poor had chasubles, and a great amount of them lived within the odd walls. He couldn't get over the strange layout. No merchant district right next to the gatehouse? How were these people handling their trash and their sewage?

Artorian didn't smell anything off, though the stream very likely helped with that. Better safe than sorry! He flooded his Presence with starlight Aura, and kept it tightly bound at skin level without any light emanation. Fighting off disease was top priority while he worked his way to the inner wall. Nothing but housing between the outer and inner wall? Maybe there would be a reason for this. The inner wall at least looked normal. He got in line for the gatehouse, behind the same merchants and Acolytes no less! Well, wasn't that just convenient.

"Let's see if anything changes."

CHAPTER THIRTY-TWO

The Acolytes did nothing different beyond sounding tired. The young Clerics spoke with groans as they complained of sore feet. No electrum changed hands, just the hand pattern. However, the merchants pulled out their money pouches, and every last one of them forked over ten electrum. What? *Ten*! That was half a gold coin! This was straight robbery.

Artorian was stopped just as before. The guards this time looked him up and down first, wondering how a beggar had gotten this far. "What's with the outdated robes? Did you lose your chasuble? We can't let you in without one."

The guards gathered closely together, so close that one more step would make it a battle formation. Artorian composed himself, wistfully speaking. "As I told your counterparts earlier, I'm a pilgrim from the far west. I'm here for the temple. It's my first time, and yes, I brought my fee."

One of the guards muscled his way to the front with an outstretched hand. Rather than give him the money right away, Artorian instead performed the copied Acolyte hand motion. The guard's smile fell, stopping in his tracks as his eyes met with the geezer's. The academic could see little rusty gears of a practically unused mind twist to life behind the scrutinizing hazel eyes. Something didn't add up, and the guard didn't know what.

The metal *tink* of electrum came from Artorian's hands. Ten pieces worth of coin showing. Rather than handing it over, he stared the bannerman down over his strange sunglasses. The old man clearly wasn't blind, so why...? A thought occurred to the guard, who had so far refused to take another step, his discomfort steadily building.

Another guard nearby had the same thought. She jerked back, and sprung to action. A thirty-something woman lurched to snatch her fellow guard by the collar. Pulling him back and quickly whispering into his ear. "Isn't it too early for pilgrims?"

The electrum loving guard that had strode forth quickly stepped aside and saluted. He snapped to attention, little gears locking in place and arriving at a conclusion. "Sir Acolyte."

Interesting. Again with the honorific? Artorian could afford to press his luck a little here as the remaining seven bannermen fell in line, each holding the salute. Artorian dropped the question with heavy emphasis on certain words. "Are you *certain*, you *don't* want a *pilgrim's* ten electrum?"

"Sir, Acolytes pay no gate fees, sir." The guard swallowed, not dropping his salute. The academic paused, not prepared for the guard to ask a question in return. "Is... is this an inspection, sir? I assure you that we of the western way gate have everything in order."

The academic nonchalantly looked away for a moment. More to hide his face so as to keep up this ruse he had just stumbled his way into. Composing himself, he made the coins disappear into his pouch. His tone dropped, and he planned his words so that he could ask leading questions while stepping past the electrum lover; pausing next to the woman who'd whispered. It was easy to add fear to those already believing there was a conspiracy.

"An inspection? I have no *idea* what you're talking about. Just as I have no idea where one gets a chasuble. What does the eastern way gate say to a person who asks where to get one?"

The bannermen were nervous. This was a trap. This was clearly a ploy by either the Inquisition or The Order to check on their work without notice. A pilgrim wouldn't know an Acolyte hand sigil; those were learned in utmost secrecy. The man had mentioned it was his first time here, but something felt wrong when he also immediately said he'd brought the fee.

If it was truly the first time here, how did he know there was a fee? How did he know it was exactly ten electrum? Had the old man talked to anyone, he would have known to secure a chasuble first, and to show up in something that didn't make him look like a beggar. This was all far too suspicious, and the outfit was just... too obvious. It was like he wanted them to know he was out of place.

Artorian was scouring his mind for details, and his thoughts landed on the Head Cleric's behavior in the Fringe. He adapted his stance to how Tarrean used to trudge around, and that minor detail was caught by eight pairs of eyes. Deagle the bannerwoman snapped to a salute for one of higher station, which informed her fellow guard that they were in deep feces if they played this wrong.

Their suspicions were true! She answered swiftly and with verbal force. "Master Cleric, it is the order of the faith that we direct those who wish to acquire a chasuble in the direction of the courier service. They are to add a writ of intent, and have it delivered with a single divine to pay the processing fee. If the faith finds this writ to be persuasive, and discovers the requestor to be in good standing, they will be hand delivered a chasuble and allowed entry into the sanctuary. There is to be no entry without a chasuble."

The bannermen shifted their stances and salutes, snapping to attention to a person of higher station. Deagle had the sharpest eyes in their little platoon. They had doubted, but if she saw something... it was usually right on the money. In Chasuble, everything lately was about money. The improvising 'Head Cleric' nodded, seemingly in approval, and took a step forward to ask something of the next person in line. This was absolutely an inspection! *Bones!*

"What does western way gate say to a person who asks where to acquire better robes?"

Chiffon, the bannerman teen that Artorian now spoke with, did his best to spill forth his answer. His painful attempt to remember made the platoon around him squeeze their eyes shut, stopping themselves from cringing. "We, ueh. The... robes. The robes are... robes! Raiment's are acquired... through the temple! Or bought... at... the temple?"

Chiffon cringed as the person he believed to be a Head Cleric rubbed his forehead with a disappointed palm. Artorian exhaled out a defeated sigh, not looking at the lad as he did. "Someone... help him."

Finding an excellent opportunity to smooth this inspection, Deagle cleared her throat. "A faithful may requisition attire at any provisionary, and they will be provided for according to their rank. A visitor may purchase attire with the permission of a witnessing Ecclesiarch, who is one rank higher than the attire being purchased."

Artorian took a sturdy step backwards, placing him back in line with Deagle, who was regretting her life choices. The old man didn't look at her, he just asked a question that was as simple as it was painful. "Then what's this I hear about visitors purchasing attire *without* a witnessing Ecclesiarch present? Quickly now, we've people approaching."

Deagle swallowed hard, some sweat forming on her forehead while the rest of her squad remained still as water. They weren't lifting a finger to pull her out of this fire. Abyss! She wasn't going to take the fall for this! "We could speak inside the gatehouse, in more *detail*, sir."

The old man peeked over his shoulder. More merchants approaching from the look of it. He could use that. "Just you. The rest of your... hard working fellows have merchants to see. I'm absolutely *certain* the entire group's reputation lies in your hands. Let's speak further inside."

Deagle turned and marched inside with a self-satisfied grin plastered on her face. The rest of her squad had neglected to help her, and the Head Cleric's wording did not set them at ease. Now it was *them* who were abyssed if she messed up!

Artorian set his stick against the shoddy wooden table as Deagle closed the studded door behind him. She pulled out a chair for him, and he cautiously did little before seating. Giving her ample opportunity to over compensate for the situation. It made him seem entitled, but that was a positive for the moment. "It doesn't look very... good, so far."

Deagle dabbed her forehead with a piece of spare cloth. "The status of the west..."

She stopped abruptly when his hand shot up, his piercing stare giving her chills. He spoke swiftly, and Deagle tried to keep her composure at the speck of good news. "I have a problem you can help me with, and if you do, I will pretend I was never here."

Sliding in the chair opposite to him, she sat upright and at attention. If there was anything she could get to give her an edge, she'd take it. "Sir!"

Artorian rubbed at his eyebrows, trying to pick his words carefully. "I'm going to let you in on a little secret. You're the only one I'll tell, so if it gets out, I'll know where to look. An Initiate royally failed at my requisition order. Now they lost my shipment, and the Initiate has *mysteriously* gone missing."

"I was informed that the... western direction, was a place things could get *done*. I don't take kindly to my raiment and chasuble being denied to me, and I'd look a complete fool telling anyone it was... misplaced. How many divines is it going to take for me to get a new set without anyone knowing?"

His finger tapped onto the table, and the C-ranker left deep dimples in the wood. It helped sell the illusion that his rank and power were aligned, even if he was absolutely bluffing. Artorian attempted to scowl like a Dwarf; they were fabulous at looking irritated, and he had recent examples to play from.

Deagle didn't flinch. "That is going to be incredibly costly."

If she had more to say, Artorian didn't let her. He snatched his coin purse from the table and threw it down. Several pieces of electrum spilled free, only to spin and reach standstill upright on their edges. All of them. Sitting back to seemingly calm his anger, he returned to rubbing his eyebrows, covering up most of his face with his hand. "Make it work."

Gathering up all the electrum, she counted it out and added it back into the pouch. "It will work, Your Grace. You have far more here than needed, is there anything else you might... want...?

Artorian copied Tarrean's grumble, and waved the request off. "Get me my needs before the end of the day, and you can have whatever remains."

He didn't even look up in time to hear the door close. Deagle had raced out, snatched two more of her bannermen, and gotten a move on. She explained things on the way, and upon hearing just how *much* electrum they were talking about, quickly found incredible motivation.

The door creaked, and a teenager managed to walk in a few paces before being overcome with shock. He had completely forgotten people had a meeting here, and since he'd seen Deagle leave, had figured it was empty. "S... sorry, sir! I'll leave!"

"It's fine. Perhaps you can help me." Artorian couldn't believe it when the same tainted greed corrupted tone of the guards met him.

"I would be delighted. I'm Chiffon, just so Your Grace knows."

He'd expected it from the forty-ish-year-olds, but the teen? That was... disheartening. Artorian could have misheard, or it could be an enthusiastic attempt to dig his way out of the abysmal showing that had occurred outside.

Artorian was getting too stressed to tell, and he needed space from the ruse. "The details are known to those who ran off. Until they're back, I desire some shut-eye, preferably without being seen."

Without a moment's hesitation, Chiffon opened the door that led deeper within the inside of the interior wall. It led to a sort of makeshift canteen, and was that the corner of a bed he saw in faint candle light? "We have cots for when everyone needs to be here, but currently it's just been a skeleton crew."

Pushing himself from the table, Artorian angrily snatched his wooden flotsam stick from the side of the table. "It will do, wake me when they're back. I wish to be here no longer than needed."

Chiffon was of the exact same opinion. This old man being here interfered with... business. He closed the door after the Master Cleric entered, and hoped never to encounter the man again. His direct superior could deal with the fallout of waking a Head Cleric; he wanted as little attention on him as possible since this hadn't gone favorably.

Artorian flicked into Essence sight when the door closed. The light went with it, and a single miniature candle wasn't going to cut it. He was essentially trapped here for the duration of the ruse, but he'd correctly guessed that money greases palms. The corruption was categories higher than his initial assumptions and that was going to be... difficult. He was out of coin to sell this bluff. The bannermen had said something about Clerics being 'provided' for and he'd have to bank on that.

Since he was here, and not at all tired... might as well rifle through everything he could find and read any material he could get his hands on. He had some time to kill, and only now realized that he didn't know the Head Cleric hand sigil. They weren't going to bring him Acolyte raiment's, but Head Cleric ones! No wonder she'd said it was going to be costly.

He slapped himself on the forehead as that thought hit him. "Crackers and toast!"

CHAPTER THIRTY-THREE

The bannermen were happy to see the Head Cleric leave; a four-striped chasuble was not easy to acquire. Deagle had swindled some profit out of it, but the deal had taken far more than she expected. Artorian wasn't interested in the details after they'd forked over the raiment and chasuble.

He'd washed up in the miniature dorm, and combed the living daylights out of his beard to make it match the requirements of the '*Cleric Handbook*' he'd found in Chiffon's belongings. He'd snuck the book back in after a read, no need to make it obvious he'd snooped.

Cedar, pine, and cypress structures dotted the land. They were two stories tall, and Artorian had to dodge pails of dirty water being emptied on the way through the cobblestone pathways. The flat roof each structure had added a bonus third floor, but from what he could tell it was mostly clothes drying territory. The flapping of cloth was a constant sound that didn't bleed away into the background.

People got out of his way, even if his progress through the city was done at a snail's pace. He wasn't fond of the attention, and had to forcibly prevent himself from addressing the issue just to keep trudging along. Artorian needed to get his mind on something. Goals. How about goals?

Lodging, meals, sunlight. He didn't have a great view from down in the tiny alleys. Puzzling out heads or tails concerning the city layout was not happening, he'd be aimlessly roaming for hours. With a slight bend of the knee, he jumped straight up. Playing hopscotch on light-bricks like it was an elaborate game when nobody was around.

Once atop the building, the sunlight on the roof alone was heavenly. This robe was *fantastic* for letting the light through. How did it accomplish that? He'd keep it in mind if he took it apart one day. If he could be fully clothed and not be hampered during active cultivation, that would be *exquisite*. He savored a deep breath as the sun's rays washed over him. How warming and pleasant it was.

"Erm... Mister? Are... you here for the laundry?" Artorian turned around with his hands behind his back, a pint-sized girl held a basket full of wet clothes. She blinked at him, and his attention was drawn to her eyes. Pink irises? He'd never seen that before.

"I'm not, but I can give you a hand if you'd like. I was just lost in thought." The caution in the child was thrown to the wind, and she smiled at the idea that she wasn't going to need to jump to get the towels over the tall hang line. She hoisted the basket over, and pulled the wet towel right out and held it up to the grandfatherly looking man.

"He' go!" It took them ten minutes instead of the half hour it should have taken, leaving the pink irised girl with a full twenty minutes to just lounge on the roof without needing to do work. She turned her head to see the old man looking off into the distance. The city was flat, and only the buildings gave it any character at all. Did they build this without a city planner? He couldn't find a straight main street no matter where he looked. Telling the difference between a shop and a home wasn't possible. Only very unique structures stood out.

"Find them?"

Artorian quirked a brow, attention turned to the little girl. "Hmm?"

She kicked her legs out off the side of the roof. "Said you lost your thoughts."

"Ah. I was lost in thought, a little different. Though lost nonetheless. See, I'm not sure where I should go. Perhaps you know? Where can an old man go if he doesn't want to be found, but that's safe enough to sleep?"

The leg kicking paused; her finger pressed to her closed mouth as the smallest cogs turned. "Mmm. Mommy would say it depends on what someone pays."

Artorian scoffed. *Again* with the corruption. If even a five-year-old gave this answer, this place was lost. "What's your name, little one?"

She flopped onto the roof. "Scilla, but everyone calls me 'hey you'."

He nodded, and kept up the questions. "Nice to meet you, Scilla. Why are your eyes pink?"

Scilla shrugged; she didn't like this topic. Her words became acid. "Dunno. Momma doesn't like it. Sis has green, and she's the big favorite. Brother has brown, and nobody looks at him twice. I've got the cursed color. That's why I sleep in the corner and eat last."

Artorian cycled Essence. Scilla had a center, but it was smaller than expected. A tiny smattering of every corruption, most of it on her back. Sleeping on the ground had something to do with that, no doubt. Her eyes were interesting and odd. They were... stripped? There was Essence damage present, though he couldn't tell any further details without a direct connection.

He scoffed, brushing the front of his robes off. "So turn them green."

Scilla laughed out loud. "That's not something that can happen?"

Artorian shot her a look of disbelief. "Sure it can, give me your hand and I'll show you."

The little girl stilled as her face scrunched together in confusion and interest. She didn't believe him, but wanted proof before she called foul and threw it in his face. Tall people making her feel better with words was worthless. She sat next to him, and gripped his offered palm.

Access was all the philosopher needed. As a non-cultivator, she didn't have a veil shielding her Center. It was just like that time under the tree when Blanket had been a little glider with two very injured legs. His Presence wrapped around the five-year-old, and she drowsily collapsed against his side as the sleep Aura coated her. Best she not be awake for this next part.

With Scilla out of commission, he was freely operating in her optics; performing a detailed scrubbing. Someone had definitely intended some foul play here: her cones and rods were scarred. An intruder had swiftly and rashly slapped an Essence effect over her irises, making them more receptive to... celestial effects? He was knowledgeable about mental effects and Essence means to invoke them. This was one of those.

She would see what someone wanted her to see. Yet, who? Wrong question. Could he *fix* this? Right question.

A few minutes of work said yes. Though... jade wasn't the variant of green he was hoping for. Dark forest green was the goal, but for some reason he couldn't affect how light and dark the irises were. Must be a lack of knowledge on his part. Either way, pink to green? Child's play. Though it was permanent. He was glad she was asleep. Had Scilla been awake she'd have screamed the entire time; this wasn't a painless process. Artorian had to move particles of corruption around in her eyes to accomplish it.

Pulling his effects back, he softly tapped her on the cheek. "Scilla. Scilla wake up..."

The five-year-old blinked, rubbing her sore, dry eyes. "Mm?"

He smiled at her pleasantly. "You fell asleep and missed the entire trick! I'm afraid your eyes are going to be stuck as green now. I'm sorry."

Scilla snorted, pushed herself up, and stamped off. More adults lying to her, as usual. Artorian smiled, counting on his fingers. He arrived at a count of twenty-three before the scream ripped from the inside of the home. He knew she couldn't resist checking. Artorian could hear the five-year-old run to her mother.

The mother didn't believe what she saw. The expected questions occurred. How? When? Why? Followed by the expected answers. Old man. Roof. Just now. So it was that, when the mother burst forth onto the roof, she was expected. "What did you do to my..."

Unlike Scilla, her mother Shamira saw the chasuble, the robes, and the rank with practiced and ingrained ease. Four vertical stripes. A Head Cleric. One rank below a Friar. If she made a fuss... her face went pale and she bowed. She had never even made it to Initiate after a decade of trying, and her chasuble reflected that. No stripes.

"My apologies for my behavior, sir. Would... would you do me the kindness to tell me why you blessed my daughter?"

Artorian played the role, just barely peeking over his shoulder. "Could you sit with me, my child?"

Scilla was shooed downstairs, her smile stretched all across her face. Her eyes were green! Full meals! No more sleeping on the floor! Shamira did as requested and threw her long hair over her shoulder. Sliding sumptuously into place next to the old man; always angling for profit. "*Yes*, my Cleric."

He waved it off, not interested in her wiles. Artorian spoke with an entirely different kind of longing. "I'm the wrong person, my dear. I just wanted... some distance. Someone I didn't know that I could speak with. Would you be that person?"

Shamira dropped her lascivious attempts, and moved right into mother mode. "Of course, Master Cleric."

He nodded slowly. "I have been gone... so long. I don't recognize any of it. I want to perform an inspection without anyone knowing I'm here. Your daughter's eyes are the fee I pay to make this next request. Would you have a spare spot I could sleep for an evening, before I discover Chasuble all over again? I don't wish to announce myself, nor barge into... well. You understand."

Green eyes held immense social benefits—their value was not to be underestimated. Scilla could now have an education without cost. Her oldest was in the Paladin Order, perhaps her youngest could... The Choir? It was safer. Housing a Cleric usually came with coin, however, housing a Head Cleric trying to remain hidden might have equally hidden benefits. The choice was easy. "Of course we do, Master Cleric. We'll find the room for you."

"I appreciate it." He motioned into the distance, then all around him. "So what happened? It's been... I don't know. Fifty years? More? What's going on?"

Shamira nodded unpleasantly. She crossed her arms and legs, her face nudging over to the northeast. "It was a long time ago, but it all started with the refugees. Do you know of the Ziggurat? Completely populated now, sprawling tent city, and has been for years and years. Some refugees came here and everything got cramped, very cramped. All the people made food availability low. That made public order hurt, which caused safety to become so poor that our graced Vicars had to set up shop here to keep things under control."

She pointed back towards the west, where the largest swath of poverty housing was seen sandwiched together. "When the Vicars settled, order was fixed. Chasubles became required, deadly punishments expanded to include petty crime, and those with money were king. Refugees are constant. Crimes didn't stop. Paying your way out of problems became even more popular, and the rules got even less lax. If you couldn't help till land, or could not pay your way into the inner wall. You were on your own."

Her hand went back in the direction it started. "So refugees gathered in the Ziggurat, and as best as I know, a few people of massive power set up there. Someone calling herself 'The Mistress', or some nonsense. More people with power making themselves feel more important. I have an opinion, but I won't voice blasphemy around you, sir. My apologies."

Artorian whispered under his breath. "I promise on my chasuble that I will not hold your words against you, please tell me everything including your personal views."

Shamira swallowed nervously. Well... he did promise. "The Ziggurat and Chasuble have a tenuous relationship. Any people Chasuble doesn't take, Ziggurat does—and I mean everyone. They turn nobody away, because even bodies have a use. For years we've thought there would be a war to spill over, and one would usurp the other. Not the case, and word on the street is..."

He nudged her on to keep speaking. "There's talk in the dark that the Vicars and the Mistress are friends. That there's a conspiracy going on between the two, but nobody knows for sure. Everyone is finding a reason to blame someone else. Food is expensive. Cloth is expensive. Everything is expensive, and making due is difficult."

Artorian patted Shamira's back, attempting to give her comfort. It didn't do anything. "I see. Ambition, desperation, and conflict must have a firm grip here. My thanks for the swift primer. Don't let me keep you from feeding your family. I'm going to sit up here a few more hours. If I could nap when the sun leaves us, that would be ideal. A little later is fine too..."

Shamira assented and left the Head Cleric to his musings. Artorian squeezed his chin, overlooking the squished together city. He liked this place less and less the more he heard. Perhaps tomorrow he'd take a quick peek into the temple. If circumstances were as dire and controlled as his landlady had mentioned... lingering even a week was not an option. Someone would catch on.

He sighed, dismissing the concern. That was tomorrow's problem.

Today, it was time to cultivate.

Chapter Thirty-four

Artorian studied the temple the following day. Both his hands rested on the walking stick while he relaxed on a bench in the sunshine, facing the myriad stairs that led up to the deceivingly old structure.

Deceiving, because it only appeared old. His memories were hazy, but he had been here before. With rough calculation—over half a century ago—when he was a small lad. He'd thought the place would have been much the same, thus the major reason he'd suggested the plan in the first place.

He'd been sorely mistaken. Nothing was the same. Structures Artorian thought he recognized were but facsimiles of their original. Constructed in their style, but in the wrong place. He knew for certain, as this stone bench was still in the right place. The chestnut tree—which had been a solid, hefty thing the last time—was now a solid ten feet thick and at least four times as tall.

Neither tree nor bench had moved, yet the structures hadn't been aligned straight to the cobblestone pathways. They'd been off center, angled away. The church's structures now faced the tree straight on, so the ruse was clear. His center smoothly rolled along, pulling in Essence in an upwards cone. It was doing as much for him as it was for the tree, the rejected energy seeping right into the soil. Additional clusters kept sprouting as the tree easily took in the high-quality nourishment.

Is this how Dawn had felt all the time? Seeing the world pass her by until only ruin and relic remained? He deeply exhaled and shook away the thoughts, resuming his people watching activities. Artorian kept tabs on the new goings on of the people and the movements of their daily lives.

One could learn much from being still and observing. People passed him by constantly, but none so much as slowed. They were all busy people with busy lives. At worst, he was in the way. As much as one could be in the way while keeping to themselves under a hefty tree that wasn't in the road.

Perhaps that wasn't entirely fair. A staunch person strolling around the temple with empowered steps functioned as some self-appointed peacekeeper; or whatever he might have called himself. Neighborhood watch? It didn't matter. The lanky figure in fashionable robes came up to him in a straight line, with all the forward momentum of a mother bear on a mission. The walk staggered to a halt as their heels dug into a mixture of cobble and clay dirt; their eyes had caught up to their hubris.

The peacekeeper, whoever they may have been, had a potent three vertical stripes on his chasuble. When their eyes caught the four stripes on the cloth of the old man, he promptly turned on his heel and veered away awkwardly. He was *not* making that mistake. Nope. Not today. He could lord his authority over anyone he wanted and stop them for any reason he could conjure up; except those of higher rank. Why a Head Cleric was just sitting on a bench was not his problem, nor his concern.

Midway back to the temple, the peacekeeper paused. His head shot a glance over his shoulder. Surely not... inspections? The man whisked himself away with great fervor, not to be seen again. Translation: he fled.

The only person Artorian did want a word with was an individual spending his time with actions rather than words. He had initially noticed the man because of the unique Aura he was coated with. From the general feel, and calm it provided to the surrounding area, it must have been some kind of restorative or regeneration Aura. He'd never seen this before, and was having a difficult time cobbling together the Essence formula. Regeneration Auras must be something specific to Clerics, yet seemed to have features similar to what his starlight Aura did; only more focused in purpose.

What looked to be an Acolyte with long brown hair in a ponytail came and went from the stairs. Each time he arrived, he held a basket full of bread and cheese. He handed these out to a flock of children that ran up to him, with naught but a smile to pay for it. They received a pat on the head afterwards. The little ones zipped back to their parents, handing over their bounty.

When the Acolyte was devoid of goods, he assured the kids he'd be back. Sure enough, a short while later he'd return with a lighter coin purse and a heavy basket. What a good lad. Didn't he have other duties to attend? So many here just about ran over one another to get where they were going.

It was well into the afternoon when the Acolyte spotted him. The thin man performed a bow, but was beckoned by Artorian's hand when he rose back up. Upon approach, Artorian could pinpoint the exact moment where the Acolyte noticed the four stripes. His entire body twitched, his step faltering. Artorian just smiled at the lad like only a patient old man could.

"Head Cleric." The Acolyte bowed again when he approached within personal greeting distance. His words dropped from confident, to concerned. "You beckoned?"

"Have a seat, my son. What's your name? I have a confusion, and require an unspoiled ear. "

The Acolyte did as instructed, and took a seat in the shaded portion of the bench. He noticed the elderly Cleric seemed to delight basking in the sun. He folded his hands and answered the question. "Alhambra, Your Grace."

"Alhambra?" Artorian tasted the word. It was sonorous, and full of melody. He liked it. A good name for a good lad. "I see many busy souls, but none seeing to the good of all these people. I've seen some of the Ecclesiarchy attempt to throw their status around like the scabbard of a sword, and others hustle while not caring who they got in the way of. You feed the people, yet what of your other duties? What happened to you, my boy?"

Alhambra scritched at the patchy start of a dark beard, though he had but scruff at the moment. His sandy skin matched it well. "I don't wish to foist my burdens upon you, my grace. It is just the fate of all who get stuck where I am."

The old man raised an eyebrow, a tiny head motion urging the lad to continue regardless. Alhambra tried not to crack a smile, he was speaking with a superior. The crack appeared in the foundations of his face regardless, this burden lay heavy on his heart. "I am an Acolyte because no higher positions are available. The quota on stations is filled, unless the faith gains more land to open new positions. My tasks are diminished, specifically so I cannot seek higher functions even if they do become available. My peers do not look favorably upon me, as they say I squander my wealth on the trivial. As if *people* are trivial!"

His tone turned bitter at that last statement, calming as he pulled himself from the emotion. "May I ask what district you field, Master Cleric?"

Artorian just nodded. "I'm on a little pilgrimage, I came from the Skyspear mountain. There's a little kerfuffle at the moment, so I decided to come visit while I still could. I intend on entering the temple, but... my heart isn't ready. I'm not sure if it will be by the time it comes for me to go back. I'm afraid to go alone, you see."

The answer seemed to satisfy the Acolyte, if only because of the volume of it. The latter part confused the man, and his minor prodding faded to the wind as his personality came to light. "You should not fear your home, Your Grace. For it is here to welcome you, always. Would you like me to go with you? I am but an Acolyte, but would be blessed to help carry your burdens... for that is the task of the Church."

He knew it! A good lad indeed. Artorian couldn't help but smile as he conspiratorially leaned in for a whisper. "In my old age, I remember there's... something I had to do to enter? Some ritual... something. I can't recall. I've been sitting here trying my best to grasp it, and it just won't come. Could you cover for me, if we go?"

Alhambra beamed. "Of course, Your Grace, I would be delighted. I know all the rules and requirements well; I am still fresh from studying!"

The Acolyte helped the Head Cleric get up. With a hand firmly on Alhambra's shoulder, the duo slowly walked straight up the stairs to the massive twelve-foot-tall ornate doors. It was even more massive up close! Nearby guards grumbled, and two more men with three stripes on their chasubles came to check up on the approaching pair. Much like the first, they made way and made themselves scarce. There was an awfully large number of shady Clerics here trying to both exert their influence and not get caught.

His ear perked up when he heard Alhambra chuckle. "Yes, my boy?"

The Acolyte swiftly regained his composure. "Apologies, Your Grace. Those two that came down and tried to bar us from entering were old classmates of mine. Their pride and greed lives in excess of their other values, and they came to berate me for approaching so close to their temple. My chasuble only has two stripes, and that means everything here. If they tell me to leave, I must listen. Regardless of the character of those who speak."

Alhambra slapped his hand to his mouth with a touch of fear. He'd just insulted those of higher station, and a Head Cleric was literally supporting himself on his shoulder. Abyss! It was exactly this kind of behavior that kept getting him stuck in these precarious positions! He was silent a moment, then a moment longer. The Head Cleric said nothing, nor did he berate him. Odd. That was not how it normally worked.

Chancing a look, the old man just winked at him, angling his nose towards the open door. His whisper was soft, but the Acolyte caught why he probably hadn't been berated. "Show me what I forgot, my boy."

Artorian released the lad, who strode forth and made complicated hand signals to the guards, the entry men, and a three-striped person seated behind a desk inside a gatehouse one had to pass before the temple could be entered. Artorian quietly followed along, smiling all the way as he kept a solid eye on all of the movements and words. He didn't try to hide the behavior either.

He was playing on the assumptions people were making. Artorian was here for an inspection, and the Acolyte was on the chopping block from how scrutinizingly close the old man got to inspect even minor motions. Even the guards could tell the Head Cleric wasn't trying to hide his attempts to check on every little detail. Artorian only noticed the Acolyte had performed something incorrectly when all the people directly nearby stiffened severely at a certain feebly motioned hand sign.

"Would you like to do that again... my boy?" Artorian sweetly smiled, copying the exact tone and expression of Gran'mama. His was soft, slow, and patient. On the surface, everything was just dandy. While Artorian was nervous he's guessed the moment wrong, some Initiates whispered sharply. They'd seen the mistake. Alhambra turned fear filled eyes upon the Head Cleric, but Artorian was already rolling his wrist as Tarrean did. The 'get on with it' motion.

On the second try, nobody reacted. Artorian decided not to act on the retry and strolled on past; his feet gently pittering against the gleaming temple floor. How does one get wood shiny? He didn't know, but they'd managed it. When Alhambra caught up and they made their way through the center of the pews, chanting began. A choir was practicing, all men from the sound of it. When the Acolyte attempted to excuse himself, Artorian grabbed him by the wrist and dragged him forward.

"Y... Your Grace! I am not allowed on the chancel, nor anywhere near the space around the altar!" Perhaps he was being dragged to the ambulatory? He swallowed hard as the Head Cleric, undaunted and in full view of everyone, dragged the lad to the front-left of the altar.

"Stand there." Artorian turned to face the people currently seated in the pews. Some common folk were present and curious. Many Initiates had gathered, not knowing what was happening. A few Acolytes were gathering up since for some reason a Head Cleric was presiding on the chancel, yet there had been no planned event for today. Nothing was on schedule for the moment, so what was this about. Had... had they missed something?

The speed of movement in the church increased to a scramble. If there was an event today, and they'd failed to set up for it... that would be disastrous. The whispers that a Head Cleric was doing an inspection grew in speed, and more Initiates spilled into the temple from their respective work stations. If there was an inspection, and someone was doing a headcount, not being in attendance was paramount to dereliction of duty. They couldn't risk it.

Artorian smiled as he remained quiet, excluding the moments where he told Alhambra to stay put. The Acolyte was a statue, but beaded heavily with cold, nervous sweat. Abyss. Abyss. *Abyss!* The old man *had* heard him, and had just waited to be inside before levering punishment.

The people with three stripes on their chasubles also made a return, hearing that Alhambra was stuck on the chancel with a Head Cleric ominously standing still and keeping him there was prime gossip fuel. Was he being demoted? It wouldn't be a surprise, given Alha's behavior and penchant to run his mouth. They filed in and gleefully sat near the front. Why had they ever been worried about this four-striped Cleric? He was on their side!

With the temple at about half capacity, Artorian turned to Alhambra. He spoke in no more than a gentle voice, but everyone stilled to deathly silence to hear it. For the words cut off their chatter swifter than a spear through the neck would.

"Take off your chasuble."

Alhambra panicked. He immediately fell to his knees, hands clasped and pleading. "Y... Your Grace! Please... not my chasuble. I will be forcibly evicted from the city! My children... they..."

The man was silenced as Artorian reached out his open palm. "Your chasuble, Alhambra."

Silence was king in the temple. Some smiled in great pleasure, others looked on in great horror. No one had missed the fact that Alhambra's title was missing. This was the fate of those who underwent inspection: it was gruesome, and resulted in the worst fate. Being revoked from the faith. Artorian kept track of those who were happy about this, as a piece of cloth made it into his hand.

The chasuble was neatly folded and laid upon the altar as Alhambra tried to keep his weeping silent. Children in the audience were forcibly stilled by their mothers after being informed that the person who had given them food was being made to stand at the altar. "Your outer robe, Alhambra."

People held their breaths as the broken man handed his robe over. It too, was neatly folded and laid upon the altar. Alhambra felt shattered on the inside. He grit his teeth and squeezed his hands as he felt his life fall apart around him. He didn't react when the entire crowd broke their silence to gasp in disbelief. With his head down and vision cast to the floor, he didn't see why. Had a blade been produced to sever his head? It might be a relief at—

He felt a soft weight added around the back of his neck. The gasping continued, and became louder. Protests from people he knew to be old classmates picked up. Angry shouts replaced silence, and at the rustling of cloth, a very confused Alhambra looked up through tear filled eyes to see the old man shake off his Head Cleric robe. Hurling it over Alhambra's shoulders, the robes gently folded around him. Alhambra didn't understand. He wasn't being exiled?

"Stand, *Head Cleric* Alhambra."

Screams of joy broke from the back pews as the common folk who Alhambra had supported for years went wild at his promotion. It had been years since anything positive had come from the Church, and ages more since it had been something positive for *them*. The three-stripes were red in the face, furious and forced to keep their silence as they watched their hated, non-corruption-friendly foe rise and lift up the end of the chasuble.

Four stripes. It had four stripes. The old man had given him his position and his rank. When a speechless Alhambra looked up, the aged Cleric had his arms out. Alhambra threw himself around the man, embracing him in a deep hug. He did not have the heart to ask why the Cleric had exiled himself just to hand over his status. "Thank you..."

Artorian leaned and whispered in his ear, words meant only for him to hear. "They will not accept this. When you leave, venture to the mountain of Skyspear. Seek the celestial scion of combat, and request the path to Dawn. Only when you find the will of fire will you find people truly deserving of your kindness. Seek it, my boy. Seek out the will of fire."

If there was ever such a thing as prophecy, Alhambra was certain that he'd heard it spoken this day. The old man was right. There was too much personal hate against him here, but with the prophecy he had a direction and a purpose. Gone were the days of aimless wandering, only *seeking* to do best for the people. He could now *actually* do his best for the people. Should he take them with? Could he? Could he chance asking? No. He had to ask. He was Head Cleric now. "What... my people. Where?"

He watched as Artorian threw on the Acolyte's robe, and snuggled his old two-stripe chasuble in place along the back of the neck. The old man just winked at him. "Do what you think is best, my boy. I have seen your heart, and know it to be *celestial*."

Artorian decided to show off a little, and cycled Essence to his eyes in a combination that made his irises shine a luminous gold. Copying the Wood Elf pattern to make it sound like multiple voices whispered in cohesion, Artorian spoke. His voice reverberated against everything in the building made of wood, especially the shining floor. "*I trust you.*"

The alteration was gone before the old man turned to walk down the main aisle, leaving Alha behind on the chancel. Stunned and speechless, Alhambra no longer believed it was a mere Head Cleric he'd been speaking to. What... what had that been? That was no person that had just spoken to him, and he was awestruck as his mind did its best to cope with the glimpse he'd seen. He had just spoken to the heavens, or the heavens had spoken to him, through an elder as their vessel. A strange old man, who even though he'd been feeding children in the square for years, had never before been seen sitting upon that stone bench.

Alhambra staggered distractedly down the aisle. He blinked and looked to see outside the massive temple doors. The old man was gone. His vision ticked up, and where there this morning had been a yellowing chestnut tree, there was now one in full spring bloom. Healthy flowers dotting its rich, dark green canopy.

Alhambra pressed his hands together, said nothing, and bowed deeply. He was going to be the news of the week, and all eyes would be on him. He did not have the luxury to ask the old man why he'd been provided this gift. He only heard the words he'd spoken, again, and again, as Alhambra's mind raced to construct plans to take him and all his favorite people away from this vile place. It would take a while to gather and convince them all. Yet, he knew who was good, and had excellent motivation to free them from the bonds of Chasuble.

His confidence wavered when classmates roared at him. Yet it didn't matter. He was of higher rank now, and he was no longer subject to their whims. He needed only to hold onto the last words that had been spoken to him; an objective truth for his self-worth to keep hold of while he weathered the storm.

"I trust you." Alhambra would not be daunted. He had people to save.

CHAPTER THIRTY-FIVE

A Dwarven hand had gripped Artorian's sleeve the second he'd left the temple, ripping him from public view. Disoriented, the old man saw a familiar bulbous nose belonging to a certain Don. It was partially hidden under a hooded Acolyte robe, clearly several sizes too large.

"Artorian, we got to go. It be worse here than we thought. The plan be drowning in the river and there ain't no reeds for us to gather air. Hurry yerself as swiftly as ye can to the north gate. Dimi already made it out, an' he be waiting for us. Don't stop for nuthin' that won't kill ya. Go. Go!"

The Dwarf-hiding robe fluttered away quickly as a still-finding-his-bearings Artorian wobbled in place. North? Sure. North sounded great. Where'd the Modsognir go? He looked, but did not see. The Dwarf was a swift boy-o when he wanted to be. Then the words had hit home: he was right, this was no place to try and stay. To the north gate it is!

"That was... noble of you, my Cleric. To rescind your position for the younger generation." A figure stepped from the side door that veered off from the main temple doorway. Artorian turned, and he immediately wondered if he'd ever seen a man with gaunter cheeks. His gauntness had gauntness, for crying out loud! Did those cheeks cave in and form spatial bag caverns? Dear celestials above! Still, he needed to swiftly make himself scarce. Better think of something.

The old man shrugged softly as he wistfully looked up to the sky, not noticing the rank of who he was talking with. He sighed and leaned on his walking stick like it was the only thing keeping him upright.

"My time is over. The end of my days has come. I returned to see the temple one last time before my long trek north. Where I believe... I will fade away. I merely saw a young man trying his best for the Church. He was merely in the right place, at the right time. I'm not sure if it was noble... I'm only glad I won't be a burden any longer. It may be difficult to tell, but I can barely even see anymore. I'm of no use to the mighty Church. May I be excused? I'd like to head out while the sun's bright enough that I may make out some fuzzy details."

A powerful, thin, spindly hand squeezed onto his shoulder. Artorian didn't need to look at the man to recognize the feeling; he knew this gentle tingling sensation well. This was a hand made from Mana, and he'd been touched by one enough to tell by mere tactile feeling. "Surely, you would offer a fellow faithful your ear?"

Artorian made sure to squint. His eyes caught the end of the chasuble. A plus symbol, two vertical stripes below it, then another plus symbol below that. Six stripes. A Vicar! He weakly smiled, hunching over as he looked up at the Mage. "I have shamefully removed myself from the Church with my embarrassing display to hand over my chasuble, without the proper... ueh... what was it called again?"

The old man sighed and shook his head. "I would, of course, be delighted to be of service, Your Grace. How may this exiled one be of service to you, Head Cleric?"

The Vicar's question had been answered before he had a chance to ask. The gaunt man raised his eyebrow. It had been a hundred years since anyone had mistaken him for something as meager as a Head Cleric, yet if the man was on his last legs and barely able to see... he supposed that it was to be expected. Unlike himself, the lesser, mortal Clerics were... fallible. Yet, perhaps there was a boon here.

Ever scheming, the Vicar twisted a sickly smile onto his face. He didn't correct the man, and walked him down the stairs. None dared interrupt. Not even the three-striped Clerics that ran from the Temple, only to skid to a halt when they saw who the old man was spending time with. The fact that a *Vicar* walked with the man solidified everything they had just witnessed. Their eyes contracted to points; this wasn't a joke.

Nothing under the heavens could convince a three-stripe to do as much as *greet* a Vicar, rather than remaining silently bowed unless addressed. Interrupting one's affairs? You'd die on the spot. They could, and would, smite you.

"No tithes to the temple?"

Artorian stopped and cupped his hand to his mouth. His whisper turned conspiratorial, and the Vicar bent in delight to hear what awful excuse the old man had ready. "Head Cleric, I wish to warn you. There are villains in your midst!"

Not the answer that had been expected. The Vicar paused in his step as well. His words were sharp and nasal. "Tell me everything, my son."

Artorian swiftly squinted his eyes and looked around. He grumbled for effect and took a step closer. "I was halted at the west gate. The bannermen there asked for papers, and not having been here a while, I showed them my chasuble. I thought, perhaps there are new rules? They tell me that everyone pays tolls now. The higher one's station, the higher one's tolls. I of course do not believe them, and get out of the way of some merchants.

"Then, my ears pick up the sounds of coin. Again, and again the merchants paid hefty tolls. I think, perhaps I am wrong? So I relent. I ask how much my portion is, they say to hand over my coin purse, and they will hand back what's left when I can prove my station. I give them my pouch, but have entirely forgotten all my hand motions. I remember the Acolyte one, yet because I wear four stripes, they call me a charlatan. A cheat!"

The old man threw a hand in the air. "Robbery I say! Yet, several younger lads with three stripes on their chasubles pull me through the gate and told me not to make a fuss. I'm staining my office with uncouth behavior, they murmur. Damage not the image of the Church, they said. I'm being an embarrassment, they whisper. I know this was my last trip, and I know I'm... faltering. My memory is... well I'd love to say it's slipping. But it's gone. I remember none of the chants. None of the motions... they still have my entire pouch. Yet... you are correct Head Cleric. I should have *fought* to bring a tithe. It's my beloved Church, after all."

Artorian stuck a finger into the air, like he'd had a thought. "Perhaps... perhaps I still can? With my life fading, and no living heirs, I should donate my life savings to the Church! What do you think, Your Grace? I could donate it to the temple, or perhaps to one of my favorite Vicars? I know it might be a pittance to them, but I respect them so. Even if the Church loses this small tool, the guiding light of my Vicars shall remain strong and vigilant. Heavens bless them, for they keep faith strong in my heart."

The Vicar with his hand on Artorian's shoulder was all smiles. "An excellent and faithful act, my son. Such a wise and gracious gift. I encourage such endeavors."

Artorian nodded, and patted his pockets for something as he emphasized words while he spoke. "I should write this down. The northern gatehouse will be my last chance to have a parcel sent. Perhaps I can... oh. No. I'm not a Cleric in good standing anymore. Heavens, how will I make them listen to me when I request them to send a letter to have my goods delivered to the temple? Head Cleric, have you any ideas to make them see to my needs? If they are anything like the western way gate, they will strongarm me into sending *them* my savings instead! What should I do?"

The Vicar lost himself in thought. He was... aware that the toll demands of the gatehouses had risen to pad their coffers. Yet he very much wanted the little treasure for himself. If he sent the old man off, he wouldn't see a single electrum of it. "Lend me your back, my son. I'll scribe a swift message for the north way gate to assist you. We do not want the affairs of the gate to interrupt the affairs of the Church."

Using Artorian's back as a table, the Vicar procured a perfect piece of embroidery edged paper from his spatial pouch. He scribbled down the following. 'See to this man's needs. Signed, Vicar Karthus'. He dated the document so it could only be used today, and neatly folded it before handing it to Artorian with a smile. "Provide this to the bannermen, and they will give you no difficulties. The Church thanks you for your years of service, my son."

Artorian took the missive and bowed the same fashion he'd seen Alhambra bow to him at the bench. The bow for a Head Cleric. He did not rise until the self-satisfied Vicar had walked away at least twenty paces. Then, he hummed to himself and checked the note's contents. Smiling, he slid the writ into his spatial pouch while skipping off to the north, walking stick abandoned next to the stone bench. It had served its purpose, and he needed it no further. Unbeknownst to him, a sneaky Scilla absconded with it minutes later.

The northern way gate was half of what he expected on arrival. Half, because there was a large merchant caravan stuck in place, and that's as far as his guesses had taken him. He could not have been prepared to see Chiffon again, this time in a bannerman captain uniform. Arguing with... Don? Yes, that upset scowl was definitely Don.

He'd planned to use the writ from the Vicar to safely squeeze his way through the gatehouse. Now... a more involved plan started to take form. He'd bluffed his way through Chasuble the entire time he'd been here. What was some icing on the cake?

Artorian mused pleasantly, fiddling with the end of his chasuble as he interrupted the conversation between the two heated children. They must have been children, given the type and amount of insults present in their conversation.

"Hello again."

"Don't interrupt me, and wait in line! I don't have time for-" Chiffon paled as he came face to face with a smiling Head Cleric, who was most certainly not wearing the clothes they'd provided him at a different gate maybe a day earlier. Deagle had told him about the inspection. Abyss!

The sudden silence made the seething Modsognir snap his gaze across the shoulder. He knew the tall, long bearded bloke. Looking back, he no longer knew the quiet, significantly paler gatekeeper that had been making a right mess of them leaving. The old man had been here a *day*, why was some random little weasel gate guardian scared? What in pyrite did this man do in a day? He decided to stay out of it as Artorian procured the nicest piece of paper he'd ever seen.

Chiffon slipped from pale to downright chalky as he laid eyes on the outstretched note. He really, really didn't want to take it. It found its way between his quivering fingers regardless, and he opened it with a swallow. Reading the contents, he squeezed his eyes and lips closed. With a sharp inhale, he handed back the piece of paper. To the Don's immense surprise, the pipsqueak bowed. "Master Cleric, I am of service."

The old man smiled widely. "Excellent. Tell me, young man whose face I'm starting to really *remember* the details of. Is money other than divines confiscated?"

Chiffon did not enjoy the mention that his particular face was being remembered by people who performed inspection work, and casually carried a personal Vicar writ in their pockets. "We do, your grace. Divines are fairly exchanged for all the wealth that attempts to enter into Chasuble after being properly taxed. We have several vaults for storage in the event an expedition crew requires some when leaving."

Artorian calmly nodded, and looked back at the caravan. "In a way, I'm glad you held up Vicar Karthus's secret little project. Though, I find it troublesome I was made to come and personally take stock of the matter. Since I'm here, you've allowed me the unique opportunity to add the addendum. Not only are you going to let the caravan through without complaint, I want all the confiscated wealth that isn't divines loaded up on this caravan. As much as it can hold. I will be setting out with them to fulfill the Vicar's private wishes. I trust this can be done as swiftly as the task... yesterday? I would very much like to forget certain faces."

Chiffon ran for his life, barging straight into the gatehouse before barking orders at the top of his lungs. Don quirked a brow at Artorian, but the infuriatingly scheming human just winked back at him. What in pyrite was going on?

An hour later, the last of the caravan carts cleared the inner circle gatehouse. Artorian sat on the last cart out, and his gaze met Chiffon's. He waved at the boy. "Goodbye, person I don't know and don't remember!"

Chiffon was soaking wet from his cold sweat, not dropping the salute until the last caravan was long, long out of eyesight. He collapsed to the ground and pressed his face into his knees. "Oh, thank the *heavens* he's gone."

"Captain, who was that?" One of Chiffon's men, equally tired from lugging heavy chests posed the question. They were rarely roused so fast and with swift secrecy.

"One of the Vicar's personal investigators, if I had to venture a guess. He had a hand-written note from the Vicar himself. Signed. Dated. Ring-Seal. Everything. I don't ask questions when a four stripe is involved. You think I was going to stick my neck out when who we were dealing with had *higher* rank? Speak of today to nobody. Today didn't happen. Take the rest of the night off. The north gate is closing early."

The aide assented, and started to pack up. "Sir, just... how much gold did we load up on that caravan?"

Chiffon groaned. "Too much."

Artorian joyfully played with his moustache. The caravan had met up with Dimi, and he couldn't believe the story from Don until he was in the back of the caravan swimming in a tub of gold coins. "I have never been so happy in me life."

Don popped up next to him, and he smiled at his massive Dwarven friend, rubies in place of his teeth before spitting them out. He raucously laughed, doing a single backstroke through a caravan hold full of money. "I know the feelin'. Artorian, you mad lad! How did... ya know what. Never mind. What's all this for?"

Artorian tiredly stretched. Tired of ruses and needing to lie and pretend his way through situations. It was time for some well-deserved, cold, hard truth. "Two things. One, to increase our options. Two... you've taken good care of me. Recall that pouch of electrum you prepared for me? Well... have a few caravans worth of gold. I'd say that makes us square, and it has nothing to do with putting a smile on all your lads' faces for leaving home. I'm responsible for an upheaval, I thought I'd get you some... recompense. I didn't want you all to scowl and bicker because of me. Consider it my apology to the clans."

Dimi blinked, and shot a look at Don. "Hold on now. All this gold. It's... for us?"

Artorian just softly smiled in return, and a tear welled up in the largest Dwarf's eye as the old man spoke. "Family takes care of family."

CHAPTER THIRTY-SIX

Weeks of uneventful travel was dull. Time on the road—when there was a road—left much time for thinking. An unpleasant dilemma for most individuals which meant that caravaneers found ways to entertain themselves on the way to Ziggurat, some more troublesome than others.

Some made garden gnomes out of stone, just to toss them into the distance at their real-life feral namesake. Others went on the hunt with throwing axes, with surprising amounts of success. One entrepreneuring Dwarf decided to get the boars drunk; that was an eventful day! Yet two events stood out above the rest. First, when they accidentally started a war.

Feral gnomes were thieving little creeps that stood only knee-high on Dwarves, and the entire feud had triggered due to a drunken enchanting attempt. Rota, a sturdy and strapping Dwarf whose jokes had latched him the nickname 'Otter', had tried his hand at scribing Runes into a set of gambling dice. While that idea was suspect all by itself, the real hubbub began when said dice went missing and a section of nearby forest up and exploded.

Rota had attempted to condense Gran'mama's explosion effect to go off if the dice ever rolled their lowest value; never considering that this was a terrible idea. The gnomes took exception to this, and the caravan was assailed by the mad creatures. Metal-tipped darts zipped through the air, stinging worse than ice wasps as Dwarves devolved into an angry horde of insults and axes.

It was a strange war. While the half-foot tall bush warriors rushed out to stab their foes to death for desecrating their favorite mushroom circle, the Dwarves invented a new sport by using the swing of an axe and striking with the flat of the blade. Scored based on how far one could club a tiny, screaming nuisance. Bonus points if it didn't kill them, since the gnomes endlessly came back to fight on for their feud. The fallen gnomes had their little hats gathered and showcased, forming an ever-increasing call to neighboring tribes that caught wind of the situation.

The chaotic activity of the first event overshadowed the mentally taxing tedium of the second. Artorian was putting Dawn's armor through endless rounds of testing. 'Find the human' stopped being difficult. They could now consistently find him when they concentrated hard enough. They'd both been in the back of a cart, and Artorian had asked Don to look away, do something else, and finally read a note. All the note was meant for was to remind Don that Artorian was in the room with him. When looking up from the note, the Don blinked in surprise.

"Ye were here this entire time? I thought you were gone!"

Artorian shook his head 'no'. His voice remained masked under a heavy *thrumm*, an effect he'd not yet figured out how to deactivate. "The entire time. I didn't even move while you were counting gold coins. What did I look like? It's not like I stopped taking up physical space."

Don rubbed his chin and lay back in the money-pile. "Well... I noticed something. 'Twas like... how do I say this? When ya go to a drinkin' hole, there's always those blokes drinkin' their sorrows away. Head on the bar, buried in the bottom of their mugs. Ya know they're there, but you pay 'em no heed. They're someone else's problem, and me thoughts put it out of mind. Yer just part of the background unless I'm specifically looking for ye."

Artorian fed Essence from his Aura back into the runic effect, and he saw Don squint his eyes at him. "Did ye just do the thing? Kill it."

"Well, any difference?"

The Dwarf grumbled with dissatisfaction. "I knew you were there, but ye blurred out of focus. That whole becoming part of the background again. If I hadn't specifically been puttin' my attention on ye in the middle of a conversation, I'd have slipped and gone back to counting gold. Speaking of... I thought of a wee problem we didn't consider."

Artorian took the helmet off, returning his voice to normal. "With the armor?"

Modsognir grunted in the negative. "We're headed to a refugee haven, and the first time we thought of this, we weren't bringing several caravans loaded down with literal buckets of gold. We'll get torn apart in there, if we even get in."

The old man pointed to himself. "You happen to know someone that can go in and take a look, before the caravan moves. If you give me about a day, I can go check the situation and report back."

Don's expression was flat. "I know what you did in one day in Chasuble, so that be a more dangerous proposition than it initially seems; no matter how innocently ye say it. Still, ain't got an easier option, and I gotta admit it's convenient. Aye. One day. Given yer track record, I'll have the caravan ready to run *away*, rather than run in. Me nose be tingling even givin ya that much."

Artorian couldn't help but gently nod. That was, after all, fair. "Very well. Escape direction?"

The question got the Modsognir right back to grumbling. "Further east and we'll hit water. There's better ways to die than bother Aquatic Elves on their beach turf. They'll think we're there for their memory stone production, and that'll be an ugly, wet way to go.

"There be nothing north but deadly mountains and crags, and across that range you're dealin' with the Lion and Phoenix Kingdoms. I want none o' that. Straight west and we'll be smack back in the mess we're doin' our best to leave. That leaves south, and I can't say I'm fond of Socorro or Morovia. One'll scorch us and leave us gasping sand, the other has grass taller than Dimi, an' even worse predators. Still, the eternal plains of Morovia may still beat out the City of Dunes. Ah hate obsidian scorpions."

Don shuddered as if he felt a chill, rubbing his own shoulders. "Ain't no good options."

Artorian sighed and rubbed his forehead. "The sects of Morovia have long since fallen. It's just overgrown wilderness now. The ligers may be bad in their preferred territory, but they're really the only problem. Everything else can be dealt with."

Don sat up in his pile of gold, curious. "What do you mean 'everything else'? Know an awful lot about a place many people won't willingly venture. Gonna add that nugget o' gold to the pile?"

The old man shrugged, trying to brush away the unpleasant topic. "We all come from somewhere, my friend."

Don flicked him a platinum coin he'd dug out of the pile, dropping the topic after correcting him on a single detail. "Brother. Call me brother."

Artorian silently smiled, nodding in assent before resuming field tests as the Dwarf removed himself from the cart; escaping his own embarrassing sappiness. Artorian was distracted by national borders, since from Don's description they no longer adhered to geographical limitations. Why couldn't kingdoms just stick to nice and convenient squares?

The Modsognir caravan encountered more and more refugees the closer they were to Ziggurat. It wasn't a major issue for the well-armed Dwarven clan, but it came with its own set of issues. Merchants they encountered began negotiations angry and hateful, and they demanded payment up front. Dwarven gold warmed their cold, cold hearts, so if merchants had food? They bought it. Alcohol? Bought it.

A great number in the caravan didn't even realize they stopped when the outer territories of Ziggurat came into view. Somehow, regardless of how much they managed to drink, no one spoke a word about their carts full of wealth. They sobered swiftly when someone wished to gander. Sacks full of feral gnomes were tossed at curious refugees with sticky fingers, leaving them covered in a ravenous, angry biting mass.

The caravan had to stop when the population density became too thick. The tent city sprawled, and the mess was as could be expected. Chasuble had a sewer system, even if hidden. Ziggurat did not; instead it had smells and concerning puddles. The Dwarves prepared themselves and their animals for a plethora of diseases, and filtered all water before boiling it. The infernal Essence that freely roamed here was so thick that a cultivator would choke on it. Non-infernal cultivators needed to seal their techniques up tightly; corruption would eat them alive in this region, and they had only reached the outskirts.

Don rapped his knuckles against Artorian's armored hip. "You're up, brother. One day. Just. *One*. If ye come back running, we're ready to roll out. So expect to find us right at the edge. We will not be moving the caravan any further into this muck than we need."

Artorian winked at his Dwarven compatriot, tucking in his beard neatly before sliding the helmet over his head. On either side of the helmet, two vertical eye-lines flared to life as the completed set linked the Runes. They interacted as intended, sapping a portion of Artorian's Essence to engage their passive effects.

They remained present unless repressed, but for the moment the old man was very happy to have a constant supply of fresh air. Regardless, he wrapped his Presence fully about his iridium gear so it didn't stain as he walked. The trudge into tent city ended up being as unpleasant as imagined. Kind words were only used in a sarcastic fashion here. There was nothing nice about trucking through a living area worse than an active warzone.

How did these people live like this? He made the question rhetorical when he realized there were more dead in the tents than living. There were crews going around piling the bodies up and bringing them closer to the center of the area, rather than the outskirts. Artorian didn't want to know why. It was clear as day something unsavory was going on here.

It wasn't until tent city gave way to an outer palisade that he found an area he could give the minimum rating of 'livable'. Initial observations made it clear that strength was everything here. Not his... favorite measurement. Ruffians crowding the gate didn't notice him at first when he muscled his way through; it was so easy to forget his S.E.P. field was active. To everyone nearby, he was Someone Else's Problem.

Or he *was*, until he reached the front of a group only to be barred by a seven-foot-tall man wielding a warhammer. Both factions of ruffians noticed him at the same time. They were confused only for a fraction of a moment before they shouted insults and attempted to strongarm him. Now, C-ranked cultivators can give roughly ten D-ranked cultivators at a time a run for their copper. A D-rank easily handled ten F-ranks. You were only an F-rank if you qualified as a cultivator. Roughly forty non-cultivators against a C-rank? There was only one outcome.

The armored figure didn't budge an inch against the combined muscle and might of easily seven burly men attempting to move him. Artorian didn't *want* to move, therefore he was immobile. His body wasn't optimal for reinforcing, but as an external cultivator, his Presence performed much the same function. He and his armor were the same thing as far as his Presence was concerned, and the forces involved were measures of energy. The math was easy: he had more.

A single step forward let Artorian bowl through a dozen screaming men, and he snatched a surprised and muscled specimen by the shoulder, only to whisk him about in a half circle and smack away five others before dropping the bruised meat-club into the mud. The path before him cleared quickly. There were grumbles, shouts, and general assertions of unpleasantry, yet the rule here was simple: might makes right.

Don't get in the way of the metal man that can use you as a baton.

Artorian hated this. There was no point in staying here! No point in trying to get the caravan here. Was there even a point for *him* to be here? He hurled another strongman out of the way when the bruiser stormed up to him with demands. He was sure the bruiser believed his shouted words to be important; Artorian found them less compelling. He did stop a moment, struck by a realization: how had the bruiser seen him?

He looked at his armored hand. The view around him was clear. He saw it with clarity and detail, but nothing about his hand looked different. He tried to switch his stealth feature off, but found he could not. It was already off? Odd. Had he removed it subconsciously when stepping into problem solving mode? The armor was meant to be responsive to him, he'd discovered that much. Did it matter? No. No, it did not. "Let's finish the scouting and go back to the Dwarves."

Artorian forgot his complaints when his eyes caught sight of a large sign ahead. It was a tournament listing for some kind of arena fight. "Glory, honor, prestige. Recognition from the Ziggurat if one makes themselves worthy. Sure. Can most people here even read this sign?"

The sign used smaller, simpler words. Yet that's what it essentially said. It wasn't the promise of prestige that attracted Artorian; it was the two names at the top of the listings. They each had a removable wooden beam as a plaque, names carved in for all to see. Artorian remembered this place now, and found an excellent reason to stay.

Position one. Grimaldus. Position two. Tychus.

His sons were here.

CHAPTER THIRTY-SEVEN

Given the social standards of Ziggurat, being cordial was utter foolishness. Artorian knew there was no point. They'd look at him strangely, and would take it as a weakness to exploit. Fights were a constant in the arena, and anyone was able to join if they could get past the factions of ruffians serving as self-appointed gatekeepers. It was swiftly apparent that the closer to Ziggurat's center one was, the better the living conditions became.

So, how to get to his sons? He'd need their attention or their presence. That likely meant doing some damage to the current standing of that leaderboard. He was secretly proud they were at the top, and hoped it was a clever ploy to get attention and get the word out. Or it could just... be who they were now. Artorian swallowed hard, he hoped the latter wasn't the case. It didn't matter. They were his boys. He'd treat them like all the rest.

Finding the large raised dais that served as one of many stone arenas was easy. Artorian strolled right up to a massive man, and helped the giant creature find his way onto a knee. The thrumming voice that erupted from the suit only helped sell that the full plate armored man wasn't here to play. "How do I get on that board?"

Gorgon the Glorious was twelfth on the board—and thus not listed, as only the top ten got a mention—and was having a good day until he found himself on a knee. With a metal hand crunching his clavicle to rubble, he swiftly found it within himself to be cooperative. "Scarf man. Speak to scarf man!"

That was plenty information. Gorgon hastily beat a retreat to a healer upon being let go. His entire left shoulder had a purple handprint on it that was getting darker by the second, and the armored figure moved on without missing a beat. Gorgon's posse had witnessed the event in stunned silence, reduced from raucous fans to confused onlookers. They exchanged glances and ran to the betting pools. Word traveled fast: there was a new fighter in Ziggurat!

Uferiel, the coordinator, pinched the bridge of his nose. How he *despised* these uncouth monstrosities of muscle and savagery. "No finesse. No finesse I say!"

He sighed deeply as yet another imposing shadow came over him. Uferiel wasn't even phased, he just prepared a new small wooden block. "Name?"

Given the red scarf-clad coordinator was in what Artorian would call 'refined' clothing, he smiled beneath his helmet. Finally someone in this area he could speak with! "'Mr. Fringe' would be an adequate representation for the purposes of the tournament, my good man."

Uferiel nearly lost his composure. Manicured nails pressed to his embroidered inner vest as his hazel eyes shot wide open, turning to regard the specter of politeness he had just been haunted by. A full, proper *sentence*? The luxury! His ears felt like they were healing from the underutilization they had suffered. "Oh, my good heavens, please do tell me that wasn't a one-off chance at proper perlocution. I'm shaken, sir. Shaken!"

Artorian nested his arms behind his back, a habit that his age wrested upon him. In the armor, it merely made him look regal. "It was not, and I do apologize for my uncouth entrance. Much of this place is crude. May I kindly register for the events?"

Uferiel blushed pink and was overcome with emotion. A tiny cheer peeped from his throat as his fingers pressed into half-fists on either side of his fangirling mouth. He was delighted!

Overjoyed! "Oh, of course, Mr. Fringe. I'll have you registered and lined up momentarily. Please do give those savages a proper thrashing. It's been so awfully long since a person of any caliber has graced my... well, it used to be a respectable sport. Now it is the 'clobbering zone'."

He sighed and carved in the name. "Arena seven, if you please. The one next to the seven flagpoles, if you can count that high... Oh! My apologies, sir! I slipped into my usual entrapments. I'm so used to offering only grunty pointing. It's over there..."

Artorian took the coordinator by the wrist, and firmly gave it a shake. "My sincere thanks. I am delighted to see such a strapping mind in charge. I was expecting ruffians to control everything in the area. Are you unharmed?"

Uferiel nearly fainted, biting back a whimpering hiccup of enjoyment at being treated with respect by another mind. Oh, his knees were weak, and cheeks were rosy pink! "Oh, oh no, sir... I am an untouchable. If anyone so much as bends a hair on my head, the Ziggurat would turn against them."

The slender man showed off a wrist bracelet made entirely of bone. A tiny opal reflected light in the center of the band. "I am marked by the Ziggurat. I can be found any time so long as I wear this, and anyone who has one is under the direct protection of the leadership. We have gained their favor through... some means or another."

Artorian pointed at the arena in question upon letting the man's hand go. Receiving a cordial nod in return, he muscled his way through the crowd and got onto the dais. It was a large, stone circle. Two squares were set on opposite ends near a stripe in the middle, and from the muddy footprints he could deduce that was where fighters stood before things began. He set himself into place and crossed his arms.

He did not have the details of how the fights worked. Artorian didn't need them. The only true victory condition was clear. Win. Win, and don't stop winning. The crowd around his arena was nothing special. He seemed to have the favor of the coordinator, but that was of little help for now. He waited only for a few minutes for the first opponent to crawl his way up the dais.

The man *crawled*, and onlookers yelled. "There are stairs! Use them!"

The armored figure covered its faceplate with a hand. To Artorian's surprise, that didn't obscure his vision. He saw right through to the other side of the hand. Helpful? Yes. Mostly odd. Still, gift horse, mouth, the usual.

"I am Rafan! I shall gut you from spleen to stern!"

Stern? The... ship...? You know what? Never mind. Artorian doubted these people even knew what the word 'anatomy' meant. He wanted this over quickly. Actually, now *that* was a thought. He smiled and spoke through his voice changer. "Ten seconds."

Rafan circled him like a rabid dog, and rusty daggers found their way into both his hands. So weapons were allowed? Good to know. Rafan hurled an insult at him, speaking with a tone that denoted a lack of... certain mental faculties that could be trained. "Ten what? What's wrong with your talky talks! You speak like dog barks!"

Artorian continued his mental countdown. "Five."

The bandolier and headscarf toting fighter lunged at him from directly behind. Against a normal person that was likely something clever. Attack from a position where your opponent cannot see. It was *something* that showed forethought.

Crack!

With barely any effort, Artorian turned and backhanded Rafan straight into the crowd. Connecting armored fist to the side of an unarmored head had expected results. The dirty fighter twitched in the mud, and bubbled out some words. Otherwise, he was out of the fight. Booing and jeering echoed around the arena. They'd come here for a fight! What was this one-hit wonder nonsense? They wanted fury! They wanted carnage! They. Wanted. *Blood*!

The armor boomed as the inhabitant put some effort into it. "I will defeat every opponent in less than a count of ten."

A count? Was that what a second was? Booing turned into questions, and greed found a new spot. Less than a count of ten was something that could be bet on! The armored figure had returned to the arms crossed position. So the fighter was confident and full of himself? Great! That would make odds all the better when someone took him down.

Uferiel was a person that played favorites. His current arena was handed off to someone else, and he quickly made his way to dais seven. No way in the *abyss* was he going to let someone else coordinate Mr. Fringe's fights. Those were his! He called out, voice sweet and sugary in a sea of shouts and death threats. "Oh, Mr. Fringe?"

Artorian turned and made his way to the edge of the dais where Uferiel stood. The man was surprised this fighter had heard him the first time, and so easily! He again felt faintness threaten him when Mr. Fringe addressed him.

"Yes, Sir Fashion?"

"Fashion?" Oh! His heart! Composing himself, Uferiel fanned himself with his hand before clearing his throat. "Is there a particular difficulty we're looking for today? It will be easier to match you if I'm more aware of your goals."

Artorian wasted not a moment, pointing at the massive leaderboard bolted to the side of a tower. "Tychus and Grimaldus. I want them *both* in my arena at the same time. I need to exchange words."

Uferiel's smile was full of overjoyed greed. All the way to the top? He had a true contender today! Given how easily Mr. Fringe dispatched of his first match in the placing round... he might actually get there. "Mr. Fringe. I would be delighted to coordinate these fights. Do you need breaks between matches? You will need to change arenas for some of the larger, more popular bouts."

Artorian shook his head before getting up. "No breaks. I will meet them *today*. Tell me when to change locations and send all challengers. Keep. Them. Coming."

Uferiel didn't even bother trying to hide his smile. "As you wish...!"

The second fight ended much as the first; an overblown fool backhanded off the stage. The third fight had the slightly smarter opponent remaining at the edge of the arena until the count hit zero, just to mess with the bets. It had not gone according to plan. Artorian only needed a single second to put the full effect of Rail Palm into motion. He didn't even perform the full art, but it still sent the challenger flying twenty feet off the stage with a caved in chest. He did not live to feel the impact of his fall.

Betting erupted. Ten seconds to defeat, or be defeated. Rapid fire matches performed at high speed. The spectacle saw many a betting man resent their loss, but nothing in the rules said they could not crawl up on the stage to fight one of the contestants. The rules didn't need to do anything: an armored backhand quickly made the attempt known as 'pulling a Rafan'.

Uferiel, while set in his ways, was a dependable coordinator. He changed the entire format of arena seven at the drop of a hat. If you registered, you got sent up right away. Given the speed at which fights resolved, a line formed in front of him as people who wanted to win the ever-growing jackpot replaced self-preservation with the hope of a one-in-a-million wonder. If only the odds had been *remotely* so favorable for the challengers.

Several aides came to Uferiel's side to help facilitate the event. Booing turned to cheering. While the carnage people sought was lacking, the constant, quick fire resolutions to fights had its own, unique draw. The first half hour of non-stop flying lessons contained nothing but non-cultivators. Those one-sided bouts were so unmemorable that Artorian yawned at the end of the last match.

Given that his armor amplified and altered his voice, his tiny yawn became an insulting bellow. The line finally thinned out of willing contestants. Even with a massive jackpot, none had put so much as a dent on Mr. Fringe. The old man looked over his shoulder. "Sir Fashion? Anytime you're ready."

Uferiel was screaming with glee. He jumped in place, arms performing little in-the-air wiggles. He was going to kill it when cashing in today's coordination logs! He'd done so much work! His pay was going to be a fat purse of *gold*. "Coming right up, Mr. Fringe!"

A figure jumped from the crowd, easily clearing ten feet before slamming down onto the arena. Cheers of support cried out from surrounding fans. Artorian couldn't immediately see the Center of this one. A veil? Oh my heavens, finally a cultivator. About time.

This match was different. Uferiel actually got up on the arena and performed an announcement. "Savages and ne'er-dowells! The preliminary rounds have ended, and we can finally set this challenger against numbered opponents. We're in the top one hundred now! Mr. Fringe now faces fighter ninety-nine: Fuego, the Firestorm! I hope you're ready, because it's about to get hot!"

Fuego was... D-rank two. Cute. His hands lit up with flames, and a minor cyclone of sorts formed on his palm. Air Essence? Artorian squinted. No... just fire. Essence plus a shape? "I mean. Why not? I'm not sure if that qualifies someone as a firestorm."

Artorian had to correct himself. His understanding of 'average' was no longer the *actual* average. D-ranks were a significant accomplishment, and he needed to remember that. He was dangerously close to the trap of seeing lesser-ranked cultivators as non-threats.

He shouldn't do that. If anything, Fuego over here might be the first actual threat he'd faced so far. Artorian decided to take the fight seriously. He smiled as the Firestorm took his position.

"Ten seconds, Firestorm."

CHAPTER THIRTY-EIGHT

A cyclone of fire enveloped the arena. Onlookers gasped and cheered when the armored figure appeared to be too scared to move. He was going to lose this one! *Yeah!*

Far from feeling fear, Artorian was *confused*. *This* was the Essence technique of 'The Firestorm'? This ability had more holes than Tarrean's favorite cheese! Was the man trying to kill him or *tickle* him with Essence? Currently it was the latter, as even a *light* field of fire Essence in his Aura made the whole attack moot.

Artorian cocked his head to the side and broke down the technique with Essence-cycled vision. Essence? Fire. Shape? Cyclone. Area? Wide. Intent? Nil. Control? Laughable. The D-ranked cultivator had fueled a half-formed technique and released it on the arena to perform a function. Undoubtedly, the effect would fizzle out when depleted of refined Essence. Even with not being great at techniques himself, he could see this one was terrible. The Essence was just spinning and expressing its unaltered concept upon the world. Fire Essence was just... there.

An idea struck the academic. Could... could he just... take it? There was only refined and fire Essence occupying the space around him. With a simple pull, it passed through his Presence coating his armor, and when it did... it was his. Artorian blinked at how easy it was. With just a thought, Fuego's technique was fueling Artorian's Essence shielding.

He needed to *know*. Even if it burned him a little, Artorian expanded his Presence to envelop the full span of the dais. No harm so far. Artorian altered the edge of his Presence into a membrane — as he didn't want any rogue infernal Essence getting in — while his Presence filtered out the unpleasantry. Conditions looked good, so... *nom*?

The burning cyclone simply ceased to be. The Essence fueling the technique stopped inside of Artorian's Presence as his will overshadowed both the technique and its owner. Neither were very sturdy... Essence looked to be molded, and the presence field was superseding a great many factors. Without effort, Artorian made it gather and come to him. It harmlessly seeped into his Aura, becoming part of his Presence.

Artorian frowned. No side effects? None? Surely not. Nothing in the cultivation life had been so easy. Fuego frowned as well, but at his outstretched hands, trying to figure out what had gone wrong. He threw out another flaming cyclone, but no fire eruption burst from his hands. As soon as the energy left him, the noticeable Presence field he was in gobbled it up. Fuego was doing little more than throwing free Essence out into the world.

Artorian was so perplexed that his count of ten stopped dead. So taken aback that he flat out asked his opponent a question: "Would you like to try again?"

Fuego threw his hands out a third time, fueling more Essence and power into the technique. Not a sliver of heat or *fwoosh* left his fingertips. Instead, he felt drained. He was sweating heavily, and his lungs drew deep, demanding breaths. Only then did he realize he was in the F-ranks. What! *How*? He thought techniques perfectly returned Essence back to the user every time, so how was he drained? The truth was simple, yet it escaped Fuego: he was wrong.

The Firestorm sank to his knees, hands shaking as he looked at them. His Essence was still draining! Fear gripped his heart, and showed on his face. "Fuego... Fuego surrenders!"

Artorian released his crossed-arm pose, and pointed at the edge of the arena. He didn't give the crowd a chance to voice their displeasure. That wasn't his concern; only continued victory mattered to him. If he could avoid killing a man in the process... that was just a better alternative. "Accepted. Leave."

The crowd broke out into screams of defiance. *Conceding?* Unacceptable! They berated Fuego as he left the arena. He didn't mind that he'd lost his spot, or that Mr. Fringe now held it. Fuego was more worried for his cultivation and his much-reduced lifespan.

Artorian mulled things over. Why had nobody thought of this before? Perhaps they had, and discovered downsides he'd not yet seen? Running the gambit, it was a safe bet that any affinity he didn't have would be absorbed as corruption, which was a good reason to be careful. A condition for this feat also seemed to be the opponent having a tenuous grasp on techniques, and a lack of intent fueling the ability. Could he test this further?

Uferiel announced the next contender. "Next up in the blood games, number eighty-five! One who needs no further introduction: Typhon of the Blades!"

A pointy-eared man clad in scarves and rags slid up the steps. He took the pose of a dagger fighter, but held a small gourd of water in his grasp rather than a knife. Artorian couldn't discern any features on what was likely an... elf? No, this was a human that had pointy ears for some reason. A mystery for another time. Artorian could discern a strong water affinity, but not much else.

Typhon activated his technique, fueling power into his gourd to create a high-pressure knife of water. It belched from the spout, and Artorian noted the same flaws as his previous opponent, so tried to sap the Essence from the technique.

Splat.

Typhon stood still as a handful of water fell to the ground. The man looked down, not sure what had just happened. Oh no... he'd wet the arena. Usually that happened with the blood of his enemies after he slashed them. His knife ignored most defenses, so it was a powerful offensive tool. He... must have done something wrong? Typhon activated the knife again! It seamlessly shaped into being while his opponent was counting down, already awfully close to zero.

Splat.

Typhon didn't have time to wonder why this was happening; a palm to the chest sent him barreling out of the arena. He hadn't even seen his opponent move, and he regularly boasted about his kinetic vision. He didn't get the chance to boast ever again, dead by the time he landed in the mud.

The armored fighter squeezed his hand open and closed. With that second cultivator, he had recouped all the costs his armor had taken from him over the last *week*. This was *fantastic!* He should attempt to use this often whenever the situation allowed. No... becoming reliant on this would only bite him in the keister.

Uferiel snorted at Typhon's loss, and announced once more. He wasn't in the slightest bothered that people he disliked were racking up eliminations. In fact, he was lining them up in hope of that outcome. Fuego remaining alive had been... unfortunate.

A line of ranked contestants prepared themselves, lining up without needing to be called. Cutting short the winning streak of a rookie was both profitable and prestigious. Not that they knew that second word, but preferential treatment was a big deal in Ziggurat. "Number seventy-four, Hestiroth the Forbidden One!"

A steam cloud wheezed onto the arena floor, forming into a bathrobe-clad human. Artorian nodded approvingly: the bathrobe was a nice touch. Cozy and snug. Artorian couldn't say he complained about the effort toward finding comfort, but then his attention shifted to his priorities. Steam? Fire and water affinity, then. Did the higher affinity of steam play a role here? That this was combat was no reason to stop learning, and he was fairly certain that this Essence combination was safe for the taking.

Hestiroth surrounded himself with a seven-foot cloud of steam the second the countdown began. Artorian saw him as if the steam wasn't even present, including the steam clone in the shape of Hestiroth's body. Was that meant as a distraction, or could it do damage? No reason to deviate from the tests!

Fhwop.

The bathrobe clad man unsheathed a curved scimitar. His plan had been to circle the armor and strike under the arm. That tended to be a weak point for full plate, as he had fought armored foes before. Still, he wasn't prepared for his fog field to just... pop out of existence. He stood there on his tiptoes, awkwardly balanced as he'd been mid-step. He fueled the effect again, but nothing happened even though he lost Essence. Then he felt dread, and tried to *stop* channeling his Essence into his steam-body technique.

Hestiroth, much like Typhon, had begun as a D-rank four. He was at F-rank nine by the time Artorian's count dropped to three. One needed exponentially more Essence each rank, even if it didn't feel like it did. Artorian didn't bother to stop counting, as there was no need to drain this man dry. The amount of Essence in each F-rank was paltry to a C-ranker. "Zero."

Crack.

Uferiel broke another wooden slat in two, and smugly threw the remains over his shoulder. He gleefully called out another victim as he advanced the count by at least ten, but skewed towards the people he wanted to see fail. "Number sixty-four, Nentendoh the Three-Pronged."

Nen was another human, this one clad in dark half plate. He paused as he walked up the stairs. Artorian was surprised to see the man's hand stop at the exact spot where he'd placed the membrane of his Presence. The D-rank six man didn't seem to be able to tell what the membrane was, but the academic took a mental note that it was in fact noticeable. Nen looked over his shoulder after passing through, worried about the effect he couldn't figure out.

"Neat trick. Been watching for a while. Can it stop all fancy effects? I'm not powerless without mine." Nen placed his hands together and pulled them apart with noticeable effort as a bolt of lightning formed with crackling thunder between his palms. Artorian went through the motions, and hit his first snag. Lightning? So it should be all air Essence if he remembered correctly? Though there was an earth affinity at play here. Drat! Not safe for absorption.

Instead, he just pressed his hind foot into the rock ground and disappeared during his forward lunge, only to reappear as his palm connected with Nen's chin, transferring the force and momentum into bone and sinew that was in no way prepared for it. *Snap*!

Nen's body remained in place, but his head did not. One needed a functional neck with a proper spinal connection for that; the man no longer qualified. His Essence fizzled into nothingness, and his body collapsed into a pile. Artorian dejectedly scooted it out of the ring with his foot, not wanting to touch the bloody corpse.

Uferiel craned to his right to watch the body hit the mud. Breaking another wooden stick in twain, he spoke his mind before really thinking about it. "Do you usually go through men this fast?"

Artorian shrugged, crossing his arms as he silently wished he'd done different tests on Nen. Perhaps he could have *stopped* the interaction of Essence, rather than absorb it? Could he negate or twist effects in his space, rather than just eat them? The thought of a meal weighed heavy on his mind as he replied. "Does one feast on a scrawny appetizer when they can see the main course?"

Uferiel shivered and announced the next contestant. Mr. Fringe was tearing through his hit list! "Number fifty-five, Zorah the Wall."

The ground shuddered as a four-hundred-pound hog of a man walked with laden steps into the arena. He wore an extra two hundred pounds in armor, making him by far the heaviest of the contenders thus far. He too stopped at the membrane, but he *flicked* it. Ow! Artorian winced. What the heck? The membrane could feel? That was news to him.

Zorah's voice was heavy and thick, the gruff rumble of a man used to eating meat every day. "A technique as a field? Pointless if it doesn't do anything except sit there. Your winning streak ends with me, metal boy. Zorah the Wall stops all newcomers."

The crowd chanted a song as the hulk rose a hand to greet them. He smiled at the hollering crowd with a row of exposed, sharpened teeth. Artorian thunked his hand to the bottom of his helm, having attempted to stroke his beard. All four basic affinities were present? Why was it that multi-affinity users were both incredibly rare, and yet bumped into him at a rate that just about made them seem common?

Zorah's equipment creaked, becoming covered in a wooden residue that thickened before hardening. Only his eyes remained visible, while the rest of him looked like it was part of a palisade. Oh, using higher nature Essence to armor oneself up by fostering wood growth on predesignated locations? Neat! Shame about the glaring weak spot. He was thankful Ember's gifted armor didn't have that problem.

Zorah roared out his challenge. "Zorah is going to flatten you!"

A beam of condensed light flashed from the tip of Artorian's armored finger. It lasted a fraction of a second, less time than lightning remained visible when it clapped in the distance. The starlight blast was a fine line, and the hole in the back of Zorah's head was all the proof Artorian needed that it was very effective against cultivators who forgot to invest into Essence shielding. Really, it was important. They should do it. The man had even been C-rank one. *Had.* Not a surprise when four affinities were involved.

Thud.

The crowd was still half-chanting by the time Zorah's lifeless body hit the arena floor. The noise died down slowly, not sure what they'd seen. Light moved awfully fast. Another wooden nameslate broke into pieces as with another dejected 'I don't want to touch this' foot-nudge, the fighter was 'helped' off from the dais.

CHAPTER THIRTY-NINE

Grand Vizier Amon, unflatteringly called 'the nope rope', coiled around his lesser throne in the top of the Ziggurat. The Queen had seen fit to bless him with an artful form for his many years of faithful service, and merely sitting on the throne was no longer possible.

The fifty-foot-long crystal cobrafied man still had arms, yet his legs were a thing of the past. He now shifted with true serpentine motion. His vermillion scale-coated body pressed what used to be his human spine against the cushioning of the throne, and golden hued rings coated him in an interlocking hook pattern. Amon's fingers steepled in their usual fashion.

Observing the heaving messenger collapsed on the floor before him, he sipped the air with a thistle forked tongue. His cobra hood stirred, inflated lightly, but comfortably eased back into place; there really wasn't a reason to be upset. The messenger had run for dear life to deliver his task as swiftly as possible. So the mortal was a little out of breath... how could he blame the limited for their limitations?

Uncaring of the plights of lessers, the Vizier glanced out of the large stone openings to regard the ever-growing fields of people. The unceasing death was pleasing. The cobra indulged in the gathered infernal Essence for a moment as an opal the size of a pearl drew energies from the region up to the apex of the Ziggurat. The best fresh breath was one steeped in *power*.

The messenger had their back patted by a figure with a lime-green glow oozing from its skeletal mouth. This small action pulled Amon from his musings; it didn't seem to matter how many moths he crushed to dust. They came endlessly, and no amount of security could keep them from finding an audience with him. He'd stopped trying, even if he had no use for their favors.

The messenger regained enough breath to speak, forming the proper bow with assistance. "My... my Vizier! I bring urgent news."

Of course it was urgent. Nobody ran for their life to deliver something mundane. Amon reminded himself that his superior mind couldn't be matched by his servants. Their sluggishness... it was to be forgiven. Again, they were doing their best. Like ants. His scaled hand rolled on his wrist, beckoning the servant to continue.

Hastily and with some panic, the messenger relayed his words. "In the last wave of refugees, an unmatched warrior has arisen! He tears through the blood games as I speak, and has already breached the ranked listing!"

Amon wasn't impressed. Many warriors entered the ranked list only to fail after a few days of climbing. There was nothing special here. His slithering voice softly whistled as he worked the words out of his reformatted serpentine mouth. It was so much more *difficult* to speak without lips. "Inssssufficient... merely a temporary shock to my system. In a few more days, the games will settle as they always have."

The messenger's panic increased, and his gaze pleaded with the quiet onlookers in the room. The guests lounging about did not speak, they had not been addressed nor given permission. They would not help him today. "My... my all-knowing Vizier. The warrior has not been in the games for even an *hour*! He breaches the thirties as I relay this message, and has sustained not a single scratch of damage. Nor does he seem winded! He has declared a challenge to the top two on the leaderboard, and the survival rate against him has been..."

The messenger ceased and bowed as the Vizier's finger steeple broke from formation. This was *not* news that pleased his master, and he abyss well knew it. The slithering voice snapped out with expected sharpness. "*My* system, undermined by a single paltry servant? It shall not be so. Who has survived thus far?"

Rising upon being addressed with a question, the sweating messenger attended the command. "Fuego, my Vizier. The man conceded and was allowed to leave the arena by the warrior. All others have fallen... in less than ten seconds."

Now Amon's interest was piqued. A serpentine eyebrow lifted, or what could be mistaken as one. It was difficult to tell on a scaled face that held the barest semblance of a human pattern, yet was for the majority, cobra. "This nuisance will either be added to my fold, or removed outright. Emerald Eyes, fetch your brother and see to this whelp.

"*Nothing* is unharmed after an hour in the games, and if it were a person on the caliber of our Queen, they would not have bothered with it to garner my attention. It displeases me that this has become my problem. If the nuisance is judged worthy, send him up to see me so we may add another to our fold. Otherwise... the usual."

Tychus stood, eleven feet tall and built like a volcanic castle. He sported more muscle than most rich people had coin. After bowing cordially to the Vizier, his heavy, thumping footfalls left the hallowed Ziggurat halls. The messenger didn't quite understand how the massive man managed that effect on a stone floor, but didn't have the luxury to find out. A massive mouth snatched him up before he even had the chance to scream. A convenient snack for the Vizier!

Tychus had to duck in a few places to not scrape the top of his head against the stone pathways. It hurt! He had to hurry, his brother wasn't in the Ziggurat, and he had to play fetch before rushing back to the blood games. Where Tychus was bound to the Vizier, Grimaldus was tied to 'The Mistress'. Their bonds had different connections and connotations, based on the differences in their abilities. After all, who in power doesn't want a pet necromancer these days? Was it in style?

Tychus jumped twenty feet and decided not to think about it anymore. His impact on the ground thundered for only a moment before he took off at speed. While the Vizier oversaw local operations in the Ziggurat, The Mistress preferred her quiet gilded mansion, staffed with her personalized art projects. Her faux-Elves. The hefty man from the Fringe shuddered at the thought. Why did anyone like the idea of being disfigured for someone else's enjoyment? He couldn't get it through his skull, but to its credit, his skull was very thick.

Why someone would want a mansion half hanging from the side of a cliff was also something Tychus didn't quite understand. Perhaps only because he'd flipped a bench by sitting on the end of it, launching the person beside him. One who had mysteriously found his head smashed through the ceiling. That had been a good day at the tavern, back when they had a tavern. Every day, something else was being torn from anything resembling a structure by the sheer amount of people venting anger or needing a floor.

Caw!

The oversized infernal corvid made its presence known with its usual impatient impunity. Its beak flicked left and right as it hopped about on a gnarled perch, head tilting at the swiftly approaching...

Fwumph.

The corvid screeched and flew out of the way as the figure barreled past its perch, kicking up enough wind as it went to send the corvid skyward. It landed, now on a slightly more crooked perch.

The vast and lavish pristine structure opened its doors as Tychus slowed. Luxurious paintings and ostentatious drapery lined alabaster walls, and there was to be no running in the halls. Numerous beast furs lay underfoot, muting his heavy footfalls as he turned corridors. When he found the one with suits of polished and posed armor lining the walls, he knew he was in the right place; or *would* be when he reached the end of this endless hall.

Full plated guards barred the double-set elephant-tall doors, their grip tight on crossed halberds tugging weapons out of the way on Tychus's swift approach. One could tell when another was in a hurry. After the guard hammered a fist against the reflective bronze, chains clinked and the grunts of a dozen men were heard as they once again saw to their task. Mechanisms in the wall creaked to life, and the pathway opened inward.

Tychus was ready for the heady scent of lavender bursting from the throne room. It was awful and overpowering. He was also allergic, and it made him sneeze mightily. Lit braziers filled the busy room, illuminating the expansive space as a golden figure worked her slender touch over an unrecognizable mass of flesh that used to be someone's face.

The massive man skidded to a halt, petals under his feet making him slip just an inch before bowing. "My Queen."

No amount of being in a hurry made one demand time from the Mistress. She would address you on her terms. Luckily for the son of the Fringe, she was impatient today, displeased with her current sculpture. "Speak..."

Tychus remained bowed, and servants adorned in a great number of gold bracelets made way. "My Queen, my

Vizier has summoned my brother and I to the blood games, we are to quell an upstart."

Her dismissive hand gesture sent him from the room. Tychus had learned it was better to go willingly, even if he hadn't received an answer. Some people were just... different. He didn't understand what made The Mistress *so* different, only that she was impossibly more powerful than the Vizier was, and the Vizier could floor him and his brother. He knew that lesson well, they'd tried plenty of times. He'd treated them like amusing ragdolls, and the ceilings were still stained by their bloody defeats.

The Mistress clicked her tongue, fist pressed against the underside of her chin. She really wasn't making any headway on this sculpture. Honestly, how hard could sculpting a crocodile head onto a person be?

"Emerald Eyes, see to your brother... Your Queen does not wish to be disturbed for any reason until my doors open."

An unremarkable man rose and bowed. Seemingly mediocre and common in every way, save for his lime green eyes, Grimaldus cordially performed the required bow and stepped from the throne room silently and at a hastened pace. Passing the elephant doors, he said nothing until they clanged to a close.

He didn't need to inform the halberd wielders, who crossed weapons to bar entry. They'd somehow heard their Queen regardless of where she was. Grimaldus's flat face broke into a sly smile as he saw his brother waiting for him with crossed arms, sporting an equally mischievous smile. "Brother..."

Tychus belted out a laugh, and bumped fists with his brother. The bump turned into an elaborate set of playful hand movements. Neither of them had ever properly grown up. Tychus slapped a hand on Grim's back, who coughed and stumbled forward. "Ty! You're still far stronger than me! Do take care."

The walking castle had done it on purpose, so his brotherly grin hadn't died in the slightest. "Is it not usually the other way around? You always protect me, big brother."

Grimaldus laughed out loud, though it was practically a whisper in comparison to his massive brother's bellowing. He playfully poked his kin in the ribs as they trotted into a swift walk. "Oh, *I* am the big brother today? What happened to all your bluster last week?"

Tychus grumbled, mumbling while looking away as he tried really hard to pretend he wasn't disgustingly ticklish. "Was the infernal talking. Hush. You already know what we're doing?"

A playful, deep sigh left his stretching brother, who was beyond pleased to have any reason to get out of the mansion. Constant cultivation made him so *horribly* sore. "I've been stuck in the pit, only got out this morning. I've missed the entire week since our last chat, and you weren't exactly yourself."

Tychus was glad to be outside as fresher air met them. He sneezed hard, nose beet red from all of the lavender petals that had attacked it. A hidden handkerchief came to the rescue, and the big man was glad for it. His speech sounded muted with his nose so stuffed up. "Some upstart is making a mess out of the games, got into the thirties in about an hour. Likely higher now, but we should make it in time in case he cracks his way up the ten's. Nine tends to give people a run for their copper. Odd thing is that the challenger asked for both of us, at the same time."

Grimaldus nodded. "But it's *my* turn."

"No, it's not. It's *my* turn," Tychus rumbled as they both dropped into a run.

His brother wasn't having this. "No, you went last time, it's my turn!"

They bickered and snapped back and forth the entire way to the arena, arriving with a full-on slapping fight. Their banter was cut short when they heard Uferiel announce a victory not from a side arena, but from the main middle dais: the one with packed bleachers.

"Number nine goes do~o~own!"

CHAPTER FORTY

"Well, this is disappointing." Artorian heavily sighed, fingers nudging the front of his helmet as if trying to rub at his brows. It didn't quite work with armor on, so the itch remained. The man hadn't quite realized he'd said those words out loud. That was supposed to be a quiet thought, so he noticed it as the crowd around him exploded in jeers. Great.

Number nine had been something of a favorite, and what was left could only be described as an artful canvas of handprints. The jump into the top ten ranking had forced the academic to put some actual effort in, but his enemies were all one-hit wonders or one-trick ponies. Abyss, he had even *gained* a cultivation rank with these bouts. Artorian floated about the precipice of C-rank seven... though the armor was greedily drinking it all in. Perhaps he wasn't holding back as many of the functions as he should.

Artorian was relying on it a little much, but not being hurt upon impact was just... such a *massive* boon. Blades were a laugh, but that one bloke with the hammer had put an actual dent into his chest. The harm was repaired as the armor took in Essence from his Aura to mold back into shape; it was good to know it could do that, even if it was a touch costly.

He should have known better, and really should have dodged. Unfortunately, curiosity killed the c'towl. The armor needed testing, even if in hindsight the time and place was a terrible idea. Blunt damage on heavy armor? Definitely felt that one. The force had carried right through and punched him in the gut harder than dwarven fire-brandy on an empty stomach. "Let's maybe not do that again?"

This entirely new way of approaching fights had enraptured the studious Headmaster. If he'd had all affinity channels, would there have been anything he couldn't absorb away? He really wanted to know; it was nagging at him. Unfortunately, he had to put it out of mind as reality was simply not the case. He tried to break it down for himself as whoever the next opponent was made themselves ready. They all seemed to have coaches and a personal posse of supporters from this point on, so it could take a while.

Body layers were threefold. Vitals, internal, and external. Aura for a base cultivator matched those layers, nice and separated. Your average cultivator – upon grasping Aura – uses mostly the external Aura. That being the part that radiates effects outward, indiscriminately. Power and affected distance depends on invested Essence. Or, going a step further, Essence deemed 'active' if your Aura stores a whole bunch of everything like his did. Not an issue for limited-affinity cultivators with only one or two channels.

Separately, adding an effect to one's Aura in the vital or internal layer caused the effect to only be applied to that region, or those aforementioned parts of the whole. It would be entirely possible for a skilled cultivator, likely in the C-ranks to apply a different effect to each Aura layer. Boost the vitals with refined Essence, empower the internal layer, apply an auric effect on the outer layer. Certainly feasible.

Hammer-brat seemed to have had a grasp of his vital and inner Aura at C-rank two. Yet no more than that, sticking to a straight forward charge and smash strategy, pumping refined Essence to the muscle for temporary empowerment. It had obliterated the prior, tiny dais arena they'd been in. Yet when the lad had stopped concentrating, both his auric defenses went down, and he was so horribly off balance that a small tap turned him into a twisted rag.

Was it really so difficult for ordinary cultivators to keep their head in the game, focus properly, and keep their mental acuity? His students at the Skyspear could have manhandled this entire lineup so far, and it would have been called a sporting exit exam. If the cultivators he faced here were indicative of the average, even with most of them being ex-adventurers, then this was... well, he'd said it before. Disappointing. How were these people trained? *Were* they trained? They all defaulted to tactics that worked well in cramped places, such as... oooh! Dungeons?

He doubted most of these adventurers had faced people, rather than endless waves of monsters. A person was nothing like a beast in the wild, and he didn't know enough about what went on in a dungeon to even start a running commentary. "Right, I'm old in comparison to these youngsters."

Most had risen through the ranks swiftly, brazenly, drunk on their might and blind to the gaping mistakes in their actions. Artorian had spent years picking such details apart in his students. From how to breathe, how to walk, how to let a body simply be. All the way to refined self-defense specifically against other people.

His combat experience was war on the open fields. Maddening fights in blinding environments where all was foe. Falling through cave mouths to see your compatriots turned to... never mind. A spot on his forehead ached. He was sure that these boys and girls were all potent warriors in their own eyes, but they... he might as well have been the sole adult in a room of flailing toddlers.

The crowd shouted out endless demands, jeering between choking on bread and water as they watched the bloody spectacle. "Show us Breaking Mountain style!"

Artorian cocked his head. Again with this 'fighting style' nonsense? All those were people thinking their single little trick, or slightly more refined than the other movements were something special. Surely something didn't get a name each time it became slightly better than an average strike to the schnozz? No... no, he needed to remember what he was dealing with. That was *exactly* how it worked. It had been the same with the initiates in the Fringe, his first fan club. What had he told them? 'No' style? Ha! Actually... there might be something to that.

When number seven, Silvia the Slimy, came to the stage, Artorian broke from his theorizing. There were more ideas to be tested! He glanced her over. Why was she... sticky? No matter. The basics as usual. Artorian was starting to get very good at this, having remembered where to look for affinity channels, rather than trying to read it off someone's Aura. It took some doing, but that was a matter of practice. Earth and infernal? Oh. Ew. Nonono. There wasn't going to be any absorbing this Essence. Actually, did he even want to touch her? The identity of 'caustic acid' radiated from the slime she was coated with.

Oh! Finally someone with a grasp of Essence identity! Good heavens, he'd been *craving* something new. He knew it wasn't usually until someone's Mage days that identity was considered. Much like Presence, which is something not even end-level C-rankers tended to have access to, if they even knew they could. Merging your three Auras was possible, he'd learned it happened during Ascension, and was part of the basic Mage process. Body and mind somehow became one. Rather, he theorized that all the body layers at that point were made of Mana. No longer distinguished by fleshy, physical requirements, it became just 'body'. Full and as a whole. The Aura followed suit. He wanted to find out for sure one day.

He extended his Presence as normal before reconsidering. He'd already forgotten Silvia wasn't an absorb-friendly target. What had he just mentally said about keeping proper focus and acuity? Artorian, you hypocrite! He verbally sorted himself out by starting his count. "Ten seconds."

His opponent appeared to roll out a whip of sorts at the confirmation they'd started. Inspecting it, the whip seemed to be an essence-made weapon meant to apply her acid coating effect. Perhaps to latch onto an opponent at a speed one could normally not react to?

Silvia screamed out and aggressively slid forward, her movements weaving as if she was skating on ice. Except... well... slime. Her whip cracked once for effect, and her second lash forward was going to melt the armor right off this grievance. He'd killed her partner! She was going to extract the bones from his still-living body for this! Silvia discovered a moment later that such an idea was little more than a passing thought. The armored figure had caught the blazing fast snap of her whip, holding the tip between his fingers as her acid effect... faded?

"Children and their tricks..." Air and celestial Essence coated his armored hand, filled with an imbued identity to 'neutralize'. He could sense the Essence was confused. Especially the air Essence didn't easily grasp what he wanted from it, even though the celestial's base identity had no such issue.

When the acid whip was caught, and the opposing Essences interacted with their direct opposites, air understood what the point was. The will directing them wanted to completely counter an effect caused by their opposites. The Essence was almost glad to do so, and Artorian noted that it was the first time he'd gotten anything remotely close to such a visceral reaction. It felt... odd? To gain an understanding that Essence was glad to do something.

The topic of study needed to wait. Wrapping the end of the whip around his hand, he jerked on the taut weapon like it was a rope, harshly tugging Silvia in. Her slippery footing sent her flopping to the ground before being dragged towards her opponent. She wasn't going to give up just because someone had her wea-!

Ding!

Taking a metal-clad punch to the face was unpleasant. Being decked while also moving *into* the fist? Doubly so. Silvia's world went starry right after being pulled up by her own weapon like it was a spring cord. Crumbling to the ground with a bloody nose and a fogged-over mind, her rebuttal sputtered out to a snore. Artorian kept a close eye on the fallen opponent. Alright, looked like sleep Aura in close proximity worked on cultivators just fine, but their Aura defenses had to be down, or nonexistent.

He gently slid his foot under the snoozing body, and relieved her presence from the arena. "Yuck!"

Silvia was caught, dropped because she was still slimy, picked back up, then dropped again as the people who touched her suffered severe caustic burns after a few seconds of continued contact. Multiple buckets of water got splashed on her to get the goop off before she could be safely carried away.

Artorian tried to squeeze his beard, but found it inaccessible as he pondered. That slime hadn't been an auric effect? It was real and physical, but clearly some kind of Essence... construct? This was new. Actually, was it? Wasn't this roughly how he'd formed a spear when in the forest? The thing Ember had told him never to do again. Granted that was a long list, but it was on there. He considered it, and decided it was different. Artorian had ripped his Aura and... made it something else? Not the best life choice. Silvia had formed a thing using Essence.

That was... well everything was made of Essence and corruption, so that seemed... feasible? How was this something he'd never thought of? He kept a running tally of discoveries, but lost track of his thoughts as he saw two familiar faces. Older, more refined, but familiar. Nobody saw the smile under the helmet. He needed to get their attention somehow.

Artorian was pointing at them before really thinking about it. Nothing easier than a challenge! He wanted his boys in talking range as soon as possible. How was he going to manage to go unheard when they were finally up here? "Hmm. Maybe something with the membrane of my Presence?

"This requires exploring."

CHAPTER FORTY-ONE

Tychus blinked at what he was seeing; frankly, he didn't really believe it. "Brother?"

Grimaldus crossed his arms, observing the conundrum as well. "Yes, brother?"

The massive man set his firm jaw, fingers drumming on his hefty bicep as the gesture was studied from afar. "I think... I think that's a challenge."

A nodding motion came from the dark man next to him, the young necromancer in complete agreement as his robes shifted into an ebony hue. "It does appear so, brother. Is it just me, or is that generally regarded as a terrible idea?"

Tychus agreed with the wisdom that had just flowed from his family member's mouth. "Generally regarded as a terrible idea, indeed! Pointing a finger at the two top contenders, in a series of matches where the results are what we *say* they are, is commonly regarded as a 'bad move'."

Since they were being pointed out, the crowd saw them. The respective fan clubs for the top two ranked arena contestants went wild. Signs with caricatures and poorly-written banners rose up, and the shouting only got louder than the wild ruckus had already been. The brothers groaned as they were surrounded by people wanting handshakes, some to awkwardly hug them without asking, and others to scream in their faces before fainting. Popularity was... a difficult nut to crack.

Tychus didn't like it one bit, and he felt cramped as claustrophobia crept in. His voice weakened as it mumbled out the discomforted request. "Grim... please do the thing."

The necromancer flicked his hands upwards, and the bones of the dead littered beneath their feet promptly snapped upright, coated with a layer of dirt. A different sort of screaming pierced the brothers' ears, as the crowd around them now fled, rather than charge. It was preferable, and Tychus inhaled deeply as the unpleasant cramped tingling faded.

Dozens of skeletons ripped free from their flesh and earthen bonds. Dark green light connecting bones as skeletal forms assembled themselves, standing up to form a protective ring about the both of them. "Still get the creepy-crawlies, Ty?"

The mountain of a man grumbled, nodding unhappily as he wiped his own arms off. Trying to remove a feeling was difficult. "Every abyssal time, too. The way this arena is structured deserves execution. So... points for consistency, I guess."

Grimaldus had a good-natured laugh. Heavens, he was happy to be out of the pit. You just didn't meet people with the mental power to put that quality of a sentence together down in the cultivation depths. The Ziggurat region was devoid of intellectualism. At least he was back with his brother and didn't have to listen to the same droning compliments, copied and parroted by other ingrates because they liked how it sounded. Abyss, he hated that pit. No, he hated the people he was stuck with in the pit. That infernal Essence gathering hole was fine by itself, it would have been even better had he been there alone.

"So what do we do about pointy the poignant over there?"

Tychus snorted, and motioned to where seats were being cleared for them. "We don't worry about it if that shiny metal can doesn't make it to us, and spend the day fishing at the lake."

His brother made the circle of repelling skeletons trudge along, taking seats when he got to the box sections of the bleachers. "The lake would be nice; I'd like the lake. Let's not count our fish before we catch them. Say shiny over there makes it. What's the plan?"

The mountain shrugged, getting cozy in a shoddy seat that was far too small for his sizable behind. "Same as usual? I do the smashing, you do the Tychus-doesn't-get-hurt with your adaptive bone armor. It still squicks me out knowing that all the bones you use for that used to be people."

Grimaldus made one of the skeletons do a little dance, just because he could. "See that? It's the same idea, just with more bones, and in a different configuration and pattern. It's just bone, brother. I just move bone in places where you'd normally get hit, and make that take the hit instead of something squishier. Is that Silvia I see getting carted off? Her face is broken."

Tychus squinted as the cart passed them by. "Bloody nose, sure?"

His brother shook his head to the negative.

"I can tell from the bone hidden behind all that meat blocking your vision. Her skull has several fractures, and all on the front. That shiny boy hits hard. Looks like a single strike too. Good to know. I'm going to have to change the configuration to the armor I'm adapting on you. Also, hand me that carrot."

Tychus didn't follow well over half of that, but reached and took one of the vegetables from the bucket before them. Why was it never *meat?* He missed the days of dried meat. He missed a lot about the old days. "Here. What do you need a carrot for?"

Grimaldus winked at him and stood. "Hey, Six!"

Sextus Palladia stopped as he looked from left to right, searching for the origin of the call. Palladia was a man in his early forties with full gladiator armor kitted on his muscled frame. His voice was gruff, having spent too much time smoking in the pit. The reply oozed disdain when he saw who he was talking to. "What do you want, *One?*"

Palladia felt a carrot hit his helmet, only to ding off and harmlessly fall to the ground as the top spot holder sneered back at him. Tychus bent over laughing as he caught the joke. "I'm rooting for you!"

It made Grimaldus sad that nobody in the crowd had been smart enough to grasp the nuance of the joke, but felt his curiosity peak when the armored figure in the arena doubled over with laughter. The man was slapping his knee, holding his midriff with his other arm before pointing at Sextus. "Ha, *haha*! Rooting? Get it? A carrot is a root vegetable!"

The brothers from the Fringe could tell that had specifically been done to make Sextus angry, and get a rise out of the warrior that had clearly not grasped the joke. Neither did he appreciate becoming the joke. Ice popped and cracked as it solidified across his armor and features, his affinity channel of water in plain view before he ever ascended the dais.

Artorian squinted. Affinities: water and fire. So that's how he was sapping the heat from the water, and solidifying it into ice. Yet, how was he getting physical structures of it on his body? It was more of this construct stuff, and the C-rank three gladiator had him beat on the skill. That was worth a point of expense at the man's fragile pride. Really up*root*ed his confidence there!

The gladiator walked up on the dais to a still snickering man in armor. Sextus twirled his spear, and somehow it made the armored figure stop its insulting outburst. He focused on the weapon, and that was something number six could appreciate. Attention on the fight. Good. The two contenders sized each other up, and Palladia had to be honest with himself. He had no idea what he was looking at.

Armor? Yes, but it was seamless. It had no visible weaknesses, and seemed flexible in places where there should have been openings to allow for mobility. On closer deduction, those four lines weren't vision slits in the helmet. It was... fire? He could tell, but how was the person inside seeing him, or reacting, with a fully closed visor? Was there even a visor?

The visuals were streamlined, but the design served to take attention away from the more dangerous details. Such as the lack of weaknesses. An additional problem was the hum of power surrounding the shiny form in a tight field, while a much larger, significantly lighter field surrounded him and the majority of the arena. Sextus did not like these conditions.

Tink.

Tink? Palladia looked down to see a section of his ice protection had fallen from his armor, and was slowly disassembling into nothingness. There was no jettison from the fallen ice, and he couldn't draw the energy back from the ice construct. Like a piece of snow under the relentless sun, it melted and was gone. That shouldn't have happened. No ice should be falling off him at all!

Tink.

A significant sheet of plating disconnected from his left shoulder and hit the dais. The arena was coated in shattered, still skittering pieces of ice before they again dissolved into nothingness. What was going on? Nobody in the crowd, or any of the close observers called foul play. Even with the people screaming for him to attack already, cold dread crept around Sextus's hands. Attacking into the unknown was dangerous, and his defenses had been compromised by a means he was unable to see. Abyss! What in Phlegeton's name was happening?

A nosy old man was cutting Essence constructs like it was a piece of scrumptious cake is what was happening. He'd tapped at a spiky bit with some hardened light, and the ice had come right off. It had been a tiny fleck, and the warrior didn't notice. The academic had a studious expression plastered on his hidden face, refining a line of water and fire Essence into a line barely the width of a scalpel. Adding the idea of 'cut', he then angled the unseen line and passed it diagonally through the points in space where ice coated the gladiator's armor.

Seeing it hit the ground, and the cultivator appearing not to understand what was going on, he tried absorbing the piece of hard Essence and came upon some revelations. He had done this before, just not in this fashion. Taking the piece of ice-like Essence apart, it had the same base construction idea as his hardened light. Wait, it had more! This Essence construct was external Aura, energized and reshaped to hold the idea of what it was. Like a container, but with a set shape unless you let it do its own thing. It was very specific on the fire to water ratio the entire way through. That explained the ice spike!

He'd expected corruption to be at play, but no such thing was found. Breaking the construct apart, he found he merely had to bathe that area of his Presence in some unseen starlight, and lance away the preset identity. Like evaporating water, the construct reverted to pure water Essence, and he ate it up without a second thought. Excellent, the fire Essence had only been used to leech away heat before dissipating. Then he did it again with the back of a shoulder plate. Same result! Excellent! Now for something a little more... aggressive?

Sextus dropped into a low combat stance, spear at the ready for a stab while his shield angled forward, ready to take a direct hit. Straight on strikes were already known to be something his opponent excelled at; he couldn't give the man the opportunity. Sextus didn't feel so good. Was he sizzling?

Pumping some extra Essence into his Aura to make sure the ice flows kept growing, he felt it... bump into something?

Something that was tightly compressing around him, siphoning away rogue Essence that left his external Aura. The feeling was also pressing him down to the ground like a weight, and his knee thumped to the arena floor as the gladiator did his best to keep eyes on his opponent as the entirety of his ice armor not immediately touching his armor melted away.

It was akin to being held under a magnifying lens. He was burning up, and fueling more water shielding to block the strange effect didn't seem to be doing anything to stop his ice from melting. This also swallowed up buckets of his Essence stores as the crippling removal effect worked faster than he could build the ice back up. The effects were so pronounced after a few seconds that a soft vapor cloud of steam started to hang around Palladia.

Artorian was having a delightful buffet of it. Weaknesses in auric defense and holes in the ice technique let him freely coat the warrior in lancing starlight, without the light ever being noticeable. Some infernal Essence that was lanced from the tip of his spear was forced to drift away. It wasn't hard to see that it beelined for the Ziggurat as soon as it passed Artorian's membrane. The vaporized water Essence, his Presence took in with ease... at first.

Palladia was putting up a fight? Could you call it a fight when someone ladled soup into your bowl faster than you could drink it? The gladiator was fueling his effects with more Essence than Artorian could reasonably absorb. Oh, look! It made clouds! How charming!

This was certainly not how either of the contestants had expected this fight to go. Whilst he still had the strength, Sextus pushed up through the extra weight, using a burst of refined

Essence on his musculature to break free. He charged swiftly, with the practice of a seasoned warrior. His spear would pierce that annoying armor with the force of his arm alone!

He'd have done so as well, if his arm ever had the power to move the spear close enough. The very space he occupied filled with a vapor and wetness that collided and clung. Sextus, midway through his charge, felt like he'd fallen into the ocean and that he was currently trying to run through water. In his confusion, he even saw the armored figure pensively nod, hearing the mumble nobody else did. "Looks like that works too..."

The gladiatorial cultivator was stuck as still as a statue but a few feet away from his intended target. Something hard, solid, and rigid had encased his joints beneath his armor. Or on his armor? It was frustratingly difficult to tell with his Aura being repressed, and when he struggled to expand it back out, felt the solid masses of Essence that had encased and immobilized him. It was like his ice, except... not utilizing fire or water Essence. A similar kind of solid Essence construct meticulously coated him, hard enough to prevent joint movement; like being bound in a cast. Actually, that's exactly what it felt like. He was entrapped in a mold.

Artorian paced around his handiwork, getting a good look at it. "Looks like I win this one. I'll take this if you don't mind, young man. It looks awfully dangerous."

Palladia the gladiator could do nothing as his opponent relieved him of his spear. The clamps around his fingers released, and let it easily slide from his grip as he was unable to close his hand to grip it tight. Making matters worse, his Essence was still being siphoned. How was he losing essence... his *ice*! Something about his opponent allowed him to rebuke the ice!

Sextus stopped fueling his defensive ability, and Artorian stopped in his tracks.

"Oh. Oh, you figured it out? About time. Any more and you'd have been so low in the D-ranks that you'd have to concede." Sextus shifted his battle plan, dropping the entire attempt of external armor, and fueling his Essence into his body instead. The armored enemy took a cautious step back. "Ooh, I wouldn't do that if I were you..."

As if the proud and mighty Sextus would listen to a distraction attempt from an enemy! With power in his musculature, he broke free of the shackles with a mighty roar! Angling his shield forward, he took a deft step, and then felt his world go hazy. His arms and legs screamed in pain, his nerves flaring with fire. Sextus collapsed to the ground in soundless agony; unable to scream from how much everything was hurting, twitching in place.

"Tut, tut, tut." The thrumming voice sighed while shaking its head. "Lost track of how much Essence you added to your muscles, didn't you? You're about to have a few unpleasant nights of no sleep. Nothing fixes an Essence overdose, just have to wait it out. Sorry my boy, you're out..."

With a foot nudged underneath number six, Artorian soft-punted him out of the arena. Keeping the spear as a trophy, of course!

CHAPTER FORTY-TWO

Grimaldus held the second carrot firmly in hand. Not a single set of teeth marks marred the surface of the orange vegetable, as the son of the Fringe remained fully enraptured in what he was seeing. He didn't actually buy what his eyes were selling. What was this ridiculousness? No wonder this upstart had been trucking through the lineup, this was *insane*! What kind of a C-ranker *increased* in power as you fought them? He was only C-rank three, and his brother one lower. Their opponent was C-rank seven, and he'd been rank six *before* the fight had started.

"Brother, I think we may need to step in before this becomes a problem. I also think... we might not be able to win."

Tychus was rarely concerned when it came to fights, but his brother had a nose for trouble. Munching on some unknown leafy greenery, he stopped to glance over, cheeks bloated full of 'rabbit food'. Some mumbling sounds came out, but a look from his brother made him swallow his food before trying again. "Why do you say that? It's just one man, tired from repeated battle."

Grimaldus slapped his forehead, groaning at his muscle head of a family member. "Ty, have you been paying attention?"

The mountain shrugged, licking his fingers clean. "I'm better at executing the plan, not coming up with it. You can see things I don't know how to. I lift. Now what is wrong?

Grimaldus firmly nudged his face in the direction of the dais. "That man started at a C-... you still don't know the rankings, do you?"

Tychus looked away to pretend he wasn't involved, and his brother sighed, covering his face with his hand to try not to be ashamed. "He's stronger than both of us together, right now. He's about where..."

The black-robed man leaned closer, whispering so only his curious brother heard him. "He's where our *Vizier* is. We're going to get rolled!"

The mountain unpleasantly shifted in his seat, expression no longer quite as ashamed, but far more concerned. "So should we just say he won, and take him to the Vizier? That's not how we do things brother. We are from the Fringe! We are defeated only when we decide we are defeated. Give not the enemy victory when you can take it for yourself. We are merely afraid of a possibility. Now come brother, use your genius. How do we win?"

For all his bluster, Grimaldus appreciated his brother's brilliant optimism, and equally brilliant smile. Really, how did he keep his teeth so white? He rubbed his temples, racking his brain. "We can't half-abyss this. We should go in at full strength from the start, with everything stacked on and ready. Forget the rules, we have to make sure to get out of the fight alive. Power up and get in the ring. Don't let anyone else fight, or that heavy armor monster is going to plow through us without a care in the world. Any more power and even my clever plans aren't going to get us anywhere. Go, go! Make a scene! I need time."

Tychus dropped his food, and jumped over the fence keeping them boxed in the private seats. He didn't like it when even his clever brother was nervous, so he kept his voice bursting with strength. "*Five!* Hold!"

Symarael locked gazes with an equally confused Uferiel, but she stopped from finishing the sign-up process. She'd expected an interruption, but not on her turn. She pressed a hand to her cocked hip, and waited for Tychus to plod on over like a bull trotting to a fence. "Two? What is it, Tychus?"

The mountain cleared his throat and leaned over her, placing a hand on Uferliel's clipboard. "No need for that, Coordinator. She's not going next; my brother and I are. You can..."

Symarael kicked the massive man in the shin so hard that he jumped around on the other leg. "What! You will *not* do the replacing of me!"

Laughter belted from the dais as Artorian hooted, watching and listening to the display his son was going through. Ahhh... still the same old tactless boy. Still had a fleck of greenery stuck to his cheek as well, and didn't even notice it. That was certainly Tychus. The two bickered for a while, but the woman stomped off angrily after feistily slapping her hand across his cheek. Looks like he was going into battle with a handprint on his face.

Tychus, cheek burning, stepped up onto the arena. He was not expecting to be addressed, and the words unsettled him. "*Tychus.* I'm... I'm so glad to see you again. Tell your brother to come over, we have much to discuss."

The mountain didn't want to approach further. 'Again'? If this was a repeat fight, he was at a disadvantage as his particular use of the infernal was as simple as he was. Still, Grim had asked him to make a scene, so a scene he would make. "I. Am. *Tychus!*"

The crowd exploded in cheers once again. They loved seeing one of their champions galivant and pace about in a small oval, hands up to draw more of their reactions. "I am the unassailable mountain, the tower of strength, and wooer of the most wonderful women!"

People snickered. They knew that last one was a joke; particularly with the very obvious handprint on his face.

The armored figure crossed his arms and cocked his head. "Are you... sure? That doesn't sound like you."

Tychus grumbled as the retort made the crowd slather on a round of laughter. *Not* the scene he was wanting to make. He wanted to put some dents in that armor, but he knew it was a ruse. He needed to wait no further as his brother stepped onto the dais. Laughter turned back into cheering as the brothers performed their fist-bump. It was always a good show when the top favorites came to brawl! "What took you, brother?"

Grimaldus shot some side-eye at the coordinator. "Unexpected *addition* to the roster. Number three is joining in as well."

Tychus threw his head back, in pretend pain. "*What?* No. Not him. I don't *like* him!"

"Evening boys... Ready to get sweaty?" Grimaldus winced at the smell of grease and sweat. Number three was as big as Tychus, but several times as girthy, and several times as smelly.

Grim glared at the man. "Wash, you oversized boar!"

Blairon the Boar, aptly named, looked sickly from how happy he was to be there. "All three of us on the stage! Isn't that just exciting? Maybe there will be *hugs* afterwards..."

Both sons of the Fringe visibly cringed, already doing their best not to hurl at Blairon's presence. Grimaldus sternly looked the other way. "Can we not."

Uferiel threw his wooden sticks into the air and stomped off. To the abyss with the rules apparently! Artorian had a look at the additional opponent in front of him. That... he agreed with his boys. This wasn't going to be allowed. "Excuse me. Three of you? Really?"

Blairon, loving the spotlight, got loud and proud. Waddling himself forward as he addressed the crowd. "I alone am enough for you, weak man hiding in his armor! My armor is my girthy and thick *meat*! My mass cannot be-"

Shink!

"I'm sorry, my boys. I just couldn't listen to that." Grimaldus and Tychus turned their sights back to the center of the arena, where a spear had impaled the brain-space of the smelly dead man.

The smaller of the Fringe brothers cleared his throat, and nudged a toe at the fat boar. Grim wanted it removed, but didn't... really want to touch it. "No that... completely understandable. We could change rings? This one is a little tainted."

The armored form strolled over, and slid his foot under the meat-pile.

"No, it's fine... just... *nyeh*!" With a wet, meaty flop, the number three arced off the arena and laid still in the mud. Nobody wanted to move that body. It could... wait.

Artorian cleared his throat and thickened the membrane on the edge of his Presence. With that simple action, he altered the light that moved through until the outside of his Presence appeared as a dark orb, blotting out the battlefield. "Better! It's about time we got some privacy."

Tychus looked around, and backed up close against his brother as the inside of what was clearly an orb lit back up. A different kind of light, but light either way. "Brother. Tell me you have something."

Grimaldus had his hands raised, but wasn't firing the expected infernal bolts of energy. Their opponent was just... standing there. He was going to reply to Tychus, but the armored form leveled a question. "Your names. What do they mean?"

The brothers pressed side to side, and Grim changed his tactics to quickly summon the bones from outside of the arena. While they crossed the threshold into the inner workings of the light sphere easily enough, he lost his connection the moment they did. The bones sizzled and began to... melt? Finally replying to his brother, Grimaldus just gave a very weak headshake in the negative. No. He had nothing. If he started attacking, his brother would get decimated.

Biting through the realization of defeat as imagined example after imagined example led to them losing. He dropped his arm and found a thread of hope, perhaps he could just answer the question. "I am Grimaldus. Son of the Fringe, necromancer of the Ziggurat, loyal to my brother, and self-proclaimed intellectual."

With a nudge to the ribs, Tychus followed suit. Not entirely sure why Grim wasn't telling him to start throwing fists. "I... ueh... Tychus. Son of the Fringe. Apex warrior of the Ziggurat, loyal to my brother, and *actual* mountain of muscle; nothing self-proclaimed about it."

The opponent nodded. He seemed satisfied with something, though neither of the brothers could tell why. Grimaldus blinked as he watched their opponent do something truly odd. The man was... removing his helmet?

"My name... is Artorian," their enemy rumbled while a long, hefty white beard spilled free. The voice of an old man replaced the thrumming depth the armor portrayed.

"Lover of naps, a pain to the self-entitled, scholar, philosopher, ex-Elder of a tiny village." The helmet came off fully, and a massive familiar smile beamed at them. "And proud father of two very much living and healthy boys, who have grown up to become men in my absence. Hello, my sons."

He bit back his emotions as best he could, but the helmet slipped from his fingers and clattered to the ground as tears ran down his still smiling face. Eyes squinted; he extended his arms towards them. "How I have missed you both."

CHAPTER FORTY-THREE

Neither Tychus nor Grimaldus knew what to say. The words were stuck in their throats, as if they were choking on coconuts. Grimaldus felt his mind race and seize up, failing to grasp what he saw. The memories in his head screamed at him, overburdened him. In front of him was the face of a man that should have died well over a decade ago. Though his memories were hazy, the elder looked exactly as his child-mind remembered. "But you're dead?"

Tychus had no such hiccup. The moment he saw the elder's face, his face fell forward, and his fists clenched so hard that his knuckles turned white. He took a step toward the old man, and blared out a howl of twisted emotions. He was both excruciatingly happy, and profoundly sad all at the same time. Not knowing how to reconcile the two, the mountain just scooped up his elder like a child would lift their oldest teddy bear. He mashed the side of his face against Artorian, and squeezed for all he was worth as tears streamed down his face.

Artorian was spun as fast as his cultivation technique when his now largest son refused to let him go. He didn't mind for the moment, glad to squeeze the giant lug. He was certain Tychus was trying to talk to him, but the words came out as malformed bleating. When his massive son carried him over to Grimaldus to show off his find like it was an animal he caught in the wild, Grim snapped from his mental stupor.

He didn't know when he'd started crying, but only now did he feel the contortions on his face as the elder wrapped his arms around his dark cloak. "B... but how?"

Artorian sniffled, not having a sleeve to wipe his face with. "Honestly, I gave you *many* clues! Did I need to make some kind of quip about choosing the worst cup, or have you been banging your head against the same hard rock your brother looks like he's been lifting for the past decade? I even named myself *Mr. Fringe* for this stupid arena just to get your attention!"

That's not what Grimaldus had meant, but he no longer cared. His fears that this was yet another loyalty test faded. This was very much the same Elder from all those years ago; nobody else would know about that stupid cup. He had loved that dumb cup. "I just... you... you can't be here!"

He silenced himself and melted into the embrace. He just didn't know how to process this situation. Tychus couldn't bear to be left out, so he scooped them both up in a bear hug. Artorian's voice cracked, but he finally got two proper words out. "Family, get!"

The trio needed a minute. Surprise reunions were taxing, and heavy on mental energy costs. When Tychus finally put them back down, their Elder didn't waste a second filling them in on crucial details. "I've missed my boys. You're the last two I've come to fetch. I'm so, *so* sorry it took me so long to get to you."

Grimaldus wiped his face clean with his sleeve, but let his Elder borrow it for the same purpose as he immediately slid in with the questions. "Last two? So when we lost contact with Astrea, it was...?"

Artorian fiercely nodded. "I've got her, she's safely in one of the regions I've made secure. You wouldn't believe the firepower that's defending that place. Wuxius and Lunella are home in the Fringe, rebuilding."

Tychus screeched in delight, a massive smile broadly plastered on his face. The mountain used Grim's robe to wipe his face, though his brother was far more grumbly and reluctant about it. "They're fine! I thought it was down to just us!"

Their Elder squeezed them both by the wrists. "Safe and accounted for. I did *promise*, after all."

Artorian was shoulder nudged by his non-humongous son. He was elated about the harmless little punch, glad to see that tiny touch still lived. Grimaldus straightened himself, already thinking about the problems that were going to come next. The fight still needed a winner, and he was being tracked. "I'd love to get out of the Ziggurat region, and especially the Mistress's grasp, but these make that difficult."

The necromancer extended his left arm, a bone bracelet sliding down to his wrist where it stopped and remained in place. A tiny opal connected the molded carbon together. He was about to explain, but the concerned and calculating expression on his Elder's face told him that he didn't need to do so. He filled in answers to questions he thought someone would ask if they were to see these for the first time.

"Can't crush it. Not for lack of trying, but it marks you for removal. There's always someone stronger, so crushing your own bracelet just turns everyone against you. It tracks my position so long as the person it is keyed to has... I'm not sure about that part, but I'd bet my favorite humerus that it would end if the person it is keyed to died. Mine is keyed to The Mistress, Ty's is keyed to the Vizier. We can't leave the Z region without them knowing, and while you seem to be on par with our Vizier, the Mistress is... something else entirely."

His son was quick on the uptake, but still Artorian ruminated. The new information was added, and he could finally squeeze a hand down his beard to think it over. After two hours of repetitive one-on-one fights, he was glad for the small, soothing comfort. "Ah, yes, my son. She's a Mage bound to a

Law that has something to do with flesh-sculpting, I'm aware of the problem. Tell me more about this Vizier, is he a good person?"

Grimaldus froze, having just heard terms he'd never encountered before dropped completely nonchalantly on a problem he'd been struggling with for years. "She's a what? Never mind. I'll figure it out. No, he is not. The Vizier is an absolute scumbag and entirely responsible for dragging Astrea, Tychus, and me all the way over here from the Fringe. There used to be two advisors, but it's believed one is dead already. So the Vizier now oversees operations in the room at the top of the Ziggurat. On that note, please tell me this bubble we're in is soundproof?"

The wily academic winked, and shoved a thumb over his shoulder. "Can you hear the crowd? Because they can't hear or see you. Thought that was fairly clear with the calm spot of space we're in. Upholding the compound effects are more costly than I'd like. So let's not dally. I can't knock the Mage down a peg, but this Vizier fellow is free game. I'm feeling warmed up and vengeful. Let's put a plan together."

***

Uferiel returned with a stiff upper lip and a heart full of rage. A small horde of raiders were at his back and disposal. *Nobody* breaks arena rules. He arrived at the main dais only to see a large dark orb taking up a good chunk of it. Many people were on the arena, poking and prodding at the semisolid... thing. This was all sorts of not allowed! "What happened here?"

The stylish coordinator stomped up the steps with guards in tow, and people who knew they weren't supposed to be there quickly made themselves scarce. Uferiel wasn't interested in appearing any weaker than he already did, and dropped a hand towards the runners. Several raiders took off after the fleeing rule breakers. They'd be caught, and they'd be publicly punished. Keeping order was paramount. He leveled his gloved digit at another coordinator that had aided him earlier. "You! Answer my question."

The aide jogged towards the head coordinator. Something was in his hand, and Uferiel recognized it as half of a femur. The middle of it was goopy, melting, and... unpleasant. He didn't want to touch it as the aide launched into a hasty explanation.

"My lord, after your leave, number three was skewered through the head by a spear. His body is... over there. We haven't touched it. The top two fighters were then swallowed by the shadowy, swirling orb. Skeletons ran into it at a certain point, but we know they didn't get very far. This is what we've recovered."

Uferiel just waved off the offer of personally inspecting the half-molten bone. He got the gist. "Continue."

The bone was haphazardly tossed away. "Since we saw what happened to the bone, we haven't wanted to try very hard in breaching that swirling dark mass. The Didact and the Mountain are both inside, along with Mr. Fringe. We're half guessing the thing will eventually go away, and we're just waiting for that to happen."

Uferiel waited a moment. Things like that tended to be said with a coinciding event occurring. The universe was jinxed like that. The aide looked over his shoulder, not certain what his superior was looking for, because nothing happened. The stylish man sighed, rubbed at his lips, and spoke.

He didn't get a word out before the ball dropped and the orb whisked away. Fans cheered and fights broke out in the stands. Uferiel pushed the aide out of the way to get a look. He saw the Mountain sitting on his butt, the Didact standing tall, and Mr. Fringe lying on the ground in the full armor he remembered seeing last.

Grimaldus punched his fist into the sky. "Victory for the Ziggurat!"

Tychus picked up the seemingly fallen Mr. Fringe, hoisting him over the shoulder as the raiders Uferiel brought stopped onlookers from storming the stage. Tychus was glad for it. No more surprise hugging... especially when Grim's protective skeleton circle wasn't available. He grumbled under his breath to his brother, raring to go. "Ready."

Grimaldus threw his dark cloak across himself with a dramatic flaunt, flouncing out of there with effortful self-important superiority. The coordinator hustled to keep pace next to them as they waltzed past him without a second thought. Incomprehensible happy noises surrounded them, and Ufieriel gladly held his tongue until they were ascending the Ziggurat steps. "My Lords, I can deduce that you were victorious. Will the contestant be... returning?"

Grimaldus shot the man some side-eye. "We're taking him to the Grand Vizier for evaluation. We will not make decisions that do not belong to us, coordinator. Would you like to come with us for the audience?"

Uferiel turned on a heel and descended the steps without a second thought. "A lovely day to you, my lords!"

Artorian mumbled softly once the man was out of earshot. "About time."

Tychus hushed back, groaning unpleasantly at his brother. "This is a terrible plan. We should try something else."

"Brother, relax." Grimaldus nudged the large bruiser. "It's a good plan, just because you didn't get to trade fists with our Elder doesn't mean I can't tell he's on par with the Vizier. Stick to the plan. You just keep the door sealed with all you've got; I'll keep the help away from the commotion. Remember that you need to play stupid if anyone comes asking. Tell them the Vizier told you to do it."

The mountain huffed. "Only matters if the Vizier dies..."

His elder giggled lightly, "My boy, you think I won't win?"

Tychus had momentarily forgotten he was carrying the person in question, and looked away. "No, I mean... sorry, Elder. I've gotten floored by that oversized snake rather often. All I'm good at is packing a lot of power into my fists. I can dish out, but I'm surprisingly brittle and cannot take. The infernal Essence we can use is strange, I don't understand it well. That's more Grim's thing. Just don't get hit by the venom he can spit. Stuff's nasty, eats right through stone."

The Mountain staggered as his ear got flicked by shaped Essence. "I'm not the Elder of the Fringe anymore. Lunella has the robes now. Call me grandfather, but you're welcome to drop the grand. Or, Artorian as I've already stated. We're going to get everyone together one way or another... even if I don't agree that we should wait for future plans to develop."

Grimaldus shook his head, but his features bled into a massive smile. The son of the Fringe liked the idea of having a dad again. He said nothing about Ty's trembling lower lip as the sniffling giant tried to keep quiet. "I would go insane without Tychus to keep me company. I too want to leave, but it would be folly so long as we're being tracked. I will try and usurp the Vizier after his death, and attempt to veer problems away from certain places. If I can sneak information to Skyspear, I will. Don't blast the person in lapis robes, I think I know how to get my hands on some. I have many questions... father. Yet, it can wait until we are secure, and not tiptoeing around a noose."

Artorian beamed proudly under his helm. Yes. Excellent... his boys were still his boys. Though, he worried about leaving them here longer. The knowledge he'd come get them if they couldn't get themselves out of this was crucial, so he'd just have to trust his lads to hold down the fort. Darn Mages! They complicated life for the little guy. How dare.

"I'll be more than glad to engage in lengthy conversations of philosophy and wit, when we're all settled. Just secure me a place to confine the Vizier, and kill as many lights and torches as you can on the way. There are many people on my list. I so look forward to crossing this new one off."

Tychus just smirked. He also enjoyed the idea of that smug snake getting its fangs cracked. "My fist-sense is tingling."

His brother laughed, relishing in the freedom to do so as they ascended the Ziggurat's stairs without any people around to stifle them. He exhaled, and a light lime-green light flickered in the back of his throat. "I so look forward to that monster being crossed off as well..."

CHAPTER FORTY-FOUR

Deep within the Ziggurat, Amon slithered back and forth in his private chambers. Something was wrong. He'd temporarily lost track of where the mountain had been, only for him to reappear at the spot he'd vanished. The tracking sense now told him that particular servant was almost to his door, but the event unsettled him still. He'd never lost track of a servant before, no opal bone bracelet just blipped in its function and stopped working for a while.

He'd question the Emerald Eyes soon. A different nearby servant bowed, vermillion scales coating patches of her upper arms. "The mountain requests audience, my Vizier. He says your will has been done, and the upstart is being delivered. The mountain says he is worthy, and had his catch not been knocked out, was already willing to join your fold."

Amon hissed in delight, the pressure relieving as stress rolled off his lengthy tail. Yes. Of course. There was no reason for concern. Of course it was another victory just waiting to come to him. The curse of the Emerald Eyes was lifted after the death of the swan princess. Everything had gone smoothly since, though he vividly recalled the peculiar way things had always seemed to go unexpectedly awry. A concern of the past!

"I grant this audience..." Bronze doors parted to reveal Tychus, prize draped over his shoulder. The Vizier saw the mountain clasp wrists with his brother and share a nod before the two parted ways.

"My Vizier, I have brought the upstart, as you desired."

A wrist motion directed the mountain to place his winnings down next to a pillar, and Tychus moved to do so as Amon finger-steepled his usual pyramid. He was delighted! Such an interesting specimen. What flawless, smooth armor! It spoke to his aesthetic, and his eyes flicked across the slumped man's features. Oh, he couldn't wait to begin interrogations!

"Leave us; you have done well." Tychus bowed, and motioned for the aides in the room to come with him. Amon didn't stop the request; the mountain had successfully guessed that he wanted prized alone time. In fact, it pleased him greatly! Even the lime-green Favor in the room slid from its seat and noncommittally bounced out of his chambers! He *so* needed time away from those bothersome moths. Hearing the metal clang as the door closed, the massive serpent slithered close, coming face to face with the slumped helmet.

"So what have we here...? Greetings, little specimen. *Gack!*" Amon choked as the suit of armor snapped its grip upwards, clamping thoroughly on the front of his throat where part of his airway forcibly collapsed shut. The silver lines mistaken as eye-holes flared bright red, and the helmet tilted up slowly to regard a surprised Vizier.

"Hello."

The Vizier's eyes opened wide, vertical eye-slits focusing as infernal Essence coursed between his fingers. His steeple broke as he stirred from the moment of surprise, preparing to bathe the entire area before him in deadly swaths of disintegrating energy. He was interrupted as the hand clamping his throat shut pulled him closer with enough force to crack-slam his face against the pillar.

Artorian was up with the swift whistle of wind, twisting out of the way as he connected pillar to face while setting his feet into a stable stance. He was already launching forward to plant a second Essence powered fist into the side of Amon's face as the cloud of caustic energy sputtered from the cobra's digits. The

Vizier snarled in a seething hiss, the blow to his face stifling his ability to see from his right side.

The lights in Amon's chambers extinguished as he slithered back, and only his own glowing eyes, and only the four red eye-lines remained visible in the room a moment later before they too vanished. Amon felt alone in the chamber of darkness. What was ordinarily a comfort was now a confusing, enraging, insufferable insult. Luckily, he did not rely on his eyes to see. Forked tongue flicking from his muzzle, he tasted the air and... tasted his enemy immediately. Everywhere.

How could someone be everywhere? He, Grand Vizier Amon, was the one whose Presence should be everywhere! Covering the world in his magnanimous might!

Artorian silently stepped around behind another pillar. Sound absorbed by his extended Presence as he built up power to begin an entire circus of effects. It had taxed him when he'd fought Cataphron that first time. This time, the burden of multiple effects would not be so taxing. Throwing his voice, he made the sound appear behind the Vizier's head. "Your people came to the Fringe."

Amon twisted into a coil, surrounding himself with a defensive cloud as a disintegrating infernal effect coated the massive serpent as if it were an extra layer of skin. Even in the pitch-black dark, his energy swirled about. Creating a visible outline as a powerful tail slam brutalized his own throne. Flattening and destroying the entire area in a swath behind him as the remains disintegrated while latent effects dissolved materials away.

Four silver lines appeared to his left. Sound erupted in a controlled, cold rage. "They destroyed my village. Scattered my family."

The pillar exploded into rubble as Amon's tail once again uncoiled with force and incredible mass. Forcing a croaking rumble to moan out from the rest of the structure. It was a terrible idea to destroy valuable support struts, but the Vizier was too engrossed in thinking about how to silence this... unexpected Emerald Eye development. He called for his aides. "Guards!"

No response came, and the bronze door remained closed. He hissed in anger, flooding the entire space of his private chambers with the caustic disintegrating foil. If he could not locate his opponent, he would make it so he did not have to. The voice was heard again, this time directly above him. He knew better than to fall for a ruse a third time.

"I was content. I was going to *pass*. Then. This."

Artorian's foot coated in Essence identity countering the disintegrating flood. He had faced worse, and he had faced better. Amon's face was crushed into the floor as his assailant plowed into his skull from above. Acidic blood sputtered from the cobra's nose, mouth, and eyes as the crunching impact splattered him on the ground.

Artorian felt his foot thunk against bone, signaling his enemy wasn't going to compress any further, and made himself scarce from the location before spikes of burning, venomous darkness splintered into the space he had occupied a second ago. It grew from Amon's head like a fire, wildly sprouting with a crackle of thunderous infernal energy.

The Vizier howled in pain, swiping wildly with his tail. He couldn't afford to keep taking damage like this. He exhaled his last breath, and a lime-green brightness built in the back of his throat, taking over the light behind his vertically slit eyes.

Artorian knew something was wrong. He felt it as his Presence... tingled unpleasantly. A higher category of power was intermingling itself into the Vizier. Mana...? Or not quite? He couldn't take the risk to have his Presence fielded across anything Mana related. A drop of it would splinter his every trick into tiny smithereens. Tutting, he pulled it all back to his form, slipping his back against an unbroken pillar as his advantage was removed.

Bathed in lime colorations, the green thrummed until it matched the beat and consistent tremble of a heartbeat. Amon's voice altered from slithered difficulty, to an undead rumble as the human aspect of his voice easily returned. He was no longer using a voice box of flesh to speak, after all. "Filthy upstart, I shall feed you to the flame of the moths. Your feeble attempts at assassination are void. I know not how you tricked my servants, but I care not. You shall not exit my chambers alive."

Artorian considered a cute retort, but thought better of it. He should start keeping a running tally of the amount of death threats and wondering if he was going to die. It was a sizable number by now. Just for fun? There would be no further talk with whatever the flesh-creature had turned into.

Sneaking a peek, a gargantuan skeletal cobra covered in crystal goop and a coral coating had replaced what had originally been a decently pretty snake. So much for blunt impact... that goop layer definitely looked like it would absorb kinetic energy.

His plan to stay in the enclosed room... alright. Bad plan. Backfired quite a bit. He should leave. Artorian wasn't going to be able to distract the thing, he couldn't get a grasp of how it sensed the world. He'd also used the element of surprise... so... run for it!

Without another thought, he bolted quick as the wind to the bronze door, but failed to reach it as a batting tail caught him right in the chest and sent him barreling back in the opposite direction. Artorian crashed hard into the now crumbly stone wall. He cried out in anguish, armor cracking and tearing from the raw strength of the blow. "Oof!"

It hurt more than an 'oof' could convey, but that's what he got before cracking with a clang against the ground. He did not roll out of the way in time for a follow up tail strike to repeatedly bash him down into the metaphorical dirt. Artorian learned what a drum felt like, funneling Essence into his armor to repair it as a proficient tail kept dribbling him. Blunt bouncing damage hurt, and the massive snake was not letting up. His vision fizzled out hard as one of the slams put a chink into a Rune that helped make the visual effect.

Artorian's world went dark, feeling only the pain of being ragdolled as he was thunked through the Vizier's chamber like a rubber ball being struck every second and a half by a gargantuan tail that didn't have the slightest problem keeping up with the rapid projectile. His Presence was neutralizing the disintegration effect, but that was a minor boon.

Faintly, he could hear amused undead laughter from the massive creature. Shielding himself with Essence and tucking in arms, he raced for ideas. He couldn't risk extending his Presence, the armor was toast, and he couldn't remove it because if even one of those slams would do to his bones what it had done to that support pillar. He was being batted around and... wait, *bat?* Echolocation!

Air Essence activated as the pounded cultivator shifted to external Aura usage, and hummed. His armor turned it into a thrum, but the air Essence fueled waves bounced across the room and came back to him faster than the massive snake was batting him around. While details were rough, the layout of the room appeared in his mind. Like a fading blueprint that was constantly updated each time a sound wave returned to him. To be frank, it was pretty fantastic.

A loud lurching metal groan of chestplate bending and twisting asunder made Amon cackle. Catharsis! He'd never felt the need to pull on the borrowed Favor power, because it was fleeting. He'd also not known it would turn him into an undead crystal cobra. His Queen would be furious with him for wasting all her hard years of work if this was permanent. He'd cross that bridge when it was time, for now he had a bug to crush. The sound the bug made went ignored, until a slicing air blade crackling with hard light forced him to swivel his head out of the way. Abyss!

Amon missed the next strike, and Artorian landed hard on a shoulder. It popped out of its socket with an unpleasant snap, but the old man was on his feet and already darting to the bronze door. He didn't have earth Essence, nor the means to affect metal. He also knew Tychus was helping to keep it shut. How could he force Tychus to let go, and get rid of the door? A thought struck him. A simple, repeated thought that must have been a universal truth. He didn't know how he'd never considered the option before, but it rang loud and true. When in doubt...

Fireball.

Chapter Forty-Five

Why use one fireball, when you could use two? Around his good hand, Artorian charged his starlight Essence. Unlike the normal identities to 'soothe' or 'lance', he tapped into a third one. Equally as natural. Equally as common. He spoke the words, not realizing he did so with as much venom as Amon was filled with.

"*Burn.*"

Spheres of power surrounded Artorian's hand. As fire, it burned a hot white phosphorous bright. He'd have been concerned about being permanently blinded by being so close to his own effect. So harsh was the brightness that if it hadn't been for his current blindness, he'd have used just fire. He didn't have the time to fine tune the light away to maximize the heat effect, and hurled one orb back at the undead snake, who sizzled from sheer proximity to the starlight effect while the other flung towards the gateway.

Would his orb be hot enough to get through a thick bronze door? He didn't know, and was unable to see the craft turn red, then orange, then white as the orb stuck to it like a sticky wet grape. Screams made it through from the other end. Well... it was successful in forcing Ty to let go, but based on his echolocation returns, a door remained. Abyss!

Glancing in the other direction, the Vizier had dodged the 'fireball' and was charging in his direction with a swift lunge. The light from the burning ball sticking to the far wall was suffering to all of Amon's existence. His body burned, his mind burned. He shrieked in maddened outcry as he shot forward, completely in the dark on why his world was made of agony.

Jumping out of the way, sadly not entirely in time, Artorian lost feeling in the same arm he'd fallen on earlier as the burning, disintegration effect coated mass slammed into his side and crashed into the space that used to contain the bronze door. Used to, as the molten slag now coated the undead monstrosity, adding a third kind of burn to the Vizier. Ha! Artorian winced, surprisingly winded by that last blow. He staggered his functional shoulder against a pillar and pulled his Aura in, covering himself in starlight Essence. Shifting to Presence, he coated just him and his gear as the echolocation information dimmed away. How was he doing?

C-rank four. Eesh, costly. He let much of his Essence flood free, feeding the self-repairing and form shaping Runes on the armor that drank it in. His protections were trashed by being pinballed across the room. Countless imprints now littered the space in his embarrassing impact positions. He chanced a breather, listening to the massive snake deal with his burning orb in the gateway.

Artorian had a moment to decide how much he was going to invest in repairing his armor. The analysis was swift: cost was irrelevant. He was dead without the hardened exterior shell. He pulled a mental lever, and let the Iridium plate have everything it wanted. His cultivation lurched, and Artorian dropped to a knee as a full three and a half cultivation ranks were ripped straight out of his Aura. The only plus was that his shoulder popped back into place from raw Essence expenditure. His fingers tingled before regaining feeling and functionality, nerves and muscle mending from the soothing starlight healing surging through his frame.

He squeezed his grip open and closed, jumping away from a thrashing strike just as he heard it coming. Artorian was too slow, and groaned as he was blown back to a mere three feet away from his still burning starlight-ball embedded in the back wall.

Oh, that had hurt! It hurt bad. His Presence was mending him, and the armor was finally reconfiguring itself into a stable protective form as he peeled himself free from the rock. Falling seven feet was no fun, but with the armor molding and forming around him, he hadn't the use of his legs to catch himself. Complaining on the ground, he remembered he could use air to soften his fall. A little too late with his face already in the crumbled gravel.

He pushed himself to his feet, and rolled his working shoulders. "Over here, you dried up carcass. I have a gift for all the misery and stress you've caused me over all these many years."

Glancing at his starlight sphere, he considered pulling it from the wall. But no. No, there was wisdom that needed tending to and just as before, the truth was clear. If in doubt, use more fireballs.

A very much on fire Amon raged and slithered towards the outline of the heat form he could see. Being undead gave an entirely different perspective to the world. He saw that which was alive, and it didn't matter if a little bit of rock got in the way. A soft heartbeat was as loud, and as irritating, as the steady thudding of war drums. Other heat signatures in the area he noticed as well, but the balls of burning light were tearing at... everything. They didn't just lance his senses, but attacked his mind, his body, his Aura, his power. It burned him at a depth he could not perceive.

Amon could not have known that starlight was a particularly potent antithesis against undead. He could not have known that the borrowing of Favor's power siphoned away his Aura to dump all the force fully into keeping up his empowered, far superior undead body. Several components of him dropped radically in defense, because the particular threat he faced was simply not something that otherwise existed.

More prominent threats he became immune to, yet he did not face melee nor weapons. Neither arrows nor spears mundane struck him, nor techniques not steeped in celestial. Facing him was a problem that functioned with celestial, but took it to a compounded category. He was fueled with maddened rage, and did not know why as memories burned away. A more serpentine, base level instinctual mind replaced him.

Artorian stood, calming himself as he focused not on the charging momentum of death, but on the numerous circling pea sized orbs that hovered around him in a gyroscopic formation. He inhaled and took a wide horse stance, spreading his arms out. Exhaling, he circled his arms. The orbs followed suit before they erupted into the size of apples, then melons. The orbs spun faster and faster, and Artorian heard a *fizz* as his sight partially restored when the vision Runes mended.

Not that it did much. The blinding brightness directly around him caused the view to melt into a crackly, uncertain, shifting screen of frazzled and fuzzy static. The Runes couldn't process or render a view where so much energy was interfering. Only hazy bits and pieces made it through in a muddled greyscale.

The first sight that properly processed made him tense in fear. More in panic than through actual planning, he thrust his hands forward in a *gnnn* of heart-gripping fear, not having known before just how close his opponent had been. The gaping, hungry, venomous fang-filled maw of the biggest crystal cobra he'd ever seen lunged at him, only to take a chest full of sequentially launched orbs that tore holes right through the undead's weakened defenses.

As with the others, the solar orbs stuck to the far wall, smoldering the surroundings as their light lanced and scalded layer after layer from the Vizier's mutated body. For a moment, Artorian believed victory was in his grasp. He lost that feeling as the gaping maw snapped shut around his being. Even if the head of the cobra had been ripped and rent from the rest of its body, it wasn't neutralized. Important life lesson: even a beheaded serpent head could still bite.

The scream that erupted from Artorian matched the shrill sound of venomed fangs piercing through iridium armor. The massive, curved bones stabbed deep into his being, and the weight of the skull alone pinned him to the ground.

The Vizier's borrowed undead light winked out. The lime-green light vanished from existence in the span of a single breath. Across the area of the Ziggurat, bone bracelets crumbled as the opal keeping them together fractured and pulverized from feedback shock. Tychus too watched his restraint dangle, tumbling from his wrist before becoming bone dust on the floor. He grit his teeth when it happened, infernal Essence still restoring the damage done to his hands from sudden door burns.

Elation replaced pain. He was free!

Bursting from his hiding place, he ran as fast as he could to the Vizier's chambers. Acrobatics snuck him through the wrought and wrecked hallway, and some blinding lights inside of the chamber were winking out one at a time. When he shoulder-checked through the rocks to form a new passageway, the dying light of the last orb was swiftly weakening. It was enough for him to see the slumped figure of his grandfather, pierced through by both of the gargantuan serpent's envenomed fangs.

"Elder!"

Artorian drew a labored breath. His Presence remained pulled around his form, doing what he could to prevent the crystal venom from getting into his vitals. Even with intricate knowledge of the venom, the quantity of it that he was fighting off was going to result in a loss. He didn't heal as fast as he needed to during purging. This was accounted for by the fact that he still had two very sizable fangs piercing him, and getting those out needed to be a slow and carefully monitored process. Just tugging them out would kill him. He'd in no way heal the gaping damage left behind with the pitiful Essence he had left.

Where was he? D-something? D-rank five. Ew. *Here comes another few years of recovery.* He pushed weakly against the snout. It didn't budge. Crackers and toast! Faltering and about to lose hope, he heard the voice of his son. *Cough*. "Ty... Tychus! Break the fangs!"

The Mountain was at Artorian's side with the speed of darkness. The environment reacted to his heavy expenditure of Essence and pushed him along as light faded. With a glance, he could discern the situation was dire. Clear directions helped significantly, and with a roar he smashed through the brittle, greying fangs using a hammerfist. Both loudly shattered. Without that support, the entire head fell sideways. Gently flaking away in the remains of the dying starlight.

Artorian didn't know how many more words he was going to get out. It didn't feel like either of the stabbers had gone through his lungs, but it hurt regardless. "Ed... edge of the refugee camp. Dwarven caravan. Two axes behind a stein of ale as sigil. Hu... hurry please."

Tychus was a doer, not a thinker. Scooping his grandfather up, he took in the need with the same direction and haste as he did when Grim laid out a plan. There didn't need to be questions. Only action. Like a hurled projectile, Tychus shoulder bashed his way out of the Ziggurat as an unstoppable obsidian electricity coated freight train. His footfalls thundered with each impact, and the approach of his charge was noticed by all.

People who didn't literally jump or throw themselves out of the way in time were bowled over and used as flooring. Palisades exploded into splinters when the massive man barreled through, Artorian kept tight and safe within his arms. Tychus could feel blood that wasn't his seep from between his fingers, and his grandfather hadn't spoken a word since going limp in his grasp. That venom was doing its work.

No thinking. No *thinking*! Thinking led to second guessing. Assumptions. Worries. There was no time for those. There was only time for the one thing he excelled at: charging in a straight line.

CHAPTER FORTY-SIX

Don Modsognir squeezed the bridge of his nose. Several more of his clan stood in a loose circle with him, while a very confused Dimi held a dapper gnome in an upturned hand. This was a topic that... honestly, it would help if they had a philosopher present. What this intelligent Gnome was telling them was difficult to understand, and he for one didn't have enough firebrandy in his caravan for this kind of talk.

He'd been searching for excuses that would let them end the conversation, and at first he'd been delighted when thundering steps seemed to beeline towards his caravan. The joy had dropped like a rock in his stomach. He'd mistaken the massive man coming their way for Dimi from sheer size, but the Iridium cradled in his arms stood out. The slumped figure in the arms of that massive man was enough for him to make snap decisions.

"*Dimi!* Our human is comin' in hot. Intercept and poultice! The rest of you lot, Caravan in motion! Destination Morovia." Don moved to the front of the group and got everything moving. The Gnome stared for a moment, then hopped away upon seeing the commotion. His time would come.

Dimi snatched a major health potion from his belt and hustled in the direction of the incoming... he didn't know what that was, but he didn't want to be in the way of it. He'd never seen a man that was him-sized. No wonder people thought he was a fright when he bolted towards them. Dimi held up the reflective glass of the potion, and the approaching darkness comet must have noticed because the charger slowed down.

Half out of breath and heaving from a run that he hadn't stopped for far longer than was healthy, Tychus coughed out a single word as his heart pounded in his chest. "Help!"

He could recognize a potion when he saw one, and the massive Dwarf had strode straight toward him from the very caravan his Elder had described. Ty's arms felt like hewn stone, and his legs were slabs of granite. Stopping made the strain and expenditure catch up with him, and the rest of his words didn't make it out at all.

Dimi twisted off Artorian's helmet with surprising ease, and dunked the lip of the potion over into the drooling mouth after tugging the cork out with his teeth. "Hold his head up higher! Don't let him choke on the preparation dose."

Tychus was still in doing-what-he-was-told mode, and didn't think twice before following orders. Neither man said anything about the other. It didn't matter that a giant half-dwarf was handling a variety of poultices with the practiced ease of a juggler, or that an equally massive man had thick black veins coursing under his muscle while infernal Essence still crackled across patches of his ashen skin. The focus of both was on triage, and Tychus had automatically defaulted to the support role. The adopted son of the Fringe and the adopted son of Modsognir spoke without words.

The right combination of healing, cleansing, and purification potions went a long way to stabilizing their joint charge. Artorian woke and drew a breath, eyelids flickering a moment. Hazily, he saw his son. The edges of his lips curled up into a smile, and his metal hand laid upon the massive knuckles of his boy. "You... did good. My son. Protect... your brother."

Tychus set his jaw, and handed his grandfather over into Dimi's experienced arms. They didn't know it, but the sudden loss of the Vizier was causing a commotion behind them as the hierarchy collapsed. His Elder was right. He needed to get to his brother, so he let his grandfather go off with the caravan that his old man trusted to get to safety.

His reply didn't come in time to be heard; Artorian was out cold again. "I... I will... father."

Dimi didn't believe his ears, but didn't have the luxury to question the statement. He connected his gaze with the frowning, massive, clenched-jaw man. "We'll get him back to his usual peppy state. He'll be back for ya, I'm sure of it. Old codger doesn't let nuthin' go."

Inhaling sharply, Tychus squeezed his hands into steadied fists. He gave the dwarven healer a stern nod before turning to backhand a snooping thief. One of many interested in the goods of a well-stocked poultice-master. The son of the Fringe understood what he needed to do, and accepted the meaning the dwarf was trying to relay. "Go."

Dimi hurried back to an already leaving caravan as the mountain turned to handle... local discord. Jumping into the back of the last cart, Artorian was laid on the thick blanket hiding the treasure trove of coin. Those broken off fangs didn't look pleasant. Dimi saw to step two of what looked like long days of considerable intensive care. Cursed *pyrite*! It hadn't even been the entire planned day and they were back on the move already.

Between getting the armor off and finding additional secondary wounds that needed tending, Dimi offhandedly watched as the region they left devolved into all-out civil war. Uncivil war? Yeesh. A wet cough brought his attention back to where it was needed. Fixing this... was going to take a while.

EPILOGUE

Artorian opened his eyes to a lovely sky. His first, properly lucid breath was pleasant and light, filled with nostalgia as the scent of overgrown bluegrass gently brushed over his senses. Was he five years old again? How long had it been since he'd lain in the endless wild fields?

He knew better than to sit up, and instead performed a self-checkup. Oh. *Oh my*. That didn't look great. His Presence still wrapped around him nice and tight, but the energy in it had significantly drained to keep him afloat. A worthwhile trade. The Essence he could get back. The life, he could not. So what's the damage?

The stab wounds in his lower abdomen had healed and closed, but not exactly properly. One of his kidneys was just gone, with matching damage around the other wound. He didn't find any remaining crystal venom, and that was a good thing. While this damage was going to dampen his already questionable physical fighting abilities, an injury like this would have permanently crippled an internal cultivator.

Artorian knew he wasn't getting up for at least a few weeks as his vitals healed, and his cultivation core mended some minor issues with refined Essence before spinning up into gear. Good news: he lived. Both his boys lived, and knew he was coming back. Astrea was safe in Skyspear. Lunella and Wux were safe in the Fringe.

His exhale relieved metaphysical weight from his shoulders as he tore a mental checklist up into ribbons. Every item was checked, and it was no longer needed. Now came phase two of the master plan. Gathering enough power to gather them all, and bundling them in a safe, single location.

A high-pitched voice he'd never heard before piped up behind him. "Ah, you're awake... excellent!"

Artorian raised a single eyebrow, tilting his head back as he pulled himself mostly out from his Center. "That voice does not sound familiar to me. Hello there, have we met before?"

The sound of minute movements let it be known that the creature moving wasn't very sizable. To Artorian's confusion, a spiffily dressed gnome walked into view and stood at his hip with patient poise. A leafy green vest smoothly fit over a tunic and breeches; a diminutive matching pointed cap nestled on his head while lensed clockworked glasses whirred lightly as he changed the focus on them.

"A delight to make your acquaintance, good human. My name is Deverash Editor Neverdash the Dashingly Dapper! Please feel free to call me Dev, or Dev Editor if you feel the need to be formal."

Artorian moved a finger forward, meaning to poke the gnome in the belly just to check if he was hallucinating. The gnome, however, took it as a cordial greeting and grasped the outstretched finger with both hands before giving it a shake!

"Well met! I've so been looking forward to conversing with you. I've been told you're a more cerebral conversation partner that can appreciate a proper academic argument."

The old man cleared his throat, and pulled his finger back. He found some nearby water, and had himself a drink before answering. "Ah, well. I'd say I'm decent at some verbal back and forth. My name is Artorian, current Headmaster of Skyspear Academy. Though, I expect that to change when the caravan gets back there. My injuries don't lend themselves to being able to teach adequately."

The small gnome held up a hand to indicate a request for a pause. Artorian broke off from what may have devolved into a lengthy blabbering session. It wasn't every day you spoke to a gnome. Speaking of, he'd never known any mention of gnomes to exist outside of references that some of their leftover technology had been found. Deverash piled up some cloth and climbed it like a hill before seating himself.

"Delightful! I'll fetch the poultice master shortly, though from what I can see, you're stable. You've been out for weeks, and if that high tier core of yours hadn't been passively turning, you wouldn't have made it. We... err... *did* have to make some unpleasant decisions on your behalf. I apologize for that, but it was necessary for your survival."

Artorian deeply frowned. "What kinds of decisions?"

Deverash pressed his fingers to his mouth a moment, goggles scanning the old man over. "You've partially descended into your cultivation pool at the moment, I believe? Have another look, I'm certain it's very apparent what I had to break. Now, I *assure* you that I was careful. Your actual core is unaffected."

Concern peaking, the old man dunked into his own center and quickly looked around. Body? Damaged but it'll work out. Main solar gyroscope? Present and functioning. So... what was gone? Everything seemed present... oh.

His mind zipped to the glittering, fractured remnants of his pearlescent webway. The entire thing was Essence dust and pearlescent material. Better to just... He absorbed the pearlescence just like it was Essence that needed to be broken down and refined. The entire thing was gone. Not crippled, or slightly damaged, or broken into chunks. The entire webway that had separated the inner and outer spaces of his center had been dusted completely.

Well, that was a bit of a setback. Ascending back to reality, he exhaled hard and turned his head to face the still calmly seated gnome. "Let me guess. The diversion of Essence back into the core wasn't conducive to making sure Essence went to my vitals instead. Since I likely could not eat, and that webway was preventing my Essence from keeping my body running..."

The gnome was already nodding hard enough to need to hold onto his tiny green hat. "I'm delighted you came to the conclusion so swiftly! As I said, no damage to the actual core. I apologize for essentially crippling part of your cultivation. I was told you'd understand adherence to priorities."

The academic didn't have words for a moment. Not having that webway was going to significantly increase the time that was needed to climb back into the upper C-ranks. He needed to ascend into Magehood to take care of his next batch of problems. Said problems had escalated to the realm of slighted Vicars and a betrayed self-important Flesh Mage. This was outside the realm of what C-rankers could handle, and he would not have Dawn to rely on for quite some time.

"I..." Another sigh left him. "Yes, yes, I do understand. If it meant I lived to have this conversation, I can't even hold it against you, and am thankful for your assistance in my continued wellbeing. Though, I will preface that I am terribly confused as to how a gnome is speaking to me, Dev. I was under the impression that... actually I don't know what happened to gnomes as a race or even what to guess. Would you mind filling me in on some basics? I'm aware the caravan encountered a feral variant during the travels, but you don't appear... of their persuasion. Now that I've affirmed my immediate wellbeing is certain, curiosity is stalking the c'towl."

Deverash rubbed his tiny hands together in anticipation. He'd been awaiting this question and couldn't wait to expound into a thorough talk. The dwarves couldn't handle his chattering, and he'd managed to give them headaches by word choice alone, but the tiny gnome didn't need to hold back here.

"Oh, I'm *so* glad you asked!"

AFTERWORD

We hope you enjoyed Annex! Since reviews are the lifeblood of indie publishing, we'd love it if you could leave a positive review on Amazon! Please use this link to go to the Artorian's Archives: Annex Amazon product page to leave your review: geni.us/Annex.

As always, thank you for your support! You are the reason we're able to bring these stories to life.

About Dennis Vanderkerken

Hello all! I'm Dennis, but I go by a myriad of other nicknames. If you know one, feel free to use it! I probably like them more. I'm from Belgium, and have lived in the USA since 2001. English is my 4th language, so I'm making due, and apologize for the inevitable language-flub. I still call fans ceiling-windmills. The more shrewd among you may have noticed some strange sayings that may or may not have been silly attempts at direct translations! Thank you all for bearing with me.

I started writing in the The Divine Dungeon series due to a series of fortunate circumstances. I continue writing because I wanted to give hungry readers more to sink their teeth into, and help them 'get away' for a while. If you have any questions, or would like to chat, I live on Dakota's Eternium discord. Feel free to come say hi anytime! Life is a little better with a good book.

Connect with Dennis:
Patreon.com/FloofWorks

ABOUT DAKOTA KROUT

I live in a 'pretty much Canada' Minnesota city with my wife and daughter. I started writing The Divine Dungeon series because I enjoy reading and wanted to create a world all my own. To my surprise and great pleasure, I found like-minded people who enjoy the contents of my mind. Publishing my stories has been an incredible blessing thus far, and I hope to keep you entertained for years to come!

Connect with Dakota:
Patreon.com/DakotaKrout
Facebook.com/TheDivineDungeon
Twitter.com/DakotaKrout

About Mountaindale Press

Dakota and Danielle Krout, a husband and wife team, strive to create as well as publish excellent fantasy and science fiction novels. Self-publishing *The Divine Dungeon: Dungeon Born* in 2016 transformed their careers from Dakota's military and programming background and Danielle's Ph.D. in pharmacology to President and CEO, respectively, of a small press. Their goal is to share their success with other authors and provide captivating fiction to readers with the purpose of solidifying Mountaindale Press as the place 'Where Fantasy Transforms Reality.'

Connect with Mountaindale Press:
MountaindalePress.com
Facebook.com/MountaindalePress
Krout@MountaindalePress.com

Mountaindale Press Titles

GameLit and LitRPG

The Divine Dungeon Series
The Completionist Chronicles Series
By: Dakota Krout

A Touch of Power Series
By: Jay Boyce

Red Mage: Advent
By: Xander Boyce

Ether Collapse Series
By: Ryan DeBruyn

Bloodgames: Season One
By: Christian J. Gilliland

Wolfman Warlock: Bibliomancer
By: James Hunter and Dakota Krout

Axe Druid Series
By: Christopher Johns

Skeleton in Space Series
By: Andries Louws

Chronicles of Ethan Series
By: JOHN L. MONK

Pixel Dust Series
By: DAVID PETRIE

APPENDIX

Abyss – A place you don't want to be, and a very common curse word.

Adventurers' Guild – A group from every non-hostile race that actively seeks treasure and cultivates to become stronger. They act as a mercenary group for Kingdoms that come under attack from monsters and other non-kingdom forces.

Affinity – A person's affinity denotes what element they need to cultivate Essence from. If they have multiple affinities, they need to cultivate all of those elements at the same time.

Affinity Channel – The pathway along the meridians that Essence flows through. Having multiple major affinities will open more pathways, allowing more Essence to flow into a person's center at one time.

Affinity Channel Type – Clogged, Ripped, Closed, Minor, Major, and Perfect. Perfect doesn't often occur naturally.

> Clogged: Draws in no essence, because the channel is blocked with corruption.

> Ripped: Draws in an unknown amount of essence, but in a method that is unpredictable and lethal.

> Closed: Draws in no essence, because the channel is either unopened, or forcibly closed.

Minor: Draws in very little essence.

Major: Draws in a sizable amount of essence.

Perfect: Draws in a significant amount of essence. This affinity channel type cannot occur naturally. It is very dangerous to strive for, as the path to this type leads to ripped channels.

Alhambra – A cleric that lives in Chasuble. Kept down for the majority of his career, he remains a good man with a good heart. His priorities for the people allot him a second chance, one derived from an old man's schemery.

Artorian – The main character of the series. If you weren't expecting shenanigans, grab some popcorn. It only gets more intense from here on. He's a little flighty, deeply interested, and a miser of mischief. He is referred to by the wood elves as Starlight Spirit.

Assassin – A stealthy killer who tries to make kills without being detected by his victim.

Astrea – The nightmare.

Aura – The flows of Essence generated by living creatures which surround them and hold their pattern.

Baobab – A wood elf with innate fire resistance. Strong-willed, this woman can handle the heat.

Bard – A lucrative profession deriving profit from other people's misery. Some make coin through song or instrument, but all of them love a good story. Particularly inconvenient ones. This includes Kinnan, Pollard, and Jillian.

Beast Core – A small gem that contains the Essence of Beasts. Also used to strip new cultivators of their corruption.

Blanket – The best sugar glider. Blanket defends. Blanket protects.

Blight – A big bad. Also known as a Caligene, this entity can take many forms. Widespread and far-reaching, this thing has been around for over a millennia, and enjoys scheming to play the long game.

Birch – A friendly set of wood elves, of the Birch-tree Variant. They're friendly and well meaning, even if limited in what they can do. They like scented candles, particularly vanilla.

Blooming Spirit – The Wood Elven equivalent of Aura. See Aura.

Boro – A trader in exotics, this man allied himself with the raider faction. He assists in swindling deals, and robbing villages blind after flooding them with gold that they will not keep.

Cataphron – One of the Skyspear headmasters. Uses the Imperius body technique of the Iron-Shelled Mastodont Kings.

Celestial – The Essence of Heaven, the embodiment of life and *considered* the ultimate good.

Center – The very center of a person's soul. This is the area Essence accumulates (in creatures that do not have a Core) before it binds to the Life Force.

Chants – Affect a choir-cleric's growth, and overall fighting ability. A Choir war host in action matches the chant of every other. Each voice added to the whole increases the power and ability of each person whose voice is involved, through celestial and aural sympathy.

Chasuble – The name of both a particular type of scarf worn loosely around the neck, and the name of a Major church-controlled city. Chasuble scarves are marked to show the rank of the person wearing them.

Church – 'The' Church, to be specific. Also known as the Ecclesiarchy, is one of the few stable major powers active in the world. It has several branches, each operating under different specifications.

> The Choir – The Face of the church, they carry to torch and spread the call far and wide. Operates as exploratory force and functions on heart and mind campaigns. The Choir's special function is to use harmonizing sound to buff and empower every member included in the group-effect.

> Paladin Order – The Fast-Attack branch, these mounted warriors function as cavalry would. The mounted creatures in question vary greatly, and most members employ a high-ranked beast for these purposes.

Phalanx Sentinels – The Siege or Hold branch, the Sentinels are a heavy-armor branch that specialize entirely on securing locations. They are well known to be notoriously slow, and just as notoriously impossible to uproot from a position.

Inquisitors – The Information gathering branch. This branch remains secretive.

Church Ranks – There are multiple Ecclesiarchy ranks, stacking in importance mostly based on cultivation progress.

Initiate – A fresh entry to the church faction, the lowest rank. Generally given to someone still in training.

Scribe – An initiate who failed to become a D-ranked cultivator, was trusted enough by the faction to remain.

Acolyte – Achieved by becoming a D-ranked cultivator. The third lowest rank in the church faction.

Battle Leader – A trusted acolyte who shows promise in the fields of leadership and battle.

Head Cleric – A high D-ranking cultivator, or a person who has been a Battle Leader long enough for their achievements to grant them their personal unit. Head Clerics are trusted to go on missions, excursions, and expeditions that differ based on the specific church faction.

Keeper – Ranked equal to a Head Cleric. People who specifically keep administrative records, and interpret ancient texts. Keepers famously do not get along, and hold bitter rivalries due to said interpretations of the scriptures. Keepers tend to be Head Clerics who failed to enter the C-ranks.

Arbiter – Achieved upon becoming a C-rank cultivator. An Arbiter is a settler of disputes of all kinds, whose authority is overshadowed only by those of higher rank. Otherwise, their say is final.

Friar – A B-ranked Cultivator in the church faction. Friars are glorified problem solvers.

Father – An A-ranked Cultivator in the church faction. A Father may be of a high rank, but has fallen out of favor with the upper echelons of church command.

Vicar – An A-ranked Cultivator in the church faction. The de-facto rulers, movers, and shakers, of the church faction.

Saint – An S-ranked Cultivator in the church faction. They do as they please.

Choppy – The prime woodcutter in the Salt Village.

Chi spiral – A person's Chi spiral is a vast amount of intricately knotted Essence. The more complex and complete the pattern woven into it, the more Essence it can hold and the finer the Essence would be refined.

Cleric – A Cultivator of Celestial Essence, a cleric tends to be support for a group, rarely fighting directly. Their main purpose in the lower rankings is to heal and comfort others.

Compound Essence – Essence that has formed together in complex ways. If two or more Essences come together to form something else, is is called a compound Essence. Or Higher Essence.

Corruption – Corruption is the remnant of the matter that pure Essence was formed into. It taints Essence but allows beings to absorb it through open affinity channels. This taint has been argued about for centuries; is it the source of life or a nasty side effect?

C'towl – A mixture between cat and owl. Usually considered an apex predator due to the intermingling of attributes and sheer hunting prowess.

Currency values:

> Copper: one hundred copper coins are worth a silver coin
> Silver: one hundred silver coins are worth a Gold coin
> Gold: one hundred Gold coins are worth a Platinum coin
> Platinum: the highest coin currency in the Human Kingdoms

Cultivate – Cultivating is the process of refining Essence by removing corruption then cycling the purified Essence into the center of the soul.

Cultivation technique – A name for the specific method in which cultivators draw in and refine the energies of the Heavens and Earth.

Cultivator – A cultivator is a silly person who thinks messing with forces they don't understand will somehow make life better for them.

Daughter of Wrath – A ranking female servant to the Ziggurat, that showed promise and was given troops to lead.

Dawn – The name taken by Ember as her S-ranked incarnation. A full perspective change from her original self, new options and a new life have opened before her. While the way of being Ember espoused still exists within her, room for the new is now possible.

Deverash Editor Neverdash the Dashingly Dapper – Also called Dev, or Dev Editor. A gnome that retained his intelligence, and may have quite the impact on adventures to come.

Duskgrove Castle – A Location within the Phantomdusk Forest. It is the primary hideout for the main antagonist.

D. Kota – An initiate in the choir, who has grand aspirations of becoming a scholar.

Distortion Cat – An upper C-ranked Beast that can bend light and create artificial darkness. In its home territory, it is attacked and bound by tentacle like parasites that form a symbiotic relationship with it.

Dimitri – Also goes by Dimi-Tree, due to his size. A mix between a dwarf and a giant, this brash and brazen mountain loves to dabble. Doing a little bit of everything, he has a reputation that there's nothing he can't fix.

Don Modsognir – Goes by Big Mo. Leader of the Modsognir clan. Responsible for trading and caravan operations. Known to be a troublemaker, he has an impeccable link of loyalty to his family. He enjoys finery, nice suits, and better company. He's got the heart of a king, and the trouble making penchant of a feisty five year old.

Dwarves – Stocky humanoids that like to work with stone, metal, and alcohol. Good miners.

Eucalyptus – A wood elf skilled in defensive and protective essence techniques.

Ember – Secondary main character: A burnt-out Ancient Elf from well over a millennia ago. She's lived too long, and most of it has been in one War or another. She finds a new spark, but until them suffer from extreme weariness, depression, and wear. Her sense of humor lies buried deep within, dry as a cork. Ember enjoys speaking laconically, getting to the point, and getting fired up. She will burn eternal to see her tasks complete. No matter the cost, and no matter the effort.

Electrum – The metal used as Chasuble's currency. These coins are collectively known as 'divines' due to the very minor essence effect on them that keeps them clean. Their worth and value differs greatly from the established monetary system many other cities use, specifically to undercut them.

Elves – A race of willowy humanoids with pointy ears. There are five main types:

> High Elves: The largest nation of Elvenkind, they spend most of their time as merchants, artists, or thinkers. Rich beyond any need to actually work, their King is an S-ranked expert, and their cities shine with light and wealth. They like to think of themselves as 'above' other Elves, thus 'High' Elves.

> Wood Elves: Wood Elves live more simply than High Elves, but have greater connection to the earth and the elements. They are ruled by a counsel of S-ranked elders and rarely leave their woods. Though seen less often, they have great power. They grow and collect food and animal products for themselves and other Elven nations.

> Wild: Wild Elves are the outcasts of their societies, basically feral, they scorn society, civilization, and the rules of others. They have the worst reputation of any of the races of Elves, practicing dark arts and infernal summoning. They have no homeland, living only where they can get away with their dark deeds.

> Dark: The Drow are known as Dark Elves. No one knows where they live, only where they can go to get in contact with them. Dark Elves also have a dark reputation as Assassins and mercenaries for the other races. The worst of their lot are 'Moon Elves', the best-

known Assassins of any race. These are the Elves that Dale made a deal with for land and protection.

Sea: The Sea Elves live on boats their entire lives. They facilitate trade between all the races of Elves and man, trying not to take sides in conflicts. They work for themselves and are considered rather mysterious.

Essence – Essence is the fundamental energy of the universe, the pure power of heavens and earth that is used by the basic elements to become all forms of matter. There are six major types are names: Fire, Water, Earth, Air, Celestial, Infernal.

Essence cycling – A trick to move energy around, to enhance the ability of an organ.

Faux High Elf – A person who has the appearance of a High Elf, but is not actually one. It is a 'Fake' Elf, who takes the position in name only. A mockery and status-display rolled into one.

Fighter – A generic archetype of a being that uses melee weapons to fight.

Fringe – The Fringe region is located in the western region of Pangea. It has been scrapped from maps and scraped from history, by order of the Ecclesiarchy.

Gathering webway – A web of essence created around one's center. For the purpose of gathering and retaining essence. This was the first method concerning essence refining techniques. It should never be sticky.

Gilded blade – A weapon, status title, occupation, and profession all in one. A Gilded blade is a weapon of the raider faction. They are brutally efficient at a single thing, and terrible at everything else.

Gran'mama – Ephira Mayev Stonequeen is Grand Matron of all the centralized Dwarven clans. She goes by Matron, or Gran'mama. While not a royal, she tends to be treated like one due to the vast respect she holds. She also keeps the great majority of land contracts.

Hadurin Fellstone – Supposed head healer of the motley Fringe expedition crew.

Hadurin Fellhammer – Grand-Inquisitor Fellhammer. Executor of the Inquisition, Lord of the Azure Jade mountain, and slayer of a thousand traitors. While not fully of the dwarven race, he is short, portly, jovial to a fault, and as sly as a certain old man.

Hakan – A gilded blade, She is the main antagonist of Axiom. Her personality is as unpleasant as her fashion sense. She's snide, cuts to the chase, and speaks abrasively without much poise or respect to anyone else.

Hawthorn – A set of wood elves that has taken it upon themselves to guard and patrol the edges of the forest. They are generally abrasive as the threats they come home with aren't taken seriously enough. Or abundantly happy to see you, with matching southern cadence and happy reed-chewing style. Rules are actually guidelines. Make no mistake. In any other setting, Hawthorne would be a dastardly set of troublemakers.

Incantation – Essentially a spell, an incantation is created from words and gestures. It releases all of the power of an enchantment in a single burst.

Infernal – The Essence of death and demonic beings, *considered* to be always evil.

Inscription – A *permanent* pattern made of Essence that creates an effect on the universe. Try not to get the pattern wrong as it could have... unintended consequences. This is another name for an incomplete or unknown Rune.

Irene – A Keeper in the Choir. There is more to her than meets the eye, and is far more powerful than she initially appears to be. Do not argue with her about scripture. This world-weary Keeper plays with subterfuge like children play outside. Though when able, she speaks with her fists. Her rage meter is tiny, and fills with a swiftness.

Jiivra – A battle leader in the choir, she aspires to be a Paladin. She has the potential to become truly great, if only given the opportunity. Young, and full of splendor. She's hasty, sticks to order, dislikes surprises, and answers to them with well-measured responses.

Jin – The child of Tarrean and Irene, a Keeper in the Fringe.

Lapis – A mineral-mining town in the vicinity of the Salt Flats. They refine the color Lapis into varying shades of Blue, and are a prime exporter. Lapis Is located in the Fringe.

Maccreus Tarrean – Head Cleric of a choir expeditionary force. His pride is his most distinguishing feature, next to that ostentatious affront known as his armor. Short and portly for non-dwarven reasons, this blundering Ego-driven voice blusters through life like a drunk through a tavern. Elbows first. His ability to craft schemes is as sharp as a dull, smooth rock. His Charisma unfortunately doesn't notice and charges on anyway.

Mahogany – Chosen leaders of the Phantomdusk Wood Elves. As a congregation of Sultans, they care deeply for their people. Forced to make difficult decisions on behalf of the people as a whole, they function with the full permission of the S-ranked council. Which is less active than they'd like it to be. A good soul, they speak with deep voices.

Mages' Guild – A secretive sub-sect of the Adventurers' Guild only Mage level cultivators are allowed to join.

Mana – A higher stage of Essence only able to be cultivated by those who have broken into at least the B-rankings and found the true name of something in the universe.

Mana Signature – A name for a signature that can be neither forged nor replicated, and is used in binding oaths.

Marud – Choir second-in-command Battle Leader, of the second expeditionary force to the Fringe.

Meridians – Meridians are energy channels that transport life energy (Chi/Essence) throughout the body.

Memory Core – Also known as a Memory Stone, depending on the base materials used in their production. Pressing the stone to your forehead lets a person store or gain the knowledge contained within. As if you'd gone through the events yourself. Generally never sold.

Mob – A shortened version of "dungeon monster".

Morovia – A world region located in the south-eastern section of the central Pangea band.

Necromancer – An Infernal Essence cultivator who can raise and control the dead and demons. A title for a cultivator who specializes in re-animating that which has died.

Nefellum – Head Cleric of the second expedition force into the Fringe.

Noble rankings:

> King/Queen – Ruler of their country. (Addressed as 'Your Majesty')

> Crown Prince/Princess – Next in line to the throne, has the same political power as a Grand Duke. (Addressed as 'Your Royal Highness')

> Prince/Princess – Child of the King/Queen, has the same political power as a Duke. (Addressed as 'Your Highness')

Grand Duke – Ruler of a grand duchy and is senior to a Duke. (Addressed as 'Your Grace')

Duke – Is senior to a Marquis or Marquess. (Addressed as 'Your Grace')

Marquis/Marquess – Is senior to an Earl and has at least three Earls in their domain. (Addressed as 'Honorable')

Earl – Is senior to a Baron. Each Earl has three barons under their power. (Addressed as 'My Lord/Lady')

Baron – Senior to knights, they control a minimum of ten knights and therefore their land. (Addressed as 'My Lord/Lady')

Knights – Sub rulers of plots of land and peasants. (Addressed as 'Sir')

Oak – A set of wood elves that embody the purest spirit of flamboyance. Rules might exist, but Oak won't care to listen.

Olgier – A trader from Rutsel, whose greed greatly exceeds his guile.

Olive – A wood elf who is very down to earth. A little greasy, he likes to dig holes and hidden pathways.

Oversized infernal corvid – Really big raven with the Infernal channel. D-ranked creature. Intelligent. Moody.

Pattern – A pattern is the intricate design that makes everything in the universe. An inanimate object has a far less complex pattern that a living being.

Phantomdusk Forest – A world region that borders The Fringe. It is comprised of vast, continent-sprawled greenery that covers multiple biomes. Any forest region connecting to this main mass is considered part of the whole, if entering it has a high mortality rate.

Presence – In terms of aura, this refers to the combined components that aura encompasses. Ordinarily a Mage-only ability. Presence refers to the unity of auras and them acting as one.

Ra – Lunella's first daughter, who causes an amount of trouble equal to the amount of breaths she takes.

Ranger – Typically an adventurer archetype that is able to attack from long range, usually with a bow.

Ranking System – The ranking system is a way to classify how powerful a creature has become through fighting and cultivation.

> G – At the lowest ranking is mostly non-organic matter such as rocks and ash. Mid-G contains small plants such as moss and mushrooms while the upper ranks form most of the other flora in the world.

> F – The F-ranks are where beings are becoming actually sentient, able to gather their own food and make short-term plans. The mid-F ranks are where most humans

reach before adulthood without cultivating. This is known as the fishy or "failure" rank.

E – The E-rank is known as the "echo" rank and is used to prepare a body for intense cultivation.

D – This is the rank where a cultivator starts to become actually dangerous. A D-ranked individual can usually fight off ten F-ranked beings without issue. They are characterized by a "fractal" in their Chi spiral.

C – The highest-ranked Essence cultivators, those in the C-rank usually have opened all of their meridians. A C-ranked cultivator can usually fight off ten D-ranked and one hundred F-ranked beings without being overwhelmed.

B – This is the first rank of Mana cultivators, known as Mages. They convert Essence into Mana through a nuanced refining process and release it through a true name of the universe.

A – Usually several hundred years are needed to attain this rank, known as High-Mage or High-Magous. They are the most powerful rank of Mages.

S – Very mysterious Spiritual Essence cultivators. Not much is known about the requirements for this rank or those above it.

SS – Pronounced 'Double S'. Not much is known about the requirements for this rank or those above it.

SSS – Pronounced 'Triple S'. Not much is known about the requirements for this rank or those above it.

Heavenly – Not much is known about the requirements for this rank or those above it.

Godly – Not much is known about the requirements for this rank or those above it.

Refining – A name for the method of separating essences of differing purities.

Rune – A *permanent* pattern made of Essence that creates an effect on the universe. Try not to get the pattern wrong as it could have... unintended consequences. This is another name for a completed Inscription.

Rosewood – Wood elves with an unbreakable passion for fashion, and making clothes.

Royal Advisor – A big bad. Direct hand to the Mistress, the Queen and Regent in charge of the Ziggurat. Lover of the Cobra Chicken, and Swans.

Salt Village – The main location of Artorian's Archives one, where the majority of the story takes place. It is located in the Fringe, and is a day's journey from the Lapis Village.

Salt Flats – A location in the Fringe. The Salt Village operates by scraping salt from the Salt Flats, a place where the material is plentiful. It is their main export.

Scar – Known as 'The Scar'. A location in that Fringe that includes the Salt Flats as one of its tendrils. It is rumored to be a kind of slumbering dungeon.

Scilla – A small girl that lives in Chasuble. She is afflicted by an effect that caused her irises to permanently turn pink.

Sequoia – Wood elves that will not be forgotten, even without them speaking.

Shamira – Scilla's mother. She is a resident of Chasuble, and not particularly happy about the conditions there.

Sproutling – A title for a child in the Fringe who has not yet been assigned a name, and thus is not considered an adult. Until a certain key event, this includes the famous five: Lunella, Grimaldus, Tychus, Wuxius, and Astrea.

Skyspear Academy – An Academy present on the world's tallest mountain.

Socorro – A desert in the central-band, eastern portion of Pangea. It used to be a place for something important. Now there is only sand, and ruin.

Soul Stone – A *highly* refined Beast Core that is capable of containing a human soul.

Switch – A village Elder of the salt village in the Fringe region. She croaks rather than speaks. Though that's only if she speaks.

Usually she complains. Loudly, and in plenty. If forced to interact with Switch, consider stuffing one's ears with beeswax.

Tank – An adventurer archetype that is built to defend his team from the worst of the attacks that come their way. Heavily armored and usually carrying a large shield, these powerful people are needed if a group plans on surviving more than one attack.

Tibbins – An Acolyte in the Choir. He has a deep passion for all things culinary, and possesses a truly unique expression. He means well, but there's something about his poor luck that keeps getting him in someone's firing line. Sweet, loves to cook, and loyal to a fault. Tibbins is just in the wrong place at the wrong time. His voice tends to tremble when he is uncertain.

Vizier Amon – A big bad. Direct hand to the Mistress, the Queen and Regent in charge of the Ziggurat. Things will get better before they get worse. Unless maybe one can pull the strings of a few favors. Sang with serpentine tongue. His time as grand vizier was short, becoming more nope than rope.

Yvessa – An elven name that means: 'To bloom out of great drought.' She is a choir-cleric going up the ranks, and holds incredible promise. A girl of destiny. A demon-lord with a spoon. A caretaker who gains wisdom beyond her years from the kind of abyss she has to deal with. Her voice gains energy as she ages, as does her spirit.

Ziggurat – Both the name of a region, and a large building central to it. Ziggurat is the current raider stronghold where all their activities are coordinated from. The hierarchies here are simple and bloody, but the true purpose of the place is to serve as a staging area for necromancer needs.

Made in the USA
Columbia, SC
04 November 2022

70507505R00240